RISING FROM ASH

JAX MEYER

This is a work of fiction. Names, characters, businesses, places, events, locales, and incidents are either the products of the author's imagination or used in a fictitious manner. Any resemblance to actual persons, living or dead, or actual events is purely coincidental.

Copyright 2019 by Jax Meyer

All rights reserved. No part of this book may be reproduced or transmitted in any form or by any means, electronic or mechanical, including photocopying, without written permission from the author.

Cover Illustration by Gwen Katz

Cover design by Amanda Walker

Story development by Em Stevens

Editing by Claire Jarrett

Published by Jax Meyer

First Edition - July 2019

❦ Created with Vellum

To my wife, whose life experiences I shamelessly borrowed to create Phoenix. I hope you'll make chicken nuggets for my birthday until the day I die. I love you.

Disclaimer

This book contains sex. It does not contain gratuitous sex, but if you do not wish to read the sex scenes for any reason, I understand. Beyond consensual sex, there are no other potential triggers to be aware of besides vague references to abuse.

CHAPTER ONE

PHOENIX

*T*he phone rang and Phoenix made the mistake of answering blindly.

"Hey kiddo."

Phoenix berated herself before answering, "hi Dad."

"What are you up to?"

"Same as every afternoon. Getting ready for work." *Which you'd know if you cared about anyone besides yourself.* She didn't have time for honesty today, having slept through her alarm, or she might finally call him out for his lifetime of bullshit. But that would require an hour long blow out, not a quick phone conversation. Better to discover his agenda quickly, because her dad never called without wanting something from her.

"Oh yeah. You still working at Hooters? I don't think I'd get an ounce of work done if I worked there. I don't know how you do it."

"They're just women, Dad, and I stay plenty busy cooking."

"Women with big knockers and tight shorts showing off their assets." He laughed at his own awful pun and Phoenix rolled her eyes. She knew having a family that accepted her sexuality was a luxury, but sometimes that acceptance went too

1

far. For example, her dad didn't know the first thing about appropriate parent-child relationships and treated her like one of his crude friends.

He knew Phoenix loved women, and thoroughly enjoyed her frequent hookups, but he failed to grasp that she always treated them with basic human dignity, unlike him. Granted, not all of the women she slept with agreed, but she honestly tried to be respectful.

"What do you need Dad?" She cut him off before he went on a misogynistic tangent that he'd believe was complimentary of her coworkers rather than demeaning.

"What makes you think I need something? Can't a dad just call his only daughter and talk?" Phoenix bit back her retort. *A dad?* Sure. But not *her* dad. She learned that lesson long ago. She'd heard of these mythical fathers who cared about their children more than themselves and called merely to talk, but her dad was not one of them. He always had an ulterior motive.

She remained silent, waiting him out while finding her ugly non-slip work shoes. Not even she could make them look cool, but falling on her ass in the kitchen would do nothing for her reputation and likely land her in urgent care with a medical bill she couldn't afford.

"I don't have time for this today. What exactly do you need?" she asked again, allowing the frustration into her voice.

"I need a place to crash for a little while. Brenda kicked me out again and—"

"Stop right there." Phoenix steeled herself against his forthcoming arguments. "I'm sorry you're having a tough time but I can't right now. I don't have the money to move you out here, or support you, nor do I have the space. And you can't afford to live here on your disability payments. I need to finish getting ready for work. Call one of your friends or apologize to Brenda."

"But we're family."

His whiny tone set her off, her anger getting the best of her. "And if this hadn't happened a dozen times before maybe I'd consider it. But I can't. Try listening to your psychiatrist for once and take your meds so you don't burn every bridge you have. You're going to have to figure this out yourself, like a grown up. I have to go before I'm late. Goodbye." She hit the end call button hard, which wasn't as satisfying as slamming it, but would have to do.

Phoenix grabbed her keys and slammed the door behind her, cringing when she remembered her neighbor had a young kid and prayed she hadn't woken him from a nap. She stomped to the car, plopped heavily into the seat, slammed the door, and screamed. Twenty-eight years with an immature, childish father who never took responsibility for his life was quickly approaching peak frustration. What would happen when she finally lost it? And why did she feel guilty for telling him no? She screamed again at the impossibility of the situation.

"Fuck him, and his shit."

Phoenix scrolled to her 'pissed at dad' playlist, cranked the music, and threw the car into gear.

Phoenix sat in the parking lot, her eyes closed and the deafening music silenced, trying to brush off her foul mood before going into the kitchen. Normally she liked to arrive fifteen minutes early, but thanks to her dad she only had ten to get in the right mindset. She wasn't sure how the waitresses handled their shitty days. The amount of harassment they dealt with on a normal shift would set Phoenix off, especially in this mood.

Good thing she was safely in the kitchen where the guys were either afraid of her or in awe of her reputation with women. Most of them were decent enough guys. If only she could say the same of Scott, her new manager and the owner's son. Their father and son relationship wasn't the problem though. Scott was one of those mediocre men with an inflated sense of importance who went to college but was useless running a business.

Phoenix was still hoping Mr. Moore would wise up and put her in charge. She'd been a cook or manager in multiple restaurants for the past decade and worked fast food since she was 15. She'd been at this particular Hooters since moving to Colorado two years ago. By now she knew every aspect of the business and ran the kitchen like a machine.

The waitresses loved her because she understood the connection between getting the food to the customer quickly and the waitresses making more in tips. It didn't hurt that she also treated them like human beings, with thoughts and feelings, unlike too many of the customers – and Scott. Customers she could ignore, but Scott ruined the invigorating work environment she used to enjoy.

A car zipping into the spot next to her pulled her attention away from her thoughts. She almost smiled at the bright green sports car. A tall, shapely blonde in the customary Hooters uniform stepped out and bounced over to Phoenix's window, which she lowered. "Are you sulkin or stallin?"

"Just waiting on you sweetness," Phoenix said as she fell into their easy flirtation, her light southern Indiana accent slipping out as it tended to do when talking with Bri thanks to her north Texas accent.

Bri was easy to like and fun to flirt with, but despite the occasional hookup they were simply friends. Sometimes Phoenix wondered if Bri wanted more, but she hadn't said so, for which Phoenix was grateful. Bri was a rare exception to her 'one and done' rule which ensured Phoenix would never get caught up in a messy relationship. The last thing she wanted was to distance herself from Bri, but she would if she had to.

"While I'd like to think that's true, I don't buy it," Bri said confidently. "What happened?"

Phoenix gave her a loaded look. "My dad called and asked to move in with me."

"Shit. Tell me you said no."

"Of course, I'm not a masochist."

"Not even for the right woman?" Bri asked with a challenging smirk. Phoenix rolled her eyes but smiled regardless. Bri grew more serious. "I know you're smart, but parents are a challenge, no matter how shitty."

Bri's smile fell for a moment as her eyes unfocused, likely thinking of her own parents. Bri and Phoenix had bonded over drinks one night, sharing their tales of running to Colorado to escape abusive and unsupportive families and they'd been friends with occasional benefits ever since.

Phoenix raised her window and Bri stepped back giving Phoenix room to open her door. "I know I shouldn't let him bother me. This is what he does. He burns through his friends, or in this case his girlfriend, and leans on me to support him until he finds someone else, which would be more difficult if he was here."

"I'm barely making rent as it is, I can't move him out here. Then he'll never leave and I'll go certifiably crazy dealing with him. Even if affordable housing existed anywhere near Denver, I can't have him that close." Phoenix leaned against her car door, already tired and her shift hadn't begun. Bri joined her, nudging her hip.

"Is there anything I can do? I know you're not big on roommates but I'm not bad company. Maybe if you didn't have to worry about money every month your dad couldn't stress you out as easily. Plus, I have some very nice noise canceling headphones for your date nights."

Her emphasis on date nights made Phoenix chuckle to herself. One night stands, even if they included dinner, weren't exactly the normal definition of date nights. Phoenix didn't date, preferring uncomplicated flings over risky relationships. Nor did she bring women back to her apartment. But she appreciated the sentiment.

Phoenix gave Bri's hand a quick squeeze. "I'm sure you'd be a great roommate, but I like my space. Putting up with Scott and working overtime occasionally to pay the rent is worth it for now. Though I should probably start looking around for another job, just in case." Phoenix pushed off the car, resigned to her fate for the evening. "We better get in there before Scott gets his panties in a wad."

"We still have a few minutes. Besides, he won't say anything. You intimidate him because he knows you are smarter and get way more ass than he ever will."

"Small comfort when he's the one making all the money while I clean up his mess."

Bri wrapped her into a hug and whispered in her ear. "Maybe I can provide some comfort tonight?"

Phoenix chuckled, ignoring the tingle in her center. "Always tempting. Ask me again after work."

"Find me if you change your mind before then. These windows are almost impossible to see into at night, if you recall."

Phoenix kissed the side of her head affectionately. "As if I'd forget."

Bri sighed as she turned toward the employee entrance. "Someday, someone is going to get their hook in you and I'm going to miss this."

Phoenix shook her head as they walked side by side. "I've managed this long without being caught. I wouldn't worry, unless there's a new breed of fisherwoman in the world I don't see myself getting hooked any time soon."

The night was unusually busy for a Wednesday thanks to the Colorado Rockies baseball game. Being the second week of September, the season was winding down and the Rockies were expected to make the playoffs this year. Given the number of cheers Phoenix heard over the din of the kitchen, she suspected they were winning, which made for happy customers spending money.

The game ended around ten, so by the time eleven rolled around she had every non-essential item broken down and soaking to be washed. As Phoenix scraped the grill of meat residue, Scott came back, smelling strongly of alcohol. Apparently he'd taken advantage of the recent slow down to drink away his daddy's profits.

"Not too bad tonight," he said, walking behind her. "Looks like you've worked your little tush off." Phoenix ignored him until his hand connected with her ass. She spun around, grabbing the offending hand, and snarled at him. "If you ever touch me again, you won't have a hand. You understand me?"

Scott's eyes were wide, just now realizing what he'd done. He laughed awkwardly. "I'm just having some fun. Lighten up."

Phoenix still held his wrist firmly, her voice like steel. "I don't know what you think is fun about this, but you aren't man or woman enough to look at my ass, much less touch it. This is your only warning."

He swallowed hard. When she thought he might wet himself, Phoenix released his hand and he scurried away like the rat he was. Phoenix stared daggers at his retreat before turning back to the griddle. Anger, no, not anger, rage built in her gut, but she couldn't walk out on this job. Not without something else lined up, which pissed her off even more. Adrenaline flooded her body and she wanted to run. The only reason she stayed was the refusal to be irresponsible like her father. This was yet another way her parents' mistakes impacted her life, even when they weren't physically around. She picked up the scraper with renewed vigor, determined to leave as quickly as possible.

Fifteen minutes later Bri stepped into the kitchen but pulled up short at Phoenix's expression.

"Woah, who pissed in your shoes?" she asked Phoenix, who was wiping down the prep table.

"Scott."

Bri walked closer and spoke quietly. "You wanna talk about it? We could get some drinks down at Gracie's."

"Thanks, but I really don't think that's a good idea," Phoenix said, glancing at Bri. "If I get drunk in this mood I'm liable to get into a fight or break something and I don't feel like going to jail tonight."

"And I'd rather not have to bail you out. If you change your mind, I'll be up for a while. Call anytime." Bri kissed her on the cheek and walked to the break room. Phoenix sighed. Bri didn't deserve Phoenix's anger, even tangentially. She knew she wouldn't take Bri up on either of her offers tonight. She redoubled her efforts, finishing her remaining tasks in record time before bolting out the door.

After the frustrating events of the day, Phoenix found herself driving aimlessly, her favorite Tool album cranked almost to the point of hearing damage. *I should fucking quit. See how he likes it when the kitchen falls apart because he has no clue how to run a restaurant.*

The album ended, the unexpected silence causing her to look around. She blinked to be sure of where she was. Yes, that was her aunt Diane's house, and a light was still on inside, despite the late hour. Diane was the only living relative that never asked anything from her. The last thing Phoenix wanted to do was burden her aunt with her dad's latest shenanigans, especially this late, but she needed to talk to someone who'd understand. Diane made the decision for her by opening the front door and yelling from the lit porch.

"Are you going to get your ass in here or do I need to drag you in?"

Phoenix grinned and turned off the engine, knowing Diane would absolutely drag her in if necessary, even while wearing cotton pajamas. Phoenix bounded up the steps and into Diane's welcoming arms.

Diane held her tight while she asked, "I assume your father called you today?"

Phoenix melted into her aunt's hug, her shoulders relaxing before stepping out of the embrace. "Right before work where my creep of a manager slapped my ass."

Diane's eyes opened wide. "Does he still have his hand?"

"For now," Phoenix said flippantly.

"That's my girl."

Phoenix warmed at her aunt's compliment. This was why she'd chosen Colorado, to be near the only family member still alive who truly loved her. "How did you know he called?"

Diane ushered Phoenix inside before locking the door behind them. "He called me this morning. I told him to leave you alone, but you know your father. You can't tell him anything he doesn't want to hear."

"Which is why I hung up on him after a few minutes." Phoenix flopped into a wooden kitchen chair feeling much older than she should.

Diane walked to the fridge and pulled out a bottle of beer. "Good for you. You've taken care of him long enough. It's time he learns how to be a grown up."

Phoenix barked out a laugh. "Have you met him?"

"One can hope at least." Diane handed the open bottle to Phoenix.

"Thanks." Phoenix took a long drink, downing half the bottle without trying. "I'm just glad there are three states between us so he can't show up unannounced. I don't think I could kick him out. The guilt is too strong." Phoenix's voice betrayed her sadness. "Fuck, I'm 28 years old and exhausted. I shouldn't be avoiding my dad because he refuses to take his medication or hold down a job and be a normal adult."

"Do you remember what your grandmother always said?"

"There are worse things than being small and having jackasses for parents," Phoenix said with a sigh. "But I'm not small anymore and I'm tired of parents who only call when they need money." Phoenix took another long drink of her beer absentmindedly. "Did I tell you mom called last week? She had the decency to call at a reasonable hour and ask me about my day before asking for money. I caved and send her fifty bucks." Phoenix shook her head, disappointed in herself.

"I don't blame you. A person can only take so much. What was the money for?"

"Moving. It's harder to say no to her when she's working and still coming up short. I can't make her go to rehab, and as long as she's a functioning alcoholic I doubt she'll see the problem. Am I enabling her?"

"Fee, you have such a big heart. Maybe you are enabling her, but you'd feel guilty if she ended up homeless over fifty dollars you could have provided."

"Augh, I hate this. I shouldn't feel guilty about their life choices. Why can't I live a normal life without constantly worrying about my parents finding a way to use me?"

Diane patted Phoenix's free hand in sympathy. How many times had Phoenix asked that very question? Too damn many.

"You've had it unnecessarily hard, and I'm sorry for that. You want another beer?"

"Can I crash on your couch?"

"Always, you don't need to ask."

"Then yes, but I can get it."

"Shush." Diane moved to the fridge before Phoenix could pull herself up. "You've been on your feet all night while I've been sitting on my ass playing games. Which reminds me, it's your turn in Boggle, didn't you see the notification on your phone?" She handed Phoenix the open bottle and sat in the chair next to her.

"I was waiting until I could bring my A game, otherwise I don't stand a chance against you," Phoenix replied before taking a drink from the new bottle. As much as she wanted to banter, her heart was too heavy tonight.

"Why couldn't I be your kid, Diane? Then Dad would simply be the weird uncle I only see at holidays."

"Because us lesbians don't reproduce nearly as well as horny teenagers. Besides, I partially raised that boy and look how well that turned out."

"You and Grandma did your best. It's not your fault he won't take his damn meds or take responsibility for any part of his life." The familiar anger rose in her gut and she fought it back down. Why get angry about something she knew wasn't going to change?

"Bipolar is a complicated disease. I'm not making excuses but we didn't know as much then as we do now. And now it may be too late." Diane squeezed her hand again. "I'm sorry I couldn't do more for you growing up."

"Stop. You were my bright spot, along with Grandma. My fairy gaymother. And now, without Grandma, you're all I've got." Phoenix took another drink of the beer, enjoying the warmth spreading throughout her body, relaxing her. "I wish you really were a fairy, then you could find me a long term solution to the Dad problem.

"You never know. For now, tell me something fun from your life. Any new hires with promise?" Diane waggled her eyebrows.

"You're almost as bad as Dad."

"Hey, now, there's no need for name calling kid. And I'm old. Women my age don't have breasts like that anymore."

Phoenix laughed. "You're only 56. You could have some of your own if you threw down twenty grand for a boob job."

Diane dismissed her with a wave of her hand. "Natural is better, even when gravity takes hold. But I can still look and appreciate your coworkers."

"Why not stop by tomorrow night? All the boobs you want on display, might as well enjoy them. Just try not to drool, it's embarrassing."

"Perky breasts and my favorite niece's cooking? Count me in."

Phoenix was putting away the blankets from last night when Diane called her from work.

"How's my favorite niece? Did you get enough sleep?"

"I did, thanks for letting me crash." Phoenix always slept best at her aunt's house, even if the couch was a little small for her 5'10" frame. Something about knowing her aunt was in the next room allowed her to relax in a way she didn't even in her own apartment. "What's going on?"

"Remember last night when you asked me to find a solution regarding your dad?"

"Yeah..."

"Well, have you ever considered the Pole?"

Phoenix almost choked on her spit. "The pole?! How does dancing solve my problem with Dad? He practically lives at strip clubs."

Diane laughed for a full minute before stopping to explain herself. "Sweetheart, you are a beautiful woman but no, that wouldn't solve the problem with your father. I meant the South Pole. You know, that place I'm responsible for staffing as part of my job?" Diane laughed again and Phoenix joined her.

"Oh, right. Well clearly the answer is no. Why?"

"For the past month or so I've been ensuring every position in the US Antarctic Program was filled for the upcoming summer and winter seasons. I had a cook cancel their year-long contract at the South Pole today and I need to fill the slot ASAP. There's a waiting list, but none of the candidates know where they are on it. If I pull some strings and fast track your application you could be on a plane to Antarctica in a month, six weeks tops, offering you a year of freedom from your family."

Phoenix was stunned. A whole year where no one could ask her for money. Or turn up unexpectedly to crash at her place. Or ask her to drive them somewhere without even offering to pay for gas. Was that truly possible? "Seriously, Diane? That would be amazing."

"You're qualified for the job, but I need you to know what you're in for. The work won't be a problem. You're working mostly with frozen food and whatever fresh food is flown in before winter or is grown in the small greenhouse. Creativity will be required but I'm not concerned about your abilities on that front. What you've never experienced is six months of darkness, or being in close proximity to the same 45 or so people for months at a time."

"But I'll be free of my parents?"

"Yes. No phone calls in, just access to emails and instant messenger unless there's a true emergency and then I will call you over the satellite phone."

Phoenix's heart raced at the possibility. "How long until you need a decision?"

"Before you go to work, at least to start the application. Ideally you'd be leaving as soon as you pass the physical because the crew currently at the station are waiting to come home."

Phoenix didn't hesitate. "Get me the application."

"I'll email it over now. Can you complete the application before you leave for work?"

"Sure, I can do that," Phoenix replied, walking to her aunt's laptop across the living room.

"And Fee, don't be mad, but I have to address one more thing."

Phoenix tensed and cautiously said, "ok..."

"The South Pole is a small community, and much smaller in the winter. If you approach women the same way you do now... it could cause problems."

The full implication of her words took a minute to register. "Wait, are you asking me to be celibate? For a year?"

"Not necessarily. But I need you to understand, there's nowhere to run. You'll see the same people every day, so if you sleep around someone is bound to become jealous and ruin the station dynamics. I really don't want a phone call saying you're causing trouble."

Two equally strong desires pulled at Phoenix. She couldn't disappoint her aunt. But no sex for a year? Was she capable of such a feat? She didn't go a week without sex unless she was sick.

"Are you telling me the cost of a year without family drama is to abstain from sex?"

"If that's the only way to avoid drama while you're on the ice, then I guess I am."

Nothing was ever simple where her family was concerned. But what other option did she have? She thought moving to Colorado would be enough to escape her parents, but she was wrong. If this was her best option, she'd have to find some other hobbies to keep her hands occupied.

"What do you think, kiddo? Still want that application?"

The pet name her dad preferred gave her the strength to commit to this new path. She needed to try something different. How much worse could Antarctica be?

"Yes, I do."

Three weeks later, Phoenix's orientation package arrived in the mail, and the next day she gave Mr. Moore her two-week's notice. He wasn't thrilled but Phoenix presented the trip as the opportunity of a lifetime. She didn't bother telling Scott, knowing he'd take her action as a personal insult, and he didn't disappoint. Scott was predictably livid when he learned she'd gone straight to his dad to give her notice.

Waiting so long to resign meant she'd be working until three days before her flight, but she wasn't comfortable quitting until everything was in place. In three short weeks Phoenix found someone to take over her apartment lease, moved as much as possible into her aunt's garage, and sold the rest. Realizing a reprieve from her old life was fast approaching gave her the much needed energy boost necessary to accomplish every task.

Her last shift at Hooters was like any other Friday because work still needed to be done. But after closing, Bri rounded up most of the waitresses and hauled Phoenix down to Gracie's, their favorite bar, for drinks. Phoenix turned down a few offers for company, but she left in an Uber with Bri for a proper send-off of uncomplicated and satisfying sex. Phoenix even stayed overnight. She'd never admit it, but Bri's unwavering friendship was a comfort in the face of so much change.

Saturday afternoon Phoenix found herself in Diane's living room trying to make sense of the piles of clothes and belongings in front of her. Like everyone else heading to Antarctica Phoenix was restricted to two pieces of luggage, no more than fifty pounds in weight each, and one carry-on bag to hold her life for an entire year. She'd be allowed one load of laundry a week, but how much variety would she want? It wasn't like she could run to the store if she got bored with her wardrobe.

Diane entered the room and handed Phoenix a cup of coffee. "Figured you'd need some fuel after your night of debauchery."

"That's an understatement." Phoenix took a drink of the hazelnut blend made just how she liked it, with a touch of cream and sugar. After setting the coffee down on the end table, Phoenix returned her attention to the clothes on the floor. "What do they provide again? I've lost track."

Diane retrieved the program handbook from the kitchen table, found the page on clothing and gear, and read the list out loud. "Let's see. When you're in Christchurch, before you fly to Antarctica, you'll be issued a water bottle, all of your cold weather gear and work uniform. They've sent a list which tells you what they supply. It consists of: a balaclava, a neck gaiter, a fleece hat, leather gloves, liner gloves, mittens, snow goggles, fleece pants, snow pants, long underwear shirts and pants, wool socks, a fleece jacket, a parka, and boots."

Diane gestured to the chaos in front of them. "Sounds like all you'll need to pack is clothing for when you're off shift, exercising, or enjoying spring in New Zealand."

Phoenix sat down cross-legged in front of her shorts and pants, grateful to have a task. Diane left the room and returned shortly, standing in front of Phoenix, a gift bag at the end of her extended arm.

The corner of Phoenix's lip curled up at the unexpected present. "What's this?"

"Something to make your life easier. They should be the right size, even with long underwear underneath."

Phoenix snatched the bag excitedly and emptied the contents in her lap. She picked up the brown bundle and her eyes grew wide. "Carhartt pants? Diane, these are expensive!"

"They aren't that bad, and you need a quality pair to last the year. Think of them as your Christmas present, since you won't be here." Diane's voice wavered at the end. She quickly walked into the kitchen, likely to compose herself. The Murray's weren't known for expressing sadness easily, but this was a unique situation so Phoenix wouldn't bring it up.

Diane called from the kitchen. "What do you want for dinner, Fee?"

Just like that, Phoenix knew how to repay her aunt. She hopped up, retrieving her wallet and keys. "Don't even worry about it because I'm cooking." She gave Diane a kiss on the cheek as she passed through to the door. "Heading to the grocery store. Any requests?"

"You know me, I love everything you cook."

"So, cabbage rolls?"

"Perfect."

Cabbage rolls weren't commonly served in restaurants, making them a special treat for them both. Phoenix would also purchase the ingredients for biscuits and gravy in the morning. And if she found a fresh turkey at the butcher, she'd surprise Diane with an early Thanksgiving feast tomorrow. She could enjoy the leftovers while Phoenix was flying halfway around the earth. It was the best she could do on short notice.

When she returned, Diane had tamed the chaos, organizing Phoenix's clothes into small piles instead of mounds. All Phoenix had to do was choose what she was bringing. The task remained daunting, so she focused on unpacking the groceries and prepping dinner. Diane joined her, peeling and dicing potatoes that would be mashed and covered in a tomato gravy before too long. They spoke as they worked efficiently together.

"Mom called when I was shopping. She sounded a little rough, but she didn't ask for money. I'm taking that as a win. I promised to write occasionally but reminded her that mail isn't an option after February when the planes stop flying in. We'll see if she remembers."

"Did you tell her to call me if she had questions or needed you to know anything?"

"Yep."

Diane nodded and silence fell, heavy with Phoenix's unspoken question. Since she'd explained to her father where she'd be going for the next year he'd ghosted her, refusing to answer her calls. Phoenix wasn't going to chase him, so made sure he knew when she was leaving and left the decision to say goodbye up to him.

"Have you spoken to Dad?" Phoenix hated how small her voice sounded. This time away would be good for her.

"Nope, he's ignoring me too. Funny thing is, I think in his mind that's a punishment when really, it's a vacation."

Phoenix's face fell subconsciously.

"I'm sorry Fee. For you this probably does feel like a punishment. Sometimes I wish I could reach across the miles and smack my baby brother. You don't deserve his bullshit."

Phoenix smiled ruefully. "Well, that's why I'm leaving, right? At least he's consistently an asshole now that I don't play his games. I can leave this country guilt free instead."

"Exactly. But don't let him dominate your trip. Make this experience a stepping-stone for you to discover who you want to be instead of living in survival mode."

"I will," Phoenix answered earnestly.

While the food cooked, Phoenix finalized her packing and made a list of everything else she needed to purchase tomorrow, including headphones and as many sketch pads and pencils as she could afford. If Diane expected Phoenix to stay out of trouble, then she'd need a distraction. She was a passable artist and this would be the perfect time to reconnect with her artistic side and also an excellent way to keep her hands busy.

Then she returned to the kitchen to start making coleslaw.

"I still can't believe you're cooking Thanksgiving dinner. You are the best niece I could ask for."

"Well, I was thinking you could freeze some leftovers, and then on Thanksgiving it would be like I'm here," Phoenix swallowed hard against the emotions welling in her chest. "You're on your own for coleslaw since it won't freeze."

Diane responded playfully, covering for the sadness in her eyes. "You know I survived Thanksgiving before you moved out here. I can make my own coleslaw."

"But will it be as good as mine?" Diane shrugged but smiled at Phoenix's boast. "That's what I thought."

Phoenix used every last drop of hot water in Diane's house when she showered Monday morning to prepare for her journey. Her flight would leave later in the afternoon, taking her to Los Angeles just long enough to catch her twelve-hour overnight flight to Auckland, New Zealand. Then it was another short hop to her interim destination, Christchurch, New Zealand. She'd spend two days in Christchurch before receiving her issued clothing and continuing on to Antarctica. In less than a week she'd be at the South Pole, limited to just two showers a week. That was challenging enough, but those showers were restricted to two minutes long. Two minutes! She was unsure how she'd handle that part, but she'd soon find out.

Breakfast was a plate of leftovers from her off-season Thanksgiving dinner: turkey, dressing, and mashed potatoes covered in gravy, coleslaw, and green bean casserole. Thinking ahead made her wonder what Thanksgiving would be like at the South Pole. Excitement filled her at the thought and kept her going as they loaded Diane's car with her bags. Soon they were off to Denver International Airport.

They kept their conversations light, but Phoenix knew her aunt was struggling. Diane was happy for her, sure, but living in the same city meant they saw each other weekly at minimum. Going a year without the possibility of hearing Diane's voice, and vice versa, would be difficult for them both.

With Phoenix checked in and her bags heading to the plane, they paused before security. Phoenix reminded herself that they'd email and chat frequently in an attempt to control her emotions.

"Well kid, you better get going. Discover the joys of airport shopping while you kill time. Remember, passport on you at all times until you get to the Pole. Call me when you get to McMurdo so I know you made it safely."

"I'll be allowed to call from McMurdo? I thought Antarctica only had satellite phones."

"That's true of the South Pole," Diane clarified, "but McMurdo is on the coast so has much better internet access. The phone numbers are local, too, thanks to the wonders of internet phones. They are considered an extension of our offices here."

"Nice. Then I'll definitely call you when I arrive. Thanks."

They embraced, eyes glistening by the time they stepped away, and Phoenix turned to the security line without looking back.

CHAPTER TWO

PHOENIX

What did I get myself into? Phoenix squinted in the sun as she stood in the doorway of the large gray US Air Force airplane. She found her wraparound sunglasses in a coat pocket which allowed her to survey her surroundings more easily. They'd landed on a far reaching ice sheet that served as the airfield for McMurdo Station, Antarctica. Ahead she noticed small buildings that reminded her of ice fishing huts and a few vehicles with tracks or oversized tires. In the distance were mountains, but McMurdo station wasn't visible yet.

McMurdo was a US research station located on the southern tip of Ross Island, just off the coast of the continent. McMurdo served as the entry point for everyone journeying to the South Pole still 840 miles inland and was a brief stopover for Phoenix.

The icy air was in stark contrast to Christchurch. When Phoenix had boarded the plane a few hours earlier, it had been a warm spring day. The last two days would be the only natural warmth she'd experience until next year when she passed through New Zealand on her way home.

New Zealand had been a dream for Phoenix's reawakened artistic side, with incredible views of the harbor from Mount

Cavendish. She could have spent a month sketching and exploring Christchurch's architecture, but that would have to wait. The US Antarctic Program dictated her agenda and she was needed at the South Pole so that last year's cook could go home.

Antarctica was the opposite of New Zealand in many ways and Phoenix began to second guess her decision as her face grew increasingly cold. In New Zealand she'd had the opportunity to escape if she changed her mind. It wasn't easy but it was possible. In Antarctica there was nowhere to run that didn't result in a quick death from the elements. No matter what happened, Phoenix would have to face the challenges that lay before her – like a grown up, she admitted begrudgingly.

Phoenix gathered her courage, ignoring her churning stomach, and followed the crowd to their transportation to town.

The airfield was far enough from McMurdo that they needed to be bussed to town. As she drew closer the true scale of the bus before her became apparent. The tires on Ivan the Terrabus, as it was so lovingly named, were almost as tall as Phoenix. She couldn't help feeling small, especially when looking over the ice sheet toward the ocean.

Ivan was not built for speed, so Phoenix had plenty of time to avoid thinking about the fact that she had just landed on an airfield built on sea ice. A few feet below was the ocean. How many times had she heard that climate change made the Antarctic ice shelf unstable? They couldn't mean this ice, right?

Phoenix turned to the older man sitting next to her and struck up a conversation. Jimmy was also heading to the Pole to be the station electrician. He was a veteran, both of the Army and the Pole, so Phoenix peppered him with questions.

"Do they really enforce the two-minute shower limit?"

Jimmy chuckled. "Unfortunately, yes. But you figure out how to wash up pretty quickly."

"What about boredom? I guess it can't be too bad if you're back again."

"Everyone gets bored, but that's true of life off the ice too. You'll be surprised at how much there is to do. Besides the obvious visual entertainment in the lounges there's plenty of live music to enjoy. Most people enjoy teaching classes about their research, or hobbies. If you want to learn something new, chances are someone already knows it and will teach you."

Phoenix smiled, her anxiety easing. "That sounds great. What are your hobbies, Jimmy?"

"I enjoy playing pool after work, or darts, but I also play the guitar. Sometimes I stand in as a bartender, and I often end up as the station's barber."

Jimmy was a larger man, with a scruffy beard. She couldn't imagine him as the barber type, but before she could inquire further, he asked about her hobbies.

"I've really only planned to sketch in my downtime and catch up on shows and movies. I also enjoy boxing and plan to use the fitness center frequently to avoid going stir crazy."

"Sounds like a good start."

The trip took about an hour as Ivan plodded along and Phoenix found Jimmy easy to talk to. Now that she knew at least one person in her new home, the unknown life before her wasn't nearly as intimidating.

By the time she'd processed through customs, which was nothing more than a table of ceremonial stamps which they were allowed to add to their passports to their heart's content, she was exhausted and starving. Antarctica was on New Zealand time but her body was struggling to find a schedule. She'd spent entirely too much time traveling and an eighteen hour time difference wasn't helping.

Thankfully she was soon escorted to her allocated room, where she dropped her bags, and was then shown to the cafeteria in the same blue building. Despite arriving between breakfast and dinner, she was pleased to see that the station had a 24-hour pizza bar and a table of desserts available. After eating her fill Phoenix returned to her room and unceremoniously passed out, completing her first day in Antarctica.

When Phoenix awoke twelve hours later she didn't feel quite so jet lagged or anxious, allowing her to take in her surroundings. Her room was small but not cramped. There was a second bed, but no sign of a roommate. Noticing a phone, Phoenix checked her watch which was set to local and Denver time zones. While Phoenix was up early for local time, Diane would be at work.

"This is Diane."

Phoenix couldn't restrain herself. "Diane! I'm calling you from fucking Antarctica!"

Diane laughed. "Yes you are. How is your trip so far?"

"Long. Confusing. Beautiful. Tiring. Bizarre." Phoenix paused to consider before letting her words out in a rush. "I didn't want to leave New Zealand. The architecture is gorgeous, even the buildings that are being rebuilt from the last earthquake.

"I took the gondola up the mountain, managed to avoid a panic attack, and saw the ocean and harbor! And sheep, lots of sheep. I took pictures, but also sketched a ton. I think I'm going to need you to send me more sketch pads to survive the winter."

Phoenix could hear the smile in Diane's voice, even from thousands of miles away. "I'm glad you're enjoying yourself. I'll be sure to send a care package for Christmas, just get me a list. And how's Antarctica? As cold as it looks?"

The enthusiasm ebbed slightly in Phoenix's voice. "Yes. It's cold and windy, but no worse than winter in Colorado. The mountains are volcanic. The juxtaposition of black rock and white snow will be fun to sketch later." Phoenix walked to the window, pulling aside the heavy curtains, the phone cord barely covering the distance. A three story brown building dominated her view. "McMurdo reminds me of those rustic Alaska shows Grandma liked to watch. Everything is very... functional."

"That's one way to put it. Your grandma would be proud of you for doing this. She wished you would be more adventurous."

Phoenix's enthusiasm waned some more. The only reason she was here was because she'd run away. Wasn't adventure supposed to mean running toward something more than mere survival? Phoenix couldn't remember ever running towards something.

"I think you're right, she would be over the moon about this trip but I don't feel very adventurous right now. To be honest it's a little overwhelming. This place feels like I'm on another planet but one that luckily still has pizza."

"It's a lot of change all at once but you'll adjust soon. You are more adaptable than you realize."

Phoenix wanted to call bullshit but she didn't want to spend her morning getting a lecture, no matter how well intentioned. Instead she did something even more questionable.

"Has Dad called?" She hated asking, but there was a tiny part of her that hoped he would regret not saying goodbye.

Her hopes were soon dashed.

"Sorry Fee."

It was pointless to keep asking, so Phoenix resolved to never ask again. Her father would get no more of her time or energy if she could help it. With her inner child safely hidden away, Phoenix returned to the hardened adult she'd learned to be, replying dispassionately. "Looks like we both win then."

Diane didn't press the issue. "When do you take the final flight of your journey to the Pole?"

Phoenix checked her watch, confirmed the time zone yet again, and answered reasonably confidently, "in roughly twenty-five hours."

"Then go out and have some fun. Find one of the bars or

coffee shops, something familiar. It will make the adjustment easier. Just go easy on the alcohol," Diane added knowingly.

Phoenix hugged her arms tight to her body, Diane's words landing with a thud. "Isn't being able to drink more one of the benefits of returning to sea level?" Phoenix tried to respond lightly but came off testy. "Don't worry, I know my limits Diane."

"Sorry Fee, sometimes I forget you are a grown woman. Go, have a good time and embrace the adventure. Email me when you can."

Embrace the adventure, Phoenix repeated to herself. Phoenix's stomach growled. A little food and alcohol should help that process along. Or more accurately, a little alcohol and a lot of food was what she needed.

"I'll do my best. Thanks for everything Diane. I love you."

"I love you too Fee. Stay warm."

The coffee shop was located inside a weathered wooden building attached to a corrugated metal Quonset hut. Inside, the rounded walls and ceiling were lined with wooden planks, providing the shop with a unique look. With no windows, the room felt small, but Christmas lights brightened things up.

Nothing about this room felt familiar, but the coffee was enjoyable and pushed away the jet lag for an hour or so. However, the lack of natural lighting appeared to be the stronger influence as her jet lag returned, clouding her thoughts. She decided a change of scenery was in order and headed in the direction of the cafeteria to refuel. She caught herself. In Antarctica the cafeteria was referred to as a galley. Might as well get used to the local lingo.

Phoenix sat by herself and ate quickly while simultaneously

taking note of the food. She expected barely acceptable cafeteria fare but everything she'd eaten since arrival, including the burger, fries and salad she was currently finishing, were quite good. Satiated, Phoenix approached the serving line, finding herself curious and excited about her new job.

"Hi, I'm Phoenix," she said warmly, addressing the older woman before her. She had her brown hair pulled back into a neat ponytail but streaks of gray were visible along with smile lines. Phoenix instantly liked her. There was something trustworthy about an older person with smile lines.

"Jane. Nice to meet you. How can I help?"

"Well, I'm continuing to the Pole tomorrow to work as one of this year's cooks. Do you mind if I pick your brain when you have a little time? I don't want to interfere with your system but I'd love some tips."

"Sure, if you want to hang out now I can explain how we do things in McMurdo. My understanding is the Pole works similarly, just on a smaller scale."

"That'd be great! Feel free to put me to work. It's not like I have anything else to do until my transfer."

Jane introduced Phoenix to Mickey, the baker, and George, the sous chef, who were both working in the kitchen as well. Each shared their tips and experiences and she did her best to take it all in.

As the shift wound down, Phoenix helped them clean the kitchen, unable to simply watch them work. The background hum of anxiety that had ebbed and waned throughout the day fled her body as she wiped down counters, the familiar activity grounding her within this new world. Jane gave her a nudge as she rinsed her washcloth.

"Care to join us at Gallaghers Pub? We owe you a drink for all the help. There's even a live band tonight."

"Why not? My body has no clue what time it is, might as well enjoy myself before I crash again."

"That's the spirit."

The aged wooden building reminded Phoenix of a decent dive bar. Arcade games off to one side, a long bar for serving or drinking, and a small, open dance floor. Decor was simple, with historic pictures of McMurdo Station on the wall. The band was already set up on the small stage and kicked off as soon as Jane bought the first round of drinks and Phoenix felt right at home. While the beer was unfamiliar, this was a situation she knew how to handle.

George bought the second round, and by the time Mickey bought the third round, just as the band was finishing up, Phoenix couldn't remember what about Antarctica had been making her nervous. Loud music replaced the band and Phoenix joined a crowd of people dancing, enjoying the complete lack of stress. She didn't have to worry about money, a job, or her family for the first time in her life.

After a bathroom break Phoenix lost track of the kitchen crew she'd arrived with, but before she could find them an attractive blonde a few inches shorter than her approached, drinks in hand.

"I saw you dancing and wondered if you'd like to join me. Whiskey?" she asked, offering the drink with a seductive smile. A familiar desire rose in Phoenix's body and she took the drink and downed it in one go, attempting to silence Diane's voice in the back of her head. Instead she focused on her most recent words. *Embrace the adventure.* Women were an adventure and always helped settle her nerves. Maybe one last fling would be ok?

"Thanks, beautiful. Gotta name?"

"Sierra. You?"

"Phoenix," she said, taking a step closer to Sierra to be heard over the music, speaking directly into her ear. "So, Sierra, are you staying here in McMurdo, or will you be continuing to the Pole this season?"

Sierra eyed her questioningly, but answered, "I'm remaining here in McMurdo for the summer. Why?"

Phoenix gave her a sly smile before responding. "Because I promised to behave – once I was at the Pole."

Sierra moved close, taking the empty glass from Phoenix's hand, her fingers brushing over Phoenix's and lingering. "Good thing you aren't at the Pole then." She placed the glasses on a nearby table before taking Phoenix's hand and leading her into the crowd.

Sierra was a good dancer, and that wasn't just the alcohol talking. She knew how to move her body in subtle ways that drove Phoenix wild. Phoenix let her body lead the way as their bodies fell into sync. It only took a handful of songs before they were both ready for something more. "Want to go back to my place?" Sierra asked hopefully at Phoenix's ear, her hot breath adding to her arousal.

"Well I don't remember where mine is anymore, so your place it is." Sierra laughed at Phoenix's statement and led her through the crowd, outside, and back to her private room.

*P*hoenix awoke disoriented, memories of the night before slowly poking through the fog of alcohol and jet lag, currently being helped along by the blonde standing before her wearing just panties and a bra.

"You're up," Sierra said cheerfully, pulling on her jeans. "Unfortunately I have a shift to get to or I'd let you sleep."

Phoenix nodded but didn't try to speak just yet. Her mouth was as dry as a desert. Maybe because Antarctica was literally a desert, but the drinks last night hadn't helped.

Phoenix checked her watch. Her best estimate was that she'd had four hours of sleep. She had five hours before reporting for her flight. That was enough time for a nap, a shower, and some food. Phoenix set an alarm on her watch and returned her focus to Sierra, unsure when she'd get to enjoy a view like this again.

Sierra pulled a t-shirt from her closet, and much to Phoenix's disappointment, put it on. "Thanks for last night. I had a great time."

Phoenix found her voice, though it sounded like gravel. "Me too. Though, I think I need some water." Phoenix looked around the room. "And a map, which should be in my pants. I don't even know what building I'm in. I only remember how to get to my room from the galley."

Sierra laughed. "Lucky for you, I know where the galley is. I can walk you there when you're dressed."

Phoenix gathered her clothes, finding her shoes across the small room. Once dressed she followed Sierra around the brown buildings and to the bright blue of building 155.

Sierra talked as they walked. "You know what I love? Thanks to everyone's limited wardrobe no one even notices a walk of shame."

"What's there to be ashamed of?" Phoenix asked playfully. "Shame is the last word I'd associate with last night."

"Oh, you're quite the charmer aren't you? I can see why you promised not to cause trouble at the Pole."

Phoenix laughed. "Thank you?"

"You're welcome. And if you end up back here for some R&R, you know where I live." Sierra said with a wink.

"I'll keep that in mind."

"Well, here's the galley. Thanks again for last night. Good luck Phoenix." Sierra kissed her on the cheek.

"You too Sierra."

After grabbing a muffin and juice Phoenix found her room and flopped on her bed. So much for keeping it in her pants, but Diane couldn't possibly expect Phoenix to pass up an opportunity like Sierra, could she?

CHAPTER THREE

PHOENIX

*W*here the plane from New Zealand to McMurdo seemed impossibly large, the plane to the South Pole was impossibly small. What Phoenix wouldn't give for a strong drink to calm her nerves. She was most certainly not feeling up for this adventure. But there was another person awaiting her arrival so they could return home to their family. If she backed out now, because the tiny plane was freaking her out, she couldn't live with herself.

The engines roared as the pilot prepared for takeoff. Between the engines and the foam earplugs, she couldn't distract herself talking to Jimmy. Instead she fell into another coping mechanism to calm her racing heart, reciting the state capitals in geographic order.

She started with Alaska, in honor of the icy locale, working her way down the west coast, with a quick jaunt to Hawaii, before resuming her path to Arizona. If only traveling was that easy. Her heart rate didn't slow to a reasonable level until reaching Harrisburg, Pennsylvania, which was farther than she'd ever taken the exercise on any of the prior flights.

As relaxed as she was going to get, Phoenix took the opportunity to gaze out the window at the continent below. Awe replaced fear as she watched the ice, shadows hinting at mounds and cracks. If she thought McMurdo was intimidating, it looked positively inviting now. *Embrace the adventure Phoenix or Grandma will haunt your ass until you do.*

When the plane landed three hours later, Phoenix was ready to run off the plane and kiss the ground, until she remembered there was no ground, not for almost two miles below her. The thought made her head spin. Two miles of ice. Over 800 miles to civilization. Antarctica had a way of making her feel small, yet now that she was off the plane the excitement took over. The sun beat down, warming her face against the cold. She'd never felt such cold in mid-October. Sure, it snowed last Halloween, but it wasn't all that cold and the snow melted the next day. At least it was spring in the southern hemisphere so it would get warmer in the coming months. Phoenix couldn't get any farther away from her old life if she tried.

The next two hours were a blur. The outgoing station manager, James, rustled them to the station for a brief orientation, including a stern reminder to drink water constantly to help them acclimatize to the geographical elevation.

Following orientation was a station tour. Phoenix had watched some tour videos online before coming down, but it was different in person. For one, videos don't smell. The station currently smelled of jet fuel and popcorn near the entrance. The videos also didn't allow the viewer to hear the background hum and occasional creak of the station shifting on the ice. That made Phoenix a little nervous, but she put her concerns out of her mind as they walked.

The station was laid out in C shaped halves called pods. Two stories tall, the A pod and B pod were joined by a walkway that allowed for movement of the ice below. Community spaces, with a few exceptions, made up the spine of the station, with bathrooms and berthing encompassing three of the four station legs. The gym took up the fourth leg in B pod near the main entrance.

The station held all the amenities of home except for live or streamed television. The first floor held the bulk of the entertainment spaces. Closest to the entrance, near the popcorn, was a comfortable TV room which also stored stacks of board games and videos. Not only DVDs, but real VHS tapes from decades past. For some reason, their presence added to the surrealness of Phoenix's surroundings.

Continuing along the first floor of B pod they were shown the coatroom, communications and office spaces, recycling, and the arts and crafts room. Phoenix's eyes lit up at the sheer variety of craft supplies. Perhaps she'd do more than just draw.

They crossed into A Pod through a short hallway to find a reading room with an impressive library of books, the laundry room, a currently empty greenhouse, a small store and mail room, and finally a sauna.

The beer can, as it was called, protected the external stairs between floors but wasn't heated. By the time Phoenix reached the top of the stairs her lungs actually ached from the cold and lack of oxygen. Re-entering the station she was struck by both the heat relieving the ache and the smell of food which made her stomach grumble.

She learned why as their tour guide pointed out the kitchen immediately to their right and led them through the galley which offered an amazing view of their surroundings. Next to the kitchen and galley was medical, fully stocked to keep them safe and healthy throughout the year.

They crossed back into B pod which held the science labs and other office spaces. But off to the left was the B3 lounge, a game room with a pool table, darts, a mini-kitchen and another TV lounge. The B3 segment was also the lifeboat for the station. If anything happened to make the station unlivable, B3 had its own life support to sustain the survivors until rescue could be coordinated. Phoenix refused to think about an emergency rescue scenario.

Their final stop of the tour was the fitness center which overlooked the gym. It held everything Phoenix might need to blow off steam, from weights to cardio to a heavy bag. Thinking back to her trip up the stairs, Phoenix decided to give herself some time to acclimate before testing the equipment.

After the tour they were escorted to their rooms. Phoenix's room was on the second floor of A pod located immediately across the hall from the kitchen and galley – a name that was already becoming second nature. It was the most convenient commute she'd ever had. Granted, that would have been true no matter where she lived on the station. It only took a minute or two to walk from one end to the other.

The room itself was only eight by nine feet but had everything she needed. Bed. Desk. Storage. A bathroom would have been nice, but communal facilities were situated not that far down the hall. She even had a small window which was currently covered by cardboard to keep out the sun that wouldn't set until the end of March. Peeking out the window revealed an almost uninterrupted view of the ice and snow, the sun glinting in a way that was beautiful but blinding. The cardboard would need to stay.

Phoenix had an hour before meeting her new boss, and rather than unpack she laid down to attempt a power nap. Maybe Diane had been right to caution her about drinking because she was already wiped out from the previous evening and fell asleep more easily than expected.

Phoenix awoke with a gasp, breathing fast with a racing heart, the feeling disorienting her. She looked at her watch, afraid she had overslept but it had only been a half hour since falling asleep. She vaguely remembered a warning about this experience at orientation, something about your body breathing too slow when sleeping at altitude, but whatever the cause she'd not enjoyed the experience. She tried to rest a bit more but now her mind was in fight or flight mode and it just wouldn't happen. Instead she spent the rest of the time unpacking.

Phoenix walked across the hall to the kitchen where a man, in his mid-40s if she had to guess, greeted her. "Ah, Phoenix, I was going to meet you in time for your tour but got held up. I'm Kevin, technically your supervisor, but I am not big on hierarchy. Think of me as a resource who just happens to report your every move to your aunt." Phoenix winced at the unexpected revelation even as Kevin laughed.

"Sorry, Diane bribed me with a care package of Nutella if I'd say that. I'm not going to report anything of the sort to her. But Nutella is my kryptonite. I couldn't resist."

"She's such a little shit," Phoenix said, but she had to admit Diane got her this time. "Should I worry about what else she said?"

"Only good things. She said you're pretty creative with food which you'll need given our supply limitations. And that you'd probably do better on dinner shift."

"That I would. When are my shifts?"

"Monday through Saturday from two in the afternoon until eleven. You'll help with lunch if needed, but mostly prep for dinner. You'll also be responsible for preparing mid-rats, or midnight rations, for the overnight folks. How's that sound?"

"Works for me. Who covers Sunday?"

"During the summer season people volunteer to help so you get a day off. In the winter it's a free for all with leftovers. The more we eat, the less is shipped back home."

"That makes sense. Can I help with anything now?"

"I like the enthusiasm. Why don't we start with a tour of our storage facilities? You'll find we have a rather unique system here and the sooner you get familiar with it the easier life will be."

Kevin led her to the hall and took a right, heading back

toward the entrance as he talked. "Most of our food, except for the freshies, is stored in the supply arch currently buried in snow. It's accessible through the beer can and well below freezing. That means we need coats. Mine is in the coat room next door. I'll wait for you to grab yours."

Phoenix agreed and soon returned from her room with her bright red parka.

"I forgot to mention our planning meetings. Every morning at nine we'll have a quick planning meeting for the day. Then each Saturday we plan the following week's meals. Once the menu is set you'll determine what ingredients you need and give that list to me. The next day you'll find everything you need in the walk-in cooler or on the back patio. You shouldn't need to visit the supply arch, but I'd like you to be familiar with it."

Kevin lead her to the beer can and down past the first floor entrance. He pointed out ice tunnels that housed water and electrical pipes but Phoenix had no interest in exploring them further at the moment. She could tell it became a tighter space than she preferred.

The supply arch was the opposite, a spacious cavern filled with shelving which held pallets and crates of food, not unlike a Costco back home. A freezing Costco that happened to be free to her, but also not restocked once they were closed for the winter. Phoenix was impressed and looked forward to the challenge of feeding the station with only the supplies in front of her.

The next day Phoenix shadowed Bob, the outgoing evening cook, for the rest of his shift, helping as needed. She'd already made notes of how she would change a few things so that they would be more efficient for her cooking style. They finished at eleven but she was too keyed up to go to bed. It was time to have some fun.

She remembered something about the B3 lounge being the de facto bar, but you needed to bring your own beverages. Phoenix hadn't thought to buy any earlier at the small shop, but she was confident in her ability to charm at least one drink out of someone.

She heard boisterous voices as she approached. Inside were a dozen or so people playing pool, darts, and generally having a good time. More than a few heads turned to see who entered, but it was an energetic blonde woman who greeted her first. *What was it about blondes on this trip?*

"Hi, I'm Skye. I believe you're the new cook?"

"Yeah, I'm Phoenix. Are you always that observant?"

"When a redhead's involved I am," Skye said with a playful lilt to her voice.

Phoenix had to laugh. She may not be home, but in this moment home didn't seem so far away. She was surrounded by people having a good time and was already getting hit on. It also looked like she wasn't the only queer woman at the station. "I'll keep that in mind," Phoenix replied warmly.

"Please do. Is it natural?"

Phoenix's tired, oxygen starved brain wasn't following her question. "Is what natural?"

"Your hair color. Will I have the pleasure of enjoying it throughout the summer?"

Phoenix ran a hand through her shoulder length auburn hair. "Oh, right. Lucky for you it is," Phoenix said, forgetting she wasn't supposed to be flirting. Well, actually, Diane said not to sleep around. She didn't say she couldn't flirt.

Skye's eyes twinkled in amusement. "Can I get you a drink?"

Alarm bells rang in Phoenix's head, but they were muted by the brain fog. How much alcohol could she handle while still maintaining tenuous boundaries? Phoenix realized she'd taken too long to answer when Skye chuckled.

"Come on, I don't bite. Unless you ask of course." Sky grabbed Phoenix's arm and pulled her over to the small kitchen.

"Liquor, beer, or wine?"

"I think I'll stick to a beer. I can barely think as it is."

"I have been known to have that effect on women," Skye said as she reached low into the fridge, giving Phoenix a clear view of her shapely ass through black yoga pants. Phoenix was still staring when Skye turned with a knowing look on her face. *Damn.* Was Skye sent here just to test her will, because that seemed like the type of cruel joke Diane would play.

Skye handed her an unfamiliar can, lingering just a bit before letting go. Phoenix wasn't sure how to navigate this new world where she couldn't just follow her libido, but she knew she would figure it out soon.

"So, Skye, what's your job here?" Phoenix asked.

"Heavy equipment operator," she said nonchalantly.

"Seriously?" Phoenix replied, immediately chastising herself for the reaction.

"I didn't take you for a sexist," Skye said teasingly and Phoenix stopped worrying. "I know I don't look that tough, but it's a lot of fun. And the look on people's faces when my tiny ass hops out of a massive dozer is priceless."

"I wouldn't call your ass tiny." The words slipped out of her mouth and she couldn't even blame it on the alcohol yet. Where was a chaperone when she needed one?

Skye gave Phoenix a sly smile as she cracked open a beer of her own. "How long are you here Phoenix? Wait, is Phoenix your real name or a nickname? You aren't from Phoenix are you?"

"Would you believe me if I said I'm both named Phoenix and from Phoenix?" She kept a straight face long enough to see Skye start to question her story and laughed. "Just fucking with you.

It's really my name, and I've never been anywhere near Arizona."

"Oh good, a bullshitter. This is going to be fun. Want to play some pool?" She gestured to the table where two guys were finishing their game.

"That depends."

"On?"

"If you're any good," Phoenix shot back.

"Oh, I don't offer anything I'm not good at," Skye said, and it sounded like a promise.

Dammit Diane, this is just cruel. Phoenix knew she should leave, but she couldn't make herself go. Maybe this could be a transition into her new life. She wouldn't sleep with Skye, but she could still have fun.

Phoenix let Skye rack the balls and break, once again enjoying a nice view of her ass. Should she be praising or cursing yoga pants, she wasn't sure. Skye sank a ball on her break, though Phoenix hadn't been paying enough attention to notice which.

"Solids," Skye called out, studying the table before choosing her shot. "How long are you here Phoenix?"

"The whole year."

"Damn," Skye said before taking her shot, sinking the two ball in the corner. "Wait, have you been to the Pole before?"

"Nope, this is my first time at *this* pole," Phoenix said, accentuating the pun. Skye raised an eyebrow but otherwise ignored the comment.

"I didn't think they let Pole virgins winter over," Skye said, eying Phoenix skeptically.

Phoenix heard a man behind her say, "plenty of virgins in the science lab," to raucous laughter. It was a lame joke, but Phoenix smiled enough to placate the people nearby. Skye ignored them as well, lining up her next shot.

"I may have had a little help with that. My aunt works in

staffing. She must have convinced them I'd be ok." That's when it hit her. Diane must have pulled some serious strings to give her this opportunity. She couldn't blow it by ignoring her one request.

"So you have connections and you make our food. I'd better stay on your good side." Skye leaned lower than was necessary for the shot, giving Phoenix a clear view down her shirt. It was a simple move but effective at redirecting her barely oxygenated blood flow to her center. They should have covered this in the safety briefing. Warning, avoid arousal until you've acclimatized or you may pass out.

Phoenix doubled down, though she probably shouldn't. Still in Skye's line of sight, Phoenix leaned against the table with one hip and drained half her can in one long drink. She couldn't be certain, but she liked to think Skye was as distracted by Phoenix as she was by Skye. Phoenix retrieved the cue ball and set up her shot.

"And how long are you here?"

"Until February. Then I'm spending a couple of weeks in New Zealand. I want to hike the Southern Alps before heading back home."

Phoenix's shoulders relaxed and she took the shot, sinking the nine ball. At least Skye wouldn't be a temptation the entire year, just four months. "Sounds beautiful. I haven't thought that far ahead, but planning for next year will make for a nice distraction come winter."

"From what I hear there are quite a few distractions, though I should warn you that sound carries and the walls are thin."

"Good to know, but I'll be ok. I'm doing my best to avoid complications."

"Why?"

"Don't laugh, but my aunt kinda made me promise to behave before she'd submit my application."

Skye laughed and Phoenix couldn't blame her. "Or what, she'll ground you?"

"She does have a knack for getting people to do what she wants, so I wouldn't put it past her. And she talks to my boss, so I know she'd find out."

"Guess you'll have to get creative then."

Phoenix shook her head. "Don't underestimate the power of an older southern woman trying to keep her favorite niece out of trouble."

"Don't underestimate my interest in a challenging redhead."

Phoenix laughed to herself. Since when was she a challenge? Since now apparently.

After another game of pool, and then darts, Phoenix's energy was sapped. She finished the last of her beer and dropped it in the recycling bin.

"As fun as this is, I need to crash."

"Would you like some company? No strings attached." Skye was so close Phoenix could feel her body heat. And it was her body that wanted the company, even as her mind told her to go to bed alone. It would be so easy to say yes, to lose herself in Skye for a night. But then, what if things went wrong? She couldn't run and Diane would certainly find out.

Phoenix gave Skye her best placating smile. She rarely used it *before* sleeping with a woman, but it seemed her best option.

"I'm afraid I'll be asleep the second I hit the pillow."

"Another time then?"

"Maybe," Phoenix said and headed to her room, frustrated but proud of herself for surviving her first real test of her new life.

ASH

Arriving at Amundsen-Scott South Pole Station on November 3rd was a unique combination of déjà vu and coming home for astrophysicist Ash Bennett. This was her second trip to the South Pole, though her first winter over. Just eleven months ago Ash spent two weeks working with a team to upgrade equipment on the IceCube neutrino detector. She'd loved it, so when presenting her PhD dissertation to her advisor she'd included a return trip to the Pole.

Now here she was, her future career hinging on this relatively brief time at the bottom of the world. Maybe it was a bit dramatic to think that way, but for the next year the responsibility for keeping the detector running smoothly for the 300 or so scientists working in the IceCube program fell to Ash and her colleague Jon.

Today she had no real responsibilities. No one could be expected to think clearly after days of travel crossing seventeen time zones, so she allowed the pressure to fade into the background. Her body hummed in anticipation of the adventure before her.

After orientation, and an unnecessary tour, she quickly

unpacked and found the pictures she'd brought along to decorate her walls. Ash wasn't prone to homesickness as long as she had a touch of home with her. The picture of her family was placed on her desk wall. On the wall opposite her bed hung two pictures of Earth as seen from Mars, a constant reminder of her dream to become a Mars colonist. If she played her cards just right, she'd see that sight with her own eyes one day.

On the surface, her time on the ice was meant to complete her PhD project, but Ash knew that proving herself in one of the most challenging places on earth would give her an advantage when applying for any future colonization programs. Given how far-fetched her dream was, she kept it to herself, but she never forgot.

The galley was about half full when Ash arrived. As she scoped out a place to sit, she spotted her colleague and fellow winter over Jon, who waved. She waved back before grabbing a plate and following her nose to the griddle where a tall, striking woman stood grilling steaks. The overhead lights accentuated the red in her auburn hair which was pulled back in a short ponytail under her round chef's hat. It was an intriguing color Ash realized she didn't see that often on campus, with most dyed hair landing along a vibrant rainbow spectrum.

The woman looked up and Ash caught her eyes, so light blue they were almost gray. She couldn't recall seeing a natural redhead with blue eyes. Maybe her hair color wasn't natural? Ash realized she was staring and pulled her eyes away, focusing on the food and trying to control the blush warming her cheeks.

"How would you like your steak?" the woman asked in a friendly tone that didn't hint at Ash's long glance.

Ash looked up and the woman was smiling knowingly, perhaps even a little cocky. She most likely took Ash's stare as interest which it most definitely wasn't. Not sexual interest, anyway. That wasn't something Ash experienced, but she couldn't say that to a stranger.

Ash stumbled over her words. "Oh, um, well done please." She paused, waiting for the criticism that often accompanied her order, but none came which was a welcome change.

"Sure thing," came the response, and while there was nothing overtly flirtatious in her words, something in her tone gave Ash that impression. She shook her head inwardly. Maybe she was misinterpreting things.

The woman deftly cut into a piece of meat and showed the inside to Ash, a nice light brown. "How's that? I could throw it back on for a few minutes if it's not done enough."

"No, it looks good, thanks." Ash handed her plate over, not meeting the woman's eyes, and quickly turned to the food in front of her. She added roasted potatoes, mixed vegetables, and chocolate cake to her tray knowing she'd need to increase her food intake while she was here. Dessert wasn't a splurge, but a necessity as their bodies burned significantly more calories to maintain oxygen levels and body temperature. Mandatory dessert was Ash's favorite perk of the job.

Ash walked to her table of colleagues, pushing the woman from her mind. She probably caught people staring often enough that Ash wasn't a blip on her radar anyway. Instead Ash focused on getting acquainted with her colleagues who she'd emailed frequently over the past year in preparation.

Ash found herself distracted while Jon talked about the college football season they'd left behind. Dinner service was winding down and the chef again caught Ash's eye as she spoke animatedly with an attractive blonde woman. They looked rather friendly, leaning toward each other as they talked. The new woman touched the chef more than Ash expected for acquaintances. Perhaps they were friends? Or lovers?

Rather than analyze why she cared, Ash returned to the dessert table for another piece of cake.

After dinner and hours of conversation, Ash was still wide awake at eleven at night. She expected her body would need at least a week to settle into the new time zone. For tonight she wanted to enjoy her down time, retrieving her personal notebook from her room and heading into the library for some writing. She'd started her current fanfic on the flight to Christchurch, her most challenging so far.

Ash discovered fanfic right around the time she was discovering her sexuality and looking for representation. Where the fanfic world offered her countless opportunities to read about lesbian relationships, they rarely included her experiences as a demisexual lesbian. With the year ahead of her, Ash hoped to re-imagine her favorite Buffy the Vampire Slayer characters as asexual, exploring the vastness of the asexual and aromantic spectrum. If she wrote the stories well enough, she might even convince some readers to give asexuals a chance with a relationship.

Thanks to the long flight, Ash had already setup the story and was just getting to the best part, an intimate and sensual scene between Willow and Tara. These scenes required concentration, the words slow to form on the page, so were best written in one sitting. That was her goal tonight as her body didn't seem interested in sleep anytime soon.

Tara spoke in a whisper, letting her lips brush over Willow's ear. "Close your eyes."

Willow shivered against her in spite of the hot bath they shared. Tara kissed her temple. Seeing Willow's eyes closed but crinkling with a smile, she began the spell she'd recently discovered.

Almost imperceptibly, the water moved around them, a slight current drawing it nearer. Tara sharpened her focus on one spot, where the water met Willow's skin, directing it up her arm.

Ash placed the back of her pen in her mouth as she pondered her next sentence.

"What are you writing?"

Ash's head snapped up at the voice, the interruption ripping her from her story. She blinked rapidly, reorienting to her physical space. Gone was the oversized bathtub, Willow and Tara and the sensual scene she was in the middle of writing. Instead she found herself glaring at the chef from earlier, not nearly as intriguing now.

"Oh, is it personal?" the chef asked. "I came in to find a book but got curious."

"Did no one teach you proper library etiquette? This is a quiet space," Ash said, her frustration getting the better of her. This was her one completely free night before work claimed a good portion of her brain and she'd been interrupted. How long would it take to regain her focus?

"I guess I was too busy working for a living to spend much time in libraries," the chef said with disdain.

Ash winced internally, realizing she had provoked the woman's reaction, although she wasn't sure why the chef had reacted so strongly. But then her eyes met the chef's, now decidedly gray rather than blue, and Ash couldn't back down from the challenge. The longer Ash stared, the less she seemed capable of explaining why they were glaring at each other.

Who was this woman who thought it was perfectly normal to interrupt someone when they were writing? What right did she have to be pissy with Ash when she'd been the rude one?

The woman continued sizing her up, not budging. As the seconds ticked by, logic returned and the ridiculousness of the situation became apparent. It didn't matter if the chef was being rude, or if Ash had every right to be frustrated. They were in too small a community to hate each other off the bat. Ash recognized she was being arbitrarily stubborn and broke eye contact.

Ash closed her notebook and set down her NASA sponsored space pen and gathered her composure. "I didn't intend to offend you but I was in the middle of..." Ash paused, not comfortable sharing this side of herself with anyone, much less a stranger who she'd just pissed off. "...something."

The chef's eyes narrowed in response. Ash kept her expression carefully neutral. Whatever she was looking for, Ash couldn't guess, not even after she responded with, "yeah, ok. I just wanted to introduce myself. I like to know the people I'm cooking for. But I'll let you get back to it." As she turned to leave, Ash's curiosity got the better of her.

"Wait," Ash called. The woman stopped and turned with a questioning expression on her face. "What's your name then? I can't keep calling you the chef."

"Phoenix Murray. And I'm not a chef, I'm a cook."

Phoenix? Ash remembered a recent story she'd read about a shapeshifter whose animal form was a phoenix. It was an interesting premise, but the story went off the rails into the truly bizarre. The juxtaposition of that story and the woman before her, gave her the church giggles, an annoying combination of inappropriate and uncontrollable.

"What's so funny?" Phoenix asked with an edge to her voice.

Ash wanted to stop, to apologize and somehow find her feet with Phoenix but the harder she tried the worse it got. "Nothing, your answer was unexpected. Your name isn't funny, really. I think I'm just oxygen deprived."

"Sure," Phoenix answered skeptically. "And *your* name?"

"Ashley Bennett."

Phoenix raised an eyebrow at her. "You laughed at my name but tell me this. How many Ashley's do you know?"

"More than a few," Ash replied with mild annoyance. This was why she went by Ash with her friends. Only a fraction of the Ashley's she knew went by Ash. "I'm not even the only Ashley currently at the station."

"Never had that problem," Phoenix said smugly.

"Yeah, well, we don't get to pick our names," Ash said sourly. She was not fond of smugness, not even on objectively attractive women. But she couldn't make an enemy. One day someone would interview the people she'd wintered over with to evaluate her suitability as a Martian colonist. How would it look if Phoenix told the story of their first day? Ash needed to find a way to at least be civil so she chose the only topic she could think of.

"What's the difference between a cook and a chef?" Ash asked before Phoenix could turn back to the door.

"About fifty grand in student loans," Phoenix replied, her voice clipped, but Ash caught her message.

"Ah." Apparently not as safe a topic as she expected so Ash quickly changed the subject, asking, "are you here for the summer season?"

"No, I'm wintering over. You?"

That wasn't what Ash wanted to hear. Could she spend an entire year with someone this difficult to talk to? She didn't voice her concerns, simply replying, "same."

"Then it looks like we'll be seeing a lot of each other."

"Well, you do prepare my food, so that's a safe assumption."

"And how was your dinner?" Phoenix asked as if proving a point, but Ash wasn't sure which she was making. Had she inadvertently insulted Phoenix professionally?

"It was good. Excellent actually." Phoenix nodded, appearing satisfied. "I'm curious what you'll be serving tomorrow night."

"You'll have to wait and see. I like to keep women curious."

Ash narrowed her eyes, the unexpected change in tone raising her defenses again.

"Yes, well, right now I'd like to get back to my work, if you don't mind," Ash said coolly. She hadn't prepared for the possibility of flirting women, which was ridiculous in hindsight. The chances of there being other queer women at the Pole were low, but not impossibly low. Phoenix, likely that blonde who needed a name, herself, and eventually Emily, the undergrad she'd be working with in December, proved that statistics meant little in life. She should have prepared a strategy instead of reacting poorly when caught off guard.

Confusion flashed across Phoenix's face, then anger, but none of those emotions were present once she spoke. "See you around then, Ashley Bennett."

CHAPTER FOUR

PHOENIX

*P*hoenix refused to allow her anger to show as she walked out the door, the search for a book forgotten. Proper library etiquette? What the hell? Do I look like I don't go to libraries or something? I thought this place was supposed to be a fresh start.

The irony was that Phoenix had spent significant time at libraries growing up. They were one of the few places that were free, quiet, and safe. Books became her escape, from history, to philosophy, to the classics of literature. But she never took them home. She learned quickly that the people around her saw reading as a threat.

Phoenix's body vibrated, as if the confusion of her conversation with Ashley was settling into her muscles, leaving her unsettled. Ashley didn't make sense to her. Phoenix had misstepped, interrupting her writing, but she'd started to warm up. Until the end when Phoenix had tested the waters with her curious comment. Ashley had pinged her gaydar, but maybe she wasn't out. Or maybe she didn't know she was gay? That would explain the strong reaction to a mild comment.

Ashley was a mystery for another day. After all, Phoenix had all year to figure her out. But she still couldn't shake her annoyance at Ashley's comments. How did this woman find Phoenix's sore spot so fast?

Phoenix reached her room and found a pair of shorts and a tank top, changing quickly. She knew this feeling, and she knew how to manage it, even if it was approaching midnight. Lucky for her, the fitness center had everything she needed. She grabbed her phone, headphones, a towel and her ever-present water bottle and headed down the hall.

The room was dark and empty, which Phoenix preferred. She'd trained with people often, but when working out frustrations she preferred privacy. Her music app held multiple playlists for just this occasion. Today she went for the one titled Women are Frustrating, which kicked off with Meredith Brook's Bitch. Phoenix grabbed a pair of lightweight gloves from the supply bin and began lightly working the bag, reacquainting her muscles with the movements. After three weeks at the Pole, Phoenix felt reasonably acclimated but she hadn't yet taken the time to use the fitness center. Her body settled into familiar combinations in time with the music as her muscles warmed up.

The song ended and she was surprised to feel her heart pounding as she caught her breath. How much was the altitude and how much was simply being out of shape? There was no avoiding cardio if she wanted to handle the exertion. She hopped on a bike, choosing a relatively easy setting and rode through the next song, Pink's Funhouse. Then she returned to the bag in time for a speed round courtesy of Linkin Park's Bleed It Out.

Her mind remained busy focusing on her body, the combinations and the lack of oxygen. Every pump of her heart pushed the lingering frustration from her body. Normally she'd go another three or four rounds but she was exhausted after two and ready to call it a night. She removed her gloves and pulled the headphones out of her ears when the door opened.

"Damn, done already? I was enjoying the view."

"Sorry to disappoint you," Phoenix replied lightly.

Skye stepped close and wrapped her fingers around Phoenix's biceps. Energy rushed to her center from a hidden reserve that hadn't been depleted during her workout. Damn, now Phoenix knew for certain she couldn't be alone with Skye. Her body had a mind of its own.

"I didn't know you were hiding these under your sleeves."

"How do you think I beat you at pool?"

Skye scoffed. "Based on my count, we're tied. I'm always ready for a rematch. "

"We have plenty of time, but I'm confident in my abilities," Phoenix replied with a smirk.

Skye walked around Phoenix and touched the tattoos on her shoulder blades, a variation on a traditional Borneo Rose. "You were hiding these too. I've never seen anything like them."

As tired as Phoenix's body was, her heart did an impressive job redirecting her blood flow to her center. She chastised her body as Skye trailed her fingers over Phoenix's shoulder blade and down her right bicep to the large blue dragon dominating her upper arm. The goosebumps forming on her flesh couldn't be controlled, but her lingering sour mood kept her libido in check.

"And this. What a beautiful dragon." Skye met her eyes and asked in a silky voice, "hiding any others?"

"That's all for now. I believe in quality over quantity."

"They are quality. So, are you up for a rematch tonight?" Skye asked as she took a step back.

"I'm pretty wiped and want to get cleaned up before bed. Another time." Phoenix wiped her face with a towel and wrapped it around her neck.

"Alright, but I'll be waiting." Skye left and Phoenix sighed.

Women were turning out to be a bigger challenge than Phoenix expected. From Skye, who couldn't pass up an opportunity to flirt, to Ashley who wanted nothing to do with her, Phoenix wasn't sure what to do.

Phoenix pondered this contrast as she wiped down the equipment and returned everything to its place. Skye was a challenge to her self-control, but Phoenix knew how to handle a woman's interest. Ashley would normally fade to the background with no second thought in Phoenix's old life. She didn't need everyone to like her, or even notice her. The world was too large to worry about the people who didn't like her.

Except... Phoenix's world was now tiny, and Ashley was not someone she could avoid. On the surface, Ashley was average. Straight, dark brown hair that went to the middle of her back. Average build, and a few inches shorter than Phoenix, around 5'6". Her eyes were the only part of her that wasn't average, a color she'd never seen before in eyes, an undefinable shade of deep turquoise. That couldn't be natural – could it?

Not that Phoenix could talk, she'd heard the questions about her own eyes countless times. Yes, she was naturally a blue-eyed redhead, a genetic rarity that grabbed women's attention without saying a word.

That must have been what drew Ashley's attention to her as well because Phoenix had caught her looking into her eyes more than once. Those looks could mean any number of things, but there seemed to be a lot going on in Ashley's head. If only Phoenix could discover what.

ASH

That didn't go well. Ash stared out the window at the expanse of white extending as far as her eyes could see, not processing any of it. She'd managed to overreact and offend the person that prepared her dinner. If she were writing this in one of her stories, Phoenix would be looking for ways to mess with her food tomorrow. Maybe even be planning to poison her slowly. Hopefully real life wouldn't prove to be so dramatic.

She should apologize, though. Phoenix had no way of knowing she was stepping on Ash's toes. She probably thought she was being friendly. Ash sighed to herself. Maybe Phoenix wasn't flirting with her at all.

It was funny. On her own, Ash had no issues with her sexuality. She was quite happy living her life, finishing her degree, and writing fanfic. She didn't worry about getting laid or meeting people, though she had to admit it would be nice to have someone to share her life with. Someone to come home to and cuddle with at night. Someone to love.

The problem arose when she'd try to explain to others that she was a demisexual lesbian, and while she enjoyed sex at times, she didn't feel attraction to a woman without sharing a deep connection. Even with a connection, sex wasn't a priority for Ash. For reasons she still couldn't understand, that was a deal breaker. Maybe not immediately, but it didn't take long. Even expecting it, the rejection stung. Why was she not enough on her own? Why was sex more important than who she was as a person?

Putting herself out there, and the resulting rejection, hurt too much to risk on casual interest. The problem now was she hadn't found an elegant way to turn a woman down, or clarify her lack of interest, leading to exchanges like tonight's with Phoenix. She was a writer and a scientist, how the hell could she not find a way to navigate these situations? Maybe she could work it out with her fanfic, but not tonight.

Ash stood, her creativity disappearing into the recesses of her mind. Her interaction with Phoenix left Ash with many questions, but she recognized she wasn't being fair. She'd apologize to Phoenix the next time she saw her and try to find some common ground so they could become casual acquaintances instead of mortal enemies.

The next night at dinner Phoenix was conspicuously absent from the line when Ash passed through. Even if she had been visible, the serving line wasn't the best location to talk. With her sleep cycle still out of sync, Ash went to bed shortly after dinner but awoke at 11:30pm. Slightly annoyed, Ash decided to make the most of the situation and write. Before Phoenix's interruption last night, Ash found the library a nice place to write and headed there again. To her surprise she found Phoenix already there. Phoenix looked up when Ash walked through the door and she stopped, second guessing her decision.

"I'm being quiet. Proper etiquette and all that. You don't have to leave."

Ash took a cautious step into the room. "I'm sorry, I was disproportionately rude to you last night."

Phoenix angled her head, reminding Ash of a confused puppy. "Disproportionately rude? Does that mean there was an appropriate level of rudeness you'd find acceptable?"

"I don't know," Ash answered while shaking her head. "It just came out. I should have stuck with the classic, I'm sorry, I guess."

A smile tugged at Phoenix's mouth. She appeared to find Ash amusing, and Ash wasn't sure how she felt about that. It was better than pissed off she guessed.

"Apology accepted," Phoenix said, returning to her notepad, drawing intently.

Ash stepped closer, curious what Phoenix was up to. "That's really good."

Phoenix shrugged, not looking up. "It's just a bookcase."

"I know. The fact that it looks like a bookcase, and not some random scribbles, makes it good in my book."

Phoenix gave her an unexpectedly shy smile. "Thanks."

Ash observed Phoenix for a time, unsure what else to say. Watching the sketch come to life was mesmerizing. After a minute Phoenix glanced up questioningly. Ash averted her gaze as her cheeks warmed and walked over to the window table. She really needed to stop watching Phoenix, or stop getting caught at least.

Ash pulled out her notebook, the Buffy sticker on the front designating it as her current fanfic notebook. Last night's scene remained unfinished but she wasn't sure that she could focus with another person in the room. Would Phoenix be able to tell what she was writing?

Phoenix spoke, interrupting her setup. "At risk of pissing you off again, I have to know. Why the Buffy sticker?"

Ash looked away before attempting to answer. "I..."

Phoenix's tone brightened. "Oh, come on, it can't be that bad. Buffy's a great show. I've watched the series multiple times in fact."

Ash hid her face in her hands, attempting to hide her blush. She never talked to people in person about her fanfic. Sharing her writing was too intimate to do casually, especially when in the middle of writing naked sensuality. But when she peeked through her fingers Phoenix was gazing intently at her, awaiting an answer. Maybe it was time to test the waters a little. "I write Buffy fanfic."

"Fanfic? Meaning you write stories about Buffy?"

"Sort of. She's often in the stories, but I prefer to play around with other characters. Willow and Tara usually."

Phoenix's face lit up. "I thought you pinged my gaydar."

Ash's face fell into a serious expression, though it wasn't easy. "Straight people can write about Willow and Tara too."

"Are you trying to say you're straight, Ashley?" Phoenix's eyes pinned her in place.

"I never said that. But there are straight girls writing Willow and Tara stories."

"I'd bet they don't remain straight for long. In my experience, it doesn't take much to go from fictional queers to real ones."

"Because you're so irresistible?" Ash replied sarcastically.

"Not what I was referring to, but that may also be true." Phoenix smirked but glanced out the window behind Ash. "No, plenty of women resist me without trying. What I meant was that fiction provides a safe place to be curious and learn who you are before trying it out in the real world. What do you think, does that apply to you as well?"

That hit entirely too close to home, surprising Ash. She was right, talking about this side of her was too intimate to share with Phoenix. "That's not exactly your business." Ash's tone was cooler than she intended, but she'd caught her off guard. Again. She needed a guidebook. Or a pamphlet. Ash wrote in her notebook, *your friend/romantic interest is asexual. Here's what they want you to know.* Maybe she'd write one with Cole and her other asexual friends online.

When Ash looked over at Phoenix she was drawing again, but her lips were drawn into a tight line, contempt written across her face. It was not the look of someone who'd received a successful apology. Her parents would be so disappointed if she left the situation as it was. She hated it when they made her properly apologize as a kid but looking at Phoenix she understood. In a confined community like the South Pole, real apologies kept the peace. Small communities couldn't allow conflicts to fester. How much more important was it in a society like a Mars colony? She needed to find a way to stop reacting without thinking.

"I'm afraid I'm doing a poor job of apologizing. The most important part of an apology is changing the behavior that you apologized for. I haven't done that and instead I've made your night worse instead of better." The look Phoenix gave Ash made her pause. "So... I'll... work on controlling my reactions." Ash furrowed her brow at Phoenix's expression. "Why are you looking at me like that?"

"I've never heard someone apologize so readily and genuinely before, though I'm not sure you have anything to apologize for," Phoenix admitted.

How was Ash supposed to respond to that?

Phoenix chuckled to herself, her eyes unfocused as she thought. "Hell, I'm not sure how many insincere apologies I've heard for that matter." She met Ash's eyes. "You are an odd duck, Ashley Bennett."

Recognizing the reference, Ash saw an opening and took it.

"So you watch Buffy *and* Orphan Black? Do you also watch Wynonna Earp?"

"Of course, what kind of lesbian would I be if I didn't? My lesbian card is properly stamped for Supergirl and Legends of Tomorrow too."

That cleared up one question about Phoenix. "But you don't read fanfic?"

Phoenix shrugged. "Not much of an internet person. But now I'm curious. If I Google Ashley Bennett, will I find your work?"

"Nope. No one writes under their actual names. That's half the fun. You get to be someone else."

"And hide?"

"No, to be your truer self."

The words hung in the air, their eyes meeting but no longer in challenge. Curiosity? Ash's curiosity was definitely piqued. If this had been their first conversation, over her favorite fandoms, she'd have liked Phoenix instantly instead of snapping at her. Perhaps they could be friends, but the moment was becoming too much. She broke eye contact, glancing again at Phoenix's sketch.

"We should probably let each other work now or risk this tenuous truce with inadvertent offense."

For the first time her formal tone was purposeful and Phoenix's smile warmed Ash's chest, causing it to flutter a little. Nope, not happening. Ash was here to work, not crush on the cook. As if that could go anywhere. She had yet to date a person who could deal with her sexuality for long. How could Phoenix, who appeared incapable of going five minutes without flirting, handle it? Ash scoffed to herself. *Deal with it. As if it's a chore to love someone who isn't motivated by sex.* Her body tensed, memories of failed relationships invading her consciousness.

Phoenix coughed dryly, bringing Ash back to the present. As she watched Phoenix drink from her Nalgene bottle, she tried to remember what her best friend Cole told her. *We can't project our past experiences onto our current love interests, or we doom them to fail from the start.* Her non-binary friend was wise, though their advice was not easy to follow. Not when her heart was at stake.

When Ash stopped writing, Tara was using magic to trail water over Willow's body. That wasn't a scene she could jump into, especially not while Phoenix sat nearby, so she turned to the beginning of the notebook and began reading. Soon she was lost in the story, forgetting that Phoenix was in the room as she visualized the scene.

Tara drew the water up Willow's arm and across her collarbone as Willow leaned heavily against her.

"Goddess, that feels so good. Where did you learn this?" Willow asked in a daze.

"Hush now." Tara kissed the side of Willow's neck, doing her best to maintain her focus. "Talk later." Another kiss, closer to her ear, and Willow hummed in pleasure. Tara could sense Willow adding her own energy to the spell, giving Tara even more control over the water. She encouraged more water up her girlfriend's arm, releasing it to create a waterfall over her breasts.

Willow laughed as she watched. "You can be quite silly when you want to be."

The water was noticeably cool by the time Tara released the spell, but Willow warmed it easily.

"Do you have a spell to turn this into a hot tub?" Willow asked mischievously.

"We won't know until we try."

Ash paused, closing her eyes as she allowed the outside world into her awareness again. Due to the late hour, she didn't want to start the next part of the scene, and finishing yesterday's allowed her to feel settled. She yawned, arching her back as she stretched, finally opening her eyes to survey her messy scrawl. Writing longhand took more time, but she appreciated the break from a computer screen and the feel of paper under her hands. Typing the scenes never took long, making it an acceptable trade off.

She glanced at Phoenix who sat angled toward her, which was not how she remembered Phoenix sitting when she began writing. Odd. Phoenix was drawing something new, but when she glanced up she looked back down immediately, slamming her sketchbook closed quickly.

Ash gave her a curious look. "What were you drawing?"

Phoenix shook her head, an exaggerated attempt at innocence. "Nothing I can't finish later. Are you heading out?"

Changing the subject? Phoenix was definitely hiding something, but their tentative truce wasn't worth risking at the moment so she let it slide.

"Yes, it's a bit past my bedtime but I've now finished the scene I started yesterday."

"Can I read it?"

Ash laughed at Phoenix's hopeful expression. "Nope." She closed her notebook and turned in her chair. "Are you sticking around to finish your secret drawing?"

"Naw, I'll do it another day. It wouldn't hurt for me to turn in early tonight. I might even be alert for my morning meeting."

Ash stood, slowing as she reached Phoenix. "Can I ask you a personal question?"

Phoenix appeared to size her up. "You can ask, but I might not answer."

"It's nothing that bad, just trying to satisfy my curiosity. Where are you from? I could swear sometimes you have an accent, and in the next sentence it disappears."

Phoenix's face took on a more relaxed expression, nodding slightly. "That's because I've actively worked to minimize my accent. Like it or not, many Americans hear even a hint of a southern accent and assume the person is uneducated. It tends to slip out when I'm tired or drinking. Or talking to another southerner."

"Ah, that makes sense, but it doesn't completely answer my question. Where's your accent from?"

"Southern Indiana, Evansville specifically. But I left two years ago for Denver. Haven't looked back."

Phoenix took a step toward the door and Ash followed, continuing the conversation.

"I love Denver! One of my friends invited me out a few years back and it was beautiful. Much more pleasant than Wisconsin or Minnesota weather. I love Madison, but the humidity makes summer long."

"Tell me about it," Phoenix said as they walked into the hall. "The Ohio River keeps the humidity just short of raining all summer. It's miserable. Though," Phoenix paused and a quick peek revealed her wistful expression, "sometimes I miss it. Mostly I miss the time in the middle of the night when the air cools from stifling to, well, less stifling. I'd sit on my porch and listen to the crickets chirp, the cars driving in the distance. The asshole mosquitos," Phoenix added with a chuckle. Ash nodded along, knowing only too well how annoying mosquitos were.

They passed a window and Phoenix gestured to it. "Now I live where night doesn't fall for months, and it's never hot or humid. It couldn't be more different."

This peek into Phoenix's world touched Ash more than she expected. Friendship didn't seem so impossible anymore.

"This is my second time here and yes, it's weird. But I can't wait to see the sunset for the first time because it means bright auroras will appear in the darkest skies you'll ever see. Very few people get to experience what we will this year. I, for one, am looking forward to the adventure."

Their eyes met, the same small smile on their faces.

"I think I am too," Phoenix said as they reached the stairwell in A pod. Phoenix angled toward it, while Ash took a step beyond, heading to her room ahead. "Looks like this is where our night ends. See you tomorrow, Ashley Bennett."

"See you."

Her use of Ash's full name was strangely amusing, lifting her mood the remaining distance to her room.

CHAPTER FIVE

PHOENIX

"You're eating late," Phoenix mentioned as Ashley came through the line with fifteen minutes to spare. Phoenix was most of the way through her wind down routine and ready for a break. Not that she'd admit it to anyone else, but Phoenix may have noticed when Ashley tended to eat dinner, which wasn't normally at the end of service.

In the week since their tentative truce in the library, Phoenix noticed Ashley snuck into her thoughts often. Most women Phoenix had sex with, Skye included, didn't hold her attention for long. But Ashley was so different from everyone she knew. And then there were those eyes, such a unique shade that she wished she could study them until they made sense.

"We had an issue with the detector. I'm going back after I eat to make sure the fix was really a fix. If it isn't, I'll be working until everything's working properly."

"I had a hunch you were a scientist," Phoenix replied playfully. "Which detector do you work on?"

Ashley answered simply, "IceCube, the neutrino detector."

Phoenix recalled the posters on the wall describing each experiment on site. IceCube was the easiest to remember because it was located in the ice itself, although she hadn't paid enough attention to the project to be able to discuss it in any great detail with Ashley.

"Ah, cool. Mind if I join you?" Phoenix asked, taking a risk. Ashley usually ate with the people Phoenix assumed were her colleagues.

From her vantage point in the kitchen, Phoenix observed the whole station every day. It didn't take long to work out that the scientists and non-scientists didn't often mix. Nor did it take long to determine that Ashley was a scientist who got along well with her coworkers. But that was all she knew besides their conversations in the library, leaving Ashley a puzzle without a box. Phoenix found herself wondering what Ashley's picture would reveal once pieced together.

Ashley hesitated before answering. "I don't mind. Do you need a plate?"

Phoenix turned to the warmer behind her. "I set one aside earlier. Didn't want to risk running out of sauerkraut."

Ashley scrunched her face. "Would that actually happen?"

Phoenix laughed. "Not a fan I take it?" Ashley shook her head vehemently. Phoenix suspected Ash had no idea how cute she looked at this moment. "You might change your mind by midwinter. Lots of vitamin C in sauerkraut. You don't want to get scurvy."

That earned Phoenix a smile. "Isn't your job to ensure that doesn't happen?" Ashley asked as Phoenix walked around to the dining area.

"Hence the sauerkraut," Phoenix replied as if that should be obvious. Phoenix grinned; Ashley's expression really was amusing. She could almost imagine a young Ashley refusing sauerkraut at the dinner table. In fairness, Phoenix didn't like it as a kid either. "Fine, no sauerkraut for you. What food do you like then?"

"Lots of things. Just not fermented foods," Ashley replied as she led them to a small round table.

"Ok, then what's your favorite Thanksgiving dish?" Phoenix asked, taking advantage of the opportunity to get to know the confusing scientist. With Thanksgiving fast approaching, it was the perfect excuse to be nosy. Ashley's silence just made her more curious.

"Do I need to guess?" Phoenix teased.

"No, I'm just trying to remember the real name. We call it corn bake, but I think it's called scalloped corn."

"That doesn't sound right."

"Why, doesn't it meet your standards?" Ashley asked playfully.

Despite Ashley's tone, a familiar irritation arose but Phoenix ignored it. Ashley had no idea how poor Phoenix had grown up. She probably assumed Phoenix was a foodie and was poking fun at her.

"No, I'm trying to imagine what it would taste like. Is there cheese in it?" Phoenix asked.

"No. It's just corn, creamed corn, and onions baked into yumminess."

"That has potential. Is it thick or soupy?" Phoenix's mind was already working on the recipe. It would be a great opportunity to use the creamed corn she'd noticed in storage, while at the same time make an impression on Ashley. Perhaps they could find a way to coexist consistently without annoying each other.

"It's definitely thick," Ashley answered.

Phoenix breathed out in relief. She wasn't a big fan of soupy food, unless it was soup. Or gravy. "Ok, I can imagine it now. That could be good."

"It's the best. Your turn. What's your favorite Thanksgiving dish?" Ashley asked.

"That's easy. My grandma's made from scratch coleslaw. It's

the perfect balance of flavor and a top-secret recipe that only I can make properly. Which means I only have it when I make it myself."

"Will you make it for our Thanksgiving?"

"That depends on the freshies shipment."

"I'll cross my fingers then."

Phoenix did as well, enjoying the unexpected warmth Ashley showed now that they were talking about a safe topic.

As Phoenix walked down the hall to her room, she dreamed of taking a long, hot shower. It was her favorite way to unwind after work back home, and by the end of her work week she was craving one badly. But at the South Pole water was ironically difficult to come by. They may sit on two miles of ice, but it took a lot of energy to melt the water they needed, hence the need for limited shower time. The showers didn't adjust for the person, turning off after two minutes whatever their hair length or level of filth. And that left Phoenix incredibly frustrated after a month, as without a proper shower her hair never felt totally clean.

She always felt a little dirty now, but she had come up with a solution. Phoenix spun on her heels and headed toward B pod and the B3 lounge where there was almost always a small group of people hanging out late into the night, including Jimmy.

Minutes later, after a quick stop in her room for a sketch, Phoenix was draped in a smock in the arts and craft room, about to trust Jimmy with her hair. She knew anything he did could be fixed over time but she couldn't help feeling a little nervous.

"Where did you learn to cut hair Jimmy?" Phoenix asked, trying to hide her nervousness.

"I have five brothers and my parents weren't going to pay for monthly haircuts on six boys. My dad's approach was to shave our heads bald so I taught myself and got pretty good at it. Then, when I was in the service, guys were always happy to trade a beer or two for a barracks cut."

He must have sensed Phoenix's concern because he chuckled good naturedly. "Don't worry, I won't give you a high and tight. Unless that's what you want of course."

"I'm gay, but not that kind of gay. I don't think I can pull off hardcore butch. But I need it short so it actually gets clean when I wash it. I drew a picture of what I have in mind."

Jimmy took Phoenix's sketch of a short faux hawk that would be easy to wash and style if she wanted but would also look decent if she did nothing. It was the style she'd secretly dreamed of but never had the balls to ask for. Now was the perfect time.

"Can you do it?"

"I'll do my best. I think I can get close enough."

A little thrill went through Phoenix when the first long lock of hair fell to the floor. There was no going back now. The hum of the clippers vibrated against her skull and another layer of her old self fell away. It was a fresh start, however the haircut turned out.

After approximately 15 minutes, Jimmy set down the clippers and ruffled her hair. It felt so strange, like the parental affection she rarely experienced. "Almost done, kid."

Phoenix smiled. Jimmy was one of those guys that called anyone under 40 a kid, but he did so affectionately. Her mind wandered. What would it be like to have a grandfather like him? Her mom's dad was distant, not an affectionate man by any means. Once Phoenix made it clear she was into girls, he was even more distant and she couldn't find it in herself to care. Why bother with family that didn't seem to care about her in return? Her dad's father was dead long before she was born, so she had no idea what kind of grandfather he would have been.

Jimmy ruffled her hair again, ran the comb through it and studied it from all angles. "I think we're done. If you notice any spots I've missed let me know."

They didn't have a mirror in the room so Phoenix thanked him and rushed to the bathroom. From her first glance she couldn't control her smile. It was her, but it wasn't. Her eyes looked brighter, her mostly gray eyes more blue. She felt lighter. And she couldn't wait to see what her hair would do with a little styling gel.

She wiped off as much of the stray hair as she could while dry, then rushed to her room for her toiletry bag and a shower.

The first thing she noticed was the water on the back of her head, more intense now without hair. She used too much shampoo, not realizing the short cut would require far less, but the extra suds made it easier to wash away the tiny hairs. She wished she could have stayed in the water longer, but she knew the drill. Two minutes flew by, but even that brief time left her feeling like a new person.

She toweled off and took a look in the mirror. Her auburn hair was messy, pointing every which way. It felt clean as she played with it, forming it into a faux hawk. She beamed at herself in the mirror. It was perfect. She owed Jimmy for this and wanted to find him to thank him with an appropriate amount of enthusiasm.

Phoenix wandered the station, peeking into rooms to no avail. It was already after midnight. Maybe he'd gone to bed? As she walked back toward her room, she heard Skye from down the hall, her words drawn out in surprise.

"Holy shit. Phoenix?"

Phoenix flushed with heat. Skye caught up with her and stood close enough to run a hand through Phoenix's hair. Goosebumps covered Phoenix's skin from Skye's fingers brushing the back of her neck. Skye's breasts brushed against Phoenix's arm, awakening parts of her she was still learning to manage. Phoenix felt her reserve crumble under Skye's touch, the weeks without sex feeling longer for the months spreading in front of her.

Skye took half a step back. "Your hair looks hot."

"Just my hair?"

"I haven't seen the rest of you yet."

Arousal surged through her body and Phoenix made a decision. "Did you mean what you said? No strings?"

"Not even a stray thread."

Phoenix smiled, wrapping her arms around Skye's waist and pulling her tight, the familiar feeling of a woman's body against hers easing the tension created by fighting the impulse. Skye wrapped her arms around Phoenix's neck and kissed her hungrily. Phoenix met her intensity, losing herself to the moment.

Somewhere in the back of her mind Phoenix heard footsteps, but it was Ashley's annoyed voice that broke through the haze of lust. "You have rooms. Find one."

Phoenix stepped back from Skye but didn't respond. Their eyes met, a shadow crossing Ashley's face when she realized who she'd interrupted. Phoenix couldn't know what Ashley was feeling in that moment, but she appeared more than just annoyed.

Skye took her hand and pulled. "Whoops. Your room or mine?"

Phoenix was still watching Ashley storm down the hall, wondering how badly she'd just screwed up. Had she damaged their tentative friendship? Phoenix could almost feel Diane's palm on the back of her head, but the damage was already done, she might as well see it through.

"Yours is fine," Phoenix mumbled before finally turning to follow Skye to her room.

ASH

Ash knew she had no right to be as upset as she was, but she was exhausted after a long day repairing the detector and she was once again taken off guard. The last thing she expected as she went downstairs to her room was a very public display of affection. It took a moment to recognize Phoenix sporting a new haircut, but she should have known. She'd seen her chatting with the other woman many times and they always looked friendly.

Well, it should simplify their tentative friendship if Phoenix was having sex with the blonde. The blonde? She really needed to learn the other woman's name so she could call her something besides 'the blonde.'

Ash stormed into her room and paced. *Why am I pacing?* It wasn't the first time she'd seen unwanted PDA. It may have been the first at the Pole, but it certainly wouldn't be the last.

She turned on her laptop, hoping the satellite was in range so she could message one of her online friends. It was so strange only having internet for about half the day. Never in her life had she experienced so little internet. She'd heard stories from her

ASH

parents about growing up without it, but they might as well have been speaking of the dark ages as far as she was concerned.

Since middle school she'd been online unsupervised, making friends around the world. At first, they'd talked about their favorite TV shows and video games, but as they grew older talk turned to sexuality. That's when the internet became invaluable. She could find fans of her favorite shows anywhere, but she couldn't find many queer kids in rural Minnesota.

Even among the queer kids, it took many years to discover the asexuality spectrum and narrow down her place on it. Her simplest approach was to view the spectrum as a line, with full asexuality and it's complete lack of sexual attraction at one end and allosexuality at the other. In reality she'd prefer to explain the asexuality and aromantic spectrum in three dimensions, but it was too complicated for most people to define, including herself on most days.

Ash wasn't sure where her personal experience with demisexuality would fit. She'd read books where the demisexual character started just like her, but then they'd make that deep connection with a person and they'd move a lot farther along that line toward the allo end than Ash had ever experienced. That's why she identified more with the ace community than the allo or demi community. Even in a relationship with someone she adored she felt closer to the asexual end of the spectrum.

Her inability to concretely define her own experience made her fellow aces her most important friendships. They helped each other figure themselves out, providing support as they navigated a world where they were rarely recognized, accepted, or understood. Tonight she needed to talk to a fellow ace, someone who understood where she was coming from.

The laptop finally connected to the internet and she breathed a sigh of relief. She opened the group chat and asked if anyone was online. She hadn't stopped to figure out what time

ASH

it was for everyone. It varied too much to matter anyway. If someone was on, they were on. The time was irrelevant.

Cole's message soon came through. *Ash! How's life at the end of the earth?*

Ash relaxed. Her brilliant and wise friend Cole was just who she needed to talk to. They always knew the right thing to say when someone was spinning in confusion.

Cole! I miss you. Life is... different here. I'm not sure how long the satellite is available for us to chat. Mind if I just dive into my moment of crisis?

Of course not, Cole replied. *What's going on?*

Ash explained her interactions with Phoenix and how they got along, at least for brief moments until one of them did something to trigger the other.

And then, a few minutes ago I practically ran into her making out with a woman in the hallway. I didn't recognize Phoenix at first because she'd cut her hair, but then I walked away and I can't stop thinking about the situation. Ash sent the message quickly and waited for Cole to do their thing and sort her out.

Do you normally react this strongly to PDA? Cole asked.

No. That's why it's confusing. Normally I say yuck, roll my eyes and move on.

Cole's status showed typing for quite a while, but they only replied with a few short words, *sounds like we need to talk about this Phoenix.*

Ash sighed. *I know where you're going and you can stop. Sure, she's interesting, an amazing cook, and could probably be a fun friend. But she's also super allo, if that's a thing. Do allosexuals have a poster boy and girl? If so, Phoenix would be one. I think she's hard-wired to flirt at every opportunity. And I'm 99% certain she's having sex right now, with someone she can't have known for more than a month.*

Cole sent back a GIF of a person raising a questioning eyebrow. Ash laughed and sent back a GIF of a person rolling their eyes, before sending a reply. *Just say it Cole.*

ASH

Is it possible you're interested in her as more than a friend? You're spending a lot of energy on someone who's just an acquaintance.

Ash started to reply with a vehement no but stopped herself. It had been a while since she'd been romantically interested in anyone, though it was never apparent to her when she met them. It took time for those feelings to develop, for a friendship to form and for an emotional connection to become apparent. And yet after a few conversations with Phoenix, Ash had already felt that tingle of interest. She thought she'd effectively squashed that curiosity but the evidence against that claim was mounting.

She didn't know enough about Phoenix to understand what she felt or wanted. When Phoenix wasn't frustrating, she was intriguing. Were Ash's attempts to get to know Phoenix because she needed to peacefully coexist with everyone on the station or did her interest run deeper?

I don't know her well enough to say, Ash finally replied. *These same things would push my buttons as a friend, wouldn't they? I don't want a friend who can't accept all of me.*

Maybe you should get to know her better and find out if there's something there. This isn't something you can reason out like physics. It has to be lived.

Have you been watching romantic comedies again? Ash scowled, and since Cole couldn't see her scowl, she sent them a GIF of a baby scowling.

I may have just read a romance novel featuring a non-binary ace and read it twice in a row. But my point remains. Get to know her. See if there's anything there. Give her a chance. She might surprise you.

Ash wasn't ready to give in yet. *And when I get hurt, again, will you admit those books are just fantasies and not based in reality?*

Only if, when you don't get hurt and you've found yourself in a relationship that makes you blissfully happy, you write me a romance novel all about it.

Ash laughed out loud. *Psh!*

You laugh, but are you seriously telling me you haven't noticed how your names work together? Phoenix and Ash?

Ash sent another eye rolling GIF back to Cole.

The phoenix rises from the ashes. I can't make this shit up. It's a sign Ash. Just try to get to know her. If all you gain is a friend, that's still a good thing. And if you discover something more, then isn't it better to find out rather than wonder what if?

You're cut off from romance novels, Cole.

Just try, Ash.

To get to know a woman who's having sex right now? Really?

Yes. Because right now, neither of you knows if you have, or could have, romantic feelings. You haven't given her the chance to decide. If she fucks that up then not only will I stop going on about romance, I'll send you a massive box of cookies.

Why are you the only person online right now? I need someone to balance out your eternal optimism.

Don't you do that enough on your own? Cole replied and Ash could almost see them smirking at her in challenge.

Alright, you win. I'll try to ignore what I know is happening and just be her friend. I like my chocolate chip cookies barely done, so they are soft. Remember that when you send me that care package.

Cole ignored her. *Phoenix and Ash... Pash has a nice ring to it, don't you think? I could make a poll and let our friends vote on it while you're cut off from the internet. Then, when you do get together, we already have your ship name.*

Ugh... Ash sent them a GIF of a toddler flipping someone off angrily, which made her laugh. Ash wouldn't admit it, but she felt better already, though she still didn't believe in Cole's optimism. She would take her time getting to know Phoenix.

Alright, change of topic. Tell me everything else about the South Pole.

CHAPTER SIX

PHOENIX

*P*hoenix always awoke early on Thanksgiving. At the South Pole, Thanksgiving was celebrated on the fourth Saturday in November instead of Thursday, as happened in the United States. The timing meant everyone had the next day off.

Thanksgiving was Phoenix's favorite day of the year. As she entered the galley for coffee, she spotted Ashley sitting quietly by herself. They hadn't spoken except for a few words at dinner for the past two weeks, and Phoenix was certain it was purposeful on Ashley's part.

"Hey stranger," Phoenix said companionably while approaching Ashley who was slumped over a breakfast of oatmeal and coffee, hoping to keep things civil but needing answers. "You planning on avoiding me forever? Because it's going to be a long year if you are."

"I'm not..." Ashley looked up, and for the first time was wearing glasses over her tired eyes, still that same undefinable color. They must be natural after all. In spite of her fatigue, Ashley looked rather cute in glasses, less sexy librarian than adorable nerd.

Sleep challenged everyone at the Pole which made coffee popular at all hours. Ashley's cup was still half full, so Phoenix guessed she hadn't been there long.

Phoenix hesitated only for a moment. Maybe it would be easier to get the truth out of her when she was tired. "Bullshit. Care to fill me in?"

"Why do you care? There are at least 100 other people here. Why does it matter if I am or am not avoiding you?" Ashley's tone was genuinely surprising, going beyond normal grumpiness to sounding annoyed with Phoenix specifically.

Phoenix knew she'd pushed too hard, so answered in a conciliatory tone. "Because in a few months the summer season will end and most people will go home, leaving only 45 of us to ride out the winter. Wouldn't that be easier if we were friends?"

"You ambushed me before coffee so we could be friends? On what planet does that make sense?"

"Hopefully this one," Phoenix replied cheerily, relying on her charm to smooth things over.

Ashley shook her head slightly. "You can start by getting me another coffee with extra cream and sugar. Somehow I don't think this one will be enough."

Phoenix grinned at the opening Ashley had given her and jumped up to retrieve the cup of coffee.

"How are you so awake?" Ashley called from behind her. "Is there a stash of extra potent coffee hiding in the kitchen?"

Phoenix turned before replying. "That's top secret and you don't have clearance." Ashley gave her a look that said she wasn't amused. *Damn, she's really in a mood this morning.* "Ok, in all seriousness, I'm excited because today is our Thanksgiving celebration. It's my favorite meal of the year, even if it starts too damn early in the morning."

"Oh, I had forgotten." Ash's tone was hesitant, but she didn't voice her doubts. "Does it feel weird to celebrate on Saturday?"

"I've lost track of what day it is anyway. I think the whole lack of sunsets is messing with my internal clock. I'm pretending it's Thursday."

"I guess that works on your planet, the one where you risk conversation before coffee," Ashley said before taking a drink, hiding the hint of a smile at her lips. Phoenix tried to restrain her own grin. She liked this side of Ashley. Definitely worth risking pre-coffee ire.

"Why is Thanksgiving your favorite meal? It seems like a lot of work to me."

"For one, I'm good at it. I've been helping my grandma cook Thanksgiving dinners since I was old enough to tear bread for dressing. Every year I'd learn a little more. By the time I was a teenager she didn't even check my dressing anymore, it was my dish. As she got older, I did more and more until she orchestrated and I did everything." Phoenix smiled wistfully, then turned to Ashley. "Is it a lot of work? Yes. But it's satisfying. When the entire table is quiet because they are all eating happily, that's the best feeling in the world."

"I can't even imagine it. We make a turkey, sure, but we use Stove Top dressing."

Phoenix gasped and clutched at her chest. Ashley burst out laughing. It was the least reserved Phoenix had seen her, and she wanted to see more of this side of Ashley. "Tell me you at least made mash potatoes from scratch and didn't use instant."

"No, we made real potatoes. But the gravy..."

Phoenix held up a hand, signaling her to stop talking. "That's enough. I can't take any more."

Ashley grinned mischievously. "The pie was frozen."

"Sacrilege."

"And the cranberry sauce came in a can," Ashley said pointedly.

"I'm actually ok with that," Phoenix said seriously.

"Really?" Ashley asked. At Phoenix's nod they both dissolved into laughter.

"It sounds like tonight's dinner will be an upgrade from your usual Thanksgiving meal."

"All of your meals are an upgrade from frozen dinners," Ashley admitted.

"Ironic since most of my ingredients start frozen or canned, but thank you."

Ashley glanced at the drink station before her face fell and she looked down at her plate.

Phoenix looked from Ashley to the drink station and saw Skye.

"Ah." Phoenix flashed back to the look on Ashley's face when she ran into her and Skye. The pieces didn't quite fall into place, but they were at least lying face up now, showing hints about the picture emerging. Not seeing the picture clearly, Phoenix knew she needed to tread carefully.

During Ashley's avoidance, Phoenix had come up with multiple reasons for her reaction and she'd hoped Skye wasn't the reason. She didn't know Ashley well enough to know what approach to take, so she chose the direct approach, given how successful it was earlier.

"Is Skye the reason you've been avoiding me?" Phoenix asked gently.

Ashley's eyes remained focused on her plate so Phoenix continued. "I'm sorry we got carried away. Skye blindsided me when my resolve was low. It won't happen again." While the sex had been satisfying enough, it wasn't worth the potential fallout.

"So that's her name," Ashley mumbled just loud enough for Phoenix to catch. Looking up with furrowed brows, Ashley asked, "What does that mean, your resolve was low?"

"Well, I promised my aunt, who got me this job, not to sleep around while I was here," Phoenix replied shyly, surprising herself. Sex, or the lack thereof, was not something Phoenix was shy about.

"I underestimated the power of the perfect haircut to attract women. Or at least one woman in particular who promised no strings attached fun. Then I saw your reaction and knew why I was warned to keep it in my pants. Beyond the jealousy my aunt mentioned, not everyone is as comfortable with physical displays of affection and that creates awkward situations. I'm sorry, it was... inconsiderate to succumb in the hallway."

Ashley took another drink of coffee, remaining silent as she gazed into her cup, and since Phoenix wasn't sure what else to say, she waited. After several heartbeats Ashley's shoulders relaxed.

"Well, it is a great haircut," Ashley admitted, lightness returning to her voice. "It's hard to believe you aren't beating women off with a stick."

"It's a good thing, too, since there's a shortage of trees here," Phoenix quipped. Ashley's mouth curled up, though she appeared to be fighting it.

"No strings attached. That's a real thing?"

"Occasionally. There are a lot of people who say that's what they want, until they change their mind and want a relationship. Skye appears to have really meant it. We had fun, but we aren't together, and she hasn't shown any signs of wanting to be. I'm not even sure how that would work in this environment. She's leaving in two months, and I'm not. It would be weird, even if I wanted a relationship, which I never have." Phoenix recognized she was thinking out loud. "Sorry, that's a really long way to say, yes, it's a real thing. But it's never a guarantee."

"Ok," Ashley said before taking a bite of oatmeal.

When it became clear Ashley didn't have anything else to say, Phoenix had to ask, "so you like my hair?"

"Um, well, objectively speaking it looks good." Ashley fidgeted with her oatmeal. Phoenix couldn't resist the urge to poke her a little.

"Objectively speaking? So I don't need a stick to fight you off too?"

"No, no one has to worry about needing a stick with me." Ashley colored and chuckled awkwardly. "Gah, that sounded so weird. Why are we talking about this?"

Ashley was proving to be a tougher nut to crack than she expected. Good thing Phoenix enjoyed a challenge, but she also knew when to back off, most days at least.

"Safer topics then," Phoenix said smoothly. "Tell me about your research."

Ashley relaxed with the change of topic. "I'm a PhD candidate working on the IceCube project. How familiar are you with it?"

"Briefly. I sketched the big round ball on display and read the poster," Phoenix said, purposely sounding ignorant for comedic effect.

"Can I see your sketch?" Ashley said excitedly, apparently ignoring Phoenix's playfulness.

"As long as you explain how it works with your research," Phoenix replied in a teasing tone.

"I was already going to do that," Ashley shot back.

"And I was going to show you anyway so keep going." Phoenix felt her chest lighten at their banter. It didn't matter that she hadn't thought to show Ashley her sketch, it was fun to play.

"Ok. Well we have 5,160 of these digital optical modules, or DOMs, strung into an array covering a cubic kilometer below the ice, hence the name IceCube. The ice creates a unique environment to detect neutrinos which only interact with matter when they collide physically with another molecule. Because this is so rare we needed a very large area to work with. That's why we built it at the Pole."

"Impressive. What about this interested you enough to spend years in school and a year of your life here?"

"I'm helping answer fundamental questions about the universe which is relatively rare in physics these days. Most people end up working on practical research, which is also important. The thing is, a lot of people think we already know all the basics, but we don't."

Ashley grew more animated as she talked, and while Phoenix didn't understand everything Ashley said, she enjoyed watching her share this part of her life.

"There's this meme, that after Einstein we knew how the universe worked, except for the small stuff, the big stuff, the hot stuff, the cold stuff, the fast stuff – you get the picture. Neutrinos are some of the small, fast stuff. When they collide we trace their trajectory backward to learn where they originated in the universe. We also know how much energy they carried. This gives us information about areas of the universe that we can't observe in telescopes. Where that knowledge will lead, who knows. That's why we do the research. To understand the unknowns."

Phoenix found herself transfixed as Ashley spoke. It took a moment for her to realize when Ashley was done.

"Wow. All that information from a bunch of these guys?" Phoenix opened her sketch pad to the page showing a round glass ball about the size of a basketball.

"Yeah. The DOMS are our eyes, picking up the faintest of blue light emitted after a collision." Ashley continued studying Phoenix's sketch. "You're really talented you know. I wish I could draw. I've never been that creative."

"But you write. Isn't that creative?" Phoenix asked, genuinely confused by Ashley's statement.

"It's different. Someone else created the characters and worlds they exist in, I'm just putting them in a different setting. I'm not creating something from scratch."

"I don't know about all that. I'm usually sketching something already in existence. It's no different from what you do. It's arguably less creative, in fact."

Ashley pondered her statement. "I guess you could be right.

But I still don't feel that creative."

"What if I read one of your stories and decide for myself?" Perhaps reading Ashley's writing would answer some of her questions.

"I don't know."

"Do you let anyone else read them?"

"Some of my friends." Phoenix shot her a look and Ashley clarified, "Online friends. I don't have to see their reaction in person. It's different."

"I can see that. But I'm a pretty forgiving reader. If you give me the chance I can show you," Phoenix said, surprised at the subtle shift she felt with her words, weightier than intended. Clearly it was time to change the subject. "So what do you like to do when you aren't working or writing?"

"Besides avoiding you?"

Phoenix's smile lit up her face uncontrollably. "Yes, besides that."

"Well between that and work, I haven't had much time for anything else. During the summer we're expected to work as much as we can to maximize our results. After losing the detector for a day, and running verification tests the next, I've worked the last two Sundays trying to catch up. And in about 2 weeks I'll be mentoring an undergrad who's here on her winter break. While she's here we'll be shoveling snow off the surface detectors and doing other maintenance. It's a rather busy time for the next month and a half. I'm really looking forward to having tonight and tomorrow off."

Phoenix's free time was running short, considering all she wanted to cook today. Volunteers had helped with the formal dinners all week, from baking pies with Maria the baker to prepping side dishes. More would be helping today, but there were certain dishes only Phoenix could make, and they had to be done before the first of two scheduled sit down dinners tonight. However, she wasn't ready for her time with Ashley to end.

Phoenix asked, "Which dinner service did you sign up for?"

"The first one, which is why I'm up so early today. I have some work to do before enjoying the evening."

"Perfect." Ashley eyed her quizzically, but Phoenix ignored her questioning gaze. "Well, I have a ton of cooking to do. I'll see you at dinner. Without Stove Top." Phoenix winked and stood to go.

ASH

The detectors must have known it was a holiday because nothing eventful happened all day. That left Ash with way too much time on her hands to think. She kept coming back to thoughts of Phoenix and their conversation that morning.

Ash knew she wasn't a morning person, preferring to start the day quietly, which is why she normally ate breakfast alone. She hadn't seen Phoenix at breakfast before, but that wasn't unusual for people who worked late at night.

What was unusual was Phoenix's ability to make Ash laugh, even when she was grumpy from lack of sleep. There was something truly unique about Phoenix. While Ash had been curious about Thanksgiving dinner before, she couldn't wait to taste Phoenix's food now.

After dinner Ash planned to enjoy her night off playing tabletop games with some of the other station nerds. She wasn't sure how much time she could take to play, not with her dissertation looming like a cloud over her. Currently that cloud was a medium gray, the type that hid the sun but was unlikely to rain on her. She'd prefer to keep it that way, especially after the storm clouds of the past two weeks.

ASH

Reminded of her dissertation, she opened her documents and re-read the email from her advisor listing points she needed to address with her research. It wasn't long, but only because the subtasks weren't explicitly spelled out. That was for her to determine, to prove she had what it took to be a true research scientist instead of a lab assistant.

She'd had an idea about one of the tasks and opened her notebook to organize her thoughts. For whatever reason, her brain worked better when writing on paper. She always backed up her notes and ideas electronically, but paper was her go-to, whether organizing research or writing fanfic.

She'd made satisfactory progress by two when Jon sat in the seat next to her. She filled him in on the uneventful day and excused herself, too excited to sit still anymore.

The whole station was likely excited for the upcoming meal. Certainly Ash's desire to head to the galley early was just for the food, wasn't it? She could already hear Cole calling her out, but she could ignore them since they weren't online. For now she'd pretend this was nothing more than the excitement of the station, good food, and a few extra hours off of work.

After dropping her notebook and laptop in her room she climbed the stairs to the galley. There were people everywhere, a hum of activity that was definitely not normal. Given the scale of this dinner, serving half the station at a time, Ash shouldn't have been surprised by how many volunteers were helping decorate and cook. Now she felt guilty for not volunteering earlier. Sometimes she got too involved in her research, but that was why she was there, wasn't it?

She spotted a flash of Phoenix's hair and Ash wove her way through the crowd to reach her. Phoenix greeted her with a big smile, her energy as high as it was that morning.

"Hey, are you here to help?"

"If I help, do I get to eat faster? It smells delicious."

ASH

"Well, flattering the cook doesn't hurt. How are you with fire?"

Ash opened her eyes wide. "Fire? I really have been doing Thanksgiving wrong."

Phoenix chuckled. "Probably, but I mean for candles. The tables are almost ready for them. Everyone gets their own candlelight dinner tonight."

Ash's romantic heart, normally dormant, did a little leap before she tamped it down. *Was Cole's romanticism contagious?* "That sounds nice. I'll get right on it." Phoenix gestured to the table of supplies before disappearing into the kitchen.

Ash chatted with the other volunteers as the room came together. The windows were covered, simulating the darkness that wouldn't fall for months. Someone switched the TVs to display a log fire, and Ash lit the candles that ran in a row down the center of the long tables. They even had cloth napkins and napkin holders. Ash was impressed. It looked like a completely new room and far too fancy for people who barely showered.

Phoenix soon joined her, surprising Ash with a quiet request. "I have a surprise for you, but I need you to test it for me."

Ash eyed her suspiciously. "Should I be worried?"

"I know it's edible. But I need to know if it matches your expectation."

Ash gave her a quizzical look. What had Phoenix done?

"Just come with me." Phoenix took Ash's hand and pulled her behind the serving line. The act was unexpected, but felt strangely natural, like of course she'd be holding Phoenix's hand right now. Phoenix's hand was larger than hers, warm and mostly soft, but with callouses that came from working with her hands all day. How many stories would Phoenix's hands tell if Ash could study them?

Phoenix only dropped her hand once they were in the kitchen, a twinge of disappointment arising in Ash's chest. *Ugh,*

Cole, this is all your fault. She couldn't even yell at them because that would be further evidence of their theory. She needed less wise friends who wouldn't put ideas in her head.

Phoenix cleared her throat and pulled Ash back to the moment. She stood in front of a covered dish holding a spoon, looking expectantly at Ash. She didn't want to admit how lost in thought she'd been.

"Yes?"

Phoenix's eyes sparkled. There was that glint of blue again. "Close your eyes."

Ash raised both eyebrows.

"Trust me. I don't play when food is involved."

"You better not," Ash said before closing her eyes, not nearly as nervous as she expected. Phoenix took food seriously, Ash could trust her in this situation, right? The ting of the metal cover was a good sign.

"Now open your mouth."

Ash did as she was told, though she felt a little silly. People could see them if they cared to look. She soon forgot all about them as Phoenix lightly held her chin and placed the mystery food into her mouth. Her heart raced in reaction to the intimate touch. Phoenix released her hold and Ash rocked forward slightly. Distracted by her absence, Ash took a moment before closing her mouth to taste the food.

Sweet but salty, firm yet soft. The taste of sweet corn and onion balancing each other perfectly. It was the corn bake she'd described last week. Her eyes flew open as she swallowed. "Phoenix, it's perfect. How did you make it without a recipe?"

"Recipes are for amateurs," Phoenix said with a grin before letting her concern show. "It's what you wanted though?"

Moisture unexpectedly pooled behind her eyelids and Ash averted her gaze. "I didn't realize I wanted it this badly until I tasted it. I can't believe you went to all this trouble for me."

"It wasn't any trouble, really. Besides, that look on your face was worth it."

Ash looked up and Phoenix averted her gaze quickly. The room felt different. *Phoenix* felt different. Ash wanted to understand, but she didn't know how to ask Phoenix what she was thinking in a way that wouldn't be awkward. Instead she asked, "Can you eat now or do you have to wait?"

"Are you inviting me to join you?"

Ash did her best to lighten the mood. "Well, you did go to the trouble of making my favorite dish."

"Then I'll get these dishes uncovered and we can eat. There's nothing else for me to work on for a while."

With each subsequent lid removal, new aromas hit Ash and it felt more and more like Thanksgiving. They walked to the front of the serving line and Phoenix bellowed, "Time to eat!" Everyone in the room lined up, the hum of excitement palpable as the smells filled the room.

Ash led Phoenix to the end of the table, a lit candle and a plate of dinner rolls front and center. *It's not a date, it's just a special candlelit dinner that Phoenix made partially for me. Crap, this sounds like a date.* Ash's nervousness ticked up, unsure what was happening between them, if anything. Thankfully she had the perfect distraction – a heaping plate of food.

Ash dove in, trying a little of everything. The turkey was moist and flavorful. The dressing wasn't over seasoned. The gravy was exceptional. Ash looked incredulously at Phoenix who was watching her eat. "Did you make this from scratch?"

"Shh, not so loud. I didn't have the time to make enough for everyone. Once this is gone everyone else gets canned gravy." Phoenix leaned in and asked, "What do you think?"

"I don't think that haircut is your most dangerous quality. I'd fight someone to get more of your food." Phoenix shot her a questioning look. Ash didn't know why she'd said that, it came out before she'd thought it through, but it was clearly true.

Phoenix's food disarmed her. "Your grandmother would be proud."

"I'm glad you like it."

Ash looked at Phoenix's plate. "Aren't you going to eat?"

"Now that I have your verdict, yes."

Ash watched as Phoenix took a bite of turkey with gravy and closed her eyes contentedly. Phoenix opened her eyes and looked up to the sky before meeting Ash's gaze.

"Ever since she died, I thank my grandma for her guidance when a meal turns out well," Phoenix explained quietly. Ash wasn't sure how to take this revelation. The more time she spent with Phoenix, the more she was surprised by her depth. Cole was right, she needed to give people more of a chance.

"This is easily the best Thanksgiving dinner I've ever had, and I think most would agree with me. I'm grateful your grandmother taught you to cook."

"She'd be pleased to hear you say that."

They ate quietly. Ash finally understood the truth in the idea that the stomach was the shortest path to the heart. There was something about good food prepared with love and passion that tasted better. As she finished her plate, Ash noticed that, instead of feeling nostalgic for home, she felt nurtured. All that remained to make this meal perfect was a slice of pie.

"What's your pie preference, Phoenix?"

"Normally I love a good fresh apple pie, but since these came from a canned mix I will have to go with pumpkin."

"Whipped cream?"

"Of course!"

Ash grinned as she stood. "I'll grab us both a piece then."

It's not a date. It's not a date. It's not. A. Date. If she repeated it enough perhaps she could maintain enough emotional distance to keep her head on straight. She knew practically nothing about Phoenix and she was here to work, not find a girlfriend. They were becoming friends. That was all.

She set the small plate of pumpkin pie in front of Phoenix who eyed it, and then her. "Enough whipped cream?"

"It's easier to take it off than go get more. But if you don't want it I'll eat it."

Phoenix covered her plate protectively. "Not a chance."

Ash took a bite, enjoying the smooth texture and sweetness, topped off with the pillowy whipped cream. Just a few bites and her meal was complete. But did that mean their time together had to end too?

"So, what now?" Ash asked. "Do you get the night off?"

"Most of it. I'll make sure everything is ready for the volunteers handling the next dinner service since I've already put in my hours for the day. Then I'm free to lie around like a beached whale." Phoenix rubbed her belly, and Ash mirrored her.

"God, I know. I might need a nap to survive tonight."

"Are you going to the after party in the gym? Apparently that's the place to be." Phoenix's voice was casual and sincere. However, Ash wasn't in the mood for loud music.

"But it's not the only place. I'm gearing up for a night of nerdy fun in the big TV lounge. You're welcome to join me."

"And how do nerds have fun? Play chess? Watch Star Wars?" Phoenix was teasing her and Ash realized she liked it, and not just because of her happy food coma.

"Sometimes. But tonight is all about tabletop games. There was talk of Settlers of Catan and Munchkin, but there's a huge stack of games to choose from, including chess," Ash added with a smirk.

"Never heard of those games."

"I could teach you," Ash replied quickly, then caught herself. "I'm not really selling this am I? I swear, the games are really fun, even for a non-nerd like yourself."

"How do you know I'm not a nerd?" Phoenix asked playfully.

Ash matched her tone, throwing her question back at her. "Are you secretly a nerd Phoenix?"

"I guess you'll have to wait and find out." Phoenix pushed back from the table.

"So is that a yes? To game night?"

"I'm game," Phoenix answered with her cheekiest grin.

"Puns? That's one check in the nerd column."

Phoenix stood, leaving the comment unanswered. "Meet me back here in an hour?"

Ash pushed her chair back and stood. "After all the work you put into this meal? Let me help and we'll go over together when we're done."

CHAPTER SEVEN

PHOENIX

Phoenix and Ashley walked side by side to the large lounge near the main entrance to the station. The furniture was rearranged, with extra tables and chairs setup for multiple games at a time. Phoenix didn't recognize any of the games currently in progress, but that didn't surprise her. Everyone was having a good time at least.

"It looks like everyone is busy," Ashley observed. "Do you want to play something together or wait?"

"Let's play." Phoenix couldn't wait to see what kind of player Ashley was. Would she be competitive? Easy going? Ruthless? Phoenix wandered over to a stack of games on an end table. She idly wondered if she'd be sick of them all by the end of winter. When was the last time she'd played an actual board game and not an equivalent app on her phone? Maybe five years ago, before her grandma died? That time they'd played Boggle and Scrabble before her grandma kicked everyone's ass, including Phoenix's, at poker. There was no getting by that woman.

Phoenix pulled Scrabble out of the pile. "How's your Scrabble game?"

"Better than yours."

Phoenix laughed, not expecting that reaction but loving it. "Oh really? Care to make a friendly wager?" Ashley's confident exterior broke just a little, but Phoenix had to give her credit for not backing down.

"What kind of wager?"

"If I win, you let me read the story I rudely interrupted the day you arrived." Phoenix threw it out there like it wasn't a big deal, but she knew better. She was dying to know what Ashley spent so much time writing but not showing people. It might be awful, but in her experience the people that hid the most had more than enough talent, they just couldn't see it for themselves.

Ashley swallowed hard. "Ok. And if I win... you draw me something that I'll determine later."

Phoenix smiled. That was a win-win in her book. Ashley may be confident, but she wasn't good at negotiating. Phoenix extended her hand and said, "Deal."

Ashley took her hand and firmly shook it. Another surprise. Ashley was not one of those girls with a limp handshake. Her hand was soft, a mark of computer work rather than manual labor, unlike Phoenix's lightly calloused hands. But for all the softness of her hand, Ashley's grip was confident, earning Phoenix's respect.

Ashley took the box from Phoenix. "We'd better find a table."

It only took a few turns to prove Ashley a worthy opponent. For all the skill Scrabble required, it literally depended on luck of the draw. If you didn't choose the right letters it was harder to build high scores. Luckily Phoenix rallied with some strategic word choices so they were basically tied as they reached their last letters.

Phoenix almost laughed when she pulled the perfect letter from the bag. She paused, just long enough to grab Ashley's attention, before placing q-u-e-e-r-l-y down, the q landing on the triple letter score.

Ashley shook her head before looking at Phoenix wide eyed. "You either cheated or you're the luckiest person on the station."

"I don't need to cheat, I'm that good. Especially with sufficient motivation," Phoenix replied with a smirk.

"I can't believe my story is sufficient motivation, or that you're this good at Scrabble. You've been holding out on me."

"Maybe if you weren't working so hard to avoid me, you'd have learned this by now." Phoenix tried to keep her tone light, but from the way Ashley's face fell the words had hit a nerve. Phoenix kicked herself. They'd been having too good a day to get prickly now.

"I'm sorry, that was meant as a joke but still shitty to say. And if I'm being honest, I was holding out on you." Ashley furrowed her eyebrows and Phoenix felt just as confused. Where was this desire to confess coming from? That was a question for later because she couldn't back out now. "Remember the first fight we had? I lied when I said I was too busy working to spend time at libraries. Well, not exactly lied, but I misled you. I was busy working as soon as I was able as a teenager, but I also spent a lot of time in libraries as a kid. And I've played a lot of word games with my grandmother. Scrabble. Boggle. Balderdash. There are a lot of random words locked inside this brain." Phoenix tapped the side of her head in emphasis.

"Why did you lie?" Ashley asked, without apparent judgment.

"I assumed you saw me as nothing more than uneducated white trash. It's often easier to let people believe their misconceptions than fight to correct them." Phoenix couldn't believe she was admitting so much, and while sober no less. What was it about Ashley that made her keep talking?

"What? Oh no, I didn't think that at all. You interrupted a really nice scene that I wanted to finish that night. Plus I was jet lagged and oxygen deprived, so I lashed out. I would have said the same thing to anyone who interrupted me. I'm sorry I made you feel unwelcome." Ashley's gaze seemed to bore into her soul at that moment and Phoenix couldn't handle it. She was too close. The truth too easy to see if she looked close enough, and that wasn't allowed. Not in her world.

"Fine, you're sorry, I'm sorry, hey do we have Sorry somewhere?" Phoenix asked with a self-satisfied grin. "You can try to get me back."

Ashley shook her head. "I don't know if I should give you points for cleverness or just call you a dork."

"Points, definitely." Phoenix picked up the game board and poured the tiles into the bag which Ashley held, smiling wordlessly. Phoenix had said too much but that was easily remedied thanks to all the distractions. She placed the board back in the box.

"Best two out of three? If I choose wisely I can reclaim my honor," Ashley said as she added the bag and tile holders to the box. Phoenix added the cover and took the box with her when she walked to the back of the room.

"As long as you realize I already won our bet, and you owe me your story, I'll play as many games as you'd like."

"Damn, well I had to try," Ashley said as she surveyed the room. "Right now it looks like we have people playing Settlers of Catan, Ticket to Ride, and Munchkin." Ashley motioned for Phoenix to follow. "Munchkin is fast and easy to learn, though the strategy takes time to develop."

Phoenix observed the game currently being played as Ashley explained the rules. It seemed simple enough. Draw cards, perform an action, and if you beat the monster you move up a level. One player asked the table for help and another offered up a trade so they wouldn't die. But then another player played a curse, which caused the two cooperative players to groan as it interrupted their strategy. This was growing more complicated by the second.

"Are there instructions I can read? This is a lot to keep track of."

Ashley found the box and handed the instructions to Phoenix. She giggled at the humor. Parts of the game were confusing but watching made more sense now. And with two players at level 8 of 10 the ruthlessness of some players also made sense. She asked Ashley questions and felt she had a good enough grasp to jump in when the game ended.

Phoenix made a few strategic errors but had fun even as she fell behind. Ashley tried to help Phoenix as best she could without peeking at her cards. Competitive without being ruthless was something Phoenix appreciated.

The fun of Munchkin, besides the ridiculousness of the cards, was that anything could happen at any point. Players could get lucky and rally, like Phoenix did. Before long she was on level nine along with Jon and Eric, Ash's colleagues, whose names she'd caught over the course of the game.

Phoenix drew a high-level monster. While she'd traded for some good armor earlier, the chances were still too high that she'd die on her own. Phoenix looked at Ashley, pleading with her best puppy dog eyes.

Ashley scoffed. "As if that would work on me. I want tangible goods. Care to revise our bet?"

Eric perked up. "Oh? What kind of bet?"

"That's private," Ashley replied, probably not realizing that was the worst way to diffuse a situation. This could be fun.

"Very private," added Phoenix, purposely making the situation worse through her tone.

Ashley blushed but fired back, "you aren't helping."

"I didn't know I was supposed to." Phoenix turned to Eric with a sly grin. "She doesn't like to share."

"My writing!" Ashley interjected. "I don't like to share my writing. Which is what the bet was about."

Phoenix chuckled to herself. Did Ashley think that was

going to help? Phoenix knew better and was just waiting for someone to twist her words. As if on cue, Eric asked, "why not? Is it porn?"

Ashley growled in frustration. "No. And for that I'm not helping any of you anymore."

Phoenix laughed. In spite of her frustration Ashley was still sitting at the table, but Phoenix had pushed things far enough.

"Ok, ok. I'll give you an IOU that you can cash in whenever you want."

"You sure that's a good idea? You don't know what I want," Ashley challenged.

No truer words had been spoken. "I trust that you're an honorable person who will ask for something of equivalent value."

Ashley's gaze remained on her for another moment before responding, "You've got yourself a deal."

Phoenix took the card Ashley offered that guaranteed a win, as long as no one screwed her over. Eric held a card in his hands, as if considering a move, but Ashley stared him down. He set the card down and leaned back. And with that, Phoenix won her first game of Munchkin and her second game of the night. She pumped her fist in the air, earning a laugh from Ashley. Phoenix met her eyes. "I owe you."

Ashley smirked. "Yeah, you do."

"Aww hell, get a room already," Eric teased. Ashley turned red and Phoenix wondered again what she was thinking. Maybe she didn't like people knowing about her sex life. Or maybe she was shy about sex in general?

"We have rooms," Phoenix said as she stood. "And I'm about to head to mine a winner." Phoenix faced Ashley. "I'd like to collect on our bet before you find a way to conveniently forget."

Ashley stood quickly and walked to Phoenix. "Like you'd let me."

"I don't want you to stall either. Now lead the way."

Safely outside the hall, Ashley stopped and turned on Phoenix. "Why did you encourage them?"

Phoenix took a step back. Apparently Ashley wasn't as cool with everything as she thought. "Because it was the only way to minimize the rumor mill. The more you push the truth the more they assume you're lying."

"That's so illogical."

"It's human nature which is never logical. But now we'll be slightly less interesting to them."

"Really?"

Phoenix nodded and skidded to a stop before running into Skye. Christ that woman had bad timing.

"Hey there sexy, where have you been?" Skye had clearly been drinking, but she wasn't slurring too much. Hopefully she wouldn't say or do something careless to set Ashley off after Phoenix had finally started to see who she was behind her professional facade.

"Just playing some games with Ashley here. I take it you went to the party?"

Skye ignored the question. "Games huh? I can think of a few games we could play together."

Ashley's discomfort was unmistakable. That was what she was afraid of. "No thanks. I'm going to get something from Ashley's room and then go to bed. It's been a long day and I'm beat."

"Alright then. Another time?" Skye asked seductively.

"Yeah, maybe," Phoenix soothed, wanting out of the situation as soon as possible, not that she had any intention of playing games with Skye besides pool or darts. She hoped Skye's behavior was due to drunken flirtation, and not a sign that her definition of no strings attached was different from Phoenix's. She really didn't want to sit down and go over it with her.

Phoenix turned toward Ashley who was looking intently at a picture on the wall.

"Interesting picture?"

"Very."

"Uh huh. So, where's your room?"

Ashley led her into A pod in heavy silence. Phoenix wanted to ask what she was thinking about, but the hallway wasn't the right place, so she waited until they were safely inside Ashley's room. She hesitated, realizing how little space there was for two people in the room when you weren't lying in bed with them. Phoenix wasn't sure how to proceed.

Ashley woke up her laptop. "Did you bring a laptop or tablet with you? The final drafts of my stories are on my computer."

Phoenix nodded. "I brought a tablet, but I'm not very familiar with how to transfer a document to it."

"Oh, that's easy, I'll just email it to you if we have internet. If not, there are other tricks using the intranet." Phoenix watched her login and pull up her email. "Looks like we're in luck. Type in your email address and I'll send it over." Ashley looked back at her and pushed away from her desk.

Phoenix leaned over the keyboard, brushing her arm on Ashley's as she typed in her email. A shiver ran through her before she stepped away. Surely that was a side-effect of only having sex once in the past month and a half, not due to Ashley herself. Ashley wasn't Phoenix's type, not that type made much of a difference in the end. She was nerdy cute, blending in until you got to know her. Then she was fun and easy to get along with.

And yet, if Phoenix hadn't shifted her focus from sex to her new job and drawing would they have become friends? Highly unlikely. Ashley would be someone she greeted at dinner and nothing more. Phoenix wouldn't know how fun she was to banter or play Scrabble with. If Phoenix had learned one thing this past week it was that she preferred spending time with Ashley to being ignored by her. The revelation hit her like a truck. What else had she missed in her life by keeping women at a distance? Who else? Even Bri was only allowed a peek into her life. Phoenix caught her balance on the desk as her world tilted. It really was time for bed.

"You ok?" Ashley asked with concern in her eyes.

"Of course, just tired. I think the adrenaline has fully worn off now. Did you send your story to me?"

Ashley drew her lips tight. Phoenix touched her arm lightly and Ashley didn't pull away. *Good, some touch is ok with her.* She kept her voice gentle. "Ashley, I promise I won't judge you. I know what it's like to put a bit of yourself into art. But it's also never the whole picture. I won't assume anything. I'm just really curious about this thing you spend so much of your free time doing. Please send the file."

Neither moved for several breaths until Ashley turned to her laptop and hit send. Phoenix gave her a gentle smile. "Thank you for trusting me."

Ashley nodded. She opened her mouth to speak, but nothing came out. Phoenix gave her upper arm a squeeze. "I'm going to check my email before we lose the satellite. And then I'm going to sleep for at least 10 hours, if I'm lucky. I'll let you know when I've read your story."

"Thanks."

Phoenix had already turned to leave when Ashley added, "goodnight Phoenix."

Phoenix turned with a small smile. "Goodnight Ashley."

ASH

Ash stared blankly at the door, her heart pounding in her chest. Phoenix had her story. Phoenix was going to *read* her story. She sighed. Phoenix was about to learn her secret, either by asking questions or assuming the story was her fantasy. Ash pulled out her chair and sat down hard. The satellites were still up, but she couldn't handle a chat just yet. There was too much to unpack from the day. Was it still the same day as Thanksgiving dinner? She took a deep breath and started writing an email to Cole.

I sent Phoenix my story.

I'm trying not to panic, but maybe if I explain to someone else how this happened, I will be able to sleep and save my panic for her reaction. Prepare yourself for a long email because it's been an eventful day and I'm not sure what is or isn't relevant anymore. Oh yeah, and hi Cole.

Ash typed furiously, describing the day as best she could remember, starting with breakfast. She tried to avoid sharing her feelings but realized Cole would insert their own interpretation and decided to treat it like a writing exercise. It wasn't her story per se, but a character who'd had a day just like hers and felt just like she did. The extra distance helped, and she managed to get the bulk of the story down in an hour.

> I don't know why I went along with this bet. You'd probably say I wanted her to read it. What better way to introduce someone to asexuality than through fiction? I don't use the word in the story, but she has to figure something out, right? She's too smart not to.
> So, it looks like I have to tell her soon. She surprised me a lot today, maybe she'll surprise me again and be that unicorn who just gets it and doesn't make it a big deal?
> I'm going to try to sleep. Thanks for listening to my day. I'll let you know what happens.
> P.S. I wrote this late Saturday night (aka our Thanksgiving) but the satellite is now gone. I've got it queued so it should send while I sleep. I plan on sleeping in and then avoiding Phoenix as much as I can. Just kidding. Or not. Ugh, the wait is torture, and at the same time I don't want to know. I'd better end this before the P.S. becomes as long as the email. Thanks Cole!

Ash submitted the email and opened her music app. Hopefully the sleep-inducing music would do its magic and she'd get some rest.

♠

Ash still wasn't used to the complete darkness in her room no matter what time of day it was. She had an interior room, which made it easier to sleep; the sun couldn't sneak past the window coverings. But it was disorienting in the morning. Without setting an alarm she wasn't sure what her body would do without normal cues.

Saturday night she'd set her alarm for 10:00 am, just to keep herself from oversleeping and destroying her schedule. Most days she was awake well before it went off, but she'd slept fitfully, her mind busy replaying the day. The alarm was met with a groan as she hit the snooze and snuggled tighter under the covers. When the alarm went off ten minutes later, she almost turned it off but knew she'd regret it. Instead she dragged herself out of bed and groggily stumbled to the bathroom carrying her toiletry bag.

The lack of showers was a challenge, so Ash washed up every day with a washcloth at the sink. It used minimal water and made her feel more human. There wasn't much she could do about her hair. Dry shampoo helped, but it wasn't recommended for everyday use. Her long-haired colleagues recommended bringing an excessive number of hair ties which was good advice. Today was definitely a 'hair up' day. If only she'd look as good as Phoenix in a short cut, her life would be easier.

Ash took longer than usual cleaning up. Was she stalling or just tired? Ash couldn't answer that question, which told her it was probably a bit of both. She doubted Phoenix had read her story last night, but she was still nervous to see her.

Oh! Cole's email! She'd been too tired to check if her email sent last night. She hurried through the rest of her tasks and shuffled back to her room.

There was Cole's email. But there was also a reply from Phoenix. Ash's stomach churned nervously. Phoenix couldn't have read the story already could she? The timestamp showed Phoenix had only sent the email five minutes earlier. She definitely hadn't read it yet. What could she have to say already? There was no way Ash would be able to focus on anything else so she clicked on Phoenix's email first.

ASH

> Ashley,
> Just wanted you to know I got the file and loaded it up to read.
> Thanks for inviting me to game night. It was the most nerdy fun I've had in a long time.
> Rematch?
> Phoenix

She's already awake. And reading. Shit. Her heart raced. Her palms were sweaty. She clicked on Cole's email before the anxiety took over completely.

> Holy shit Ash, I'm so proud of you. My romantic heart is all aflutter from your email. You spun a captivating tale and I can't wait for the next chapter.
> You'd better not hide in your room all day. Be brave, my adventurous explorer. You can do this.
> I expect an update in 24 hours.
> Love you,
> Cole

Surprisingly few words, yet they managed to work in aflutter, she thought sarcastically, but they were right. She had to be brave, at least long enough to eat. Then she could hide in her room and write.

⚱

Ash brought extra food back from the galley so she could stay in her room, writing in peace. She managed to avoid Phoenix during her brief excursion, and by evening her anxiety was barely noticeable. Until the knock at her door.

"Who's there?" Ash asked, torn between wanting it to be Phoenix and hoping it was anyone but her. If she was lucky it would be Jon needing help, giving her something else to think about.

"Land Shark," Phoenix called through the door, mimicking the classic Saturday Night Live sketch.

Ash smiled in spite of herself. *Dammit, how does she get to me so easily?* Ash decided to play along, surprised both knew a sketch that was older than they were. "I know this trick. Who is it really?"

"Your biggest fan."

Ash scoffed and opened the door. Phoenix greeted her with arms raised, which she clamped around Ash's arms repeatedly while making chomping sounds. Ash laughed at the ridiculousness of it all and ran back into her room. Phoenix closed the door behind her, their laughter slowly dissipating.

"You should be more careful Ashley. Today it's your biggest fan, but tomorrow, who knows? It could actually be a land shark. Or its more dangerous cousin, the ice shark."

Ash restrained another laugh, worried what would happen if she actually encouraged Phoenix. She might end up tackled on the bed, a far more awkward situation than their current one.

"My biggest fan huh? I'm more inclined to believe the land shark."

"I bet I could find a shark costume in the arts and crafts area. Or make one. I can't be the only person who'd want a shark costume."

"Sometimes I don't know what to do with you," Ash admitted, smiling as she shook her head.

"Is that why you are avoiding me again?"

"I'm not avoiding you," Ash said defensively. "I'm just hiding in my room."

"And the difference is?"

"Answering the door when you knock," Ash replied smugly, secretly pleased at her answer.

"Does that mean you were going to let me in without a shark

attack?" Phoenix asked playfully, but with a genuine question to her voice.

"Most likely."

"Good to know. Have you been out to eat real food today?" Phoenix asked.

"I stocked up at breakfast," Ash said impatiently, her nerves getting the best of her. "But that's not why you're here, is it? To attack me and check on my eating habits?"

"No," Phoenix admitted. "I wanted to ease into it, but that's not what you want it seems. So why is it easier to believe I am a land shark and not your number one fan? You're a really good writer. Why aren't you writing real novels?

Ash scowled, having heard some variation on this question too many times before. "Are you saying this isn't real writing?"

"That's not what I meant." Phoenix furrowed her brow, struggling to find the words. "It's just, I think you could write something more—"

"I write what I enjoy writing," Ash snapped, her temper getting the best of her. "It doesn't have to be for anyone else but me."

Something in Phoenix's expression stopped Ash in her tracks. Time stood still and everything that relied upon it. Her thoughts. Her breath. Her heartbeat. Phoenix didn't deserve this reaction.

Phoenix spoke before Ash could apologize, almost too quiet to hear. "Why do I always say the wrong thing around you?"

Her vulnerability was so unexpected, it triggered something in Ash that she'd never had words for. Her walls crumbled.

"For the same reason that I am lashing out at you again," Ash admitted with a sigh. "I've been thinking about this. I imagine that everyone has a minefield around them that no one else can see. Sometimes we can't see them ourselves, or forget they are there until someone else steps on one and we explode." Ash took a breath to center herself.

"Some people only have a few mines and you can spend your whole life together without triggering one. But other people have mines that are so sensitive that getting anywhere near them sets them off." Ash looked at her floor, uncomfortable with her own admission but unable to stop herself. "I have some sensitive land mines."

Phoenix picked up the analogy. "And I was raised by assholes that don't care about minefields. They selfishly stumble through them, completely unaffected by the explosions going off around them and the trail of bodies they've left in their wake. I know the feeling of being set off and it sucks."

Ash flinched when Phoenix touched her arm but looked up when Phoenix spoke again.

"Hey, that analogy explains a lot. How can you not see that you're a good writer?" Phoenix asked sincerely. Ash had to look away again. "Oh, is your writing a land mine?"

"Sometimes, such as when people imply I'm wasting my time writing fanfiction. But in this case I am writing about my biggest land mine. And that's making me extra sensitive."

"Woah ok, I don't want to be blown up again. Is there any way you can guide me through this minefield?"

Why did Phoenix need to be so sweet right now? If Ash told her who she was, and why she'd written that story, and she reacted badly, it would hurt so much more. "We might be pushing the limits of this analogy."

"Can you tell me when I'm approaching a mine at least?"

"I can do that."

Phoenix smiled so sweetly it made her heart ache.

"Can I compliment you now?" Phoenix teased.

"I'd rather you didn't."

"But is it a land mine?"

"No."

"Great, because I really want to tell you what I thought."

Ash suppressed a smile. "I guess if you have to."

"I really do. I also have to admit that I didn't know what to expect. But this was a well thought out story. I didn't plan to read it in one sitting but I got sucked in. You have a talent." Phoenix paused for effect. "How am I doing so far? Am I about to blow up?"

"Not yet."

"Good, but I think I'm about to hit one of those mines. Because those intimate scenes were sexy as hell. We definitely didn't see that on TV." Ash braced for the judgment that had to be coming. Phoenix must have seen it, because she asked, "Are you going to warn me off?"

Should she? She wanted to, but as hard as it would be to hear Phoenix's criticism, it wasn't going to get any better with time. She needed to see where Phoenix was heading while she could still rein in this crush she was developing if need be.

"No, I'm not."

"But you want to?"

Ash sighed heavily. "Just say what you want to say Phoenix. Please."

"Why didn't they have sex? They did everything else but stopped short."

"They wanted sensual intimacy, not sex."

"I don't think I understand. If it was me, I would have fallen apart in that tub. That spell, I could almost feel it right along with Willow. If I was Tara, I wouldn't want to stop before making Willow come. That would be the best part, seeing her lose herself because of me."

Ash's face fell. She knew Phoenix wouldn't understand, but she'd hoped.

"I said something wrong. Do I need to duck and cover?"

Ash smiled sadly. "No. And that's not remotely close to the worst comments I have heard."

"Will you explain this aspect of your story then? Because I'm confused."

"I reimagined Willow and Tara as asexual. For them it's all about the sensuality and intimacy. They don't need an orgasm."

"Asexual. I feel like I should know what that means, but I don't. Does that mean they don't like sex?"

"Not necessarily. Asexuality is defined by a lack of sexual attraction, not by whether they have or enjoy sex. Within the context of the story, I haven't decided where each falls on the spectrum yet. This story was meant to show the beauty of sensual intimacy."

Phoenix was silent as she processed Ash's words. As the silence lengthened, she wondered if it was a good or bad sign. She didn't want to interfere with Phoenix's process or explain in greater detail until she was ready, so she waited. Her pulse beat faster as the silence stretched and Ash found herself fidgeting with her pen.

"So they went to bed happy, not frustrated?"

Ash cocked her head at Phoenix's unexpected question. "Right."

"Huh."

Huh? Ash couldn't help it. Her chuckle slowly built into full on belly laughs, the stress and worry releasing as she laughed. Phoenix just might be part unicorn.

"What's so funny?" Phoenix asked.

"Of all the responses I've heard, and expected, 'huh' has never been one of them." Ash smiled at her, unsure if she'd ever know what to expect from Phoenix.

"What do— Wait, I don't think I want to know. I feel like I just disarmed a land mine and don't want to push my luck." Phoenix looked at the wall beside Ash. "Why not tell me about the pictures next to you. From the red hue, I'm guessing that's Mars?"

Ash turned to look at the pictures, regaining her control. "Good guess. This one is a simulation of what Earth would look like from the surface of Mars." She pointed to the next picture.

"This is an actual picture taken by the Curiosity rover that landed on Mars in 2012. It's just a printout but Earth is visible in the original high resolution images."

Phoenix moved to look more closely, and Ash became keenly aware of her presence stuck between Phoenix and her computer desk. If she moved a fraction of an inch they'd be touching and not just sharing body heat. How would it feel to simply lean against Phoenix? Would Phoenix hold her, caress her, kiss her? And that was the problem, she didn't know what Phoenix would do, but she didn't seem the type to stop at a kiss. Ash wasn't certain if she wanted a kiss or not either. Besides, Phoenix was enough of a distraction as a friend. If Ash blurred the lines, things could become incredibly complicated.

"Where is Earth then, in both pictures?"

Ash sucked in a breath to clear her head. "This bright dot here," Ash said as she pointed to the computer generated image, "and right about here on this one." Her arm brushed Phoenix's chest as she reached for the second image and her cheeks warmed. Phoenix didn't react, maybe this was entirely one sided?

Phoenix squinted and leaned in before taking a step back again. "It really puts the distances in perspective. Why these pictures? They aren't objectively beautiful—" Phoenix stopped herself, eyes wide as she looked at Ash.

"Not a land mine," Ash assured Phoenix. "You're right. These are far from the most beautiful pictures of Mars, or Earth for that matter. But they remind me of what I'm working toward."

"Mars?"

"Exactly. In our lifetime, we're going to send people to Mars as colonists and I'm determined to be a part of that group. That's part of the reason why I'm here. If I can show I've already spent time in an isolated area with a small group of people, then I believe that will be what sets me apart from others."

"Wow. That's a really big dream. I don't know if I could do it.

I didn't even plan to come here, it just sort of fell together at the last minute. Not that I'm a scientist, but if I was, I'm not sure I'd have the courage to go."

"They'll need more than scientists in a settlement. It's no different than here. You need people who are experts in their field, but also others who are generally handy and hardworking to keep everything running. It's even more crucial when the journey is most likely a one-way trip. Colonists would be committing to living out their lives on Mars."

"And that appeals to you?" To her credit, Phoenix didn't sound judgmental. That was better than most people when she told them about her dream.

"It would be the adventure of a lifetime. Hell, two lifetimes! The opportunities for scientific discovery are unimaginable, and I'd help form a new civilization. Do you remember the history of American colonization? They traveled by boat for approximately four and a half months, which is almost the same time it takes to travel to Mars. They knew they were never returning to England. This is our generation's chance to explore the unknown, with a lot less bloodshed."

"Strangely enough, that never occurred to me, but the parallels are intriguing. However there's a difference between a romanticized version of exploration, where so many still died, and risking your life on a planet that you can't even walk on without carrying life support."

"Looks like I'm more of a badass than you are," Ash teased. "What are you going to do when the last plane leaves for the winter? Seven months, almost no chance of rescue?"

"Well, I was hoping you'd keep me distracted."

Ash's breath caught. *Don't overreact*, she repeated to herself.

"I fully intend to beat you at every game on station by the time the first summer plane arrives in October," Phoenix added with a smirk and Ash breathed again. She really needed to stop reading into everything Phoenix said.

"You can try. But now that you've read my story, you're going to need something else to wager."

"Oh, I'll think of something."

Ash's mind wandered, and apparently Phoenix's did as well because she fell silent.

"Well, I should let you get back to your work. I'd hate to interfere with your newest story," Phoenix said.

"After hiding in here all day, I should probably spend a little time in the library and get some sunlight before bed. Thanks for finding me tonight. And for so deftly navigating my minefield," Ash added, feeling herself lean towards Phoenix. She hesitated for half a breath before stepping forward and wrapping Phoenix into a hug. "I can't express what it means to me."

Phoenix gave her a squeeze and Ash forgot why she'd avoided embracing Phoenix. Their height difference meant Ash's head landed near Phoenix's shoulder, allowing her to feel more than hear Phoenix's chuckle.

"If I knew you gave out hugs in exchange for not pissing you off, I might have tried harder before."

Ash smacked her lightly on the back but smiled to herself. It felt good to touch her, to hug her in genuine affection. She maintained a professional distance from everyone else and now understood how much she missed the physical connection that friendship provided. Ash backed away reluctantly and grabbed her notebook and pen. "Shall I walk you out?"

"You'd better, I might get lost in this mansion of yours." Phoenix followed Ash out. "You know, if they find a way to bring you back from Mars, the Earth governments will give you a mansion as a thank you for risking your life for humanity."

That made Ash chuckle. "The Earth government? You might read too much science fiction."

Phoenix paused at the stairwell, looking like she wanted to say something else but didn't. Ash eyed her questioningly, but Phoenix only said, "Thanks for tonight. See you tomorrow."

Ash nodded. "See you." She watched Phoenix turn and walk up the stairs, more confused than ever. Ash walked past the library straight to the coat room and found her parka. She put on sunglasses and walked to the second-floor balcony.

The sun shone almost directly above as they were less than a month from the winter solstice. She let the brisk air fill her lungs, giving her something else to think about besides the past two days. That lasted for all of thirty seconds though.

Ash hated to admit it, but it seemed Cole's words of encouragement were working. And while she'd looked forward to Cole's cookies, it didn't compare to her relief at hearing that simple little word. Three letters, barely a word at all. Huh. Who knew three letters could hold so much possibility?

For a moment, Ash allowed herself to hope that Phoenix wasn't just part unicorn. What if she could truly accept Ash for who she was? A breeze blew into her hood, sending a shiver down her spine. It was a nice dream, but this wasn't fanfic, and the outcome wasn't up to her alone.

CHAPTER EIGHT

PHOENIX

The week following Thanksgiving, the first of December, gave Phoenix few opportunities to speak to Ashley at all, much less alone. More scientists arrived as the summer season hit its stride, including a few from Ashley's project.

Without Ashley around, Phoenix spent more time in the B3 lounge where she'd relax with a drink. It reminded her of home, usually in a good way. She loved shooting the shit with Jimmy and whoever else was up late, listening to stories of life off the ice. It seemed everyone at the Pole had traveled extensively on adventures Phoenix had never dreamed of. No one in her family traveled much, and for the first time she was seeing how much life she'd been missing.

As outgoing as Phoenix was, she also enjoyed her quiet time, which is when she'd gravitate to the library to draw or read. More accurately, Phoenix spent her time thinking while enjoying the sun streaming through the windows. During those quiet moments Phoenix found Ashley's story rattling around her brain.

Phoenix tried to understand what Willow and Tara experienced in the scene Ashley wrote, still blown away that it could end when it did. The story brought up an entirely new approach to relationships and also gave her an insight into a life that Phoenix never knew existed. The more she thought, the more questions she uncovered so that by Saturday she was bursting with the need to talk to Ashley.

Not interested in community movie night, Phoenix wandered over to the library where she was ecstatic to find Ashley at the small table by the window. Ashley looked up and let a smile slip out before catching it. Such a small gesture, but it was real and warmed Phoenix's heart.

"I've been thinking about your story all week," Phoenix said without preamble, her thoughts tumbling out now that she finally had Ashley alone. "Willow and Tara were perfectly matched. Both were happy with the level of physicality they chose," Phoenix paused to look for warning signs from Ashley, but only saw curiosity in her eyes. "But what if they weren't perfectly matched? What if one was asexual and the other person was..." Phoenix stopped, not knowing the word she was looking for.

"Allosexual. That's the word for people who experience," Ashley hesitated before completing her thought, "what people think of as normal sexual attraction, though I don't know how anyone can quantify what normal is," Ashley replied before looking down at her notebook, appearing slightly uncomfortable. Phoenix sat sideways on the couch, giving Ashley her full attention.

"Even among asexuals, their physical needs may be different. But statistically speaking, the challenges are greatest between asexuals and allosexuals because they often view intimacy in fundamentally different ways," Ashley continued as if she was giving a lecture. But then her tone eased, becoming more casual.

"Fanfic, and even a lot of traditional fiction, is a fantasy. It's an escape from the challenges of real life. Willow and Tara fit together because I wanted them to. It rarely happens like that in real life."

Phoenix knew that too well, which was why her next question surprised herself. "But it has to work sometimes, doesn't it? It's rare for people in any kind of relationship to have the same sex drive, for instance."

"Yes but look at the rate of divorce. How often do people divorce due to differences in the bedroom?" Ashley asked pointedly.

"I don't know. In my experience, there are far bigger issues at play than a mismatched sex drive."

Ashley considered her words before responding. "My best friend Cole would agree with you. A couple who relies solely on sex for intimacy will likely fail no matter the pairing."

"I should probably know this already but what is non-sexual intimacy?" Phoenix asked sheepishly. This felt like a really basic question that any 28 year old could answer, but clearly she was out of her depth.

"Intimacy isn't about any particular action, but the connection between people. Look at the examples of physical intimacy in my story. For allosexuals they associate these acts with foreplay, like kissing and caressing, but for an asexual that can be the main event, so to speak," Ashley said, her voice regaining that clinical quality, a stark contrast from the emotional scenes Phoenix had read. Then again, not everyone could speak comfortably about sex so she left it unaddressed.

Ashley paused, surprising Phoenix when she spoke again. "The lightest touch can be more intimate than sex, if you're open to it," Ashley added shyly.

I wouldn't know, Phoenix admitted to herself. Had she ever allowed herself to be truly intimate with a woman? She had come close a few times, but nothing felt like the connection Ashley wrote in her book.

"Intimacy is more than physical though," Ashley said, pulling

Phoenix out of her memories. "Willow and Tara could reach that level of physical intimacy only because they were emotionally connected. They shared their feelings, dreams, hopes and fears, as stereotypical as that sounds, but that openness was necessary to build a strong relationship. They created magic together, literally and figuratively, because they were connected beyond the physical. When a relationship has that, they are better prepared to handle differences in the bedroom, though it's not easy. No relationship is."

Phoenix barely noticed her pulse and breathing increase. Did intimacy really require showing that much of herself to another woman? Who would want her if they knew who Phoenix really was? "Well, Dr. Bennett, thank you for the lesson. I have a lot to think about."

"Not a doctor yet, but you're welcome. I wrote the story to show people one example of asexual intimacy, but I haven't discussed it with a reader before."

"Hey, I'm not just a reader, I'm a fan. I might start an online fan club," Phoenix teased, enjoying the opportunity to lighten the mood.

"You wouldn't," Ashley replied, aghast at the suggestion.

"Oh yeah, the Ashley Bennett fan club. No, not that Ashley Bennett. Or that one. The future Martian and writer."

Ashley fought another smile and Phoenix knew she had her. "Not everyone can have a unique name Phoenix."

"I guess you'll have to become the most famous Ashley Bennett then, and it won't matter."

"Now you know my plan. And why I don't write under my real name."

Phoenix wasn't sure how she missed that fact, but her document didn't include a title or author that she noticed. "What name do you write under?"

"Are you going to look me up when you get back to your room?"

"Of course! What kind of fan would I be if I didn't?" Ashley appeared to be considering her options, so Phoenix raised the stakes. "You know I can just enter the first paragraph of your story into Google and find you. I'm not completely internet illiterate."

"Fine. But remember, this is for fanfic. And I came up with the name when I was 14."

Phoenix leaned forward, waiting.

"It's... back2ash, with the number 2," Ashley responded hesitantly. "Because vampires are turned to ash, and I go by Ash with my friends."

"Aha, you do like puns! Does that mean I can call you Ash too? I mean, as the president of your fan club, I think I've earned the privilege."

Ash blushed. "I think your standards are entirely too low. Wait, do you have a secret online life running fan clubs? That would explain your low standards."

"No, I'd just run yours. I'm loyal like that."

"You're impossible and full of shit," Ash threw back.

"That's also true. But I'm still a fan of yours, Ash." The name was new, yet natural on her tongue. She wasn't an Ash when they met, but seeing this side of her, Phoenix could see that Ash was just waiting to come out of hiding.

Ash suppressed another laugh. "If I let you call me Ash, will you promise not to form a fan club?"

"For now."

Ash may have sounded annoyed, but Phoenix knew she wasn't. She did, however, change the subject.

"Are you excited for Christmas? I saw the mural hung by the tree. I assume you drew it?"

"Normally I'm not into Christmas, but here it's different. Nothing commercial or materialistic, so it's more fun. And I needed a project to work on."

"Planning any more? Because I just had an idea." Ash's eyes

sparkled, stirring something in Phoenix that made her want to say yes no matter the idea.

"What if you did a sketch of the IceCube array lit up in the shape of a Christmas tree?"

Phoenix had seen the posters of the project often enough to see Ash's idea without effort. "Consider it done. I wonder if I could do something for each program."

"It would make you even more popular than you already are. You might end up with a fan club of your own."

Phoenix ignored the comment, already thinking about possible designs. Perhaps a Christmas tree constellation above the dark sector where the telescopes were housed. Santa flying his sleigh around a weather balloon. Yes, this would be a fun project.

"Phoenix?"

"Huh?" At Ash's expression Phoenix guessed she'd been distracted longer than she realized. "Sorry, I was thinking about the drawings. Would you mind if I got to work on them now?"

"Not at all. Besides, I was supposed to be working too."

Phoenix said a quick thanks before turning to a new page and diving into her first idea.

ASH

Before meeting Phoenix, Ash kept her work and personal life separate without issue. Compartmentalizing allowed her to focus on research while at work and leave it behind when she left. She was then free to be Ash, the writer, in her down time. Phoenix's praise was uncomfortable, but Ash could admit her writing continued to improve, in part because of her focus. That made her all the more frustrated when her focus was barely present Monday morning.

Ash was alone in the IceCube section of the science lab, having come in early to finish the script she was writing to address one aspect of her thesis. Programming wasn't her forte so when the script failed to work as planned, the internet was a welcome distraction.

She couldn't afford these distractions, not with their undergrad assistant Emily arriving in under two weeks , but every time she set the programs running she'd find herself thinking about Phoenix. For instance, she now knew that blue eyes and red hair was so rare that it only occurred in .017% of the population. By those statistics there were merely a million people in the entire world with that combination. Phoenix was literally one in a million. *Of course she was,* Ash added sarcastically to herself upon the discovery.

Staring at a blinking cursor rather than typing anything into her dissertation draft, Ash sighed. She'd found herself once again lost in thought at how quickly her friendship with Phoenix had developed. Each conversation felt easier and Ash wished she saw Phoenix alone more often, until she remembered that Phoenix still didn't know Ash's secret.

How could she not guess already? Phoenix danced all around the issue without bringing Ash's life into it. At this point it would be easier if Phoenix just asked because it felt weird to bring it up now. *Oh, by the way Phoenix, I wrote that story because I'm on the asexual spectrum. What? Why is that relevant? Oh, no reason.*

Except Ash knew she was developing a massive crush. She felt that tingle when Phoenix talked excitedly about food, or what she loved about her favorite fandoms. She noticed the affection fill her chest when Phoenix managed to ask about asexuality without being an asshole. She even noticed the crush growing incrementally watching Phoenix draw, a little wrinkle forming between her eyebrows when she was intensely focused on her work. And those eyes, with just the hint of blue that drew her in. It reminded her of the detector, the ice so clear until a neutrino collided with a water molecule, producing a trail of blue light in its wake. That blue was rare but held the secrets of the universe. What secrets did Phoenix's eyes hold?

Seriously Ash? What secrets do her eyes hold? Get a grip.

There was no way she could work until she let these thoughts out. Ash took a look around before opening the chat window for Cole.

I blame you. Ash didn't really, but she knew it would get a reaction out of them.

Ha! For something good I hope. Cole was too smart to take Ash's bait.

That remains to be seen. Ash knew she didn't have forever to talk, so she decided to dive into it. *I can't get her out of my head. Phoenix?*

Yes, of course Phoenix. Who else?

Sorry, couldn't resist. Why is that a problem?

Ash shook her head. *Let's make a list. 1. I'm too distracted to work.*

Cole replied with a shocked emoticon.

Yeah, and I have to stay focused to get my dissertation done. I don't have time for such a massive distraction. 2. I don't actually know her, so why is this happening? I know things about her, but only fragments of her life. She's hinted at family troubles, but nothing in detail. How can someone so elusive be so distracting?

Ash waited impatiently as Cole typed, hoping for wisdom.

Let's start with number 2. You haven't known her for that long. Do you feel like she's ever lied to you?

Ash had to think about it. Phoenix did admit lying when they'd first met, but she'd explained herself. And since then, Ash thought she'd been truthful, just guarded.

No, I feel like she's hiding herself, but I don't think that's just about me. I suspect she's hiding from everyone.

Sounds like she needs more time. You have ten or eleven months ahead of you, so let her come around. If it really bothers you, ask. But don't expect her to pour out her darkest secrets after a month. It's not like you've shared yours.

Fair point. But aren't secrets a red flag? Ash didn't believe they were with Phoenix, but she couldn't trust herself with something this important.

They can be. But from your prior emails, it doesn't sound like she's keeping secrets so much as testing the waters and only showing you small parts of herself at a time. She might be afraid that you'll run if you know everything about her.

Ash knew that feeling well. *She asked about relationships between allos and aces last night. She still hasn't asked about my sexu-*

ality, it's all in context of the story, but the story is on her mind. Which now means her thoughts on asexuality are on my mind, instead of the script I should be fixing and testing.

Will telling her about you help you focus?

I don't think so. She's approaching it so unexpectedly, I want to let her get there on her own. And if she doesn't then I'll have to tell her. I don't know what she's working through, but she's not asking questions flippantly. Nor has she made any jokes, or ignorant comments. Maybe I completely misjudged her at the beginning? I just don't know.

Maybe she doesn't either.

Ash didn't know what to do with that idea. How were they supposed to figure this out with so many unknowns?

Ash, do you know what you want?

Ash looked at the wall, her gaze unfocused, hoping for answers that just wouldn't come. What she wanted was too dangerous to admit to herself, much less Cole.

I can't want... anything. There's too much at risk. Ash made a mental list. Her dissertation. Her career. Her heart. And that last one was the most terrifying of them all.

Cole sent a hug GIF before adding a message. *You can't control what you want. Fighting it causes more of a distraction than embracing it. At least, that's my theory. You don't have to act on anything, but maybe if you stop fighting your feelings you'll be able to focus again.*

I don't know if I want her like that, but I want to know more about her. Ash searched for an analogy. *I feel like this is a job interview. Her resume is intriguing, and I'd like to call her in for an interview. But I don't know if she's going to show up or not, so I haven't invited her.*

You haven't even told her there's something to interview for. Invite her when you're ready. Unless you're interviewing other candidates for your heart?

I walked right into that one, didn't I? Fine. I'll see what happens. If she doesn't start opening up, I'll ask her about it. Maybe.

Be strong like an Amazon my friend.

Ash smiled at the Buffy reference. *I'll try.*

Do or do not. There is no try.

Wrong fandom you dork! But Ash was smiling again, the pressure of the situation reduced to a simmer. She could focus on work again.

Cole sent a GIF of Yoda brandishing his lightsaber. Ash sent them back a GIF of Buffy spinning a stake.

You know, most Jedi make wonderful ace characters. Maybe you should expand your writing horizons.

I can already imagine Phoenix's reaction. She keeps gushing over my writing and wondering why I don't write something that isn't fandom.

Maybe one of her deep, dark secrets is that she's a Star Wars nerd.

Ash laughed out loud. *I'll be sure to make that my first question. I'd better get back to work now. Thanks for the talk. Will you email me later and fill me in on everything going on in your life? I hate only chatting when I need something.*

As long as the time you would spend talking to me is spent talking to Phoenix, I'll let it slide.

You're a hopeless romantic Cole.

No, I'm a hopeful romantic. There's a difference.

CHAPTER NINE

PHOENIX

*C*hristmas morning felt like any other day at the Pole until Phoenix went to breakfast. Excitement vibrated in the air as everyone bustled around, preparing for the yearly race around the world. It was a time-honored tradition, the race crossed through every time zone on a two-mile track, allowing the participants to claim they'd walked around the world. While some trained so they could run it, plenty of others walked the course at a slow pace. And still others decorated the heavy machinery and drove a slightly larger course to keep the pedestrians safe. It was a highlight of the summer season.

The event would be fun but Phoenix was focused on her gift giving afterward. She'd spent the past two weeks making holiday themed sketches for each program that would decorate the galley for Christmas dinner. More importantly, she couldn't wait to see what Ash would think of her gift. But first Phoenix had to find her. And walk around the world. Talk about an eventful day!

When Ash didn't appear at breakfast Phoenix decided to try the science lab. She assumed Ash planned to participate in the race, but she hadn't confirmed.

The science lab was empty so Phoenix walked to Ash's room and knocked quietly on her door. She tried one more time, louder in case Ash had headphones in. A loud thunk confirmed Ash's presence so Phoenix waited, curious as to the cause. After a minute the door flew open and a harried looking Ash stood before her in purple and gray flannel pajamas.

Phoenix didn't bother to hide her amusement. "Merry Christmas?"

"Shit! I overslept. I didn't miss the race, did I?" Ash asked while reaching for her clock.

"No, you still have a half hour." There was something extra endearing about frazzled Ash. "Why don't you get dressed and I'll grab you something to eat, unless you want to wear your pjs on your adventure around the world."

Ash looked at her clothes sheepishly. "I'll change." She lifted her head to look at Phoenix. "Thanks for waking me up."

"No problem. I'll meet you outside your pod."

When Ash emerged ten minutes later, she no longer looked like she'd literally fallen out of bed. Instead she was the same level of scruffy as everyone else and dressed in enough layers to stay warm.

Phoenix offered her a cup of coffee and bowl of applesauce. "Take your pick."

Ash grabbed the coffee, took a big drink once she realized it wasn't scalding, and began walking down the hall to the main entrance where their parkas were stored. Phoenix walked alongside, giving her time to wake up, knowing how grumpy Ash could be in the morning.

Ash detoured to the lounge next to the coat room. "Can I have the applesauce?"

Phoenix handed her the bowl. "You know, we have time. If we head out a little late no one will care." Phoenix set a bag of trail mix on the end table.

"Thanks. I can't believe I overslept. I never do that."

"You've also never lived where the sun doesn't set. That can throw anyone off."

Phoenix watched people pass them on their way outside, giving Ash space. Most people spoke excitedly, snippets of conversations caught as they dressed. The stream of people slowed as the race start time passed.

Ash downed the rest of her coffee. "Ok, I'm ready to walk around the world."

They donned the rest of their extreme cold weather gear and sunglasses, an absolute necessity. Snow blindness was a real danger, especially when spending almost an hour in the sun.

Outside bustled with a good percentage of the station spread over the course. Those running were already halfway complete. The walkers stretched the remaining distance. Snowmobiles decorated with flags continued buzzing around the separate course.

"Wow, this is something," Phoenix said, admiring the view.

"Definitely the most unique Christmas morning of my life," Ash replied. "I may have missed all the holiday parades, but we made our own. And there's even a balloon." Ash gestured toward the weather balloon that was decorated with antlers for the occasion.

"There were parades on Christmas morning?" Phoenix asked, genuinely confused. Her experience with holidays was complicated. The only reason Thanksgiving was relatively untainted was because it required starting so early, she always slept at her grandma's the night before which meant her parents didn't have much opportunity to screw her morning up.

Ash turned to look at her. "I believe there was only one, the Disney parade. But we watched the earlier parades too. They can be cheesy, but I enjoyed the marching bands and giant balloons."

"When I watched parades, it was to see if a balloon got loose." At Ash's questioning gaze Phoenix added, "I may have been bored. Or an asshole. Or both." Phoenix shrugged. "The jury is still out."

Ash looped an arm around Phoenix's elbow, sending an unexpected rush of heat through her. She liked Ash touching her, perhaps a bit too much.

"I'm going to go with bored and lacking in awareness. I just can't see you as truly an asshole."

Phoenix sighed. "I wish I could agree with you but there are too many people who could make a strong case against your statement."

Ash didn't respond and soon Phoenix was lost in the feeling of walking arm in arm, unsure if it meant anything, or if she wanted it to mean something.

Much of the course was walked in comfortable silence, the air too cold and thin to carry on a long conversation. Phoenix wondered how long it had been since she enjoyed touching someone without any expectation of sex. Maybe when she'd been twelve?

She may have agreed not to sleep around out of respect for her aunt, but now she was learning new things about herself. Without the constant stress of her family and job she didn't need the distraction of a woman. Not that she wasn't feeling the lack of companionship, but she could take care of her own needs. Two months in, finally relaxed, she could admit that lack of sex was worth the physical distance from her family.

Given their late start, they were among the last to return to station. It was the longest Phoenix had spent outside and she felt invigorated, if not a little tired.

As they removed their coats, Phoenix became impatient. She couldn't wait to see Ash's reaction to her present. "I have something for you, but it's back in my room. Can I meet you in a few minutes?"

Ash looked at her quizzically. "Why don't I just follow you to your room?"

"Uh, well, if I tell you why then it isn't a surprise. Please meet me at your room." Phoenix didn't give her a chance to ask more questions as she rushed down the hall and up the stairs to her room. Within minutes she was at Ash's door, a sketchbook obscuring her gift.

Ash opened the door at Phoenix's knock, curiosity written all over her face.

"Just wait out here. It will only take a minute," Phoenix said excitedly. At least she hoped that was all Ash heard in her voice because she was also uncharacteristically nervous.

"I can't believe I'm going along with this," Ash said as she shook her head. "Ignore the mess."

"Too late, I've already seen it. Besides, my room is a disaster in comparison."

Ash took her place outside and Phoenix stepped in the door, laying out the drawings as soon as the door closed.

Moments later everything was set. "Ok, you can come in."

"No, I can't," Ash's muffled voice called through the door. "I don't have my key."

Whoops. Phoenix opened the door and retreated to the far end of the small room as Ash looked around cautiously. When her eyes drifted to the wall Phoenix held her breath. A smile tugged at Ash's lips as she spoke.

"What is that?"

"That is the hottest Christmas gift for space geeks around the world. What you see is a paper doll of Dr. Ashley Bennett, famous astronaut, placed in an inspiring poster of Mars. We see her gazing upon Earth from the surface of Mars in fulfillment of her lifelong dream. In her bio it says that's her favorite pastime." Phoenix's heart beat loud in her chest, awaiting Ash's reaction.

Ash's grin widened. "It is, huh?"

Phoenix's smile mirrored Ash's. "Definitely. I know it's hard to tell with that suit on, but she hasn't finished terraforming Mars."

"Have you been reading up on Mars colonization?"

"Did you know there are no fewer than five books on Mars in the library?" Phoenix asked in response.

"I did not."

"You should check them out. Would hate to see you get behind on your dreams." Phoenix kept her tone light but earnest.

Ash grinned and moved close to the pictures. "That's amazing, Phoenix," she said as she looked back.

"That's not all." Phoenix reached for the notebook and handed Ash a drawing in the style of a trading card. It included a portrait and facts about astronaut Dr. Ashley Bennett, including that her favorite TV show was the well-known classic Buffy the Vampire Slayer. Her favorite color was purple and her favorite food was anything cooked by celebrity chef Phoenix Murray. Her heart kept pounding in her ears, worry sneaking into her consciousness as she wondered if the gift was too silly.

Ash read the card and then threw her arms around Phoenix's neck, knocking her off balance in surprise.

"Woah. They were just drawings," Phoenix said, a little embarrassed.

"No," Ash whispered before releasing her hold on Phoenix. "Do you know how many people believe me when I say I want to live on Mars? How many take me seriously?" Ash didn't wait for Phoenix to respond. "Almost none."

They stood awkwardly, Phoenix unsure what to do facing Ash's emotions. She thought about her own dreams, but quickly realized she couldn't remember having any dreams that mattered. Adding 'celebrity chef' to Ash's card was a joke, not a serious dream. But that wasn't what Ash needed to hear right now.

Ash needed someone to believe in her outlandish dream,

even if the thought of fulfilling it meant she would no longer be in Phoenix's life. The thought gave Phoenix pause. Since when did she think so far ahead about anyone in her life? She shook off the question and returned her focus to their conversation.

"I'm sorry. I don't know why people feel the need to shit on people's dreams like that. In the end, someone has to go to Mars. Why not you?"

Ash hugged her again, not as forcefully, allowing Phoenix to notice how Ash melted into her body. The act was so intimate, like Ash was hiding nothing from her, and Phoenix didn't want to hide from Ash anymore either. She stiffened at the realization until Ash eased her grip and began to move away.

"Sorry, I didn't mean to invade your space like that."

Phoenix held her tighter. She didn't know what was going on with her, but in that moment her body's desire for touch won out.

"It's ok. You can hug me anytime you'd like. It's not a bad Christmas present, actually."

Ash pulled back suddenly. "Oh no, I don't have anything for you. I didn't think—"

Phoenix interrupted her apology. "I don't expect a present, I just had an idea and went with it. Besides, you gave me two hugs." Phoenix gave her a mischievous smile, one that usually got women to smile whether they meant to or not. Ash once again proved herself uniquely able to resist Phoenix's charm offensive.

"That's not remotely the same, Phoenix."

Phoenix lifted two fingers to accentuate her point. "Two hugs Ash. I think you underestimate the value of your hugs."

"Shut up." Ash blushed and Phoenix was pretty sure her heart would dance right out of her chest.

"Ok then, why don't you write me a story?" Phoenix said without thinking.

"I'm afraid to ask what you want me to write about."

"Hmmm..." Phoenix made a show of thinking, but she really wasn't sure. "What would you write about if you weren't writing fanfic?"

"I don't know, I've never tried. I like writing fanfic. I don't have to come up with the characters or world's they exist in, just rearrange them into the stories I'd like to read."

"Well, what if we create something together?" Excitement rose in Phoenix's chest as the idea took form. "I can draw, and you can write. We can make a comic!"

Ash didn't respond, apparently stunned by the suggestion. Phoenix tried to convince her, determined to make this happen.

"Wouldn't that be easier? We can create the world together and you won't need to write the setting because I'll draw it. It might just keep us sane during the winter."

"I— Wait. Have you ever drawn a comic?"

"Have you ever written one?"

"No."

"Then we'll learn together," Phoenix said enthusiastically.

Ash's expression was impossible to read. She appeared to struggle with the decision, which was unexpected. Just when she thought she had a handle on the scientist she threw Phoenix for a loop.

"What if we disagree on the storyline?" Ash finally asked. "I don't want to ruin our friendship over a disagreement."

"We won't let that happen. If it doesn't work out, then we stop. It's not a contract, just something fun to do." Phoenix may have thrown the idea out there on a whim, but she was already committed to it and desperately wanted Ash to agree. "Please? For Christmas?"

"Since you asked nicely..." Ash's voice trailed off noncommittally.

Phoenix pumped her fist in celebration. "Yes!"

"Really? You're that excited?"

"Would you rather I practically knocked you over with a

hug?" The words were out of her mouth again without thinking and Ash blushed, so Phoenix did just that, wrapping her tightly in a hug.

"Three hugs in one day might just go down as the best Christmas so far," Phoenix spoke low into Ash's ear. Did she detect a shiver, or was that wishful thinking?

Ash stepped back uncomfortably. Maybe it wasn't wishful thinking after all. "Don't you need to get to work? I expect another perfect holiday dinner from you."

Phoenix didn't want to leave, but Ash appeared to need some time alone. Besides, she was right. For as many volunteers as she expected, she was going to be kept busy in the kitchen.

"Yes ma'am. One extra special dinner coming up. See you there."

ASH

"This roast is perfect Phoenix. It's so good, I don't even miss Christmas dinner back home," Ash said, savoring the rich flavors of the beef.

Phoenix just smiled knowingly and took a bite of potatoes.

"The pictures turned out great too," Ash added, interested to see if Phoenix would take the compliment or not.

"I guess they weren't too bad, and it was amusing to hear everyone's reactions. Thanks for the suggestion," Phoenix said, a pensive look on her face.

Ash smiled inwardly as she took another bite. That was almost an acknowledgment of her talent.

"I can't remember the last time I got to draw so much. I need to stock up on supplies before we're cut off for the winter."

"Phoenix, I hope you realize that you're kind of killing this Christmas thing. Between your food and the drawings, I think you've managed to cheer everyone up in some small way."

"I guess there's a first for everything," Phoenix said, emotion clouding her face.

"Why do you say that?" Ash asked, confused. Thanksgiving

and this morning showed her how excited Phoenix could be on a holiday, but her excitement was tempered now.

"Christmas wasn't exactly the most fun growing up. Too much stress caused by not enough money. Add in the rotating cast of step-siblings and I don't have a lot of good memories."

"Ah." Ash wanted to know more, but it didn't feel right to push and make Phoenix feel worse. She wasn't sure what would make Phoenix happy, but she had to try, softening her voice for her reply. "From what I've seen, that couldn't have been your fault. You've already made my Christmas pretty special."

Phoenix gave her a humoring smile in response, clearly not free of her past.

"What are you doing after dinner?" Ash asked, trying to distract her. "I hear there's a live band tonight. If I remember correctly this one is made up of maintenance guys."

Phoenix looked up, a spark returning to her eyes. "What, no epic gaming night?"

"Probably, but we have all winter for that. Wouldn't you like to do something else? Live music could be fun."

"Will you dance?" Phoenix asked with raised eyebrows.

"That depends," Ash said coyly.

"On?"

"The band. The alcohol. The darkness. My mood."

Phoenix laughed. "And here I thought you were flirting for a second."

Ash felt her cheeks warm as she wondered why she'd begun flirting. She knew why she'd backed off at least. Phoenix didn't know about her asexuality, and flirting without a clear understanding of what it meant would get complicated. So why flirt at all? Was she developing real feelings for Phoenix? Ash sighed inwardly. She really needed to talk to Cole and Phoenix to start sorting this out. But not now. Not on Christmas Day.

She'd apparently been silent for too long because Phoenix answered her original question. "I think the party will be fun.

And maybe I'll get you to dance." The playfulness was back in Phoenix's eyes, and Ash suspected she was in for an interesting night.

The band was already on stage when they arrived, playing an upbeat number that Ash didn't recognize but was enjoyable. Multicolored LED lights decorated the gym, creating a more festive atmosphere than she'd expected. There was even a tree in the corner made of spare parts scrounged from recycling and lit with more lights. Groups of people milled about, watching the band or chatting with each other animatedly. It was just like any other bar with a live band, except this was the South Pole. Instead of a bar, punch and snacks sat on a table in the back.

Phoenix saw her glance toward the drinks and asked, "Want some punch? If you chase it with a shot you'll have a good buzz going in no time." Phoenix pulled a fifth of vodka from her cargo pants' pocket. Ash hadn't seen Phoenix drink often, so it was surprising to see her with a bottle of liquor. Not that it was a big deal, they were both adults. And a shot would help her relax.

"Ok, I'll give it a shot." Phoenix raised an eyebrow in response. "Yes, pun intended," Ash said with a laugh. Phoenix placed a hand on her low back as they walked to the table, moving through the growing crowd. Ash stiffened, unsure of Phoenix's intentions, but relaxed when her hand didn't stray. If anyone else there had touched her so intimately Ash would have shuddered, and yet with Phoenix she felt cared for, not patronized. Ash groaned to herself. Her body was not making it easy to keep the friendship line in place.

Phoenix dropped her hand at the table to pour the vodka into their cups before adding the punch. She handed Ash a cup and lifted hers for a toast. "Merry Christmas, Ash."

Ash returned the toast and took a long swallow, hoping to minimize the taste. As they finished the drinks, the band switched to a song she knew. Her body moved without her noticing and Phoenix set her cup down to grab Ash's hand, momentarily stealing her attention from Phoenix's words.

"What?" Ash asked, loud enough to be heard over the music.

Phoenix leaned close to her ear. "Dance? You want to?"

"Do you promise not to laugh?"

"You can't be any worse than they are," Phoenix said with an encouraging smile, gesturing to the room. Ash looked around, realizing that Phoenix was right. Dancing did not require skill, just a bit of courage, and hers was boosted by the alcohol warming her belly and the smile on Phoenix's face. She nodded and let Phoenix lead them away from the table and to a space off to the side of the main crowd.

The music overpowered her self-consciousness so she let her body bounce to the beat. It wasn't that she never danced, but the intimate dancing she saw on TV was such a foreign concept to her that she normally avoided these situations. But Phoenix wasn't encroaching on her space, just moving with ease next to her, a relaxed smile on her face. This version of Phoenix was breathtakingly beautiful, without a care in the world.

After another song, Ash excused herself for a drink, minus the vodka this time so she wouldn't overdo it. Turning, Ash was startled to see Skye dancing rather close behind Phoenix. Her stomach dropped, and as much as she wanted to look away, she couldn't. Skye had no qualms about Phoenix's personal space – though that seemed to be normal for her. Nor did Phoenix seem to mind. The rational part of Ash's brain knew that people danced together all the time without it meaning anything. The irrational part of her brain also reminded her that people use dancing as foreplay, and that's the thought that took root. Besides, Skye was making her intentions very clear as she pressed against Phoenix's body, her lips deliberately brushing over Phoenix's neck.

Phoenix spun and spoke to Skye, and then her eyes met Ash's. Yet again, Skye stood between them, a stark reminder of who Ash wasn't. Her heart sank and she turned to the exit, needing to escape. The bright lights in the hall stunned her momentarily. Ash let her eyes adjust, which was all the time Phoenix needed to catch up to her.

"Ash, where are you going?"

"I think I'll go to bed. You should stay. Have fun with Skye." Ash hadn't meant to say that last bit, but it slipped out and the look of hurt on Phoenix's face confused her more than anything else. She hadn't meant to cause Phoenix any pain, but Ash was afraid she would continue to hurt her if she stayed any longer. She began walking down the hall toward her room.

"Ash, please stop. I don't want to be with Skye, which is what I just told her. I want to hang out with you."

Ash wanted to believe her, but it was so hard. She kept walking.

"I don't understand. Can we please talk?" Phoenix asked, pleading as she walked beside her.

Ash made a split-second decision and stepped into the library, pulling Phoenix in behind her, but then immediately released her hand. It was time, whether she wanted it to be or not. She motioned for Phoenix to sit and began pacing.

"There's something I need to tell you, but I don't want to tell you, because it will probably change how you feel about me, even though we're just friends. Or maybe it won't and I'm worrying for nothing. Hell, I'm honestly surprised you haven't figured it out yet."

"Ash?" Phoenix interrupted, "unless you're a mass murderer, I don't think there's much that would change my opinion of you."

Ash continued to pace, hands in her jean pockets while her mind raced, ignoring Phoenix's attempt at levity.

"But you are worrying me. Just tell me what has you so upset."

Ash stopped and stared out the window, the bright sun adding a surreal element to the night as she tried to find a starting point. "Remember when we talked about land mines? I told you I would do my best to warn you, but I never told you what my biggest land mine was. Well, Skye just stomped all over it."

Phoenix scrunched her eyebrows. "Yeah, she is a bit of a stomper, isn't she? I guess it's appropriate that she drives heavy equipment."

Ash smiled in spite of herself and turned to look at Phoenix. "How is it that everyone assumes that fanfic is autobiographical fantasy, except you?"

Phoenix looked even more confused and Ash silently cursed herself for making this such a big deal. Her hesitation wasn't helping the situation. Time to be an adult and just spit it out. Quickly. Ash closed her eyes and took a deep breath before letting the words tumble out.

"I'm demisexual. It's part of the asexual spectrum. That's why I wrote that story, and while I could have lied and sent you something else, I wanted you to know.

"I thought it would be easier if you asked, but then you didn't, and I didn't know how to tell you. Until tonight when I saw Skye dancing with you, and I knew I couldn't hide this part of me anymore. She set me off because she reminds me of everything I'm not and can't be for someone."

For a moment, everything was still. Ash stood frozen, arms wrapped around herself, barely breathing. Phoenix hadn't moved, except her expression which told Ash nothing of what she was thinking. If she were religious, Ash would be praying frantically. Instead she listened to the pounding in her ears and willed herself to be calm.

When Phoenix finally spoke, her voice was even. "I don't think Skye is a standard you should aspire to."

Ash blinked. "What?"

"You are so much more than Skye. Sure, she's fun, and without the request from my aunt to minimize sex I probably would have enjoyed her company frequently without a second thought, but there's no connection. No intimacy, that's the word you used, right?"

"Yes," Ash said, her throat suddenly dry. "But she has no problem with physical intimacy, which is what most people want."

"She has no problem with physical touch, but intimacy? She and I are a lot alike. There is no real intimacy, just temporary release," Phoenix said, a mix of sadness and disappointment coloring her words. "Until I came here, I gave sex no second thought, as long as I kept my walls firmly in place. But now that approach to life feels hollow. Like eating candy all day, eventually you need food of substance. I think, for the first time in my life, I need more."

Ash was stunned. She'd assumed so many things, about Phoenix, about Skye, none of which was fair or accurate. Yet she wasn't ready to give up her position.

"But it's not that simple. Maybe Skye is a bad example, but she's the one who's here."

Phoenix stood and slowly walked to Ash who swallowed hard, looking toward the floor. She felt too exposed and wrapped her arms tighter around herself.

"Can I hug you?" Phoenix asked from mere inches away. Ash didn't answer, just wrapped her arms around Phoenix's waist and let herself be held by strong, sure arms.

Cole was right. She needed to give Phoenix a chance. But

acceptance from a friend was very different than acceptance from a partner. As she listened to Phoenix's heartbeat, she knew that at least a part of her wanted more than just friendship. But her head was still blaring warning bells of danger. *You don't know enough about her. She doesn't know what a relationship really means. What if this blows up? Or what if it doesn't? What does that mean for both of us in ten months if we do find a way to make it work?*

Ash willed the thoughts away, knowing they'd return later with a vengeance, and took a deep breath, relaxing into the embrace.

"Feeling better?" Phoenix asked quietly, still holding her.

Ash didn't want to answer because she didn't want Phoenix to let go. But not answering would be weird.

"Yes, thank you."

Phoenix loosened her grasp, but Ash wouldn't let her go, so Phoenix kept her arms loosely around her.

"Not better enough?" Phoenix asked tenderly.

"Or maybe you underestimate the value of your hugs too."

She felt Phoenix's chuckle and squeezed again before Ash reluctantly relaxed her hold as well. Phoenix took a step toward the small couch, tugging on Ash's arm encouragingly. She followed but paused, unsure where to sit. Phoenix extended her hand.

"My hugs are just as good on the couch, if that's what you're wondering. But if that's too much, I'll give you all the space you need."

Was it too much? Ash's body moved before her mind could overthink the moment and sat right next to Phoenix, who wrapped an arm around her shoulder.

"If you're up for talking I'd like to ask you something," Phoenix said gently.

Ash's stomach churned, but she'd opened the can of worms. She could always choose not to answer a question, but her response remained hesitant. "Ok."

"Who hurt you so bad that you were afraid to tell me?"

Ash took a moment to enjoy the warmth radiating from Phoenix's very being. Her gentleness was a surprise, definitely not what she expected from the person she'd met just two months ago. Had she been wrong from day one, or had this place changed Phoenix? Or was it a little of both?

"No one person did anything particularly awful. It's like death by a thousand cuts. Actually, more like a thousand papercuts."

"What's the difference?"

"If someone is standing in front of you with a knife, you know what's coming. But a papercut sneaks up on you. Occasionally I can see a person's proverbial knife, but usually I'm blindsided. When enough people react like there's something wrong with you, or even stranger, that there's something wrong with them when you aren't attracted to them, you expect rejection from everyone. It becomes the only way to protect yourself."

Phoenix pulled her tighter. "I'm sorry people are assholes."

Ash rested her head on Phoenix's shoulder. "Thanks."

"Have I been an asshole?"

Ash smiled up at her. "No. You've been amazing. Unexpectedly so, which makes me a little paranoid. Would you mind if I asked you some questions?"

Phoenix answered without hesitation. "Not at all, though I can't imagine what you want to know."

Now that she had permission, Ash wasn't sure what to ask. She'd seen the effect Skye had on Phoenix before. What was different now? Ash took a deep breath. "I don't know how to ask without sounding like I'm judging you."

"That's foreboding."

Ash turned in place, putting a little space between her and Phoenix. "It shouldn't be. I just don't understand you. From the first day I saw you in the galley talking with Skye, I saw how sexual you were, for lack of a better description. In case you somehow missed this realization, you exude sexual confidence. So that night in the library, I was already on guard. That's why I pushed you away at the slightest hint of flirtation.

"And that sounds egotistical in hindsight. I'm not saying I thought you were seriously flirting with me, it's just... I don't want to lead anyone on. Or end up in an uncomfortable conversation about being asexual with someone I don't know. What if I read them wrong and they laugh at me or say any number of awful things about asexuality not being real, or that it's a hormone imbalance or, even worse, that they could fix me."

Phoenix's eyes narrowed. Was she angry on Ash's behalf? Ash couldn't be distracted by exploring Phoenix's reaction in case she lost her train of thought. Ash rushed ahead to verbalize her thoughts.

"All that is to say, when you got here, you seemed really into Skye. And then there was the infamous hallway incident. It didn't appear like Skye's interest was one sided. But tonight, you followed me out rather than enjoy a night with her. And I don't understand why, to any of it really. Does that make any sense at all?"

"I think so? But hell Ash, I don't think I understand it either," Phoenix admitted. "And since you're being so honest, I should be, too. I'm not sure who I am anymore. When I arrived, I was still adjusting to this new life, one where I don't use sex to escape. That left a vacuum though. I've been filling it with exercise and other activities, but they're not the same.

"Flirting with Skye was fun and it felt good to be wanted, but I had no intention of sleeping with her. She caught me off guard, and apparently I was lonelier than I realized because I forgot all the reasons I was supposed to refrain. She promised no strings attached, so I took a chance.

"What most surprised me is that it didn't help, not really. We had fun, but something was missing. That's why I turned her down tonight, and Thanksgiving night as well. I'd rather hang out with you, especially if you're handing out hugs, than have empty sex." Phoenix winced, and Ash wondered if the reaction was subconscious or not.

"Does that answer your not entirely clear question?"

"Intellectually, yes. But personally? The thought of having sex with anyone, even the most beautiful woman on earth, without having emotional intimacy is completely foreign. I don't even think it would work."

"You've had sex?" Phoenix asked, surprise evident in her voice.

"Yes," Ash said with a small chuckle. "Still do, in fact. Are you up for a little asexuality 101?" Phoenix nodded and Ash continued.

"One of the largest myths around asexuality is that we don't like sex, but that isn't always the case. Asexuality is defined by a lack of casual sexual attraction. For some that means never experiencing it, but I'm a little different. I'm demisexual, which is still part of the asexual spectrum because on an average day I also don't experience sexual attraction. For whatever reason, my brain doesn't even consider the option without an emotional connection and a romantic interest."

"Before I recognized my asexuality, I thought there was something wrong with me. Rather than express my lack of interest I gave in to my girlfriends' desires. It didn't go well. Now I'm learning to approach sex and relationships in a way that doesn't negate my own needs. It's a work in progress."

"Sounds complicated and challenging. I'm struggling to understand what it feels like to not be attracted to people," Phoenix said.

"And I'm struggling to understand what it feels like to be attracted to random people. Isn't it distracting?"

Phoenix laughed. "Yes! But it's also fun, especially when the feeling is mutual. There's a spark of excitement that's almost intoxicating."

"Until it isn't? Like with Skye?"

Phoenix thought her question over before responding. "Even then there was the excitement, and intoxication, but it left me with a hangover I haven't forgotten."

The explanation clicked in Ash's brain, allowing her to relax. "I like the analogy, it helps."

"Thanks. Feel free to tell me to piss off, but I'm still wondering about the sex part. Why did you have sex if you didn't feel like it?" Phoenix was genuinely interested in her answer.

"Oh. Well, I didn't want to disappoint the woman I was dating and made the best of it. I liked her well enough, but there was something missing because I never developed that real desire to have sex with her. Not that I had the language to understand the situation then. I broke it off and decided to focus on my degree instead. Physics is infinitely simpler than trying to date when ace, which is slang for asexual," Ash clarified at Phoenix's confused expression.

Phoenix nodded in recognition. "I want to say that I understand."

"It's ok," Ash said, patting Phoenix's thigh. How was she the one offering reassurance now? Could this situation be any stranger? "I might regret asking, but has anyone come onto you and you didn't feel the desire for sex?"

"Do you think I'm merely an animal, letting my hormones drive my actions?"

Ash reacted quickly. "No, I don't," but then Phoenix smiled, and Ash smacked her in the stomach.

"Ow! Ok, too soon. I get that now." Phoenix rubbed where Ash had slapped her. "Seriously, of course there are times. Even today, Skye's dancing felt good, but the interest wasn't there."

Phoenix hesitated for a moment. "I don't fully understand

what is happening with me, but I don't feel the intense drive for sex like I did before I arrived. So maybe I understand you more than you realize."

The desire to touch Phoenix washed over Ash and she went with it, wrapping an arm around Phoenix's waist and resting her head on her shoulder. Phoenix leaned back, making it easy for Ash to relax alongside, feeling Phoenix's chest rise and fall. She couldn't believe how natural they felt together. Did Phoenix feel the same way?

"You just reminded me of another question," Phoenix said.

Ash furrowed her brows. What else was there to discuss? Phoenix gestured with her free hand to the space, or lack thereof, between them.

"This. I didn't get the impression you were a very physical person before you hugged me. But, now?"

Ash's cheeks warmed. "I am, with friends and people I trust. But it's easily misunderstood, so I try to keep it in check." She stopped short of admitting how lonely that distance made her feel.

"Thank you for trusting me." Phoenix sounded like she had more to say, but didn't, and Ash wasn't going to press her. If her head spun from their conversations, she could only imagine what Phoenix felt.

"Thank you for not freaking out."

They sat together in silence, Ash wishing she'd had the courage to ask Phoenix if she had any romantic interest in her. But for now, she was content in Phoenix's presence. Cole was going to love this story. Phoenix looked more like a unicorn every day.

"Is this the weirdest Christmas ever?" Ash asked, amused at the turn of events.

"What, you don't run around the world and then come out every Christmas?" Phoenix teased.

"No, but maybe I will make it a tradition. Minus the running. And the coming out. So I guess that just leaves Christmas hugs."

"Sounds pretty good to me," Phoenix added softly.

Ash yawned, and a glance at the wall clock told her it was already after 11, but she was enjoying the calm silence too much to get up. She nuzzled a bit closer to Phoenix, her breath deepening.

Phoenix's voice was quiet when she spoke a minute later. "If you fall asleep here you're going to regret it in the morning."

"Ugh, when did you become the voice of reason?"

"Must be a Christmas miracle."

Ash took one more breath curled against Phoenix before sitting up reluctantly, immediately missing the closeness. They walked to Ash's room in silence, and Phoenix said goodnight with another hug. All the while Ash wondered if she would find the courage to go for what she wanted.

CHAPTER TEN

PHOENIX

Phoenix returned to her room following the morning kitchen meeting, hoping for a nap but finding it impossible. Ash's story remained open on the tablet beside her. After their discussion last night, she hoped the story would provide greater insight into Ash and her experiences.

Even knowing about Ash's sexuality, nothing about the story felt different than any other romance until the end. Willow and Tara became close in Ash's story as they practiced magic. They were emotionally connecting, in ways Phoenix had never allowed herself to fully experience. And they were becoming more physically intimate as a result, just without the sex.

The story tugged at her heart, much to her annoyance. Phoenix was not a sucker for romance. She didn't dream about finding the one person who would complete her. That was nonsense. Her interest in the story wasn't about her, it was a way to understand Ash. Her friend, who she enjoyed cuddling on a couch with and the reason she'd rejected sex with Skye. Phoenix shook her head and dragged herself out of bed. All this thinking was getting her nowhere so she gave up and headed to lunch.

At the galley she spotted Ash speaking animatedly with a younger woman. Cute, strawberry blonde, with black rimmed glasses, she could easily pull off the sexy librarian look if she wanted to. Phoenix idly wondered if there was something about astrophysics that drew subtly attractive women to it as she walked up behind Ash unnoticed. Phoenix wrapped her arms around Ash's shoulders, causing her to startle.

"Morning," Phoenix said with a chuckle. The blonde gave Phoenix a curious look while Ash relaxed in her arms.

"Christ Phoenix, a little warning next time? And what's this morning stuff? It's almost one. Have you only just woken up?"

Phoenix gave Ash an extra squeeze before releasing her and sat in the next chair. "I couldn't get to sleep last night, so after my early meeting this morning I opted for a lazy day rather than walk around grumpy like *someone* I know."

Ash's expression betrayed concern, but she didn't verbalize her thoughts. Perhaps because they had an audience. Phoenix hoped her words would ease her concern enough for now.

"Nothing to worry about but we can talk about it later. Who's your friend?"

"Oh, this is the undergrad assistant I told you about, Emily. She got in an hour or so ago. Emily, this is Phoenix, the best chef here but she also happens to be an artist. She drew all the Christmas pictures on the wall." Ash gestured to the wall near the doors.

"I told you, I'm a cook, not a chef, and far from the best, but it's nice to meet you," Phoenix said while giving Ash a look. While she appreciated Ash's praise, she wasn't comfortable with the expectations that came along with it.

"She's also too modest," Ash said, giving Phoenix a nudge, "but you'll learn that at dinner."

"Dinner? I feel like I should be having breakfast. This time difference is confusing," Emily said.

Phoenix smiled. "Yeah, I'd say you get used to it, but you

won't be here long enough for that to be true. However, if you're really craving breakfast tonight, just ask and I'll whip something up for you."

"Really?" Emily asked.

Ash joined her. "Yeah, really? You never gave me that option."

"That's because you hated me when you first got here."

"What about now?" Ash asked indignantly.

Phoenix shrugged. "Now you need to suck it up like everyone else."

"Why is Emily an exception?"

Phoenix replied smoothly, "Because she's your friend."

"That doesn't make any sense!" Ash said with a laugh. Phoenix loved her laugh and her chest swelled at the sound.

"Hey, don't expect logic before coffee."

A chuckle from across the table reminded Phoenix that they had an audience. "Anyway, I'd better eat before my shift starts. See you at dinner."

Phoenix squeezed Ash's shoulder before walking away, lighter than when she'd arrived, conscious of the two sets of eyes following her.

ASH

"You two seem close," Emily observed after Phoenix walked away.

"Yeah, Phoenix has been the biggest surprise of this trip."

"Are you two together?" Emily asked knowingly.

"We're just friends," which surprisingly hurt to admit out loud.

"You sure about that?" Emily asked pointedly.

Who knew Emily was so ballsy? "It's complicated. But at this exact moment, we are only friends."

Emily gave a halfhearted shrug. "She's hot though."

Ash squelched the surge of jealousy and replied dryly, "Yeah, that's the general consensus." Ash preferred to keep her private life separate from her professional life, at least when it came to her asexuality. While she knew Emily was queer, she didn't want to get into what may or may not be happening with her and Phoenix, especially when she didn't know how Phoenix felt about her.

"Let's talk about your schedule. Once you're unpacked, meet me in the lab. We'll go over everything there and keep things light. Most people are recovering from last night's party anyway so it should be quiet. But tomorrow we'll all be out at the site, measuring and shoveling snow off the surface array. Try to get as much sleep as you can tonight." Ash just hoped she could take her own advice.

By the time dinner rolled around Ash felt almost as tired as Emily looked. She excused herself and retired to her room, hoping to either catch up on sleep or find a way to silence the thoughts keeping her up lately.

Ash flopped on her bed but didn't move, just letting her body release all the tension from the day. Her eyes drifted to the pictures on the wall, to her avatar gazing at the sky, and her thoughts drifted to the artist.

She spent a lot of time thinking about Phoenix, wondering just what she was hiding. Most of the time Phoenix was funny, carefree, thoughtful, and far more considerate than she'd imagined. But then Ash would compliment her and a hint of something else came through. She'd referenced her family more than once, and not always in a positive way.

A small part of her worried, what if Phoenix wasn't who she appeared? But those concerns were forgotten in Phoenix's presence. And what did the past really matter right now? Here, everyone had the chance for a clean break from their past because they were so far from civilization.

Maybe her concerns weren't really about potential red flags, but Ash wanting to know Phoenix better. Even now, as much as she needed the rest, Ash wanted to be near Phoenix. Phoenix made her feel, what exactly? Ash's eyes fell on Phoenix's sketch again, trying to get into her head. Phoenix had listened to her and took her seriously. Phoenix made her feel seen, and that was a potent draw.

What she didn't know was whether her crush on Phoenix

would fade into friendship or blossom into love. She'd fooled herself before thinking a friendship could be romantic, back in undergrad. But there was something missing when they'd kissed at the end of their first date. Luckily they'd both agreed they were better as friends and still laughed about it to this day.

Was that the solution here? Just kiss Phoenix and see how they both reacted? For all she knew, Phoenix saw her strictly as a friend. Somehow Phoenix didn't seem the type to hold an experimental kiss against anyone.

Time would tell. If the opportunity arose, maybe she'd take it and put her concerns to bed. Then she could focus on work again.

CHAPTER ELEVEN

PHOENIX

How is it already New Year's Eve? The week since the most bizarre yet best Christmas of her life had flown by with minimal time spent with Ash. She'd seen the soon-to-be-Doctor Ashley Bennett, astrophysicist and now mentor a few times, but only briefly as she was now responsible for Emily and spending her social time with her colleagues. Ashley was pleasant enough but not as much fun as Ash.

Phoenix understood when Ash explained that they'd be working long days on detector maintenance, though she was surprised physics required so much manual labor. She also explained that Emily needed to learn a lot in a short time, but the timing was crap.

More than anything she missed talking with Ash. They'd had a rocky start, more than a few prickly moments, but that made it all the sweeter when they got along. And they got along rather well now.

Without Ash, Phoenix could have filled her time in the lounge, but it lacked appeal, leaving her with too much time to revisit Ash's questions from Christmas. Phoenix realized how much she was enjoying her new life. The people around her respected her. Appreciated her. Valued her. They expected nothing of her except to cook them delicious food. All of which was missing from her life back home. And once she relaxed her creativity exploded.

If it wasn't for Ash shaking up her world Phoenix would have likely settled into the comfortable habits of many of the non-scientists, playing cards, watching movies, shooting the shit, and drinking. Skye would be an enjoyable distraction and her life would look a lot like it had before she arrived, but without the pressure of her family. That thought saddened her. Diane would be so disappointed if she returned home the same person she'd left.

Phoenix hadn't discussed the comic idea with Ash since she'd originally suggested it. She had an idea that she wasn't sure Ash would be into, but she had learned a lot from her fanfic and thought maybe it would help both of them to build on it. She just needed a chance to talk to Ash about it.

That's why she was glad it was New Year's Eve. Most people left work early and had the next day off as well. Being on the same time zone as New Zealand, they would be among the first to ring in the New Year. The truly dedicated would continue celebrating as each time zone struck midnight, but that type of celebration held no appeal tonight. She was waiting for Ash who rushed in at the end of dinner service.

Phoenix instantly brightened. "Hey, I was about to make you up a plate. Long day?"

"A little hiccup with the system, but it gave me the chance to show Emily some troubleshooting techniques."

"Do you have to go back to work tonight?" Phoenix asked, trying to hide her disappointment. Since when was she needy?

"No, it's working again so we're free to attend the battle of the bands tonight."

"You and Emily?"

Ash gave Phoenix a funny look. "No, you and me silly. I've spent too much time with my coworkers this week. Unless you want me to invite them?" Ash said teasingly.

"No way. I've shared you since Emily arrived." Suddenly shy at her admission, Phoenix changed the subject. "Let's get you fed."

Phoenix snacked as Ash ate and filled Phoenix in on the mundane events of the week. Some of the references went over Phoenix's head, but she didn't care. She finally had Ash to herself. When the conversation lagged, Phoenix decided it was safe enough to bring up her idea.

"I know you've been busy, but have you given any thought to my Christmas request, that we try writing a comic together?"

Ash winced. "I knew I was forgetting something but there's been so much on my mind..."

"It's ok, I understand. I have an idea for you, which you're free to veto."

Ash propped her chin in her hands, giving Phoenix her full attention. "What is it?"

"Well, it's only part of an idea. A baby idea."

"Is it an actual baby? Babies are cute, especially animal babies. Ooh, what about a sloth baby? I've always wanted to cuddle a baby sloth. Can you draw me cuddling a baby sloth?" Ash teased and Phoenix laughed realizing she was being ridiculous. This was Ash. The worst she could do was say no.

"No," Phoenix said, still laughing. "I was thinking about your fanfic, how it helped me begin to understand asexuality better. Something about seeing it in context, between two people, was easier than reading definitions in an article."

Phoenix saw hesitation in Ash's eyes and softened her approach. "I mean, you need to be comfortable with this too, but if we made a comic with an asexual character wouldn't that help you and other people like you? Maybe you wouldn't have to be so afraid to come out to someone new."

Ash scrunched her eyebrows as her lips formed a thin line. "I don't know Phoenix. I have no idea how to create characters. And it hits so close to home, it took a lot to write Willow and Tara's story."

"That makes sense. I don't know how to develop characters either." Phoenix pondered the situation. "Maybe we don't need to. Maybe we can do a comic about us."

Ash cocked her head. "How so?"

"Well, we could document our discussions in some way. The things you teach me, we tweak them and turn them into a comic. Add some funny bits. Remove the more personal details, generalize, whatever we need to do."

"That could work," Ash said cautiously. "We could even scan and publish them online as we go."

Phoenix's heart lifted. "Yes! That would be great. A webcomic that's semi-autobiographical, though we don't have to say that if we don't want to."

"No, I think that would be good to share, so they know it's based on real conversations."

"I agree," Phoenix said, barely containing her excitement. "This is going to be so much fun."

Ash's expression gave Phoenix pause. "What?"

"I don't want to dampen your enthusiasm, but once we start posting, we're likely to attract trolls. I don't think I can handle reading the hurtful comments that are inevitable."

"Leave that to me. I'll read them and only tell you about the good ones. I'm used to dealing with assholes that try to push people's buttons." Hell, her dad was a source of constant practice. No troll could be worse.

"Any other objections?"

"I'm in, but I reserve the right to object later."

Phoenix laughed giddily. "Of course. Can we begin the festivities?"

"Yes, I'm so ready for a night of fun," Ash said as she stood to deposit her dishes in the dirty bin. "I need to change first. Why don't I meet you there?"

"Sure. I'll run upstairs and snag a drink. What's New Year's Eve without at least a little alcohol?"

"I think that's still New Year's Phoenix," Ash replied dryly.

"Technicalities." Phoenix playfully bumped her shoulder and headed to her room across the hall.

The gym was full when Phoenix arrived, everyone out to support their colleagues and friends who were competing in the battle of the bands. She waited just outside the door so she wouldn't miss Ash's arrival. Ten minutes later Phoenix wondered what Ash was doing to take so long. A moment later the reason for the delay was clear. Ash's hair was down, a rare and pleasant sight that certainly took more time than simply changing into a clean pair of jeans, an almost dressy shirt and purple Chuck Taylors. Phoenix failed to hide her grin.

"You look nice."

Ash appeared nervous, replying shyly. "I brushed my hair."

"And it looks nice." Phoenix offered her arm without thinking. Ash considered her for a second before looping her arm through. And that's when Phoenix realized how quickly the night turned from friends blowing off steam to something approaching a date. It was too late now. If she retracted her arm Ash would definitely get the wrong impression. She'd have to keep reminding herself it wasn't a date until it stuck.

Phoenix steered them toward the drinks table, dropped Ash's arm and retrieved the fifth of vodka she'd opened at Christmas from the pocket of her cargo pants. She took a quick shot and chased it with punch before offering the bottle to Ash.

"Not yet. I'm pacing myself."

Phoenix returned the bottle to her pocket and followed Ash a few feet away where the crowd was thinner.

"Did I tell you Jon's band is playing first? They're going to play all Barenaked Ladies' songs."

Phoenix groaned. "Why?" she dragged out in a whine.

Ash laughed. "Because they want nerd points. It all started with the theme song to Big Bang Theory and before they knew it, their set was entirely Barenaked Ladies' songs."

"Please tell me they're at least decent?"

"We're about to find out."

Phoenix attempted to control her reticence as Jon and four other guys took to the stage. She may not be a fan of the music, but the guys performed well, and when Ash nudged her during the first song Phoenix decided to enjoy it and dance. They closed the three-song set with the Big Bang Theory theme, which as expected had the crowd singing along. Phoenix had to admit she was having fun.

They talked as the bands changed.

"Do you play any instruments?" Ash asked.

"No, that required money we didn't have, so I didn't even ask. Maybe someday I'll learn guitar, when I'm not working all the time."

"You could learn while you're here."

Phoenix shrugged. "Maybe in the middle of winter but I like focusing on drawing. It's soothing. You?"

"No, on music or art. I'm pretty good at being a fan though."

"Are you a fan of mine?" Phoenix asked before she could stop herself. She was having a good time and the flirting just slipped out.

"You know I am," Ash replied quietly, then added more confidently, "why else would I agree to make this comic with you?"

"Because I'm incredibly persuasive?"

"Maybe. Try to use that power for good, ok?"

Phoenix's heart warmed. *Not a date*, she reminded herself. The next band began their sound check, providing a convenient distraction for which Phoenix was grateful. She wasn't sure they were talking about the same things, and she didn't want to find one of those land mines again.

The next band played heavier rock and Phoenix let loose, laughing at Ash's attempts to headbang, which lasted all of five seconds before she shook her head and jumped around instead. It was so damn cute.

The song ended and Phoenix couldn't resist teasing her. "Did you hurt your brain?"

"I might be concussed. Check my pupils," Ash said with fake seriousness. Phoenix met her eyes and forgot what she was supposed to do. It would be so easy to lean in and kiss her. Phoenix blinked to clear her head. This was Ash, her friend, and Phoenix didn't kiss her friends anymore. Especially her asexual friends.

"Uh, I think you'll be ok, as long as you avoid any further headbanging."

"I'll take that under advisement."

The rest of their set was more subdued but still fun. The third group was a blues band. They slowed things down a bit and Phoenix was pleasantly surprised when Ash took her hand and pulled her close. Phoenix wrapped her other arm around Ash, embracing her as they moved together with the music.

Phoenix's body came alive with the closeness. With anyone else she knew where the night would lead. Now she felt like an unsure teenager, where nothing was known, including whether her friend was really just a friend.

Ash leaned back after the first song. "Is this ok?"

"Of course." Phoenix danced with women all the time, why should this be any different? *Because this is Ash and you haven't been laid in six weeks.*

Phoenix attempted to focus on the band, but there was no way to ignore how good Ash felt in her arms. The light brush of her ass against Phoenix's pelvis. Ash's back against her breasts. If it had been anyone else that contact wouldn't have been an accident, but with Ash she didn't assume anything.

The last song was upbeat and Phoenix reluctantly let Ash go. To continue holding her would have looked strange and definitely not friend-like.

When they finished the last song, Phoenix needed a moment and walked back to the table for her second drink and Ash's first. Skye intercepted her, a beer in her outstretched hand. "I figure I owe ya."

Phoenix took it with thanks and watched her walk back towards the front of the crowd and close to— Oh, that might be a problem.

"What was that about?" Ash asked, following Phoenix's gaze.

"I had a talk with her and asked her to back off. She didn't realize she was causing problems and apologized." Phoenix caught another glimpse of Skye and she was definitely on the prowl.

"Ash, how well do you know Emily?"

"That depends on why you're asking."

"Is she normally into women?"

"Yes, that's part of the reason I've been working with her instead of Jon. Why? Who did she find?"

"Skye."

"Oh." Ash took a drink of Phoenix's beer, much to her chagrin, but then surprised Phoenix with her response. "Well, she's an adult and only here for another week. I'm sure she knows what she's doing."

Did Skye only bother Ash when she was around Phoenix, or was Skye no longer an issue since they'd talked over Christmas? With only one band before the New Year countdown now wasn't the time to ask.

The last band took to the stage, playing popular songs that had everyone singing along. They ended their set with R.E.M.'s anthem It's the End of the World as We Know It, which was strangely appropriate given their location.

All in all, the bands were good and Phoenix joined Ash in cheering enthusiastically for them all, diluting her vote to be meaningless.

The lights dimmed as the announcer directed everyone's attention to the projection on the wall which showed a video of the festivities in Auckland, New Zealand. The clock read 11:59 and 30 seconds. The brightly lit ball waited for its time to move, signaling the end of the year.

Ash drew near to Phoenix's side and slid her arm around Phoenix's back, resting her hand on Phoenix's hip. Phoenix tried to remain unaffected. Ash was just a friend. If she repeated it enough maybe the nerve endings in her body would get the message.

With 10 seconds left, the ball on camera began its descent as the crowd counted down. With two seconds left, Ash moved in front of her, pulling Phoenix's attention from the screen. She barely registered Ash's *happy New Year* in the noise of the celebrations.

The cheers disappeared the moment Ash's lips touched hers gently, as if asking permission. *Still a friend,* she thought, until Ash's tongue brushed across Phoenix's lips, a sweet invitation to more if Phoenix would allow her in. And allow her entrance she did. Phoenix parted her lips, meeting Ash's tongue with her own, heat exploding in her body like the fireworks on the screen.

Not just a friend. This was new and wonderful and as they continued to kiss, terrifying. Phoenix didn't have enough words for the complicated emotions exploding inside her. Her heart raced, but not only from excitement. What was she doing?

Phoenix pulled back, Ash's eyes half closed as she struggled to comprehend Phoenix's reaction. It was too much, too confusing.

"I'm sorry," was all Phoenix said before turning and rushing from the room.

ASH

Ash stood frozen and confused as Phoenix rushed away. Someone bumped her from behind, breaking the spell and allowing her to move. She jogged out the door and down the hall, calling after Phoenix. She took the stairs two at a time, regretting it when she reached the top and felt short of breath, but she finally saw Phoenix, hands stuffed deep in her pockets, head down, shuffling quickly down the hall.

What had she done? Her only goal was to confirm her feelings for Phoenix were more than friendly and see if she felt the same. And for about ten seconds she thought the answer was clear. Her stomach did that flip of excitement, her body flushed with heat, and when Phoenix kissed her back she wanted to keep kissing her forever. Until Phoenix pulled away with pain in her eyes and Ash's heart smashed into the floor.

Ash walked as fast as she could without scaring Phoenix away, catching up with her before she turned into the berthing area.

"Phoenix?" While Ash's voice was barely above a whisper, she knew Phoenix had to hear her, but she continued walking past the bathrooms.

"Phoenix, I'm so sorry. I didn't mean to hurt you." This got a reaction and Phoenix finally looked at Ash.

"You didn't hurt me," she said with a sad smile.

"Then tell me what's wrong before I freak out."

Phoenix took Ash's hand. "Not here. My room."

Ash allowed herself to be led, still confused, to a room in the far end of the pod. Phoenix escorted her in wordlessly, gesturing for her to sit on the bed. Phoenix sat at the opposite end, far enough away that Ash would have to reach to touch her. The air was thick with tension, but Ash didn't want to rush Phoenix with whatever she was struggling with. She'd already made enough mistakes today.

"Why did you kiss me?" Phoenix asked finally, not meeting Ash's gaze.

Not once in the past week did Ash consider the possibility that Phoenix would be upset with a kiss. Her heart sank into her stomach but Phoenix deserved the truth.

"I had to know if my feelings for you were romantic or purely based on friendship. Sometimes it's hard to tell the difference." Phoenix peered up through her lashes but didn't otherwise respond. "I'm sorry, that wasn't fair to you."

"And what did you decide?"

"Do you normally kiss your friends like that?" Ash asked lightly, recognizing the importance of understanding Phoenix's reaction. She'd already assumed too much.

"Yes? No? I don't know. You are unlike anyone I've ever known. Most of the people I call friends are really acquaintances that occasionally have side benefits."

"Oh." So much for the perfect plan. The kiss had apparently clarified her feelings but had complicated Phoenix's. "Phoenix, I don't kiss my friends like that."

"I didn't think you did."

"Does that mean you didn't feel anything?" Ash asked shakily.

Phoenix looked at her fully now, her face filled with emotion. "The problem is I felt too much."

Ash furrowed her brows. "I don't understand."

"I don't either. Until tonight, I'd been successfully avoiding my feelings for you. So, when you kissed me, I thought it was a friendly New Year's kiss. Until it wasn't."

Ash could barely breathe. Or think. She couldn't come up with a question, but thankfully Phoenix wasn't done.

"I don't know what I'm doing Ash. You're amazing, and I love spending time with you. But I don't know what to do with these feelings, and I sure as hell don't know what to do with a relationship. If you were anyone else kissing me, I could easily determine what you wanted. But you're different. All the signals I learned to read don't mean the same thing with you. I'm afraid of making a mistake and hurting you while I try to make sense of it all."

Ash's stomach clenched. "So you ran away because I'm asexual?"

"No, I ran because of who I am, not who you are. I don't know how to do this"—Phoenix waved her hands in the air—"feelings stuff and I panicked."

"All I wanted tonight was to find out if I wanted something more than friendship, and I do. But if you don't—"

Phoenix reached for Ash's arm. "No, I do. But relationships are uncharted territory for me. I've never even considered one before you. I don't know how that works, with anyone, but especially with you. Because if you weren't asexual we'd already be naked by now."

Ash didn't notice herself reacting, but she must have, because Phoenix quickly clarified, "And that's one reason why I left. I won't pressure you into something you don't want."

Ash's heart ached at Phoenix's sincerity and consideration. She extended her hand. "Will you come closer? That's all I want right now, to feel you close to me."

"I don't think that's a good idea."

Phoenix's words hit her in the gut. "Why not?"

"Because you aren't looking for a hookup. Hell, for the first time in my life, I'm not either. But I'm not the girl you bring home to your parents. I'm the girl you sneak out of your house to meet until you find the socially acceptable girl that fits in your world. Or the girl you bring around to purposely piss your parents off or to make someone jealous. I'm not good enough for you."

"Do you think I'd kiss you if I thought any of what you said was true?" Ash retorted, moving closer to Phoenix, beginning to understand.

"Ash, you're this brilliant scientist who's going to Mars someday and I'm just a cook who barely finished high school and whose aunt pulled strings to help her escape her family. You earned your position. I'm just lucky to be here."

"Phoenix, you're more than qualified to be here and everyone knows it when they eat your delicious food. As for your education, who cares? Did you forget that you beat me at Scrabble? But you know what matters the most to me? You've treated me with such kindness and respect I'm still in awe. Even tonight, I took a risk and you were a perfect gentlewoman." Ash brushed her hand over Phoenix's cheek. "I'm not better than you."

Phoenix leaned into Ash's hand, her eyes closed. There was a vulnerability Ash had never seen from her, pulling at her heart.

"When I kissed you tonight, I had no destination in mind. I was opening a door to see if anything was on the other side. Maybe I was wrong and should have discussed this with you first, like a mature adult. But I didn't, and we're here now." Ash turned Phoenix toward her, feeling more confident with a woman than she ever had in her life. "Can we try again? No expectations. No pressure. Just a kiss of possibility?"

Emotions too complicated for her to read churned in Phoenix's blue-gray eyes. Ash stilled, waiting for Phoenix to make her decision. After an eternity, possibly two, Phoenix's face softened and she reached up to cup Ash's cheeks in her hands. Ash's heart was beating so loudly in her ears she could hear nothing else, but she didn't need to. Phoenix leaned in, gently taking Ash's mouth with her own, lips barely meeting, and she felt the door of a new future cracking open.

For all Phoenix told her, Ash was certain there was more she wasn't admitting to. Now that Ash knew, she would be careful and let Phoenix set the pace as she worked through her demons.

Ash let her hands fall to Phoenix's side and focused on Phoenix's lips, so tender as they kissed, but also restrained and Ash wasn't sure if Phoenix was holding back for herself or Ash. In case she needed a sign, Ash parted her lips slightly and sucked on Phoenix's bottom lip, eliciting a quiet moan which made Ash's heart leap. Their experiences may be different, but Ash wanted Phoenix to feel as good as she did, if not better.

Phoenix slipped a hand behind Ash's neck and deepened the kiss, their tongues caressing each other in a slow exploration and Ash melted. This was so much more than she imagined. She found herself falling into Phoenix, her arms wrapping around Phoenix's waist, drawing their bodies together. As she ran her hands up Phoenix's back, she shivered but didn't break the kiss. Instead her touch grew more confident, one arm wrapping around Ash's back as Phoenix increased the intensity of her lips. The kiss was dizzying, making her even more grateful for Phoenix's strong grip on her.

After several minutes, Phoenix broke the kiss. Ash gazed at her as they both caught their breath. The storm she saw earlier was gone, replaced by black pools of desire.

"God Ash, I feel like a virgin again. I can't remember when a kiss had such an effect on me."

Ash flushed at Phoenix's candor. "Is that ok? It's not too much, is it?"

"No, just different. Besides, I can always take care of myself later," Phoenix added without even a hint of embarrassment. Phoenix's ease in talking about her own needs made Ash more comfortable.

"Oh, good. Because I really like kissing you." Ash placed a quick kiss on Phoenix's lips to accentuate the point. "I don't, however, want you to suffer. Will you tell me if it becomes too much?"

"Yes. And I'm happy to follow your lead, but will you tell me if I'm about to cross a line?"

Ash smiled coyly. "Not only will I tell you when you're about to cross a line, I'll tell you when the line has moved. Sex probably won't remain off the table." Phoenix's eyebrows lifted slightly and Ash smiled. "But not yet. I think we both need to get to know each other better first. There's no rush."

"Got it. So kissing?"

"Strongly encouraged. Along with cuddling, hugging, and hand holding."

Phoenix drew Ash tight to her body and Ash closed her eyes, feeling completely safe in Phoenix's arms. She hummed in pleasure, memorizing the feel of Phoenix, not looking forward to leaving soon. But it was late and she was quickly growing tired.

"Are you working tomorrow?" Phoenix asked, sounding sleepy herself.

"Only if the detector misbehaves. I think I'd like to get a little writing done, maybe while you're working so I can focus."

"Are you saying I'm distracting?" Phoenix asked with mock indignation.

"Definitely. Between you monopolizing my thoughts, and spending extra time with Emily and the team, I haven't done much writing this past week." Ash hadn't intended to share all that, but her walls were down. Trusting that Phoenix wouldn't push, and that she was in control, allowed her to relax.

Phoenix kissed Ash on the neck, making her shiver in pleasure. "Good to know. If you're up for it, I was going to go rock climbing after dinner, burn off some extra energy."

Ash furrowed her brow. "There's a climbing wall here?"

"In a nondescript building out in summer camp. I'll show you tomorrow if you come with me."

"I'll let you know tomorrow," Ash said before she yawned and extricated herself from Phoenix's arms. "But for tonight, are you going to gallantly escort me back to my room?"

Phoenix hopped off the bed and bowed solemnly. "M'lady, would you do me the honor of escorting you home?"

"Why of course, good knight. One never knows what dangers lurk in the shadows."

Phoenix stood, held the door open with her foot and extended a hand, which Ash took. Outside the room Ash looped her arm through Phoenix's, giggling. "Your British accent is atrocious."

"You're one to talk! For it being your game, I'd think you'd be better prepared," Phoenix teased.

"I'm a writer, not an actress, but it can be fun to play."

Phoenix cocked an eyebrow and Ash nudged her. "Somehow I don't think those thoughts are so gallant."

"Apologies m'lady." Phoenix lifted Ash's hand to her lips. Ash's chest swelled. How could she think of Phoenix as only a friend? Cole was going to tease her mercilessly for this development, and she'd let them because without their prodding she'd still be trying to figure everything out from afar.

At her door she turned to Phoenix, taking both of her hands in her own. "My gratitude, brave knight. How shall I repay you?"

"Perhaps you could spare a kiss?"

Ash couldn't stop the swell of affection filling her body as she reached to kiss Phoenix on the cheek. Ash pressed herself close, resting her head against her chest, and whispered, "Happy New Year Phoenix."

"Happy New Year Ash." Phoenix kissed the crown of her head before Ash finally turned and retreated to her room, happier than she could remember being in years.

CHAPTER TWELVE

PHOENIX

Not for the first time Phoenix was grateful to work the dinner shift. Sleep just wouldn't come between memories of the evening and her body's stubborn reaction to that kiss. Her body was easy enough to quiet, but her mind? She felt like a teenager with her first crush. But even as a teenager she hadn't allowed herself to get too close to anyone. She'd seen too many bad relationships, been burned too often by her family, to risk her heart.

Sex was easy. And all she'd ever needed until Ash snuck her way in. Now she was all twisted up, torn between wanting to run to her and from her at the same time. With anyone else Phoenix could scratch the itch and leave, but not with Ash. For one thing, Ash wasn't into casual sex. And for the other, where would she go? At the end of the day she was going to be living in a giant box for the next 10 months.

With nowhere to run, Phoenix finally had to face her feelings, and she had no clue how to do that. Sitting in front of Ash, it was easy to follow her heart. But left alone with her thoughts, her fears soon made themselves known. She couldn't shake the feeling that this was a bad idea. Ash didn't know who she was off the ice, and if she did, maybe she wouldn't think Phoenix was worth being with.

Phoenix shook her head, returning her focus to the chicken she was preparing. At least she could cook with her eyes closed, because deciding what to do about Ash dominated her thoughts.

She still hadn't come up with a solution when Ash came by for dinner, greeting Phoenix with a smile that lit up the room. Her heart leapt, but then fell as all her fears came rushing back to the forefront of her mind. Phoenix made an excuse about being too busy to eat with her, but the knowing look in Ash's eyes, tinged with pain, affected her. It was a bullshit excuse, and they both knew it. But Ash didn't push, instead finding a table to herself. This was why they were a bad idea. She was sure she would end up hurting Ash.

Phoenix busied herself with cleaning, a convenient excuse to stay in the kitchen. Ash startled her, asking, "Do you still want me to go climbing with you?"

The question brought Phoenix to her senses. Faced with the real Ash, instead of the hypothetical one she'd eventually hurt, weakened Phoenix's resolve. Her heart finally won the battle with her mind. The thought of losing Ash before they'd even begun was worse than the fear of any future pain.

"Yes."

"Are you sure? Because I don't have to go if you want to be alone." Ash's eyes were sad, and Phoenix assumed she was the reason. Phoenix didn't want to be that person anymore, the one that unintentionally hurt women who cared about her, but wasn't sure how to be someone else. Now she could only hope Ash had the patience to let her figure it out.

"I don't want to be alone; I want to be with you. I promise." Phoenix lightened her tone. "Pick you up at nine? Kevin gave me permission to take off a little early tonight."

"Like a date?" Ash asked, cautiously hopeful.

Phoenix felt a shy smile form. A date had never held this

much appeal before Ash. "Yeah, exactly like a date. Just dress comfortably."

Two hours later, Phoenix was actually nervous as she knocked at Ash's door, partially dressed for the outdoors and carrying a small bag with supplies. Ash answered with a tentative smile, already dressed in snow pants and her light fleece jacket. Phoenix's stomach settled in Ash's presence, which told her all she needed was to stop thinking so much. Phoenix leaned down for a hello kiss. Not enough to awaken her libido, but to remind her what was important. Ash.

"There you are," Ash said, taking her hand and searching her eyes. "Are you doing alright?"

"Too much thinking. Not enough doing." Ash stiffened slightly before Phoenix caught her words. "Not like that. I can't just sit around and think or I end up making a mess of things." Phoenix wrapped an arm around Ash's waist. "I don't want to make a mess of this."

"Me either, but I don't think you will," Ash said sincerely.

Ash didn't need to hear Phoenix's doubts, so she kept them to herself as they walked to the coat room to retrieve their matching red coats. Even with strong sunglasses, the never setting sun made her blink rapidly as she adjusted to its glare. Add the shocking cold which stole her breath and Phoenix remembered why she went outside less often than a lot of others. If she didn't change her patterns and start going out more she'd go stir crazy before the sun set this winter.

They walked arm in arm across the snow to summer camp, just a few minutes away. Summer camp was originally an overflow area from when the station was a large dome, supporting a much smaller crew. But as the number of projects, and thus the volume of support staff increased, summer camp was built to handle the lodging and supply needs. Now a good portion of those simple buildings went unused, except the ones they still used for daily needs like storing supplies, vehicles, fuel and maintenance facilities. Before long they arrived at a small, single story plywood building, indistinguishable from the other small buildings except for the climbing wall sign.

"Are you sure there's a climbing wall in there?" Ash asked as Phoenix reached for the door handle. "What is this, the TARDIS?"

"No, but that would make the station way more interesting. We'd have a swimming pool, possibly in the library!" Phoenix opened the door and flipped on the lights, illuminating the room covered with artificial holds along the walls and ceiling.

"You watch Doctor Who?" Ash asked, her attention focused on Phoenix rather than the room as she placed her sunglasses in her coat pocket.

"You sound surprised."

"Well, you didn't list that as one of your fandoms. That's worth two nerd points I think."

"Wait, why are you only tallying nerd points? Shouldn't I get cool points too? Rock climbing has to get me a point or two. Tattoos. Great hair." Phoenix shot Ash a mischievous grin. "Are you biasing this little experiment to obtain the result you want?"

Ash paused and then answered with a smirk. "Yes. But only because I think it will annoy you."

"You'll need to work harder than that to annoy me."

"That's a nice change, isn't it?"

Phoenix pulled her in for a kiss. Her lips were cool from the walk, so Phoenix took her time warming them up before answering, "Yes. I'd rather kiss you than argue."

"Me too," Ash said with a wistful smile.

Stepping away, Phoenix removed her coat and reached for Ash's when she shrugged hers off. After hanging them on the coat rack, she turned to see Ash taking in the cave-like room, mouth agape.

"I was wrong," Ash said, scanning the room one more time

before facing Phoenix. "It's not the TARDIS because it's smaller on the inside."

Nerdiness hadn't been a quality Phoenix found herself attracted to often, but with Ash it was endearing.

"What's the opposite of the TARDIS?" Phoenix asked.

"An anti-TARDIS? Like anti-matter particles, they'd destroy the Universe if they met."

"So, a Pandorica? That destroyed the Universe when it exploded."

Ash eyed her quizzically. "What don't you know about?"

For a moment Phoenix considered explaining that knowing a little about many topics was a survival trait, allowing her to fake her way through different social situations. But that could quickly turn into topics Phoenix didn't want to discuss yet.

"World peace. I just can't wrap my head around it."

Ash shook her head. "Well that is a tough one."

Grateful to have avoided a deeper discussion, Phoenix returned to the topic in front of them.

"Have you been climbing before?"

"Not really. I tried one of those portable walls they bring out for events, but the rope was so tight it felt like I was being pulled up more than actually climbing."

"Yeah, I hate it when they do that. Just because you're a woman they think you can't do it yourself? Bullshit." Phoenix gazed around the room. "This is going to be a little different from what you've done before. Technically this is referred to as bouldering. No ropes since we aren't climbing up in this short room. In this case you traverse the room laterally which is only a foot or so off the ground, or challenge yourself on the ceiling routes. That's when you want the crash pads, in case you land awkwardly. The five foot drop shouldn't do any damage, but it's always best to fall off the wall in a controlled manner."

Phoenix removed her boots and snow pants. "Do you want me to go first?"

"Please, I don't know what to do with all this," Ash said apprehensively.

"That's ok, I'll teach you. First, we need climbing shoes. There are shoes you can borrow over here, along with sanitizing spray. Climbing shoes provide friction and are meant to be tight. The last thing you want is your foot to move within the shoe. It takes some getting used to, but it makes a big difference."

Phoenix found the right sized shoes and removed her socks before doing a few quick stretches to warm her body up. Then she dipped her hands in the chalk bucket and coated her palms to enhance her grip. She decided to work clockwise around the room and chose some big, easy holds to start, letting her body get used to the movements. Her muscles complained at first but once they accepted the activity Phoenix moved more smoothly, enjoying the feel of her body supporting her weight.

"Do you climb a lot back home? You seem to know what you're doing." Phoenix didn't miss the admiration in Ash's voice, enjoying the ego boost.

"Not enough, but I try to go once a month." Phoenix hopped off the wall when she reached the end, shaking out her arms which burned more than she'd care to admit. She resolved to come back once a week to rebuild her climbing muscles.

"Do you want to try now? I think you'll like it. Climbing is a puzzle. You're always looking for the next move, where to place your hands and feet so that you move efficiently through the route. There are plenty of times when the shortest route isn't the most ideal."

"Oh! It's a real-life energy optimization experiment," Ash added excitedly. "Most people assume the best route between two points is a straight line because it's the shortest, but in nature the most efficient path is often a curve, utilizing the momentum built while working with gravity."

Phoenix realized excited scientist Ash might be her favorite.

"That sounds about right. All I want you to focus on is keeping three points of contact on the wall as often as possible. That will minimize the strain on your muscles and give you more control."

"Ok, that makes sense."

Once they found a pair of shoes for Ash, Phoenix rubbed chalk over her palms, enjoying how easily their hands slid over each other's. Ash cleared her throat when Phoenix took longer than necessary, but could she blame her? Phoenix released her hands and directed Ash to the same holds she started with earlier.

"These are comfortable holds to start with. Just step up." Ash did, but rather than hug the wall like Phoenix had, her hips jutted out, placing unnecessary weight on her hands. "Move your hips close to the wall. You're wasting energy."

Ash appeared to try but was either too unaware of her body to adjust, or it was too difficult.

"Can I help?" Phoenix asked.

"How?"

Ash's arms started to shake. Phoenix gently yet firmly grabbed high on Ash's hips and pushed her toward the wall. Ash's head spun around, but Phoenix held her confidently. "Does that feel better?"

"What?" Ash's voice cracked a little.

"Did that take the weight off your arms?" Phoenix asked, suppressing a smile.

"Oh, yeah, it did. Thanks."

"No problem. I'm going to let go now, so try to hold that positioning before trying to move."

Phoenix took half a step back, leaving chalk marks on Ash's hips, but kept her hands up in case she fell.

"Now try to take a step. Start with your lead leg. Decide which hold you want to move your right leg to first, then shift your weight to the right using your hips."

"Phoenix, in case you didn't notice, I'm not exactly athletic. That was too much information."

Phoenix placed her hands on Ash's hips again. "Relax," she said quietly. "Let me move your hips for you."

Ash swallowed hard. "Is this why I'm here, so you can get your hands on me?"

"No, that's just a bonus. Now relax, I have you. Just reach out with your right foot."

When Ash's foot was securely on the hold, Phoenix shifted Ash's hips to distribute her weight between both feet.

"Do you feel that, how your weight is balanced on your feet, but not your hands? Now find a new hold for your right hand."

Ash reached frantically for a big hold while Phoenix held her hips against the wall. With her hand firmly on the rough hold, Ash relaxed and beamed with pride.

Phoenix praised her enthusiastically. "There you go! See, it's not so bad once you understand the process. Try it yourself now."

Ash moved a few more times before jumping off the wall. "I'm so out of shape!"

"I like your shape," Phoenix said, her voice low as she wrapped Ash into a hug from behind, warmth filling her. "But if it makes you feel better, I'm feeling it too. I've only got another couple runs in me."

The room was warm enough for Phoenix to remove her t-shirt, revealing a tight racerback tank top which was more comfortable to climb in. Phoenix chalked up again while studying a lower ceiling path that cut through the room, standing there for a few moments as she worked out her starting point.

"As you get better, you can really push yourself and work on the ceiling routes." Phoenix locked one foot into a big hold, positioned her hands, and pulled her other foot up. She felt the position immediately, realizing she'd been overconfident as she struggled, dropping before reaching the other side.

She caught Ash staring and thought she knew that look. From others she saw desire, but with Ash she wouldn't assume. "See something you like?"

Ash blushed lightly. "I've never watched muscles move like that up close. The way they work together, shifting from position to position, I could almost see the force vectors as you moved. It was mesmerizing."

She wasn't exactly sure what Ash was talking about, but the admiration in her voice was obvious. "You know, if anyone else looked at me like that, I'd think they wanted their hands on me."

"Oh, I do, just not in a way that lands us naked on these crash pads," Ash said unapologetically as she covered the space between them. "I want to know more than your head. Or your heart. I want to know your body, too."

Phoenix's body burned as an emboldened Ash ran a finger from Phoenix's shoulder, down her arm in the space between her bicep and tricep, both swollen from effort. Arousal surged in Phoenix's center and her throat went dry. Ash may not have meant to be seductive, but it had the same effect.

"I don't care why you want to touch me, as long as you do."

There was a question in Ash's eyes, but she didn't ask, which made Phoenix incredibly curious. "What?"

"Even without any intention of sex, my touch doesn't bother you?"

"Oh, I'm bothered. And very hot." Ash winced and Phoenix realized she had very little time to disarm this land mine. "But that's not a bad thing. There's nothing malicious in your touch, nor do I feel like you're teasing me. I feel like you're an entirely new breed of human. Instead of assuming I know who you are, and how you want to interact, you're a clean sheet of paper."

"I'm a sheet of paper?" Ash's face pulled into a confused expression.

Phoenix hoped this new analogy would make sense because she was making it up as she went. "Yeah. When we first met, I realized you weren't like other people, but didn't know why. I kept trying to fit you into a picture I already knew and understood. At Christmas it all came together, so I threw out all the pictures I tried to match you to and started from scratch. Since then I've been sketching in bits and pieces as I learn more about you."

"Last night gave me a lot to think about, but I'm doing my best not to extrapolate and assume who you are. So when you touch me, I'm not upset that it isn't going as far as I'd like, I'm ecstatic that you're doing so. Talking nerdy science in that appreciative tone like you just did feels amazing and also adds to the sketch that is uniquely you."

Phoenix looked deeply into Ash's expressive eyes. "Don't change who you are for me. Don't hold back or hide your impulses because you're afraid it's too much for me to handle. The only way for me to get to know you, and your body language, is to show me. I'll tell you if you cross the line from exquisite to torture, ok?"

Ash fixed her with a stare that was not what Phoenix expected.

"Now what?" Phoenix asked, almost exasperated. She thought she'd been clear for once.

"Are you real, or is this some elaborate dream? Am I still lying in bed?"

Laughing, her cheeks warming with embarrassment at having shared her feelings so openly, Phoenix closed the distance between them. "Do you want me to pinch you to be sure?"

Ash reached up for a kiss, sensual and soft and so wonderful. Phoenix sighed in pleasure and gently drew Ash closer. Maybe they were both dreaming.

A hazy look filled Ash's face. "Why would I want to wake up

from a dream this good?"

Phoenix shook her head. "Good question."

"Well, since this is a dream, I might as well take advantage of it. Turn around?"

Phoenix did and shivered at Ash's light touch over her shoulder blades and the tattoos she knew were directly under her fingers.

"What do they mean?"

"It's kind of a long story," Phoenix replied as she turned around, "and I don't share it with just anyone. But since we've established this is a dream I can tell you."

Ash moved into Phoenix's field of vision, smiling encouragingly.

"Before I moved to Colorado, I went to a tattoo convention up in Chicago. There were so many different styles on display it was mind blowing. But one booth in particular drew me in. The artist was sharing his traditional tribal tattoos from Borneo.

"We got to talking about the power of tattoos, which they believe provide protection and strength, and I mentioned that I could really use some protection myself. He suggested a variation of the Borneo Rose, which is a tattoo boys get before their journey into manhood. Normally they are placed on the front of the shoulder, but I wanted protection from my past, so asked to have them on my shoulder blades instead.

"I was worried about cultural appropriation, but he said that he shares his tribal traditions freely and just asks that people respect and appreciate the meaning behind the tattoos. For instance, certain symbols should always appear in pairs to maintain balance in the powers they provide. That's why I have two, and not just one."

"Wow, do you feel the tattoos really helped? Do you feel stronger and protected?"

"Aren't scientists supposed to roll their eyes at that sort of thing?"

Ash shrugged. "Belief is powerful, just look at the study of placebos in medicine. I try not to dismiss people's experiences, even if I don't believe the same thing. I have my limits, don't get me wrong, but what's the harm if you feel the tattoos helped you?"

"That's rather pragmatic of you. And the answer is, I don't know. Maybe they helped me to break from home and ultimately end up here."

Ash shifted more to her back and traced the spiky outer pattern and then the smooth spiral at the center. Phoenix remained still as Ash explored her skin. "The spiral reminds me of a galaxy."

"It symbolizes the cycle of life, and the growth from child to adult. But now I'm wondering..."

Ash tilted her head, waiting for Phoenix to continue. Her idea was pretty out there, but also intriguing and she wondered how Ash would respond.

"I chose between multiple variations of that spiral, including ones that were far less galaxy-like. What if that choice was more than preference, but destiny? If we assume there's magic in the world, and these tattoos, then it's not a stretch to imagine the tattoos called to you in a language you'd understand."

"That's..." Ash stood straighter, releasing Phoenix's arm. Her thought process playing out in her features. Confusion. Amusement. Curiosity. "Well, I don't know what to think, but it would make a great fantasy."

"Cosmic soul mates, is that one of your fantasies?" Phoenix asked more seriously than she intended.

"I didn't think it was, but, I mean, adding magic to the mix? That certainly increases the appeal."

Phoenix's chest warmed at the thought. Was it secretly her fantasy as well? Where did the idea come from? Ash rescued her from her thoughts, taking Phoenix's hand and extending her arm to get a clear view of the dragon on her arm.

"And what magic is in this tattoo?"

Phoenix sucked in a breath, a spike of pain to her heart. What she wouldn't give for that tattoo to be magic.

"That's... complicated. Can we talk about it another time?"

"Sure." Ash stepped back and gave Phoenix space. "They're all beautiful. Now, do you have the energy to get back up there? I'd like to see you in action again, if that's ok."

Relieved at the change in subject, and looking to impress Ash further, Phoenix ignored her tired muscles and pulled herself up to the ceiling. Ash's fingers ran from her shoulders, down her trapezius muscles and Ash's words from earlier rang in her head.

"What's a force vector?"

"They are a way for us to show forces on an object. We draw an arrow to show the direction in a length relative to the magnitude of the force. For instance, right now there's the force of gravity pulling straight down on you. Your muscles are countering that, but given the nature of muscles those forces aren't pointing straight up."

Ash ran her fingers along Phoenix's lats. "Here they'd point the direction my fingers are moving, toward your shoulders. Now, I'm not very familiar with the intricacies of muscles, but they'd have to transition around your shoulders, meeting your chest. Then the forces would begin pointing up your arm, adding together to balance the force of gravity until you either fell or moved forward." Ash's fingers continued tracing their path along Phoenix's arms before returning to her lats.

"Move to another position," Ash commanded gently.

Phoenix moved, knowing she wouldn't last much longer, especially as more of her blood flow was currently being redirected south. No one had ever touched her like this and she didn't want to cut the moment short.

"As you move, the force vectors change directions, showing how your muscles propel you forward. It's beautiful. Your body is beautiful," Ash whispered reverently, hitting a place in Phoenix that she didn't know existed inside her. She'd been called many things, including beautiful, but never in that tone. And never so believably.

Phoenix's arms began to shake and she let herself drop feet first, realizing that this wasn't even the strangest foreplay she'd experienced. *Perhaps foreplay wasn't the right word. But what? And did it matter?*

"And now, gravity has won," Ash said playfully.

Phoenix shook out her arms to speed the return of blood flow. "No, I definitely won. And you can talk science to me anytime you want. I had no idea it could be such a turn on."

"Me either."

"Do you want to try?"

"You mean, do I want to fall on my ass, because that's the most likely result of that experiment. Can't I just admire you?" Ash asked playfully.

"While that's great for my ego, I'm fried." Phoenix sat, wiped her hands on a towel from her bag, and began removing her shoes. Ash grabbed the towel and wiped Phoenix's back.

"Sorry, I got chalk on you."

Phoenix chuckled. "You should see the back of your pants." Ash contorted herself to see and she laughed.

"This makes it look like we were doing more than climbing."

Phoenix took the towel and brushed off Ash's pants as best she could. "Guess you'll have to change later."

Ash thanked her and handed Phoenix her t-shirt.

"Did this help you clear your head?"

"Mostly. My thoughts have certainly shifted thanks to you."

Phoenix's body hummed, an interesting combination of arousal and worn out muscles. Phoenix pulled on her t-shirt and looked up at Ash. "How was it for you? Acceptable first date?"

ASH

"It was." Ash's body flushed as she thought about touching Phoenix's bare skin, feeling her muscles move beneath her hands. She turned away, hoping to hide her reaction and took a long drink of water from her ever-present Nalgene bottle.

"You know what surprises me most about you?"

Phoenix's comment caught her off guard and she turned around.

"No, what?"

"The way you touch me is so different from anyone else, deeper somehow. You don't treat me like someone to enjoy for a night and I don't know how to react."

"You know, I've thought about this a lot. And I think this is an area where asexuals have an advantage." Phoenix raised an eyebrow and Ash knew she had her full attention. "When I touch you, it's because that's the only thing I want to be doing in that moment. It isn't a ploy to get something else. In a lot of relationships, a massage isn't about making the other person feel good, but coercion for sex. There's a selfish underlying motive. But that doesn't seem to be the case for most asexuals."

Ash reached for Phoenix's bicep and gave it a squeeze. "I

ASH

hope you don't think I'm objectifying you. I'm fascinated by you and your body. While you were climbing it made me want to feel what you felt. To be in that moment with you. Maybe that's why it felt deeper?"

"Wow. I'm not sure I've ever separated touch from sex in that way. My mind just goes there."

"I might regret asking, but what were you thinking when I was enjoying your body?"

Phoenix appeared to size her up before responding. "Honestly I couldn't think. Between your hands and your sexy science words, it was all I could do to stay up there. And then after, if I'd thought you would've been into it, I would have had you pinned to one of those mats as soon as I came off the route."

Without Phoenix's earlier explanation Ash would have been concerned by her revelation. Thanks to her candor, there was more Ash could learn if she didn't let her own insecurities distract her. "On the first date?" Ash asked.

"Without hesitation. I've never been looking for a relationship, so I only went on something resembling a date to make women feel better about hooking up. But there was never any pretense about it being anything other than sex. I didn't mislead anyone but there were always those who thought they could change my mind. Which is why I had a strict 'no second date' policy."

Ash's stomach churned. Phoenix wasn't exaggerating when she said she didn't do relationships. Ash wasn't just asking her to shift her perspective on sex, but also relationships.

"Ash?"

Ash jerked her head, "huh?"

"Does that freak you out? My past?"

"A little." Ash answered honestly. "Is it actually in the past, or..."

Phoenix took Ash's hands in hers. "Would you be my first real second date, almost-Doctor Ashley Bennett?"

The ridiculousness of Phoenix's question caught Ash off guard and she laughed, falling into her embrace. The uneasiness dissipated, fading to an ignorable level.

"Dinner and a movie?" Ash offered.

"That can be arranged. How about Sunday so I'm not stuck working?"

Ash nodded her agreement and placed a hand on Phoenix's chest, just over her heart. "You know, I bet if you let this lead you instead of your head, you'll figure dating out easily."

"I'm usually not thinking with either of those," Phoenix admitted.

"You seem to be doing alright so far," Ash said before kissing her sweetly.

Phoenix held her close, arms wrapped around Ash's hips. "So how do first dates end in your world? Clearly I've been doing them wrong all this time." Phoenix's tone was playful, her eyes bright as she asked.

"We walk back to the station; you escort me back to my room and give me a good night kiss. Then you return to your room and pine over me," Ash added dramatically.

"But it's barely eleven. It's not like you have a curfew."

"No, but I think it's time to recalibrate your expectations of dating. Besides, I have a long day tomorrow and already know I won't easily fall asleep."

"Fine, your logic wins, this time. Can I have one more kiss before we go back?"

Ash leaned in, expecting a gentle kiss, but Phoenix had other ideas, cupping the back of her head and meeting her with a kiss that was immediately deep and passionate. Ash surrendered, slipping her hands up Phoenix's back and under her shirt to feel the muscles tense as they came together, no doubts about Phoenix's interest in dating remaining.

When they broke apart they both needed a moment to catch their breath. "And that is why you aren't allowed in my room tonight. Neither of us has enough restraint," Ash admitted.

Phoenix grinned impishly. "As long as it goes both ways, whatever that means for you, I'm good." Phoenix tossed Ash her snow pants and she barely caught them, stunned by Phoenix's reaction once again.

The next morning, Ash ran into Emily at breakfast, a noticeable hickey on her neck. Ash had never understood the appeal, but then again, there were a lot of things she didn't understand.

"So," Ash said, drawing out the word, "is that Skye's handiwork?" Ash motioned to Emily's neck who blushed lightly.

"Not a bad way to start the New Year. An unexpected highlight. What about you? Fun night with Phoenix?"

"Yes, but not like that."

"Why not? You're clearly into each other," Emily said a bit smugly. Ash wasn't sure how she felt about this discussion, even if she'd started it.

"But I'm not into hooking up. Besides, we have all winter ahead of us. That requires a bit more caution."

"I suppose."

And this is why it's better to maintain professional distance between colleagues. She could come out, but it felt odd. Why did it matter to anyone whether or not she had sex? She let them know she was a lesbian because it set the expectations for what type of person she'd bring to an event, if she brought a date. But whether she had sex with them? Irrelevant.

Except Emily wasn't like the majority of her colleagues. She was neither straight nor male. But she was a colleague, and if she reacted poorly, Ash wasn't certain their professional relationship would survive. The queer community wasn't inherently more accepting of asexuality, unfortunately. It wasn't worth coming out, not yet.

⛺

By Sunday, Ash was fatigued from the increased physical workload. Everyone on the team was, but their tasks were almost complete. Then Ash could return to days spent mostly in front of the computer and using the quiet time to make headway on her dissertation. With Emily leaving in two days, she looked forward to more free time in the evenings.

She'd barely seen Phoenix without a colleague around during the past week, though their stolen kisses tucked into corners or empty hallways were exhilarating. The prospect of a day off, just her and Phoenix, weakened her resolve for them to actually date, as best they could given their limitations. It would be just as much fun to hang out in her room and make out, right? Thankfully enough of her brain was engaged to stick with the plan.

Ash spent the morning brainstorming about their comic, anticipating Phoenix's interest, and took one of her two allotted showers. By the time she got home she'd probably run the shower until it was cold, just because she could.

Phoenix knocked precisely at noon, and what Ash saw made her eyes widen in appreciation. "You got a haircut!"

"Yeah, well, that's what you're supposed to do before a date, right?" Phoenix asked in a tone that sounded nonchalant, but Ash thought she heard hesitation too.

Ash beamed at her. "Yes, and it looks great. Better than the first time, I think. It's shorter on the sides and back?"

The smile Phoenix returned was genuine. "Yeah, I wanted to experiment a little. I'm undecided about this particular variation, but I love it short."

"It suits you. It's almost impossible to think of you with long hair now." Ash moved closer, realizing she'd never felt Phoenix's haircut when it was still fresh like this. She pushed the thought of Skye doing so out of her mind and reached behind Phoenix's head, running her fingers over the freshly buzzed hair.

Phoenix sucked in a breath and closed her eyes at the touch. Ash pulled her closer and kissed her, gently at first, but Phoenix quickly responded with an intensity that sent a thrill through her. Phoenix was objectively hot, and she could probably have half the women at the station if she wanted them. But she was here, with Ash, knowing she wasn't going to get laid anytime soon. Talk about a powerful feeling, but it also brought up some insecurities. What did Phoenix see in her?

Ash's back hit the door, which didn't take much in her small room, but it was enough to make Phoenix break the kiss, admitting, "If I don't stop now, I'll be doing my damndest to convince you to move our next date here and now."

The hunger in Phoenix's eyes worried Ash. As much as she liked Phoenix, she wasn't at the point of wanting to have sex. How long could Phoenix wait?

"Patience. We have the whole day ahead of us"—Ash stepped to her desk and picked up a notebook—"and I've been working on ideas for our comic."

Phoenix's face brightened. "If I promise to keep my hands to myself, can we work in here? We'll be able to speak freely that way. I doubt any common area will be empty today."

It was a logical suggestion, so Ash accepted and they got comfortable on her bed, sitting cross-legged with their corresponding notebooks. She hadn't sat like this since, well, maybe never. Yet wasn't this how TV and movies showed teenage girls talking to their friends? The visual made Ash laugh, earning her a perplexed look from Phoenix.

"I was thinking about all those movies where the giggly teenaged girls are eating popcorn and gossiping on the bed during a sleepover. The visual was too ridiculous when applied to us."

"You weren't a giggly teenager?" Phoenix asked.

"No, far from it. I was serious and focused on my studies. My friends and I had fun, sure, but I don't remember a single giggly conversation about boys or girls," Ash said, frowning.

"Plenty of girls giggled in my bed, but we weren't doing much talking," Phoenix admitted without her usual bravado. She met Ash's eyes hesitantly. "Land mine?"

Ash's lips were drawn tight. "No," she answered quietly. "Your past doesn't bother me, not really. But..." Ash wrung her hands as she furrowed her brows. She'd ignored her insecurities too long and she knew Phoenix deserved to know. Phoenix's hands closed around Ash's, stilling them. Ash focused on Phoenix's hands as she spoke.

"I still worry I'm not going to be enough for you. That in a few weeks, or a few months, you're going to want more than I am able to give. I don't know how much that is, but I can't imagine it will be as much as you want. What if that's too hard?"

Phoenix brushed her fingers over Ash's forearm and she looked up shyly. "Hey, easy. You're getting ahead of yourself."

Ash didn't meet her gaze. Phoenix moved closer to her so their knees almost touched. "Ash, I recently realized I wasn't having sex purely for pleasure, but to escape my life which has been a complete mess for as long as I can remember.

"When I discovered sex it made all the crap in my life disappear. Sex became my go-to coping mechanism. It was better than drinking and made me feel loved, at least for a moment or two."

The idea of using sex in this way was foreign to Ash but it was plausible that it worked for some. Phoenix's voice grew quieter, pulling Ash in. "The driving need for sex is gone now that I'm out of contact with my family. And it's possible you have something to do with that."

Ash intertwined their fingers in response. She suspected that admission wasn't easy. Phoenix locked eyes on her. "I still have desire. Lord I have an abundance of it. After our climbing adventure I was strung so tight it took no time at all to get myself off that night. And maybe I should be more private about masturbation, but I need you to know that so far, I am ok with all of this. With you." Phoenix squeezed Ash's hands. "I can't say I understand it, or even myself. But I'm having a blast with you, so please don't worry."

Silence fell as Ash processed Phoenix's words. She hadn't given much thought to the reasons why allosexuals had sex. Sex wasn't simple in Ash's experience; it wasn't something she got lost in. It didn't occur to her that there were reasons beyond a desire for pleasure or procreation, but she could imagine that being the case for Phoenix. What would happen when they left the ice?

Now she was definitely ahead of herself. "That helps. I'll try not to worry so much, but..." Ash paused, knowing the question would bother her if she didn't ask. "Are you really ok with masturbating after our dates? It doesn't bother me, but I don't want you to resent me?"

"Ash, I'm fine. I'm not here for sex, I'm here for you."

Ash's heart soared. "Thank you." Ash reclaimed her hand to pick up her notebook and opened it to her page of notes, ready to leave her insecurities behind.

"This is a list of topics we've already discussed about asexuality, as well as some I thought would be good to add. But now I realize that isn't enough. It's just as important for me to understand you and your experiences because I clearly don't."

Phoenix nodded. "I can only speak for myself, but I've never asked why a woman wanted to have sex, beyond making it clear that it wasn't going to turn into a relationship. So maybe there's a larger audience for both sides of this discussion."

Ash wrote down some notes, capturing her assumptions and

how they affected her interactions with Phoenix. When she finished writing, Ash noticed Phoenix's partially covered drawings.

"Can I see?"

Phoenix readily handed Ash the sketch pad. It was clear which character was which. Ash with her shoulder length hair and the taller Phoenix with her messy, short hair and tattoos.

"These are adorable Phoenix. So how do we start?"

"Since we first discussed the idea, so much has happened. We aren't just friends anymore. What if we introduce the characters, and then tell our story as it unfolds? We have control over how much we share, but there are plenty of common aspects to draw on."

"How identifiable do we want to be, because if we mention where we are, it will take almost no time to determine our identities. I'd rather not have my colleagues knowing so much about my personal life."

"True. Fake names?"

"I can't imagine you as anyone but Phoenix. What's your middle name?"

"Don't laugh."

"I'm not going to laugh."

"You laughed when I said my name was Phoenix."

Ash smiled at the memory again, but at least didn't laugh. "Sorry, but that was because I had recently read a fantasy involving a shape shifting Phoenix-human. A were-phoenix? Anyway... you caught me off guard."

Phoenix cocked an eyebrow.

"Stop distracting me," Ash said with a playful shove to Phoenix's knee. "What's your middle name?"

Phoenix eyed Ash warily. "Rayne. With a y, because my parents thought it would look cooler."

"Hey, I couldn't pull off that name, but you do. I take it you wouldn't want your character to be named Rayne?"

"No," Phoenix answered firmly. "What's your middle name?"

"Paige."

"Almost-Doctor Ashley Paige Bennett. I like it." Phoenix wrote Paige in surprisingly neat handwriting above Ash's character while Ash chuckled.

"Ooh, you should get an A name then so we can maintain some symmetry." Ash studied Phoenix until a name came to mind. "I like Al."

"Al. That's sufficiently gay. Why not?" Phoenix wrote Al above her character. Then she added more text below Paige, which Ash read out loud.

"I'm Paige. I am a brilliant scientist and a talented writer of nerdy fanfiction." Ash smacked Phoenix's foot. "Hey! Fanfiction isn't inherently nerdy."

"Who said that's what made you nerdy? Besides, I called you brilliant and talented, or did you miss that part," Phoenix said with a smirk before returning to her writing. Under Al she wrote, I am Al and I am a passable cook and artist who Paige thinks is awesome because she was raised on boring food.

"Ok new rule. You don't get to write about yourself."

"That could be interesting. What would Paige say then?"

Ash grabbed Phoenix's notebook and added, "This is Al. She can make any food taste like the best you've ever eaten."

Phoenix snatched her notebook back and added another line. "Because you have low standards."

Ash gave up on the writing. "I bet if we took a poll more people would agree with my assessment of your cooking than yours."

"Whatever. We're supposed to be writing this comic, remember?"

"I'll let you off the hook this time, but only because I am right and this is fun."

They worked for a couple of hours and Ash couldn't remember when she'd had so much fun writing. It wasn't like writing a story. This was just the two of them playing around, teasing each other, and assigning their words to avatars on the page.

There were a lot of little details to work out before publishing, including how long each comic would be, but they had time. Right now they were finding their feet, their focus, and in the process getting to know each other better.

CHAPTER THIRTEEN

PHOENIX

"What's the food you unexpectedly miss the most?" Phoenix asked as she sketched Paige sitting on a bed, just as Ash was doing now.

Ash looked up, her gaze unfocused, until a wistful smile formed. Phoenix leaned forward, not knowing what to expect, and hoping she had the ability to make it happen.

"Chicken nuggets."

Phoenix laughed. "Chicken nuggets? Are you 10?"

Ash shrugged. "You asked, I answered. I like bite sized chicken. It somehow tastes better. What about you?"

"There's this fast food chain back in Colorado called Freddy's. They have the best seasoned shoestring french fries. I can get the seasoning pretty close, but I can't make fries that skinny. Besides, they also have the best frozen custard, and fries dipped in custard may be the greatest snack ever."

"Gross."

Phoenix stuck her tongue out, feeling silly.

"Now who's 10?" Ash asked teasing her.

"As long as we're ten-year-olds together, does it matter?" Phoenix challenged back. In the back of her mind, she was already going down the checklist to put her plan into action. Flour, cornmeal, garlic, salt and pepper, paprika, and red pepper. Yes, that could work. "I have an idea for dinner, but we should start it now if we want to avoid people. Would you like to make your own chicken nuggets?"

"Seriously? They don't just come out of a box?"

Phoenix rolled her eyes good naturedly and stood, extending a hand. "Come on, you're going to get a cooking lesson. And some delicious nuggets."

Ash took her hand and stood, but continued moving into an embrace, wrapping her arms around Phoenix's neck, sending tingles up Phoenix's spine. "You know, for someone who's never dated before, you're off to a good start."

Ash's praise affected her more deeply than expected. Phoenix distracted herself from the emotion washing over her by kissing Ash before leading her to the kitchen, which should be empty thanks to being Sunday. While technically against the rules, she doubted Kevin would care if she appropriated a few supplies.

Phoenix pulled the smallest package of chicken from the freezer and placed it in a bowl of water to thaw, then talked as she gathered ingredients. "Back home I prefer a prepared mix, but here we'll make it from scratch." She set the breading ingredients on a prep table with a bowl.

"Ready to know my big secret?" Phoenix asked.

"Of course!"

"I hate measuring but I was taught to cook by feel. The food is a little different every time." Phoenix reached for the container of cornmeal. "So, we'll start with about this much cornmeal"—Phoenix poured enough into the bowl to cover a pound of chicken—"and a bit of flour to hold it together."

"If we only add salt and pepper at this point it would be acceptable, but we aren't aiming for merely acceptable. That's why I will add a touch of garlic, paprika and crushed red pepper flakes. How spicy would you like your nuggets?"

"Who makes nuggets spicy?"

Phoenix chuckled to herself. "No spice then." She added just a pinch of red pepper to the mix. It would enhance the flavor profile, but not enough to be spicy. Phoenix grabbed a spoon and handed it to Ash. "Give it a stir while I get the potatoes. Then I'll teach you how to make fries without cutting your fingers off."

Ash chuckled. "That would be a really bad end to this date."

Phoenix nodded, resisting the urge to make a joke about lesbians needing their fingers, before washing a few potatoes and depositing them and two large knives on the prep table. Then she snagged a large frying pan, adding enough shortening to handle the chicken, before turning on the burner to let the shortening melt into oil.

Phoenix picked up a knife and ran the blade along a sharpener. "Most people don't take care of their knives and it makes cooking more difficult. You can prep faster and cut more accurately if you keep your knives sharp. But that also means it's easier to slice yourself, so you want to be careful and keep the fingertips curled under." Phoenix handed the knife to Ash, who had watched her closely. "Think you can cut these potatoes into fries? Just place them in this bowl of water as you go."

Ash took the knife by the handle and answered, "Of course, as long as they don't need to be pretty."

"Will you be annoyed if I give you a line about you being pretty enough that it doesn't matter?" Phoenix asked impishly.

"That's not a very good line."

"I'm out of practice."

Ash gave her a kiss on the cheek. "We'll both practice then. What are you going to do?"

Phoenix picked up the second knife and sharpened it as well.

"Make your nuggets. Any special requests? Should I make them look like McDonald's?"

"You can do that?" Ash asked incredulously.

Phoenix chuckled. "Not without wasting a ridiculous amount of chicken. But, I'll see what I can do."

Honestly, Phoenix had never tried to make chicken into shapes, but that seemed like a fun date activity. The chicken breasts were thawed, so she laid them out, studying them like she'd seen sculptors do. It wasn't her medium, but that didn't mean she couldn't do it, just that she hadn't had the opportunity. After trimming the meat, she scored the desired shapes on the surface with the tip of her knife, then set to cutting away bite sized pieces until the shapes emerged. They were rough, but clearly what they were intended to be – two stars and two hearts.

She added each to the pile of chicken in the bowl and looked over at Ash who was just about finished with the potatoes. If she moved fast enough, Ash wouldn't even see her creatively shaped nuggets.

With the oil ready, she grabbed the nuggets with one hand, allowing her to keep the other clean for handling utensils. She was pretty sure food poisoning wouldn't be a good end to the date either. She pulled the bowl of breading to herself with her other hand and covered them all before Ash had looked up. It helped that Ash had to concentrate on her cutting.

With everything prepped, Phoenix worked on frying their dinner in small batches, ensuring the oil stayed up to temperature and their food would be perfect. The surprise nuggets were well hidden by the others, allowing them to remain a surprise.

Within a few minutes the first batch of golden brown nuggets floated in the oil. Phoenix fished one out, verifying the meat was cooked fully. Ash picked up one half, blew on it and popped it into her mouth. Phoenix scooped out the remaining nuggets to avoid overcooking them.

"Well, how is it? Does it fulfill your craving?" Phoenix asked, knowing the answer by the expression on Ash's face.

"Oh my God these are the best nuggets I've ever had. I think you've just ruined fast food for me."

"Give me enough time and I'll ensure you never want to eat out again."

"Feeling cocky today?" Ash teased.

Phoenix set down the tongs. "Confident."

Ash wrapped her arms around Phoenix's waist. Phoenix lifted her hands awkwardly. "Careful, I have a gross raw chicken hand."

"So you're at my mercy?" Ash asked with a seductive lilt to her voice that was so unexpected Phoenix couldn't control the surge of arousal in her center.

"Damn, that's unfair."

Ash kissed her deeply enough that Phoenix almost forgot about her hands. Ash tasted like the seasoning on the nuggets, which wasn't the worst way to taste test her food. When Ash stepped away, Phoenix was stunned. "What was that for?"

"Doing all this. Besides, it's kind of fun seeing you flustered. I didn't know it was possible." Now Ash sounded cocky, and damn if that wasn't a turn on in itself.

"If you don't behave, I can't finish making dinner."

Ash took a step back and popped the other half of the nugget into her mouth. Phoenix's grandma would kill them both for snacking, but she wasn't here to smack their hands. This was Phoenix's kitchen, and she made the rules.

When Phoenix was down to the last batch, she distracted Ash by sending her to get them drinks and plates. That gave her just enough time to finish the food, wash her hands, and turn off the stove.

She met Ash out in the dining room at a smaller private table, tucked as close to the corner as they could get to avoid bystanders and volunteers who would be coming around soon to set out leftovers for dinner. She set down the fries first, freeing a hand to pull out the star and heart shaped nuggets and set them on Ash's plate.

"What do you think?" Phoenix asked, not nervous exactly, but excited to share this with her.

"Oh my God. Phoenix these are adorable!" Ash stood and pulled Phoenix by her collar for a quick kiss. "And you said it wasn't possible."

"I didn't know if it was. Now eat before someone else comes in here wanting some. I don't want to get in trouble." Phoenix sat and filled her plate with the normally shaped nuggets and fries, just as excited for this meal as Ash appeared. It had been too long since she'd made anything similar. Why was that? When she returned home she'd be cooking a lot more.

"You didn't make yourself special nuggets?" Ash asked, confusion in her voice.

"There wasn't enough chicken to make more, and these taste exactly the same. I made those especially for you."

Ash reached across and set a star on Phoenix's plate, followed by a heart. "I give you... my chicken heart." Ash said with a grin before taking some of the normal nuggets in exchange.

It was just chicken. So why was her heart radiating with warmth and affection? Was Ash turning Phoenix into a hopeless romantic? Oh God, she was! Old Phoenix would never stand for it, but the look of pure joy on Ash's face prevented Phoenix from freaking out. She was too damn happy to put her guard up. All Phoenix could do was smile goofily and take a bite, wondering how much of Ash's heart she was being given, and how much she could give in return.

A few minutes later, Ash groaned as she leaned back. "Ok, I found your first dating mistake."

Phoenix furrowed her brows in concern. She was admittedly winging it all, but she couldn't imagine how she'd screwed up.

"You made entirely too much delicious food. I feel like I'm going to explode."

Relief replaced concern and Phoenix relaxed. "Good thing we're watching a movie after dinner then," Phoenix said. "I'm also stuffed."

Ash rested a hand on her belly, reminding Phoenix of a pregnant woman until she shook that unexpected, but surprisingly pleasing, thought from her mind. Seriously, what was Ash doing to her?

Ash thankfully didn't know what Phoenix was thinking and continued the conversation. "I'm ready to find a couch and digest while we watch... wait, what are we going to watch?"

"Whatever you want. Let's clean up and see what we can find."

ASH

The warmth of Phoenix's hand in Ash's drew her attention as they meandered down the hall to the cozy TV lounge in B pod. She was becoming increasingly comfortable with showing their relationship in public.

Phoenix interrupted her thoughts. "Do you want to watch Buffy?"

"This is going to sound strange but no. After all the research I did to write my stories it's hard to watch them for fun. And tonight should be about fun."

Phoenix squeezed her hand lightly. "That makes sense, strangely enough. We'll find something."

Ash couldn't help but wonder if Phoenix was this understanding about everything. It was hard to believe anyone could be. There had to be something that Phoenix would push back against.

As they approached the lounge, light and muffled sounds spilled into the hallway, a sure sign someone was inside. Everyone was well trained to turn off lights to conserve energy.

"Looks like someone else is choosing what we watch tonight. Hopefully it's something good."

"We don't have to watch anything you know. We could just Netflix and chill back in your room," Phoenix offered with a grin.

Ash looked at her, puzzled. "We aren't allowed to stream, you know that."

Phoenix pulled her close and kissed her temple. "And you apparently don't know that for most people that's a euphemism for sex. Or at least making out."

Ash's cheeks warmed in embarrassment and she looked away. Phoenix stepped in front of her as she apologized. "I was just teasing, please don't feel embarrassed. I'm not propositioning you, though making out would be fun." Now it was Phoenix's turn to look away, clearly flustered. "Ugh, I'm making this worse. I'm such an asshole."

Ash was unsure what to address first. Everything was fine one minute, the next they were spinning out of control, bumping into each other's insecurities.

Ash reached for Phoenix, trying to pull her attention back. "Phoenix, you are not an asshole simply for expressing your desires. You're not asexual. I expect you to have sexual desires that I don't. You don't have to suppress that side of yourself."

Phoenix glanced at Ash before responding. "I don't want you to feel pressured."

"I think I can tell the difference between joking and pressure." At least she hoped she could. "Besides, I like making out with you too. Which is why we're not in either of our rooms right now. Being in public should slow us down."

Phoenix brightened at Ash's admission, pulling her close by her belt loops and giving her a mischievous smile. "The keyword is should."

"I said slow, not stop," Ash quipped before giving Phoenix a quick kiss on the lips. "Come on troublemaker. You have another date experience to check off your list."

"Oh, I've had sex in a movie theater," Phoenix said before

catching herself, looking sheepish. "Sorry, my mouth is running without a filter tonight."

Ash tried to ignore the niggle of worry in her belly, perturbed that Phoenix was giving up too much to be with her.

"That's not what I was referring to. Tonight is the experience of *not* having sex while watching a movie." Ash kept her tone light but studied Phoenix. Something was off about her, and not just her ability to put her foot in her mouth. She fidgeted, tapping her fingers on the side of her leg.

"Phoenix, are you nervous?" Ash asked cautiously.

"Why would I be nervous?" Phoenix replied, unconvincingly.

"I don't know. Because dating is a new experience for you?"

"True. Or because so far we've had enough distractions that I didn't get caught up thinking about what I might be doing wrong. Or worrying about feelings. Or desires. Movies aren't nearly distracting enough." Phoenix ran her fingers through her hair roughly. "Christ, where did my filters go? Maybe a movie is what I need to stop talking."

"Would it help if I take your nervousness as a compliment? I don't know if I've ever made someone nervous before." Ash wrapped her arms around Phoenix's waist and relaxed into her, resting her head on Phoenix's shoulder. Phoenix's arms enveloped her, resting her head on Ash's.

"I don't know how you feel," Ash whispered, "but this right here is what I look forward to. This connection takes time to build, but it's worth it. That's the purpose of the dates. Not to make you nervous." Phoenix pulled Ash tighter but didn't speak for several breaths.

"This part is pretty nice," Phoenix said quietly before ending the embrace but taking Ash's hand, maintaining contact. "Shall we see what's playing in the lounge, my dear?" Phoenix asked with mock formality.

Ash nodded and finally finished their walk to the lounge. Inside were a handful of people watching a later episode of the

X-Files. "Ooh, this can definitely work," Ash whispered, pausing in the back of the room so as not to disturb the others.

Phoenix agreed, adding, "Nerdy fun for you, sexy Gillian Anderson for me. Does she really do nothing for you?"

Ash just shrugged. It would never make sense to her either. "I can recognize that she's beautiful, but that's about it."

"Just to be clear, if she were standing in front of you now, naked, offering to spend the night with you, you'd do what? Hand her a robe?" Phoenix's expression was incredulous.

Ash chuckled. "Pretty much. I mean, I don't know her. Maybe if I spent the time to develop a connection then I'd probably enjoy kissing her, but that's not something that happens in a night. You stand a hell of a lot better chance of me not handing you the robe than she does right now."

Phoenix grinned, looking equally proud of herself and a little turned on. "I'm totally going to tell people that you chose me over Gillian Anderson."

"I haven't yet," Ash teased, "But if it boosts your ego..."

"Oh, it does. Because while I get it, everyone else is going to interpret your choice as me being a stud."

It all sounded strange to Ash, but if it helped Phoenix be comfortable with their relationship, she'd go with it.

There was an empty couch in the front of the room, which Ash walked toward. They greeted the others and got comfortable, Phoenix sitting in the corner of the couch and Ash lying down, her head in Phoenix's lap.

There was a simple pleasure in lying on a couch instead of sitting on a bed or desk chair. It felt more normal, like they weren't in an isolated research station at the bottom of the world. Phoenix ran her fingers through Ash's hair, seemingly absentmindedly. Before long Ash closed her eyes, the motion so comforting she couldn't focus on anything else.

"Hey Ash?" Phoenix whispered after a few minutes.

"Hm?"

"Your hand."

Ash opened her eyes and noticed her hand was halfway up Phoenix's leg, lightly rubbing the inside of her thigh. She turned to face Phoenix who did not look nearly as relaxed as Ash felt, her breathing quickened. "Sorry," Ash said, moving her hand to Phoenix's knee.

"It's ok. It feels good. Too good, especially while watching Scully."

Ash lightly slapped Phoenix's knee and turned back to the TV, trying to remember what was happening in the show. Not that she cared that much anymore, she was simply enjoying laying on the couch with Phoenix. She closed her eyes again and enjoyed the moment, one of Phoenix's arms across her belly, the other still playing with her hair. She could stay there forever.

When the episode ended, Phoenix asked, "Has this fulfilled the date requirement?"

"Where would you rather go?" Ash asked and she looked up, already knowing the answer.

Phoenix lifted an eyebrow and Ash chuckled as she sat up and then stood, reaching for Phoenix's hand. In the hall, Phoenix pulled her close, wrapping an arm around her waist. If only Ash wanted sex, she could give Phoenix exactly what she wanted, but there was so much she didn't know about her. They'd only known each other for two months and dating a week. But Phoenix wasn't used to waiting and Ash couldn't completely put that out of her mind.

At her door, Phoenix asked if she could come in and Ash knew she wasn't ready for the night to end. She stepped aside, allowing Phoenix to pass before locking the door behind them. Phoenix was close when she turned around, but she didn't touch her. She seemed to be struggling before asking, "Can I kiss you?"

Ash was thrown by the question, but that must have been what Phoenix was struggling with, locating Ash's boundaries. A surge of affection hit her and Ash pulled Phoenix to her by the shirt and kissed her passionately. Phoenix responded instantly, parting her lips, encouraging Ash's tongue to join hers, bringing them closer than they'd been all day. Phoenix's fingers slipped under the hem of Ash's t-shirt, tickling her skin with a light touch that roamed up and down her back.

Phoenix traced her lips along Ash's jaw to her neck, sending tingles down her body. Ash released a sigh of pleasure as Phoenix continued her exploration up to her earlobes, her hot breath making Ash giggle as it tickled the sensitive skin. Phoenix paused, whispering, "Is this ok?"

"Yes...God, I wish I could give you what you want right now," Ash admitted.

"Me too," Phoenix said with a seductive growl. "How far can we go?"

Ash tugged at Phoenix's shirt. "I'd love to touch you again."

Phoenix sucked in a breath. "I know that's not how you meant it, but damn if it didn't affect me just the same." Phoenix ripped her shirt over her head and reached for Ash's. She nodded in permission, loving the ability to offer whatever she could without sacrificing who she was. Phoenix kissed the hollow of Ash's neck, and then worked her way down until she reached the top of her bra, her hands brushing along her ribs, up the side of her breasts through the fabric.

Ash longed to feel Phoenix's skin under her hands. She stepped back, sat on her bed and then pulled Phoenix to her, kissing her again before sliding to the far side of her small bed. Phoenix followed without hesitation until Ash placed a hand on her chest, stopping her from moving on top. She trusted Phoenix, but the need to maintain boundaries was greater. Phoenix immediately backed off, settling on her side facing Ash, a grin on her face.

"What?" Ash asked, confused.

"Do you have any idea how happy I am to be here with you?"

Ash's face lit up, pleasantly surprised. "Really? You aren't frustrated?"

"Not in a bad way. It's like... the anticipation before an adventure. You're in control here, I'm just following your lead."

"Is that new for you, giving up control?" Ash asked, trying to understand Phoenix.

"Actually, no. I give women whatever they are looking for. Some want me to be strong and in charge. Some want to direct the show. I'm there for all of it, as long as they aren't asking me to be emotionally invested after."

"And I'm asking you to do the opposite, to be emotionally invested without the sex."

"I'm trying," Phoenix said, concern in her voice.

Ash shifted closer so their bodies almost touched. "I think you're doing more than trying," Ash reassured her as she leaned in for a kiss. Phoenix closed the gap, their lips crashing together. Ash couldn't think anymore, running her hands along Phoenix's body to her strong shoulders. Phoenix's body showed that she worked for a living. From the strength in her muscles to the small burn scars on her hands, Phoenix was not the type to waste away in front of a computer.

"You're amazing," Ash said reverently. Phoenix shook her head slightly, finding it hard to believe in Ash's assessment of her. It bothered her how little Phoenix thought of herself sometimes. She was determined to get to the bottom of it, but first she needed Phoenix's attention.

Ash sat up and looked Phoenix square in the eye as she moved on top, straddling her hips. Phoenix's eyes grew wide. "Someday you're going to believe me," Ash said, leaning down for another kiss, but she was distracted by Phoenix's moan when her weight shifted back against Phoenix's center. Phoenix reached behind Ash's neck and pulled her down strongly, kissing Ash deeply.

They kissed for what felt like forever, their skin brushing

together, exploring each other until they were breathless. "Still ok?" Ash asked, not wanting to push her too hard.

"Yes?" Phoenix replied, her voice breaking. Ash gave her a look that told Phoenix she wasn't buying it. "But, I'm so close I think I could explode without you touching me. I should go back to my room before I spontaneously combust."

Ash gazed down at Phoenix's barely focused eyes, brushed her fingers through her hair, and wondered if there was a compromise. Only one way to find out.

"And if you didn't?"

Phoenix blinked. "What? Are you offering—?"

"To take the edge off. How long do you think you could last? A minute? Less?" Ash teased in her best seductive voice, running a finger along Phoenix's collarbone, down the center of her chest. Phoenix shuddered. Ash lowered her body to Phoenix, increasing the pressure on Phoenix's center, causing her eyes to flutter closed with a moan. Ash kissed below her earlobe and whispered, "Let me take care of you."

Phoenix answered in a raspy voice, "You're sure?"

Ash pulled Phoenix into a sitting position so she was now sitting in her lap.

"Do I look unsure?" Ash asked before pushing Phoenix's sports bra off her small breasts, brushing her palms over the nipples hardening into peaks. Phoenix's eyes were so dark only a ring of gray remained. Ash's breathing quickened, but not with her own arousal as much as the power she held over Phoenix. It was the best word she could find in the moment as Phoenix bit her bottom lip. Ash held all the control, the question was, what would she do with it?

Ash ran her hand up Phoenix's neck, cupping the back of her head and kissed her deeply while Phoenix pulled her tight. Her fingers teased Phoenix's hair, eliciting a moan as they continued kissing. Ash nipped at Phoenix's bottom lip, causing Phoenix to tremor beneath her.

Phoenix pulled back, gasping. "Can I take off your bra? Nothing else, I just want to feel you against me."

Ash nodded and Phoenix undid the clasp with practiced ease before laying back on the bed. The bra joined their shirts on the floor and Phoenix's unbridled admiration made Ash blush. Before Phoenix could say a word, Ash met her with another kiss.

Soon she lost track of everything besides Phoenix's hands on her back, their bodies molding together seamlessly. Ash even caught herself smiling, actually smiling against Phoenix's lips. What a difference trust made.

Ash let her hands and lips explore, enjoying every sound of pleasure emanating from Phoenix's mouth. She let Phoenix's body be her guide, finding the places where Phoenix reacted the strongest. Licking her pulse point, nibbling her ear, Phoenix writhed beneath her. Breathing fast, Phoenix grabbed Ash's thigh and gave it a nudge. Ash shifted her weight and let Phoenix place her leg right up against her center. Phoenix shuddered and sucked in a breath.

Knowing how close Phoenix was, Ash took a hardened nipple into her mouth, teasing it with her tongue while Phoenix ground against her thrusting leg.

"Don't stop Ash. I'm almost—" but Phoenix's desperate voice was cut off as her body clenched and spasmed. Ash watched her, finally understanding what Phoenix had said earlier about making a woman come. Without the pressure of meeting her lover's expectations, she'd relaxed and given Phoenix the release she needed. Lying below her, gasping for air, a light sheen of sweat over her skin, Ash felt powerful. Not the disappointing lover from relationships past.

Ash gazed down in wonder, not knowing it was possible for someone to orgasm so easily. They were still wearing pants! And yet, Phoenix had a contented smile on her face, and when she opened her eyes drew Ash close to her, kissing her on the forehead. "I take it back. That was way better than taking care of things myself. You are fucking amazing."

"I don't exactly know what I did to make that happen, but thank you."

"It's just you. Christ, you gave me the best orgasm I've had in ages." Phoenix studied her before asking, "Are you good? Was that too weird for you?"

"I'm good, and strangely enough it wasn't too weird. In fact," Ash paused, wondering how much to share with Phoenix, "I rather enjoyed myself. And now, seeing you happy and content eases my fears about keeping you happy," Ash answered honestly. "If you don't mind, though, could we cuddle? I'm ready to pass out."

Phoenix smiled and nestled Ash's head into her shoulder as Ash settled in. "This feels weird. I'm not used to stopping before my partner is fully satisfied."

"But I am satisfied. I promise, if and when I want more, I will tell you." Ash caressed Phoenix's belly, enjoying the smoothness under her palm. It was getting late, but the last thing she wanted was for Phoenix to leave. "Speaking of, do you want to stay tonight?"

Phoenix kissed the top of her head. "Absolutely."

🦔

Ash scrambled across Phoenix to turn off the alarm clock on her desk. Completely dark except for the pale glow, Ash woke up her laptop to provide enough light to see Phoenix without waking her. By the time she turned around Phoenix had rolled over, taking Ash's vacated spot against the wall. Ash smiled lazily and slipped back into the bed, nuzzling against Phoenix's back.

If Emily weren't around she could go in whenever she wanted. Jon wouldn't care as long as she checked in with him at some point. But showing up late set a bad example, and she didn't want word circulating that she was unprofessional. Emily was unlikely to spread rumors, but she could mention it to someone else who would misunderstand.

Phoenix's breathing remained even and the temptation to stay in bed grew stronger. Instead of falling back to sleep, Ash took advantage of the quiet to notice how different everything was with Phoenix. Comfortable. Easy. Low pressure. Not what she expected from any relationship, much less someone used to sleeping with anyone she wanted. But here they both were, half naked in her bed.

It was so easy to see herself falling in love with Phoenix. Except they didn't know each other well enough to lose her head or heart. Not yet.

Now, with Phoenix sleeping, Ash had an opportunity to observe her without interruption. Ash nuzzled against Phoenix, kissing her back. Phoenix stirred but didn't awaken. Perhaps she should test just how heavy a sleeper Phoenix was.

She traced the spiral on each of her tattoos, allowing herself to dream of a universe that brought people together. Was there a part of Phoenix who believed her own theory of destiny?

Ash wasn't sure which reality she preferred. Nothing in physics told her the universe was a thinking being, but she saw the appeal. If they were fated to meet, their relationship was important to more than just the two of them. They became heroes in their lives.

At the same time, believing her fate was entirely in her hands meant that their success as a couple was even more impressive. And yet... the tattoos drew her attention. Her scientist self scoffed at her romantic self and she gave up deciding which version of her and Phoenix's story was better.

Ash kissed each tattoo in turn before wrapping her arm around Phoenix's belly. A hint of shampoo hit her nose as she took a deep breath at Phoenix's neck.

She smoothed her free hand over Phoenix's skin, accidentally brushing against a nipple which immediately hardened. Her only other reaction was a quickening of breath. Ash was in uncharted territory, genuinely unsure what Phoenix would appreciate. Phoenix's breath settled before Ash ran her hand back down to Phoenix's belly, this time carefully avoiding her nipple, but it didn't seem to matter as Phoenix's breathing increased again.

Not wanting to wake Phoenix quite yet, Ash moved her hand, lightly tracing the dragon on her bicep, again wondering what it represented. Perhaps one day soon Phoenix would explain. Ash smoothed her palm over Phoenix's arm, firm even while relaxed, and she could almost feel her lizard brain light up, causing her to roll her eyes at herself.

Curious, Ash squeezed her own bicep. There was no comparison, though her muscles were clearly stronger after two weeks of shoveling snow. She continued her journey to Phoenix's forearm where she could just make out scars mingled with freckles that continued onto her hand. How many were the result of working in kitchens compared to the rest of her life? There was so much to learn about Phoenix. At least they had ten months ahead of them, plenty of time for Ash to make her discoveries.

What they didn't have was limitless time today, so Ash pulled herself tight to Phoenix's back, her arm low around Phoenix's hips and belly.

"Ash, what are you doing?"

"Waking you up?" Ash responded innocently before placing a kiss between Phoenix's shoulder blades.

Phoenix turned in Ash's arms. "I think that explains my dream."

"Do I want to know?"

"Probably not, but you should know you were in it, but with a lot less clothes on."

Ash replied with a chuckle. "So that's why you slept so soundly, you didn't want me to interrupt your dream."

Phoenix grew unexpectedly still, her eyes flicked downward. Had she said something wrong? She didn't think so. "What's wrong? Should I have let you sleep?"

Phoenix remained silent for several more breaths, increasing Ash's confusion. "No, that's fine, you probably saved us both from an awkward situation." Ash wasn't sure what that could be, but she was fine not knowing.

Phoenix hesitated again before finally admitting, "I'm not normally a heavy sleeper. Not unless I'm at my aunt's house. I can't relax enough."

"Maybe that means you feel safe with me," Ash offered, trying not to think too hard about why Phoenix couldn't relax with other people.

"Yeah, I guess," Phoenix replied, sounding rather dispirited and definitely not what Ash expected after such a great night.

Ash studied Phoenix's face, looking for clues. "What's wrong Phoenix? This isn't like you."

Phoenix shook her head and looked away. Ash rubbed her stomach, offering comfort. "I can't answer that."

Ash stilled her hand. She cautiously asked, "Can't or won't?"

Phoenix met her eyes, answering firmly. "Can't."

Ash's confusion deepened. "Ok. You know I'm here if you want to talk about anything at all. At any time." Phoenix nodded, but her body was still tense and on edge. Ash battled concern and frustration. Phoenix, while more open, continued hiding the most important aspects of her life. If she could just open up, maybe Ash could help. She decided to try a different approach, curling into Phoenix's side and resting her head on her shoulder.

"I feel safe with you, too. If aliens attacked, I'm confident you'd kick their asses to protect me."

Phoenix gave her a squeeze and it felt like progress. "No more X-Files for you. It gives you ideas."

Ash looked up, asking with false innocence, "but what about your Scully fix?"

"I don't need her, I have you," Phoenix said with a grin.

Ash returned her smile, but added, "I call bullshit. Would you really hand a naked Gillian Anderson a robe like I would?"

"I'd probably ask if she were interested in a threesome."

"Hey!" Ash replied, punctuated with a slap to Phoenix's belly. She knew Phoenix was kidding and left the statement unchallenged. She was too happy to see Phoenix laughing again.

"Ok, you're right. I'd give her a robe too, just for different reasons. You may feel no attraction, but I'm certain I would. I know my body. But that doesn't mean I'd sleep with her while we were a couple."

Ash kissed her chastely on the lips, realizing they both must have morning breath, but wanting to be closer to her. "That's a really good answer. Sounds like a good comic to draw up. Perhaps I'll write something after work, which I need to get to soon," Ash added, hoping Phoenix could hear how sorry she was to have to leave. "Emily's last full day is today so I can't skip out."

"You don't think she'd understand?"

"No, she'd understand, but she might mention something to our program advisors who wouldn't. I can't afford to gain a reputation for being unprofessional."

Phoenix looked more confused. "Because you're a lesbian?"

"No, because I skipped out on work for... romantic reasons. There are many people who wouldn't understand."

Phoenix's face clouded over, again leaving Ash lost as to what she'd said wrong. The ease they had moments ago was once again gone.

"I think I understand." Phoenix sat up, extricating herself

from Ash's embrace. "I know I'm not the kind of person that your bosses would approve of."

Ash shot up, too stunned to reply while Phoenix grabbed her shirt from the floor. "Let me know when I'm not a danger to your career."

"What?" Ash asked in alarm, jumping off the bed and finding her shirt. Phoenix shoved her bra in her pocket and picked up her shoes, not bothering to put them on as she took a step toward the door.

"Phoenix, stop. That's not what I was saying."

Phoenix continued to the door, speaking without turning around. "Just go to work Ash."

Ash stood there, stunned, as Phoenix walked out the door.

CHAPTER FOURTEEN

PHOENIX

*P*hoenix's heart pounded in her chest as she ran to her room. Why had she freaked out on Ash? Everything was going fine, great even, and yet here she was, running away like a child. Why?

She wanted to be rational, to return to Ash's room and apologize. Instead she ran to her room and curled into a tight ball on her bed, her eyes squeezed tight, attempting to regain control. *Olympia. Salem. Sacramento. Carson City.* With her highly developed visual brain Phoenix could see the US map laid out, but this time she struggled to hold the image until reaching Denver. By the time she made it to Baton Rouge, Phoenix was calm enough to open her eyes. Her gaze landed on the picture of Diane and her grandmother and for once she wished she wasn't so far away. She could do with a late-night chat over beer. Given the time difference, she might be able to catch her online before heading to bed.

Phoenix grabbed her tablet and sent a quick email to her aunt, asking if she was up, then distracted herself with some music. Thanks to her focusing exercise she had *Calling Baton*

Rouge in her head, so she threw on some Garth Brooks and waited. Before long an instant message popped up.

Hi baby girl, what happened?

That was the question of the hour, wasn't it? Phoenix hadn't even told her aunt that she and Ash were dating. There was a lot to fill her in on.

How much time do you have?

Diane's reply came without delay. *As much as you need.*

Phoenix decided to start with New Years, and Ash's kiss, and the dates which earned a shocked reaction from Diane. Her aunt didn't know the true extent of Phoenix's resistance to dating, but she knew enough to recognize the significance. She explained their comic, and Ash's asexuality, as best she could, and then told her about their night together, skipping the details no aunt wanted to know about their niece.

This morning, everything was great until she mentioned I was a heavy sleeper, which I'm not. Or wasn't, until sleeping with her. It should be a good thing that I trust her, right? But alarm bells filled my head, like I'd made a huge mistake in letting down my guard.

Then she mentioned needing to go to work so no one thought she was unprofessional. She said I misunderstood, but all I heard was that I'm not good enough for her, which is true. But I was an asshole and rushed off instead of handling it like an adult. Now I'm freaking out for no good reason, and realizing she must be confused as hell, but I don't know what to say to her. I can't just tell her I have issues and had to run away.

The typing notification showed on the screen for far longer than the reply required. It probably was a lot to sort out for Diane as well.

Trauma is a sneaky bitch kid. It bites us in the ass when we least expect it. After a pause Diane added, *sounds like you have a lot of feelings for her.*

Phoenix chuckled. *Too many to count.*

How much does she know about your childhood?

Phoenix sighed. *Almost nothing.* She watched the typing notification, dreading the reply. The last thing she wanted to do was explain to Ash what a mess her life was. It was so much easier to pretend it didn't exist. At least for another 10 months.

I'm not going to tell you to tell her everything, because I know that's not going to happen. But maybe tell her a little, enough to explain why you reacted the way you did.

Ok, sure, as soon as you tell me why I freaked out, because I don't get it.

Fee, have you ever trusted someone this much before? Let anyone this close to you?

Phoenix didn't have to think about the answer. *No.*

What are you afraid will happen if you let her in more?

Memories flashed in her mind, of drunken fights and heated words with more faces than she could count. Fights in bars between her friends, relationships blowing up more often than not. She certainly didn't know anyone like her who'd managed a safe, loving, and stable relationship for long. Finally, a flash of a stranger in her room. Nope, not going there. Phoenix forced her focus back to her tablet.

Assuming she doesn't run, once she knows who I really am, I can't even imagine what a healthy relationship means. What are the chances that this is different from everything I've seen? People like me don't get happy endings. So what happens when this blows up? Or hell, when we go home and live in different states?

Diane's reply quickly came in. *If you were here I'd smack you for that. People like you? There are no people like you Phoenix. You aren't your folks. You aren't the people you grew up around, content to work, drink and waste their lives away. You're so much more than that. Let me ask you, what's it been like being away from everyone?*

The unexpected question threw her. *It's been amazing. Calm. Easy. I miss you, but I don't look forward to leaving.*

If you let yourself relax, I think you'll discover even more about yourself and understand just how different you are from where you came from. And that you do deserve a happy fucking ending to your story.

How?

Well you can start by getting this 'I'm not good enough' crap out of your head. Then, find that girlfriend of yours and apologize. Tell her something about your life so she can understand where you are coming from. Let her in a little. You can't build a relationship while you're hiding everything.

Ugh, that sounds so hard.

Of course it's hard, why do you think I'm single? But you're supposed to learn from all of my mistakes and do better.

Phoenix shook her head in disbelief. *So this is a 'do what I say' moment. Great.*

Damn right it is kid. I never found that woman who was worth risking it all, but if you have, don't throw it away because you were too afraid to try.

A flicker of hope sparked in Phoenix's chest. *Fine, I'll think of something. Thanks Diane.*

Anytime Fee. Go clean up your mess and send me some pictures when you get the chance. I need to see this girlfriend of yours.

Phoenix caught herself smiling at the word girlfriend. She, Phoenix, had a girlfriend. Or hoped she still had one.

Yes ma'am. Goodnight.

Phoenix set her tablet aside and wondered if Ash would be at breakfast or work. Phoenix rushed to the galley and spotted her sitting at a table with Emily who eyed her warily. Great.

"Um, Ash, can we talk for a second? I won't make you late, I promise."

Emily excused herself before Ash could respond so Phoenix took her chair. She fidgeted with a napkin as she spoke. "I'm so sorry for this morning. I freaked out for reasons that are too complicated to tell you now. Will you give me the chance to explain after work tonight?" Phoenix looked up tentatively into cautious but forgiving eyes. Ash took Phoenix's hands in hers and she stopped fidgeting.

"I'll listen to anything you have to say, but I need you to promise not to run off again, because that's what really hurt. You didn't let me explain."

Shame churned in Phoenix's gut. "I'm sorry, I promise to stay. I didn't mean to hurt you."

Ash lifted Phoenix's hand and kissed her knuckles. "I'm just a little hurt. Still confused, but I can wait until tonight."

🎂

Phoenix knocked on Ash's door just after 11pm, hoping she hadn't changed her mind. Ash greeted her warmly, but only kissed Phoenix on the cheek. Maybe it was appropriate given how unsettled they'd left things this morning, but it made Phoenix even more uncomfortable. She didn't want things to be different between them.

"Shit, now I've made everything awkward," Phoenix admitted.

Ash shook her head and wrapped her arms around Phoenix, just as warm and comforting as Phoenix had come to expect from a famous Ash hug. Phoenix breathed her in, kissing her on the top of her head before taking half a step back. Ash took her hand.

"Come sit down. We'll figure it out."

Phoenix allowed herself to be pulled onto the bed and sat cross-legged, her shoulders slumped. "I don't know where to start. There's still so much I'm trying to understand myself." Phoenix fidgeted with her pants hem rather than look at Ash.

"Tell me what you can. I promise to listen and try to understand."

Phoenix nodded and dove in. "I had a rough childhood. My parents were young when they had me and weren't good together. The only good decision they made was to not get married. But that also meant there were a string of partners of varying quality as well as frequent moves. I learned at too young an age that sleeping heavily could be dangerous. I couldn't trust anyone, except my aunt and grandma, until you apparently."

Anger flashed as she realized how her family managed to taint what should have been the best morning in recent memory. She forced the anger back and kept her voice even as she spoke.

"When I realized that I trusted you, I was surprised but happy. I still am, really, but my brain flashed back to events I'd rather forget, warning me that it was dangerous to let my guard down, telling me I can't trust anyone. I couldn't truly hear what you were saying because my brain was in overdrive."

Ash touched Phoenix's arm, pulling her attention outward. "That sounds awful. I can't imagine what that does to a kid. Except, maybe I don't have to because you showed me what it does this morning."

"If it helps, my reaction was unexpected for me, too. I don't usually stay until morning with a woman." Phoenix glanced up, attempting a smile. "Then again, I've never had a girlfriend before. I'm breaking all sorts of rules with you."

"I'm glad you are, even if there are unintended consequences. I'm still confused why don't you think my colleagues would approve of you?"

Phoenix's gaze fell to her feet. "Maybe not all your colleagues, Jon is great. But you made it sound like your bosses weren't quite so understanding. I imagined all those college professors looking at me and seeing nothing but the white trash family I came from. That I would be an embarrassment to you if people knew about us. I barely finished high school. I have tattoos and cook in restaurants for a living, and not high-class ones. You know where I worked before here? Hooters. I wouldn't blame you if you didn't want your bosses to know that. It doesn't fit with the image of a successful scientist."

Ash opened her eyes wide. "Now *I* don't know where to start. If my colleagues have a problem with your profession, that's their problem, not mine. And if they are psychic and can know your past just by looking at you, then they might be in the wrong profession. I'm going to leave Hooters for another day, because, wow. So many questions. But you know the only part of this that concerns me?" Ash lifted Phoenix's chin to make eye contact. "That you think I would care about your past more than who you are now. If anything, your past makes you more amazing because you became this person in spite of your challenges. That takes real strength Phoenix."

Phoenix scoffed. "Strong enough to freak out because I trusted you. Strong enough to run away."

"Strong enough to come back and explain," Ash countered firmly. "Don't beat yourself up. The human psyche does a lot to protect itself. It doesn't always make sense, but it's not exactly something you can control. This, tonight, showed your strength. Thank you for confiding in me."

It was hard to believe Ash. She didn't know everything Phoenix had done in her life to survive. But the ache in Phoenix's chest was stronger than her disbelief, drawing her to Ash. She needed Ash's comfort, her affection, her surety that Phoenix mattered.

Looking up, Phoenix mustered the last of her courage to ask, "Can I just lie with you? I really need to be close to you right now."

Ash moved up on the bed and wrapped her arms around Phoenix without a word. Phoenix buried her face in Ash's chest, letting the sound of her heartbeat sooth her to sleep.

ASH

Ash didn't fall asleep nearly as easily. Her mind had raced with questions and concerns. Phoenix finally opened up and that peek was enough to realize there was so much more she wasn't ready to say, not that Ash could blame her. She'd shared enough to believe Phoenix had plenty of valid reasons to not trust people. But Ash was serious about Phoenix's past making her more amazing. How could it not? From everything Ash had seen, Phoenix cared about others, experienced genuine pleasure from making people happy, was kind and considerate. Knowing she'd become this person in spite of her background made Ash care for her even more.

Holding her all night, being trusted to provide comfort, was the most amazing feeling. Gazing down at tough, strong Phoenix peacefully asleep was something she never wanted to forget. Ash hoped the next morning would turn out better than the last.

It was Phoenix's turn to wake Ash up, nuzzling against Ash's chest. She blinked against the darkness. "Phoenix, you awake?" Ash whispered.

"Yeah," Phoenix replied groggily.

"You know, this is two nights in a row," Ash said playfully. "Are you U-Hauling me?"

"I don't think a U-Haul is necessary. Maybe a duffle bag."

"Duffle-bagging doesn't sound nearly as nice as U-Hauling."

"I'm pretty sure it's too early to debate which word is better," Phoenix said with a yawn. "So are you asking me to move in or is this your passive aggressive way to send me away."

"Well, the last two nights were spontaneous. It wouldn't hurt to plan ahead. Bring a toothbrush, pajamas, whatever makes staying over more comfortable," Ash offered.

"And if I sleep naked?" Ash heard the grin in Phoenix's voice.

"Just bring your toothbrush," Ash threw back, calling her bluff.

Phoenix chuckled and rested her head on Ash's chest again, relishing their closeness. After Phoenix's admissions Ash wanted nothing more than to be as close as possible to her. The image of them laying together just like this, but naked, caused Ash's pulse to kick up in excitement. Phoenix lifted her head and Ash realized she must be able to hear Ash's pulse quicken. Ash's cheeks warmed when Phoenix asked if she was ok, but it was too dark for Phoenix to notice.

"When do you need to go to work today?" Phoenix asked.

"Emily's supposed to fly out at 1:00 if the weather cooperates. It would be nice to see her off and go into work after."

"What about your reputation?"

"I realized that I had overreacted as well. I asked Jon if he minded if I came in a bit later today and he looked at me like I was ridiculous for even asking."

Phoenix's voice brightened. "So we have the morning together? I have so many comic ideas to run by you."

Ash couldn't help but be charmed by Phoenix's enthusiasm. "After some breakfast."

"You know what's funny?" Ash asked as they sat eating breakfast. "We've barely spoken about our lives before we got here. I understand now why you wouldn't want to, but now that we're dating shouldn't we know more about each other?"

Phoenix eyed her warily. Ash rushed to clarify.

"Not all the bad memories, but basics. And you get to choose what you share."

"I can work with that. You go first."

"Ok, basic family stuff. Your parents...?" Ash wasn't sure what she was going to ask, but Phoenix bailed her out.

"Suck. And yours?"

Ash stifled a laugh. "Don't suck. Usually. Siblings?"

"Zero to eight at last count." Ash furrowed her brows and cocked her head. Phoenix clarified, "No blood siblings that I'm aware of. Plenty of step-siblings, though I only keep in touch with one, Steph. She feels like family, even though her mom is dating someone else. You?"

"A younger brother. We aren't very close. I love him, but we're two very different people. The four year age gap was just enough to keep us from playing together and bonding early."

"So he's not a super nerd like you?" Phoenix asked with a grin.

"Hey! I'm not a super nerd," Ash replied with mock indignation.

"Really? Do we need to make a list?"

Ash leaned forward, grabbed a handful of Phoenix's t-shirt, and pulled her in for a light kiss. "You share at least half of the interests that would be on that list, nerd."

Phoenix laughed, an infectious laugh that made Ash's heart flutter. "You didn't answer my question, super nerd."

"No, he's a musician and works whatever jobs allow him the flexibility to perform. He's good, but being good isn't enough to be super successful. I think he's happy at least."

"Aha, I found something you have in common," Phoenix

exclaimed. Ash couldn't begin to see the connection, so let Phoenix finish. "You're both dreamers. Your dreams are different, but you both want the improbable."

"I never thought of it that way, but you're right. So what's your improbable dream?" A shadow fell over Phoenix's face. "Sorry, you don't have to answer. I didn't expect that to be a delicate topic."

Phoenix shook her head. "Dreams didn't keep the lights on, or food in the fridge. I was too poor to afford a dream."

"Not even as a kid?"

"I was working by the time I was ten, helping my stepdad clean out crappy apartments. Working fast food by 15 and already learning the tricks shitty owners pulled to avoid paying me what I earned. I'm sure I had dreams at some point, but quickly realized they were pointless."

For the second time in twelve hours Ash's heart broke for Phoenix. What could she possibly say that wouldn't make the situation worse? Did Phoenix need an inspirational speech? Comfort? To move on? She needed to say something so chose the safe approach.

"I'm sorry Phoenix."

Phoenix merely shrugged.

"What about now? Your needs are met, you're away from your family, and you have a super nerd for a girlfriend." Phoenix smiled at the comment. "What would you dream now?"

Ash ate more of her oatmeal while Phoenix thought over her question.

"I don't know if I'm doing this dreaming thing right, because I can't think of anything big like yours."

"Dreams don't have to be that big. What would you do if you had all the money in the world?"

"I'd open a restaurant and serve classic home cooked meals using my grandma's recipes," Phoenix replied sheepishly. "And if that's too big, maybe a food truck."

Ash reached for a hand and held it in hers. "Phoenix, you should do that! You're an excellent cook, and a hard worker. I'm certain you'd succeed."

"Sure, but with what money?"

"Maybe you'll become a famous comic artist and that will fund your restaurant," Ash offered, semi-seriously.

"You are such a dreamer, aren't you?"

"Who knows what will happen in the future? But if you don't try for a dream, you'll never reach it. And if you try but fall short, you're still further along than you would have been. I don't see a downside."

Phoenix reclaimed her hand and took a bite of her eggs.

"What did I say wrong?"

Phoenix met her gaze for just a heartbeat before looking down at her plate. "Ash, do you have any idea how much it hurts to try and fail? To have everyone laugh and tell you that you were stupid for trying? That you aren't meant for anything more than sacrificing your body until you're too hurt to work, when you get on disability and wait to die? Because that's what I heard my entire life."

"No," Ash said quietly, her heart sinking. "But I'd never do that to you. Everyone deserves to dream, to strive for more. And you know, I might be your biggest fan and a bit biased, but I think you can do anything you want to."

Phoenix gave her a rueful smile. "I don't know if that's enough, but thanks for trying."

"No problem. How about some happier topics? Tell me about the people you do like in your life, like your aunt."

Phoenix's wistful look told Ash she chose the right topic.

"Diane is an old school lesbian and my hero. She's why I moved to Colorado, and she's why I am here. She pulled some strings after a really bad day with my dad and former boss to get me into the program. The original cook backed out about a month before I left."

"Wow, a gay aunt? What was that like?"

"It helped to have someone to talk to, to know my family would be cool. I never had a big coming out talk because of it. I brought girls around after school, never boys, and made it clear that I wouldn't be bringing boys around, and that was that. Definitely better than what some of my friends dealt with. It's even better now, because she's part parent, part mentor, part friend. She calls me on my shit when I need it, like yesterday. But she doesn't make me feel like shit when she does it. It's a crucial difference."

"You told her about me? About us?" Ash suspected that was a big moment for Phoenix, given her lack of relationships. She may not be ready to open up fully, but telling her aunt must be a good sign.

"Yes, to both. I mean, I kinda had to if she was going to help."

The hope that had ballooned just seconds ago deflated a little. "You didn't want to tell her?"

"I did, but I didn't know how she'd react. What if she didn't understand how different I am here and got mad because I disobeyed her request to avoid complications? But she listened and didn't question anything. Also, she wants a picture of us, probably because no one will believe her if she says I have a girlfriend," Phoenix added with an eye roll.

"Then we'd better fix that for her. Oh, Cole and the gang would freak if I sent them pictures."

"Tell me about Cole. You mentioned them before. I take it they are non-binary?"

"Yes, I met Cole in the asexual sub-reddit. I was frustrated with how hard it was to find a romantic partner when everyone seemed to want to jump into sex. I'm just not built that way. I don't even like to kiss someone without some emotional connection. It makes dating so difficult. Everyone else agreed, a lot of people said they gave up dating because it felt impossible. But not Cole.

"Cole is an eternal optimist, a hopeful romantic as they like to say, and they encouraged me to not give up. That if I wanted to find someone I needed to be open to finding them." Ash smiled at the memory. "I don't even know what that means, but they were right. If I hadn't taken the risk to open up and give you a chance to prove you're more than just a flirt, we wouldn't be here now."

"What I hear you saying is, I owe Cole a drink or something."

"And I owe your aunt a drink." Ash softened her voice. "I'm glad you have her."

"Me too."

CHAPTER FIFTEEN

PHOENIX

The next day, Phoenix was about to make up a plate to set aside for Ash when she strolled in, five minutes before the scheduled end of dinner service. She tended to almost miss dinner once or twice a week due to work but as yet hadn't failed to appear.

"Hey stranger, I was starting to worry you'd forget to eat."

"Lost track of time, but I wasn't worried. I hear one of the cooks has the hots for me."

"Don't I know it." Phoenix set everything up so the stragglers could help themselves, grabbed a drink and met Ash at the table.

"I have some good news," Ash said in a sing song tone. "Now that Emily is gone, we can be more flexible with shifts. I spoke to Jon and we agreed that I could work the same shifts as you. No more early mornings or waiting around in the evenings."

"Really? That's great news! Maybe you can come to the gym with me now."

"Are you trying to tell me something Phoenix? With all your experience with women, don't you know better than that," Ash teased.

"Ha, no way. I'm just trying to keep these muscles you like to run your hands over." Phoenix winked at her and enjoyed the blush that colored Ash's cheeks.

Ash avoided the comment. "Anyway... date three? What do you think?"

"I think it's difficult to come up with unique ideas. What's the point of official dates again?"

"To have fun and get to know each other. There's also something to be said for creating a dedicated time period rather than just hanging out."

Phoenix tried to think of all the dates she's seen in movies. There weren't many places to go. The season was winding down already though they weren't halfway through January yet. In about a month they'd be down to the winter crew – a mere 45 or so compared to the 150 people a few days ago. She thought there was a concert coming up before more musicians left. They could play games, but they'd be doing a lot of that come winter.

With no obvious answer Phoenix changed the question. "If we could be anywhere else in the world, what would you like to do?"

"I miss swimming. And warmth. A beach would be heavenly right now. Warm, crystal clear water, white sand, walking along a boardwalk checking out the shops, holding hands and enjoying your company. That would be amazing."

Phoenix could almost envision it, though she'd never walked along the ocean in person. "That sounds nice. It's too bad we can't have a pool or even a hot tub."

"Oh, but we do have a sauna! And we can pretend it's warm outside and take a walk."

"It's called summer camp, that's almost a warm sandy beach," Phoenix added, catching Ash's enthusiasm. "We'll even have sunglasses on."

"And then we can watch a summer movie. It's almost as good as the real thing," Ash said with a chuckle.

"So, sauna after work? Hopefully we'll have it to ourselves because I didn't bring a bathing suit," Phoenix said with a wink.

"Oh, right. Do people usually go into saunas naked? That seems unsanitary."

Sexy but unsanitary images quickly came to Phoenix's mind. "We'll wipe the benches down first, just in case. And wear shorts."

Phoenix downed the rest of her lemonade and stood. "I'm going to get back to work. The anticipation of you in a sauna has me extra motivated now." She kissed Ash, lingering long enough for Ash to tug down on her shirt. Arousal surged in her center and Phoenix broke the kiss before it crossed a line.

"I'll find you when I'm done."

"You're wearing more clothes than I expected," Phoenix said when Ash opened the door.

"That's because I thought it over and realized it made more sense to go outside first, get cold, and then hit the sauna to warm up."

"You're the boss."

They walked hand in hand, first to Phoenix's room for another layer of clothing, and then to the coat room. The simultaneous blast of cold air and bright sun never failed to stun Phoenix. Definitely not a warm beach. *Think warm thoughts.* She imagined Ash in a bikini, lying on a sandy beach...that was definitely helping.

"What are you thinking about?" Ash asked.

"You. On a beach. In a bikini." Phoenix gave her a sly smile. "I needed to think of something to warm me up."

Ash shook her head and kept walking. "Glad to hear you're getting into the spirit of it. So, beaches. Ever been to the ocean?"

"Nope. Closest I got to a beach was swimming in the Ohio

River, which is the opposite of clear water and sandy beaches. We had a lot of mud and who knows how many pesticides and chemicals. But we didn't know any better and it gets damn hot during the Indiana summer. A muddy river becomes rather tempting when it hits 100 degrees with 90% humidity."

"I can imagine. I've only been to the ocean once. My parents wanted a family vacation before I went off to college, so we drove to Florida. It was relaxing."

As they approached the buildings that made up summer camp, Phoenix tried to see them with different eyes. She imagined the colors as more vibrant, murals on the side of the black Quonset huts, the snow as sand, with palm trees dotting the landscape. It wasn't easy, even for her visual brain.

"I think I need to take a little extra time in New Zealand on the way home," Phoenix said. "I didn't have time on the way down and I want to see more of the world. Starting with an ocean."

"That's a great idea," Ash said. They were both quiet for a moment, the cold air and altitude making it more difficult to talk. Ash broke the silence. "I don't want to be presumptuous, but if we could coordinate it, would you like to explore New Zealand together?"

"Will you wear a bikini?" Phoenix replied suggestively. Ash nudged her with her elbow. "Whatever you wear, I'd love to explore with you. We can redo this date when it's warmer."

"Speaking of warmer, I'm ready for that sauna if you are."

ASH

After ditching all but their essential layers, they found the sauna with some residual steam but otherwise empty. While it reheated they stripped down to only underwear, ditching the shorts idea, and wrapped a towel around their breasts in case anyone else peeked in. Ash grabbed her water bottle and Phoenix poured some of her water over the hot stones, filling the room with steam.

Ash felt herself relax instantly, her body absorbing the humidity like a sponge. Phoenix extended her hand and pulled Ash to her, avoiding the window in the door. Phoenix met her lips gently, but the moment Ash parted her lips the kiss grew hungry. Ash wasn't sure if the heat coursing through her body was from Phoenix or the sauna. Whatever the cause, Ash realized quickly that her body was responding more and more to Phoenix's presence. Excitement grew in her belly, along with the desire to feel more of her. Before second guessing herself, Ash released her towel, letting it fall around her feet and reached for Phoenix's.

The moment their bodies came together, skin to skin almost

everywhere, was exquisite. Phoenix groaned deep in her throat. Ash pulled back to see Phoenix's hooded eyes and she worried she'd gone too far.

"I'm ok Ash," Phoenix said, her voice low, before kissing her on the side of her neck, sending goosebumps down her body. Ash angled her head to provide better access as Phoenix kissed down her chest and between her breasts. Ash's breath caught before remembering where they were.

"What if someone opens the door?" Ash whispered. Phoenix stood and rested her forehead on Ash's, her eyes closed.

"If I thought you'd be into it I'd have you up against that wall right now, that's how not worried I am."

Energy shot through Ash's body, taking her completely off guard. She'd never been so affected by her partner's desires, but there was something about Phoenix. If there was even a hint of resentment in her voice Ash would have recoiled, but there was nothing but honesty. And now Ash found herself in the confusing position of wanting Phoenix to do just what she'd said.

To her credit, Phoenix wasn't acting on her desires. Instead she walked to the bench, sitting sideways and gestured for Ash to sit between her legs and lie back. Ash's body vibrated, like it was so excited to be this close to Phoenix that every atom danced in joy.

But her body wasn't the only thing to consider. Was she emotionally ready for Phoenix to make love to her? Until that answer was a clear and resounding yes, she'd keep her body's reactions to herself. She didn't want to confuse Phoenix or make her feel that Ash didn't trust her. She just needed more time.

Phoenix wrapped her arms securely around Ash and rested her head on Ash's shoulder. Phoenix hummed in pleasure, the vibration a gentle tingle against Ash's neck. "This feels so good."

Ash leaned more heavily back, craving more contact even as her mind told her to slow down. "It so does." Ash closed her eyes, enjoying the silence filled only with their breathing. If she stayed still enough it almost felt like she and Phoenix were sharing the same body. She couldn't describe it any other way and she didn't want it to end.

But her body wasn't used to the heat in the room and, coupled with the heat inside her, she needed water which was across the room by the door. Ash groaned.

"This feels too good to get up, but I really want some water. Why hasn't anyone created teleportation yet?"

"Because you haven't invented it," Phoenix spoke against her skin, before placing light kisses along her neck, kisses that made her flush even hotter which wasn't exactly helpful. But when Phoenix flicked her tongue over Ash's pulse point, Ash's need for water was replaced by need for Phoenix. Ash turned into the kiss, capturing Phoenix's mouth with hers, forgetting about the water bottle as they kissed deeply. Phoenix's hands caressed her stomach, one drifting up to cup Ash's breast, her nipple hardening under her touch. Ash turned, draping her legs over Phoenix's thigh and felt Phoenix gasp as she brushed against her center unintentionally. Phoenix pulled her closer, wrapping an arm around Ash's bare legs, the sensation sending another thrill through her as they kissed again. Ash wrapped her arms around Phoenix's neck, her fingers playing with the short hairs, content to stay until she melted into a puddle on the floor.

Ash smiled against Phoenix's lips, realizing she was practically naked, in a sauna, and wrapped in Phoenix's arms. It was one more layer removed between them, literally and figuratively. Ash couldn't be more delighted with how these dates were turning out. They had fun, and after? Ash couldn't get enough of Phoenix's kisses. Or her body, which was far from thin but held so much strength. Ash knew logically that she didn't need protecting, but a primal part of her loved being wrapped in her arms.

The steam was slowly dissipating, their bodies covered in a sheen of sweat, and Ash felt her stomach getting a little queasy from the heat. She sat up, and after a quick kiss to Phoenix's forehead hopped off the bench to get their water bottles. Phoenix took hers gratefully and both drank deeply. Ash drank too quickly, spilling some of the cool water down her chest.

"Oh, come on, now you're just torturing me," Phoenix said in a low voice, without malice. Ash closed her bottle and set it aside.

"I am? Well, how can I make it up to you?" Ash asked flirtatiously.

Phoenix pulled Ash in by her hips and bent down, licking the errant water with her tongue. Ash forgot to breathe.

"You taste so good." Phoenix slipped her thumbs into the band of Ash's underwear, tickling the sensitive flesh and pulling Ash's attention back from the haze.

"I wish I could taste you everywhere," Phoenix said, her voice heavy.

Why was she putting it off again? It was hard to remember in the moment. "Phoenix..."

"Sorry, I got carried away."

Ash pulled Phoenix to her chest. "You have no idea how much I wish I could go there with you, but I can't. Not yet."

"Not yet, huh? Is there a timeframe on that?"

"Sorry, that's even harder to predict than the next neutrino strike." She felt Phoenix shudder with laughter against her and somehow it really was ok.

They'd spent enough time in the humidity, so after wiping down and getting dressed they meandered back to the TV lounge to find a movie, though Ash wasn't sure they'd watch the whole thing at this rate.

"What kind of movies do you like Phoenix?" Ash asked as she skimmed over the massive movie selection.

"Almost anything really. Horror and comedy are my favorites. What about you, are you all about sci-fi and comic book movies?"

Ash shot her a look. "Stereotype much? For your information, I like horror and comedies too. But tonight, I'm looking for something specific, with a beach theme."

"What about Beaches?" Phoenix offered, sounding unexpectedly serious.

"Isn't that the movie with Wind Beneath My Wings?"

"Bette Midler, yes. It's a classic," Phoenix added.

"If we watch that I'm afraid I'll have the song in my head for weeks. I have to say no." Ash returned to her searching, hoping if she occupied her mind enough the song wouldn't take root in her subconscious and run indefinitely. Finally, she found a movie that would fit and pulled it from the shelf.

"Have you seen 50 First Dates? It's got a beach and Drew Barrymore."

"Of course I have. What kind of lesbian would I be if I didn't have at least a small crush on Drew?"

"The kind that didn't have a crush on Drew Barrymore, you goofball."

They stopped by the popcorn maker and snagged drinks from the galley before returning to Ash's room. Luckily her laptop had a DVD player so they had complete privacy to cuddle to their heart's content.

Ash remembered enjoying the movie but hadn't watched it with someone she was dating before. She found her attention drifting. What if Phoenix lost her short-term memory? Their relationship took time to develop. They had so many misconceptions to overcome, would it even be possible to rebuild every day?

"What are you thinking about?" Phoenix asked, pulling her from her thoughts.

"Just the movie, and us, and whether we would even be possible in a situation like that. How do you restart every day?"

"Well, first off, this is a movie. A highly unrealistic movie." Phoenix lifted Ash's hand to her mouth for a kiss. "Why don't we do our best to avoid head injuries? Then we'll never have to worry about it."

"You're right. It's silly to think even about."

Phoenix turned Ash to face her, concerned. "Hey, what's really going on?"

"I guess I'm wondering if you'd have given me a second glance in any other situation. Would we even be friends?" Ash hated the insecurity in her voice. Why was she bringing this up now? They'd had a great night and she was bringing up irrelevant doubts. *Nothing more attractive than insecurity*, she thought sarcastically.

Phoenix didn't answer right away, apparently choosing just the right response. Ash's heart pounded, hoping she hadn't made a mistake.

"Have I done anything to make you feel like I wasn't happy in this relationship?"

"No, but it's not like there's a lot of competition here. What happens when we're back in the real world?"

"Ash, I'm not with you because you're my only option. We could have stayed friends, but that wasn't what I wanted. I want to be with you. Only you."

Ash's heart warmed, but her frustration remained. "I hate that this bothers me, that I can't just enjoy what we have without negativity sneaking in."

"You're human, and at least you talk about it rather than let it fester. Hell, I'm still waiting for you to wise up and dump my ass for someone better."

"The thought hasn't crossed my mind," Ash said adamantly.

"And you know why? Because you're the only person here who can't see how awesome you are."

Phoenix had the decency to look properly sheepish and didn't argue.

"Maybe we should both stop worrying?" Ash suggested.

"Maybe I can give us both something better to think about?" Phoenix leaned in and kissed her gently, easing her fears.

CHAPTER SIXTEEN

PHOENIX

At the Monday morning meeting, Kevin announced that R&R trips to McMurdo for those wintering over would start this coming weekend. Distracted by dating, Phoenix had forgotten all about the trips that had to take place before the summer crews left. While she looked forward to seeing more than just the endless expanse of white around her, the thought of going without Ash tempered her enthusiasm.

Their meeting ran longer than normal and Ash wasn't in her room when Phoenix raced to find her. Phoenix ran across the station to the science lab. Maybe if they asked today she and Ash could visit McMurdo together.

Phoenix burst into the lab not even trying to hide her urgency. Ash's head shot up, a concerned look on her face.

"What's going on Phoenix? Why are you out of breath?"

"Because I ran here from the galley and wanted to catch you as soon as possible." Phoenix took an extra breath before continuing. "I'm scheduled to fly to McMurdo next week and want you to come with me. Do you think you can work that out?"

Ash's eyes brightened and she stood. "I'll check with Jon, but I don't see why not." Ash glanced around the room, seemingly taking stock of the people around her, and took Phoenix's hand. "Let's go find him," Ash said quietly before leading Phoenix into the hall where she ambushed Phoenix with a kiss. Phoenix kissed her back, the excitement rising in her chest at the possibilities. A mini-vacation with Ash was just what she needed.

They broke apart at the sound of someone on the stairs nearby, the footsteps coming closer and conveniently revealing Jon.

"Just the person I needed to see," Ash said enthusiastically. When he acknowledged her she jumped right in. "Would it be possible for me to take my R&R trip to McMurdo with Phoenix next week?"

"Of course. I'm not going to spend the whole winter here with you, knowing I kept you from your girlfriend when there wasn't a good reason. Especially when said girlfriend cooks my food. What day are you scheduled for Phoenix?"

"Wednesday, if the weather cooperates," Phoenix said.

"That works, we still have plenty of people here. I'll put in the request now," Jon said as he turned and walked back towards the offices.

The grin taking over Phoenix's face couldn't be stopped. She cupped Ash's cheeks and gave her a quick, but heartfelt, kiss.

"Why are you at work already? Problems?"

"Yes, we'll probably be heading to the detector site in a bit. Can I walk you back to your room at least? Then I need to get back to the lab."

Phoenix nodded and wrapped an arm around Ash's waist.

"Anything special you want to do in McMurdo, Ash? Date 4?"

"I don't care as long as I can take a nice, long shower and spend my time with you," Ash said wistfully.

"We could do both at the same time," Phoenix suggested seductively. At Ash's less than enthusiastic facial expression, she amended her idea. "Or not. But I agree, showers. Every day. Maybe twice a day. Then I can lotion you up after?" Phoenix asked carefully.

"Now that sounds wonderful."

The next week was long. Firstly, because Phoenix had to go into work three hours early to help cover lunch, and secondly, because she couldn't wait to get on that plane and have zero responsibilities for three days.

With the extra hours taking over Phoenix's free time, she was glad Ash had brought up the option of Phoenix staying over anytime. It allowed them the freedom to hang out at night, watching movies and cuddling before they went to sleep. Or just talking, which was another thing she wasn't used to doing with women.

Thanks to these conversations, Phoenix learned about the vast world of fanfiction, the most realistic plans for colonizing Mars, and just how different college was from what she saw in movies. And Phoenix taught Ash about the joys of having an old, southern grandmother who was apt to store dead rabbits in the freezer next to the Popsicles, scaring the daylights out of unsuspecting kids.

Wednesday morning finally arrived. Their flight was scheduled for late morning, whenever the flight arriving from McMurdo was ready to leave again, so there wasn't much to do but wait and watch some episodes of the X-Files in the lounge. Two episodes later they were loading up into a decidedly not-first class C-130 military transport plane, with its mesh seats along the walls and cargo strapped down in the center and rear of the plane. Phoenix followed Ash to the far wall and took the seat next to her, each tucking their duffle bags under the seat.

"These are more comfortable than they look," Phoenix observed, feeling the mesh cradle her through the padding of her snow pants.

"Didn't you fly over in one of these?" Ash asked.

"No, I came over in one of those puddle jumper things. This feels sturdier, though there aren't many windows. Looks like I'll be standing most of the flight."

"I know, the view is the best part." Ash glanced to the front of the plane and excused herself, walking over to a young woman in a flight suit. Phoenix couldn't hear what she said, but at one point Ash gestured toward Phoenix and the woman smiled. Then she nodded and Ash walked back to Phoenix looking rather pleased with herself.

"What was that about?" Phoenix asked, beyond curious at this point.

"It's a surprise," Ash said coyly.

"I'm too nervous to handle a surprise right now. Just tell me," Phoenix pleaded. Ash shook her head and crossed her arms.

"Do I need to guess?" Phoenix asked mischievously.

Ash narrowed her eyes skeptically. "Yes, I'm rather curious as to what you think I was doing."

Phoenix smirked and simply replied, "Threesome."

Ash chortled. "Keep dreaming."

"Oh, I will. That's one dream I can get behind. I can even dream higher. Like a foursome."

Ash rolled her eyes and shifted her attention to a crew member standing at the front. As he ran through the safety brief Phoenix had to bite back a laugh. When he was done, Phoenix whispered in Ash's ear, "Do you think he expected to be a flight attendant when he joined the Air Force?"

Ash giggled and gave her a kiss on the cheek. "Put your earplugs in before they start the engines, you goofball."

Phoenix did, and in just a few minutes they were taxiing to the end of the runway, the skis bumping along the ice. After turning around, the engines grew much louder than Phoenix expected, yet they barely moved. Unease brewed in Phoenix's gut and she looked toward the flight crew strapped into seats at the front. Neither of them appeared worried, nor did Ash. Phoenix cupped her hands around her mouth and shouted into Ash's ear.

"Are we going too slow?"

Ash nodded, but still gave no sign of worry. She raised her hands to her mouth and Phoenix offered her ear.

"Just wait," Ash yelled, barely audible through the earplugs and engine noise.

Phoenix furrowed her brows but Ash didn't elaborate. Instead she placed her gloved hand on Phoenix's thigh and patted it, muted by the thick layers of fabric between them but effective all the same.

A new noise kicked in, accompanied by a jolt and sudden increase in speed. What the? Eyes wide, she looked at Ash who had a huge grin on her face. She shouted a word, but Phoenix couldn't hear her. Then she pantomimed, puffing out her cheeks and slowly moving her hand up from her leg, as if she was holding something Phoenix couldn't see. When Phoenix gave no indication of understanding Ash moved her imaginary object in an arc around Phoenix before setting it on Phoenix's leg. There had to be an easy answer, she just had to think like Ash. And then it hit her. Rockets. Were they seriously using rockets? The Air Force just became a lot cooler.

The rockets shut off once they were in the air and Phoenix wondered how long it would take her heart to settle down. She began running through the capitals discreetly, not wanting Ash to see her nerves. By the time they were given the all clear to get up she felt as calm as she would get. Ash tapped Phoenix's shoulder, pointing out the woman from earlier when she turned around. The woman gestured for them to follow as she walked to the front of the plane and through the door to the cockpit. Phoenix stopped at the door, but Ash kept walking up the couple of stairs to the cockpit level. On someone else, Phoenix would have been annoyed at the self-satisfied smirk on Ash's face, but Ash was too damn cute. Phoenix smiled in return and followed her in.

ASH

The look on Phoenix's face when Allison Schmidt, the only woman on the crew, explained that she could sit in the cockpit was priceless. But then Phoenix sat in the seat vacated by one of the pilots and Ash thought her heart might explode from joy at Phoenix's child-like glee, all awe and wonder and not an ounce of the cool, confident energy she associated with Phoenix.

The pilot encouraged Phoenix to sit and then take the joystick. "It's just like a video game," Phoenix observed.

"Yes, except you're now flying a real plane." Ash was too far back to hear Phoenix's reply, but she shook her head vehemently.

He let go in the universal, no hands, gesture. Phoenix's eyes widened briefly but she tightened her grip and stared out the window.

Ash walked behind Phoenix, resting her hands on Phoenix's shoulders as she peered out the window. The expanse of white ice and black mountain peaks was more impressive through the wraparound glass.

"I'll still be lightly holding the joystick, but if you want to steer us toward that peak over there, you can." He gestured to a peak slightly to their left with one hand while holding the controls with the other.

Phoenix raised both eyebrows at him. "Is that a good idea?" she asked skeptically.

"Just turn it smoothly and you'll be fine."

"You're not going to crash us Phoenix, just try it," Ash added encouragingly.

Phoenix adjusted the controls accordingly and the plane responded, dipping and banking to the left.

"Ummm, we're pointing down more than before..." Phoenix said nervously.

"That's ok, ease back on the joystick until I tell you to stop." Phoenix followed the pilot's instructions, and soon they were level again, pointed at the intended peak.

Phoenix took another deep breath. "Maybe Ash should try now. I think I've had enough flying for a lifetime."

"Good to know we've got job security," the pilot behind them said.

Phoenix stood gingerly, appearing to avoid touching any controls which was hard considering they were everywhere.

"Your turn, hotshot," Phoenix said with affection in her voice. "Future astronauts should know how to fly, shouldn't they?"

"I don't know about that, but I'm not passing this opportunity up."

Ash had played flight simulator games, but a computer monitor and keyboard were nothing compared to a real cockpit with real consequences. The implications were intimidating, though she understood flight mechanics enough to realize she couldn't do much to throw them off course, even without the other pilot.

"Why don't you steer us back to the right," the pilot suggested.

The feel of the plane banking under her hands was unlike

the simulator. She wasn't sure she'd ever felt so powerful, not since learning to drive. Ash pulled back on the stick to compensate for the drag while she turned.

"How's that?" she asked Phoenix with a grin.

"Showoff," Phoenix replied smugly, but then wrapped her arms around Ash from behind and kissed her cheek. "Are you planning a career change now? Forget all this science and fly planes?"

"Oh, I don't know. Maybe I'll learn after my PhD, fly as a hobby. It's kind of awesome."

"Speak for yourself. I'll stick to cars and paying people to fly me places."

Ash took another long look out the front before working her way out of the seat. They thanked the crew and walked back to the cabin.

"What did you think about your surprise?" Ash asked before Phoenix put her earplugs back in. "Did you have a little fun at least?"

"Yes, when I wasn't terrified of crashing the plane. I don't know how you convinced them to let us up there, but thank you. Though I applaud you. Clearly you're more adventurous than I am."

"When you understand the science, there's nothing to fear. Even if the engines died the plane would glide and give us a chance of survival. But I'm certain we couldn't turn off the engines accidentally, so we were perfectly safe."

Phoenix eyed her doubtfully but pulled one of the soft earplugs out of her pocket and began rolling it to fit in her ear. "Too bad fear isn't logical."

"You're right, it's not. I still get nervous during turbulence, but flying in smooth air? That's just fun." Ash worked her earplugs into her ears and pulled Phoenix back to the window. There was nothing like the view from a plane, and having Phoenix there with her? Well that made it even better.

CHAPTER SEVENTEEN

PHOENIX

When Phoenix first arrived in McMurdo, the town appeared tiny, but after three months at the South Pole, McMurdo felt like an oasis. Mountains, water, hell, even oxygen which was noticeably more available at sea level. Phoenix couldn't wait to take a shower and have some fun.

They set their bags on the floor of their shared room, which felt downright massive after the small rooms at the Pole. Unfortunately, the beds were the same size, but that was minor. They had room to move for once. Phoenix and Ash explored the bathroom. They shared it with the next room, but they wouldn't have to walk down the hall for the shower or toilet, a true luxury after communal bathrooms.

Before Phoenix could ask about showers and plans for the day Ash had her shirt off, making Phoenix laugh. "I take it there's no negotiation here?"

"I have more hair, I'm showering first," Ash replied while unbuttoning her jeans. "And then I'll be nice and dry by the time you're done, and you can cover me in lotion," she added teasingly as she gave Phoenix a nudge and disappeared into the bathroom.

Phoenix's stomach tightened, a jolt of electricity running through her body. Heat built between her thighs imagining Ashley, dripping wet from the shower, lying on the bed...

Phoenix jumped up, glancing around the room for a distraction. Any distraction. She brushed aside the heavy blackout curtains and looked out the window. If she leaned into the window at the very edge she could see a hint of mountain around the brown building opposite theirs. No view this time either.

Phoenix let the curtains close and studied the bed situation. They could always throw the mattresses on the floor, but that brought up some unpleasant memories, so Phoenix walked to the bed closest to the door and pushed it up against the one nearest the window. There was still a gap, so she shoved as hard as she could on the mattress and laid down. When everything felt alright, she wiggled around because, honestly, she hoped there'd be more than a little wiggling on the bed. Better to test it out first.

The mattresses weren't nearly as secure as she liked so she stood, set her feet in a solid stance, and pushed with all her strength, moving both beds against the far wall. *And Ash wasn't in here to see me flex my muscles. Damn.* She jumped on the bed again and this time the mattresses held their positions better. It would have to do.

Ash was still in the shower, so Phoenix walked to the closed entertainment center. She picked up the remote and turned on the TV to find an announcement channel. She flipped through the five stations, returning to the station showing the first Iron Man movie which never failed to amuse her. Before long Phoenix was engrossed in the action, until Ash's voice pulled her attention away.

"You've been busy," Ash said from the bathroom door clad only in a towel. Phoenix sat up, transfixed as Ash walked toward her.

"That coming off anytime soon?" Phoenix asked, reaching for the towel.

Ash slapped her hand away. "Shower first. Then we'll talk."

Phoenix ripped off her shirt as she jumped out of bed. "Just talking?" Phoenix asked, standing close enough to see the water dripping down Ash's neck, calling to her, the pull almost irresistible.

"I guess you'll find out when you're done."

Phoenix kissed her intensely but without otherwise touching Ash. "I love it when you tease me."

Ash cocked her head. "You do? Why?"

"Because you aren't trying to be an ass, and it makes me feel wanted." Phoenix answered easily as she walked to the bathroom, adding over her shoulder, "Don't overthink it, Ash, just keep doing it."

The only reason Phoenix left the shower before she was completely wrinkled was her curiosity over Ash's state of dress. *Don't get your hopes up Phoenix, we're following Ash's lead.*

She toweled off, feeling cleaner than she'd felt in months, knowing she'd miss it when they left. But for now, they were clean and free to do whatever they wanted.

ASH

The shower left Ash's body fully relaxed in ways only the sauna had. Her mind, however, had plenty to consider. First and foremost, what should she wear? She didn't have to ask Phoenix's preference, but Ash wasn't ready to be completely naked, even if it was the easiest way for Phoenix to spread the promised lotion over her. But she couldn't tempt Phoenix like that, even if she asked to be teased.

Ash dug into her bag and pulled out a pair of panties. Nothing fancy, but they were clean and added just enough of a barrier to make her comfortable. She slipped them on before turning off the TV and reclining in bed, enjoying the silence to think.

Phoenix had been great so far, but it would be easier if Ash could let go and allow Phoenix to touch her how she wanted. They could enjoy a few days of sightseeing, showering, and sex, and Phoenix would be over the moon. *If only I could be more receptive.* Maybe this trip would bring them together enough for Ash to feel comfortable with more reciprocation?

And that opened up other questions. Ash wasn't all that experienced to begin with, what would Phoenix expect from her? What if Phoenix grew bored even after Ash was ready to have sex? Phoenix was surely more experienced and used to variety.

Heaviness settled in Ash's gut as an even less pleasant question came to mind. How safe had Phoenix been prior to them becoming girlfriends? The risks weren't all that high, but still. Ash groaned. With the question raised, she wouldn't be able to forget. Would Phoenix be offended by her asking?

When Phoenix returned from her shower she wore her towel around her waist, her hair tousled and damp, showing zero discomfort displaying her body. Ash didn't feel quite as comfortable but did her best to appear so as she reclined on the bed in just her panties.

Unexpectedly, Phoenix didn't go straight to the bed, but to her bag, pulling out a pair of boxer briefs and putting them on before dropping her towel.

Illogically, Ash felt worse about asking what she needed to ask, seeing how considerate Phoenix was. The more time that passed, the harder this discussion would be to have, so she dove in.

"I need to ask you something, but I don't want you to feel like I'm judging you. So please believe me when I say I'm not, ok?"

Phoenix stood a foot away from the bed. "Ok..."

Ash fidgeted on the bed, now wishing she was more covered, but pushed through her discomfort.

"I know the risks aren't all that high, and we were all tested during our physicals, but I also know you've had sex with at least Skye since then. I don't want to know how many other people you've had sex with, but I do need to know how safe you were."

"Oh, is that all? You had me worried for a second."

Ash's unease left immediately. At least Phoenix wasn't offended by her question.

Phoenix unfocused her gaze before continuing. "I won't lie, I don't always do the right thing. But since my last test I've been responsible. As best I know, I'm clean. What about you?"

Ash laughed out loud, in part from the ridiculousness of her question, but also as a stress release. She'd worried for nothing. "I'm sure it won't surprise you to know that I haven't had sex since my physical, so I'm also in the clear."

"Does that mean you're thinking about sex? If so, I could throw enough clothes on to track down some free dental dams if you're worried."

Ash sighed, realizing she should have anticipated that question. "Sorry to get your hopes up. I'm... thinking about it. But attraction and desire are funny things. I want to be near you. To touch you. The way I feel with you is so different from anyone else. If I could flip a switch to be everything you want, I would."

"Please don't. Not even in this hypothetical scenario. Don't wish you were different. As long as you aren't holding back because of who I am?"

"I'm not. Unless you think my lying in bed almost naked is holding back?" Ash lightened her tone easily.

"You are? I didn't notice," Phoenix teased. "I'm glad we talked but I have an even more important question. Am I clean enough to touch you now?" Phoenix took a step toward the bed but stopped at Ash's response.

"Only if you bring lotion."

Phoenix grabbed the lotion and leapt onto the bed like a big kid. "Where should I start?"

"By kissing me." Ash sat up, meeting Phoenix's mouth in the middle of the bed. They kissed passionately, Ash easing back and bringing Phoenix with her, wanting to feel all of Phoenix's body on hers, so smooth and warm from the shower. As physically close as their bodies were, Ash felt the inexplicable urge to be closer still, pulling Phoenix against her. Not even when

Phoenix's hips began to move between her thighs did she release the pressure.

Ash slid her hand behind Phoenix's head, her fingers running through her hair and Phoenix moaned deep in her throat, before breaking the kiss. "Ash," she said, her voice low, "this feels too good. If you want me to stop, I need to do it now."

Ash gazed into her eyes, appreciating Phoenix's honesty and kindness even while she clearly wanted more. Ash ran a finger down Phoenix's ribs, causing her to gasp. "And if I help you out, like I did last week? Will it be enough to not touch me in return?"

Phoenix could barely hold her eyes open, the lids heavy with desire. "Yes, whatever you want."

Ash held Phoenix's gaze while she asked, "but what do *you* want Phoenix?" She almost missed the flash of uncertainty that crossed Phoenix's face. Did she not know, or was she not used to being asked?

"Do you think"—Phoenix hesitated, biting her lower lip—"maybe you could touch me? I don't need it," Phoenix added quickly, "I have a vivid imagination but..." her voice trailed off.

Ash continued tracing her finger down to Phoenix's hip and inside the waistband of her boxer briefs. "Then these are going to have to go."

Phoenix eased off of her, but Ash didn't release her grip on the band, sitting up with her. "Let me," Ash said as she pulled the boxer briefs down, brushing her fingers along the outside of Phoenix's thighs.

Ash looked up. Was that restraint etched on her face? But not just restraint, the corner of Phoenix's mouth curved up, enough to show Ash she was enjoying herself. Ash's concerns were quickly nullified when Phoenix kicked her underwear across the room and fell into her, meeting in the middle of the bed and resuming their passionate kissing, but now Ash had a goal – to make Phoenix feel as good as she possibly could while enjoying herself in the process.

Her hands roamed while she kissed over smooth skin and muscular arms, down her sides until finding Phoenix's breasts. Remembering how much Phoenix enjoyed Ash playing with her nipples, she rubbed them with her thumbs, squeezing and teasing them to peaks until Phoenix's breath became uneven.

Phoenix broke the kiss freeing Ash to taste her skin, leaving a trail of kisses from her collarbone to her small breast. Phoenix arched into Ash's mouth the second Ash sucked the nipple deep into her mouth. Tremoring, Phoenix bit her lower lip as Ash bit down lightly. Phoenix seemed so close already and she'd barely explored her beautiful, strong body.

Ash placed a hand on Phoenix's chest and guided her back on the bed, placing her knee right up against Phoenix's sex, already soaking wet.

"Looks like you're going to need another shower soon," Ash teased, leaning over Phoenix, her hair tickling Phoenix's skin.

Phoenix grinned even as her body began to move against Ash's thigh. "Maybe you'll join me this time."

Ash flicked the other nipple with her tongue. "I don't think that would help the situation."

"You won't hear me complain," Phoenix admitted.

Ash shifted her weight back, sliding her hands over Phoenix's stomach, feeling the muscles clench beneath her touch. And then down into the wild curls of Phoenix's center. Phoenix moaned and closed her eyes when Ash ran her fingers through her folds, up and down slowly, wanting to draw out Phoenix's pleasure as much as possible.

Phoenix's hips moved against Ash's hand, encouraging Ash to move lower to her entrance. "What do you want Phoenix?" Ash whispered low. A small shudder passed through Phoenix's body but she looked to be holding back.

Ash slowed her hand. "What was that?" Ash asked coyly. "I need an answer."

Something changed in Phoenix's eyes. She reached between them and pulled Ash's hand to her mouth, sucking two finger inside. Ash's eyes opened wide. After running her tongue along both fingers, Phoenix released them, pushing Ash's hand back down to her entrance. And then, without any hesitation, she said "I want you to fuck me until I come all over your hand."

Ash shivered, the rawness of Phoenix's desire, and her own desire to make that happen, shocking her. She met Phoenix's lips with renewed excitement while covering her fingers in Phoenix's juices. Phoenix arched against her hand, her body begging for more. Ash eased two fingers inside, a moan escaping Phoenix's throat as her inner muscles clenched. She waited for the pulsing to ease before moving, following Phoenix's rhythm, enjoying the ease at which they fell in sync.

Phoenix was mesmerizing beneath her. Ash suspected this was not a position her girlfriend allowed herself often. Open. Vulnerable. Ash's chest threatened to explode. This was a taste of the intimacy she'd missed in sex, and she'd found it in Phoenix, of all people. One in a million Phoenix.

Phoenix must have sensed the change because she opened her heavily lidded eyes. Her pleading voice was barely above a whisper. "Kiss me Ash."

She didn't hesitate, and the intensity with which Phoenix returned the kiss stole her breath. They moved faster, Phoenix urging Ash to push deeper until she'd driven Phoenix over the edge, muscles convulsing around her fingers as Phoenix's body spasmed beneath her. Ash slowed her thrusts, easing Phoenix down from her orgasm as she caught her own breath. In awe of their moment together, Ash placed tender kisses over Phoenix's heart before removing her hand and sliding alongside her.

CHAPTER EIGHTEEN

PHOENIX

What just happened? Phoenix loved sex, but she didn't lose control like that. Letting a woman touch her, penetrate her, wasn't something Phoenix normally craved or allowed. But with Ash she wanted... everything. Ash made her want more from her life, from herself... *Oh shit.* Phoenix drew a ragged breath as her heart rate shot up.

The familiar churning of anxiety filled her belly, bubbling into her chest. Her breathing grew shallow and fast as realization crashed around her. Ash hadn't just been inside her physically, she'd worked her way inside Phoenix's very being, past the walls she'd erected every time someone in her family broke her heart. But Ash'd snuck by every defense and Phoenix was powerless to stop her.

"Phoenix?"

Her name sounded like it came from far away, but it broke through enough to stop her train of thought. Now all she noticed was her heart racing, making her feel lightheaded.

"Phoenix, talk to me," Ash's concerned voice felt closer now, drawing her out of herself. Phoenix blinked, fighting her body to regain focus, but she couldn't catch her breath.

"Phoenix," Ash said pointedly, reaching for Phoenix's chin and turning it to face her. "Hey!"

Ash eyed her warily. *Oh God, what have I done?* Phoenix closed her eyes and her body flushed, wanting to hide but knowing she couldn't. Not without hurting both of them. She tried to slow her breathing, forcing her body to exhale fully. Ash brushed her fingers through Phoenix's hair, the gesture giving her something else to focus on, her heart slowing to a more reasonable rate. After several long moments she dared open her eyes.

"There you are," Ash said, so gently her voice was almost a caress.

"Sorry," Phoenix replied, trying to hide her embarrassment.

"You have nothing to apologize for. Do you want to talk about it?"

Phoenix shook her head. "I... just can't right now."

"Can't what?" Ash asked cautiously, no longer moving her hand.

"Can't talk about it. I don't have words for what just happened," Phoenix replied.

Ash nodded and resumed playing with Phoenix's hair. "That's ok. I think I understand."

"You do?"

"Well, not exactly. But this is as new for you as it is for me. That's bound to bring up unexpected emotions."

Phoenix turned away, unable to face Ash and find her words. "The things you do to me, make me feel... I don't recognize myself. How do you do this to me?"

Ash rubbed her arm gently. "I don't know. Just like I don't know what it is about you that lets me relax and enjoy giving you an orgasm."

That got her attention. Phoenix needed to see Ash's reaction, not just her words, so turned back to her. "Really? I mean, I know you wouldn't do it if you didn't want to, but you're having fun?"

The look on Ash's face made Phoenix's stomach clench. Equal parts playful, sultry, and wicked. "Oh, I am. When you let me in and show me how I affect you, I feel powerful. I've never felt like I truly had control in a relationship."

Phoenix knew power and control well. To give that feeling to Ash was an unexpected but welcome surprise. "And I've had plenty of power, but not trust."

Ash intertwined their fingers. "And without trust I can't relax enough to enjoy that power. Seems to me this—" she gestured between them, "—only works because of who we are together."

Silence fell, not heavy per se, but Phoenix felt the shift, not only in their relationship, but in her life. There was no going back to the life she'd left behind. But this new one was completely foreign to her and more than a little terrifying. Her heart sped up again, warning Phoenix away from her thoughts. She had to go at her own pace or she'd end up right back in a panic attack.

How could the same person calm her and give her a panic attack at the same time? She needed a distraction.

"Can I give you that massage now? I need to get out of my head."

Concern flickered across Ash's face, but she smiled through it. "Well, I'm not one to pass up a massage by my favorite person. If it helps you feel better, then that's a bonus."

Ash's attempt at levity helped. Phoenix knew how to do light; it was the intensity of the moment that threatened to push her over again. "I'm your favorite person, huh?"

"Let's see. You keep me well fed with the best food I've ever had. You amuse me with adorable pictures. And you're an amazing kisser. Only one question remains."

"And that is?"

"Are your hands as talented as your lips," Ash said coyly.

Phoenix laughed. Ash's unexpected response was exactly what she needed. "You bet your ass they are."

Ash lifted an eyebrow. "Prove it."

Gratitude filled Phoenix's chest and she kissed Ash deeply.

Ash broke the kiss with a chuckle. "I'm testing your hands. I already know what your mouth can do."

"That's what you think," Phoenix said, letting every bit of earned confidence show.

"I hear a lot of talking," Ash challenged, "but see no lotion."

Phoenix sat up and spotted the lotion on the floor, having fallen during their fun earlier. She leaned over the bed, retrieving it and holding it aloft, victorious, earning an indulgent smile from Ash.

"Roll over," Phoenix commanded seductively before realizing her tone probably had no effect on Ash. As long as Ash didn't mind, Phoenix saw no reason to change who she was.

As Ash got comfortable, moving her hair over her shoulder, Phoenix asked, "how do you want to feel when I'm done with you?"

"Like a pile of goo."

"Not a problem," Phoenix replied confidently. She'd made a lot of women into piles of goo, just not often like this. It would be a nice new challenge.

Phoenix straddled Ash's backside, placing a generous amount of lotion in her palm. She moved some into her other palm and spread it over Ash's back in long light strokes, simply enjoying the feel of Ash's skin beneath her hands. She felt Ash sigh and close her eyes. Phoenix continued the long strokes, applying more pressure now, working deeper into the muscles.

She hadn't had all that many massages in her life, they cost too much money, but she knew her muscle groups, especially those on the back thanks to years of boxing. Phoenix followed the muscle flow, working outward from Ash's spine, visualizing Ash's lats below her skin as if she were sketching her. She was careful to avoid the side of Ash's breasts, which would not have been the case if this was part of the evening's seduction. Phoenix gave each side equal attention, slowly working her way up until reaching the traps, noticing more tension in this area. Adding more lotion she worked slowly, carefully pressing deeper into the muscles until they relaxed, Ash's soft moan just barely audible in the quiet room.

Phoenix followed her lats up her neck, to the base of her skull, her thumbs moving up and into her hair, working from the top and back down her neck, the tension slowly releasing. Phoenix placed a light kiss on Ash's neck, taking in her scent mixed with shampoo.

"Mmm, that feels so good."

"But not goo yet," Phoenix observed, moving to her shoulders and down her left arm. There was a softness to Ash, in her body and personality now that Phoenix had earned her trust. In so many ways she was Phoenix's opposite. From the hardness in her arms built over years of training and physical work, to the walls slowly crumbling around her heart, Ash's differences were appreciated. Phoenix gave her upper arms a squeeze.

"All that manual labor these past weeks has given you some muscles. Pretty soon you'll be buff like me," Phoenix said teasingly. Ash smiled but didn't otherwise respond. That had to be a good sign.

She gave Ash's right arm extra attention, placing a kiss on Ash's palm after working her way down to it. It had worked hard making Phoenix feel so damn good, the least she could do was repay the favor.

With Ash's upper body thoroughly lotioned and relaxed, Phoenix rose up to reposition herself.

"Thank you," Ash said in a sleepy voice.

"You're welcome, but I'm not done yet. You are only half goo, or maybe a quarter goo? Either way, not remotely done yet." Ash opened her eyes. "No arguing, just close your eyes."

Ash did, and Phoenix added more lotion to her hands, sitting at the foot of the bed. While she previously kept her thoughts relatively chaste, that all went out the window working on Ash's legs.

She may have been the tiniest bit disappointed when she'd come out of the shower to find Ash wearing underwear, but now she was grateful for it. Rubbing lotion into Ash's calves and up her thighs was already turning her on enough. Ash laid bare before her would have been too much. The last thing she wanted to do was pressure Ash with her own desires, especially since this massage was about meeting Ash's needs.

Having reached Ash's panties, Phoenix leaned down, placing light kisses up Ash's spine. Talented hands and talented mouths should go together after all. By the time Phoenix kissed Ash's neck she seemed to hum under her touch.

"Now how do you feel?" Phoenix whispered into her ear. Now she did hum audibly, making Phoenix grin in pleasure. "If you roll over, I'll keep going."

"You just want to touch my boobs," Ash said lazily, yet surprisingly quick in her current state.

Phoenix laughed against her body, again surprised at Ash's response. "Damn right I do." Feeling Ash turn beneath her, Phoenix rose to her knees, offering enough room for Ash to turn.

"Come here," Ash commanded quietly, reaching for Phoenix's neck, pulling her down and meeting her with a slow, languorous kiss that lit Phoenix's whole body up, tingling from head to toe. She couldn't imagine how different Ash experienced pleasure, or even what she felt now.

"At the risk of totally screwing this up, I have to ask. Do you really not feel the need for me to remove these," Phoenix tugged gently at the waistband of Ash's panties, "And make you come?"

Ash gazed up at her apologetically. "No, I really don't. But I am so blissfully happy right now, I promise you. Everything you've done is perfect."

"Wow, ok. I'm not sure I'm ever going to truly understand, but I believe you."

"Are *you* happy?" Ash asked, brushing her hand along Phoenix's cheek. Before answering, Phoenix closed her eyes and leaned into Ash's touch, so gentle and caring it made her heart ache. She opened her eyes again, not allowing herself to go down the rabbit hole that minutes before caused her to panic.

"Before I met you, I couldn't imagine a simple massage being enough for my partner or myself. But it is. And really, when I think about it, the end result should be the same, a pile of goo." Phoenix flashed an impish grin. "Whether that comes from an orgasm or a massage doesn't matter in the end because everyone is happy."

"What do you think has changed?"

Phoenix considered Ash's questions, putting the pieces together. "You. You showed me that sex isn't the only way to connect to someone. Faced with that life changing perspective, I began to look at my past with new eyes.

"When I'm with a woman, my focus is on their needs. Whatever they are, I try to meet them. Over the years I've learned how to manage my own needs without relying on anyone else, since I rarely felt comfortable allowing my partners to touch me. It's really not much of a stretch to give you what you want."

Ash's expression was a mixture of awe and appreciation. "You really are a unicorn! How did I get so lucky?"

Lucky? That wasn't the word Phoenix would use. But they'd agreed to put worries about their worth aside, so Phoenix didn't complete her thought.

With no answer to Ash's rhetorical question, Phoenix laid

next to her, tucking her head into Ash's shoulder. If this was going to blow up at some point, and realistically it would, she wanted to remember this moment when everything was perfect.

ASH

The next morning, they awoke rested and ready to explore. At least, that's what Ash thought, until they arrived at their destination where a large metal pipe poked out of the ice by about a foot. The pipe allowed access below the surface of the ice to an observation area allowing a unique view of the water. It wasn't a long walk from their room, but if they stayed outside too long there was a warming hut nearby.

"Are you sure about this?" Phoenix asked, standing beside Ash as they both looked into the pipe. Ash had to admit, it was intimidating, especially since they couldn't see the bottom, but it had to be safe.

Ash turned to Phoenix, raising an eyebrow that she probably couldn't see through the dark sunglasses. "This was your idea Phoenix. Are you going to chicken out now?"

"Jimmy didn't say how small it would be," Phoenix replied defensively. "Or dark."

"What *did* he say about it?"

"Something about it being the only way to see under the ice, a once in a lifetime opportunity, indescribable, blah blah blah."

"Well I'm still going. You can stay up here if you want, but

I'm rather intrigued to discover what it looks like down there." Ash leaned over, stepping one leg onto one of the small metal loops that served as ladder rungs, admittedly a little nervous. The pipe seemed unnecessarily small, but she didn't come all this way to leave before checking it out. She took a few steps down, leaving only her head above the entrance and made another plea for Phoenix to join her.

"Are you going to follow me?" Phoenix looked even more nervous with Ash in the tube. "It's up to you, but I know I've never kissed someone while technically being under ice. Sure would be fun to check that off my bucket list." And with that, Ash stepped toward the unknown.

Hand over hand she descended into the darkness, the light above too bright to allow her eyes to adjust, but not at the right angle to illuminate her path. Her heart leapt into her chest when her foot met the rope ladder instead of the solid metal she was used to, but once she found her footing she was fine. Three steps later she was touching the floor of the observation room, a slightly larger hexagonal space consisting primarily of windows.

Ash pocketed her sunglasses, taking in the yellowish-green light shining through the ice above, a color she was certain she'd never seen before. *Wow, indescribable is right.* The water continued only about ten feet below the ice which was bumpy instead of smooth, similar to the bottom of clouds. Occasionally shafts of ice cut down into the water like an icicle, or stalactite. That was something she'd have to ask about. Thousands of tiny fish, not even an inch long, swam everywhere. There was so much, yet so little, to take in, not unlike the rest of Antarctica.

"Phoenix, you have to see this. It's unreal."

"Is it any bigger at the bottom?" she asked, peeking her head into the tube.

"Yes," Ash said, adding the word *technically* to herself. "You don't need to stay long and I'll distract you."

"Will you take your shirt off?"

Ash shook her head. "Are boobs the only way to distract you?"

"No, but it's effective."

"Just get down here."

Ash watched as Phoenix took her first tentative steps into the metal pipe. With the sun behind her Phoenix was merely a shaky black figure. While Ash couldn't see her face, it was clear Phoenix wasn't comfortable. She stopped once her whole body was below the opening, her fast breathing the only sound in the quiet chamber.

"I take it back," Phoenix said shakily. "You'd better be naked when I get down there."

Ash chuckled to herself. "Are you a fifteen-year-old boy now?"

"Babe, I've always been a fifteen-year-old boy, but I usually hide it better."

Nothing about that made sense to Ash, but it didn't need to. At least she now knew how easy it was to motivate Phoenix, which was useful information. But she wasn't about to take her shirt off in the cold pod. She could, however, remove her parka, which she did, resting it along the wall to make more space for the two of them.

"What if you come down here and I distract you with my clothes on, but wear as little as possible once we're back in the room?"

Phoenix made a show of considering the offer, humming and hawing, until she agreed. Ash was about to make an argument about being a badass, but Phoenix continued her descent and Ash wasn't sure whether she'd be triggering a land mine for Phoenix if she said any more. Considering how rarely she'd seen Phoenix flustered, now wasn't the time. Ash gentled her approach.

"There's a rope ladder that you're about to reach. I'm going to grab your leg and guide you so the transition doesn't freak you out."

As Ash helped Phoenix onto the last steps, she heard Phoenix mumble, "I'm going to kill Jimmy for this," but Ash let it go unquestioned. Fears were illogical, and everyone's fear seemed like an overreaction to someone not experiencing it.

"Last step," Ash said, wrapping her arm around Phoenix's waist under her parka.

"I thought you said it was bigger," Phoenix said, tension in her voice as she looked around the space not much larger than the two of them.

"It is, technically. And with the windows it feels bigger than it looks."

Phoenix shot Ash a doubtful look, biting her lip and shaking her head. "Now is not the time for pulling the Obi-Wan card."

"Cole was right, you are a Star Wars nerd!" Ash exclaimed victoriously.

"Only from a certain point of view."

"You are not helping your case." Ash placed a kiss on her cheek, earning her a smile but Phoenix's body was still tightly wound.

The space wasn't heated, but it was small enough for their body heat to warm it quickly, especially after the walk down from town. "The pod will feel larger without your parka on." Phoenix continued to eye her skeptically but wriggled out of her coat with Ash's assistance. Ash took Phoenix in her arms, resting her head on Phoenix's chest. Phoenix's heart continued pounding.

"Just breathe with me and watch the fish swim by."

Ash exaggerated her breathing, lengthening it to help Phoenix slow hers while at the same time rubbing the small of Phoenix's back with her palm. Phoenix fidgeted with the unzipped zipper pull on her fleece. Ash pointed out how close they were not only to the surface, but to the bottom. It wasn't much deeper than a swimming pool. Besides, everything was engineered by the best and brightest Antarctica had to offer. Ash didn't know if that was true, but Phoenix relaxed a little as they stood there watching the tiny fish.

Phoenix tensed again at a strange, high-pitched whistle. "What was that?" she asked carefully.

"I'm not sure, but I doubt the sound belongs to anything dangerous. I doubt anything is capable of damaging these windows."

"I'm not nearly as worried about the animals as I am that the walls are going to collapse and crush me. Or someone will lock us in and we'll run out of air. Or even worse, we'll run out of air without realizing it, and by the time we do we'll be too weak to climb back out. We'll die here without even being trapped." Phoenix turned in Ash's arms to check their escape route.

Ash didn't restrain her but kept ahold of her hand, speaking before Phoenix bolted up the ladder. "We have plenty of air. But I did promise to distract you, so don't run off yet."

That got Phoenix's attention and she turned back to Ash. Their time was short, so Ash didn't waste any more time talking. She moved as close as she could to Phoenix, leaned up and kissed her slowly. Phoenix didn't respond as readily, but a little coaxing with her tongue and Ash felt Phoenix melt into her, fully committed to this one kiss.

When the cold wall pressed against Ash's back she didn't break the kiss, leaving that for Phoenix to decide. The contrast between Phoenix's heat and the cold wall was striking, adding an even more surreal element to this moment below the ice. When they did break apart, Phoenix seemed more herself, though not completely at ease.

"Better?" Ash asked and Phoenix nodded. "Good because this wall is damn cold. Warm me up." Ash pressed her back to Phoenix's front, leaning into her as Phoenix wrapped her arms tight, burying her face in Ash's neck. She wasn't sure how long

Phoenix would tolerate the enclosed space, but Ash hoped her distraction bought her another minute.

As she watched the water Ash saw a shadow, perhaps just a trick of the light, but it grew larger, taking on a form until —"Look Phoenix, seals!"

Phoenix's head shot up and they watched together as a mother and her baby swam right in front of them, the baby tight to its mother's side. They were silent, transfixed as the seals looked back at them inquisitively. How strange it must look from the outside, two humans trapped in a cage while they swam freely. After another minute they swam away, leaving Ash stunned.

"Wow, that was amazing," Phoenix whispered, "but can we go back up now? I've risked death long enough and would like my reward." Phoenix kissed the side of Ash's neck suggestively.

"Isn't it a little early to turn in for the day?" Ash asked.

"Fine, then I want a drink as my reward," Phoenix whined playfully as she put her coat on to return to the surface much more quickly than she descended.

Ash wiggled into her coat and donned her sunglasses before heading up herself. She found Phoenix bouncing around, looking a little silly.

"You alright?" Ash asked, interrupting Phoenix's movements.

"Just enjoying all this space and air. There's so much of both."

"Yes, there is. So why didn't you tell me you were claustrophobic?"

Phoenix looked into the distance, less bouncy now but rocking on her feet. "You really wanted to go, and I didn't want to disappoint you."

"I don't want you to make yourself this anxious though. I didn't know it would bother you."

Phoenix shrugged her off. "Yeah, well, I was pretty sure I could stay distracted enough. And it was my idea. We only get a few chances to do something new while we're here. I pushed through it and it was fine."

Phoenix turned and slowly started up the path back to town. "Besides, it's not like you're the first woman I've done something questionable for."

Ash wasn't sure where to go with that information. For all of Phoenix's outward confidence, there appeared to be this underlying insecurity that Ash couldn't understand. "For example?"

"Besides flying a plane and crawling down a pipe?" Phoenix offered lightly, but Ash's heart sank, along with her expression. "Umm... I jumped off a tree into the Ohio River once. I don't even remember why. Actually, I probably did that twice. And I jumped off a garage onto a trampoline. I don't recommend that."

Ash shook her head. "But why?"

Phoenix shrugged. "A pretty girl dared me? Sometimes I'm just a teenage boy with testosterone poisoning."

"But you're not 15. You're an adult, and I'd rather you tell me that you don't want to do something instead of pushing through it. What if you'd had a full blown panic attack down there?" Ash wasn't sure where her intensity came from, but she desperately wanted Phoenix to understand. She continued, hoping Phoenix would listen to her perspective.

"My needs aren't more important than yours. Not physically, and not when it comes to what we do with our free time. I love that you're so considerate of my feelings, but you have feelings too. And I want to hear them. I want to know where your boundaries are. When you need me to back off, and when you need to make new choices. I don't want you to go along with whatever I say."

Phoenix scowled at the ground as they walked in silence. Ash had nothing else to say, so left her to her thoughts. Before reaching their building Phoenix stopped outside a bar.

"Now I need two drinks," Phoenix said testily.

ASH

Ash kept her feelings to herself but didn't like Phoenix's tone or demeanor. But Ash had pushed her to this point and didn't know how to undo her words. All she wanted was for Phoenix to value herself in this relationship. Instead she'd apparently blown up a land mine she hadn't seen, and she didn't like what she was seeing in the fallout.

CHAPTER NINETEEN

PHOENIX

*P*hoenix didn't look back but she heard Ash follow her into the bar. She ordered a double shot of Jameson before turning to Ash.

"Do you want anything?" Phoenix's voice remained clipped at the judgment she saw in Ash's eyes as she asked for a glass of water. Phoenix wasn't exactly pleased with herself, but Ash really hit a nerve out there. And after putting herself in a damn pipe under the ground, just to be scolded after, she needed something to calm her nerves.

The liquid burned slightly as she downed it in one go. She ordered another double and took it to an empty table. Her head had been so loud since Ash had called her on her shit. Phoenix knew her need to please women, even on her own terms, wasn't always healthy. But it wasn't that big of a deal either. She wasn't being hurt by it, just stressed like in the pipe. So why did Ash care? She got to do what she wanted. It was fun enough. Why make it complicated?

Phoenix sipped on the whiskey, actually tasting it this time. She didn't normally drink to get drunk, as it reminded of her of her parents, but instead treated alcohol like any other food. She enjoyed the complexity of whiskey, and now that the first two shots were working their magic she could savor her drink. Ash's shoulders relaxed a touch. She must have worried Phoenix was going to slam that one as well.

The door opened and a man entered holding a guitar case. He walked to the stage and began setting up. This could be a welcome distraction.

Phoenix turned to Ash. "Do you want to stay and listen?"

"Sure," Ash answered tersely.

Phoenix was aware that she was likely pissing Ash off, but she didn't want to talk so continued sipping her whiskey while her mind ran.

This was why relationships sucked. Someone else got to decide who you should be, and what you should do. But Phoenix was fine, wasn't she? The whiskey didn't argue. And if she kept her mouth shut Ash might not either.

Ash got up, walking to the bar to retrieve pretzels and potato chips, just in time for the man on stage to begin his sound check. They listened and snacked, still not speaking and Phoenix gave a silent thanks that at least Ash wasn't pushing her to talk. Phoenix could even feel herself relaxing after a couple of songs. Maybe today was salvageable.

In between songs a familiar figure sat next to Phoenix. "Hey stranger, welcome back."

Phoenix brightened. "Sierra! I didn't know if I'd run into you again."

"You're in my favorite hangout so it was bound to happen. What are you drinking?"

"Jameson, but I'm good."

"Nonsense. Let me buy you a drink. What about your friend?"

"No thanks, I'll stick with water," Ash said coolly. Sierra nodded and turned toward the bar.

Phoenix ignored the tone, even when Ash directed it at her. "Who's Sierra?"

"Just a woman I met on the way through," Phoenix answered dismissively, finishing the drink she'd been nursing.

Sierra set a shot glass in front of Phoenix and a glass of water in front of Ash who gave her a questioning glance before taking a drink. "Thanks," Ash offered a little warmer than before.

"I'm Sierra."

"Ashley."

Phoenix watched in curiosity. She had almost forgotten that Ash didn't normally introduce herself as Ash.

"I haven't seen you around before. Are you on R&R as well?"

"Yep, one last taste of civilization until October."

Sierra shook her head. "I don't know how you do it. This place gets old fast. I can't imagine being stuck at the Pole for a year."

Phoenix answered suggestively, "We find ways to occupy ourselves."

Sierra opened her eyes slightly wider in recognition. "I'll bet you do. If I was sticking around for the winter, I'd be sure to find myself an ice wife too. Makes life more interesting and less lonely."

Phoenix didn't miss the tension returning to Ash's shoulders. Or her face. Shit. Looked like the day was getting more complicated by the second. Phoenix had to minimize the damage quickly.

"It's not like that. This happened without us trying and we're seeing where it goes, right Ash?"

Ash met her eyes and softened slightly, unless that was wishful thinking. But she agreed, and they were saved by the man on stage starting a new song. They listened politely and Sierra picked up on the conversation when he was done.

"How long are you here?"

Phoenix answered, "Tomorrow is our last day."

"So soon," Sierra replied a little disappointed. "Well, do you want to hang out tonight? We had a lot of fun last time you were here."

"That we did." Ash shot Phoenix an incredulous look. Clearly that was the wrong response. "I'm afraid we'll have to pass. I think we need some alone time tonight."

"Understood." Sierra focused her attention on Ash. "You're a lucky woman."

Ash blushed lightly, mumbled a less than enthusiastic agreement, and excused herself to the bathroom.

Phoenix probably would have worried more if she hadn't been on her fifth shot, but she had enough awareness left to realize this situation wasn't getting any better and no amount of alcohol would help now.

"Everything ok, Phoenix? Did I say something wrong?"

"No, I'm sure this is my fault somehow. Thanks for the drink, I'd better go fix this." Phoenix downed the rest of her drink and went to find Ash.

ASH

Ash heard the door and was only mildly surprised to see Phoenix. She wasn't sure what to expect from her at this point. Nor did she truly understand why she was reacting the way she was. Was this simple jealousy? It didn't feel that way, but everything was confusing and frustrating today.

Phoenix left a few feet between them and asked, "Are you going to tell me why you're so angry with me, or am I supposed to guess?"

Ash sighed. "I'm not angry, I'm frustrated. And, maybe also a little disappointed."

"Awesome," Phoenix replied without enthusiasm. "I'm used to disappointing people, so welcome to the club."

Ash tensed her fists, the frustration rising to a peak. "Dammit Phoenix, that's what I'm frustrated about. Just stop putting yourself down for five minutes, please?"

Phoenix turned away and Ash realized they couldn't have this discussion in the bathroom of a bar where anyone could walk in.

Ash stepped to Phoenix and grabbed her arm. "Come on, get

your coat. We need to talk somewhere with less chance of interruption."

Phoenix allowed herself to be dragged back to their table where she gave Sierra a quick goodbye, grabbed their coats, and headed outside. Finding her bearings, Phoenix turned toward the water and Ash went with it. Maybe she could get through to her better if they weren't in a constricted space. Phoenix finally stopped where small waves lapped against the shore. When Phoenix didn't speak Ash took a calming breath before raising the topic again.

"Why did you shut down on me back on the ice?"

"You mean when you scolded me like a child?"

"I didn't—" but at Phoenix's glare she stopped. Thinking back, she could see how Phoenix would feel that way. "I'm sorry, that wasn't my intention. I got intense without realizing you could interpret my words differently."

Phoenix stepped forward and sat at the edge of the water. At least she didn't run away. That was progress, right? Ash sat near Phoenix, leaving space but able to touch her, wondering if she could diffuse this situation.

"Ok, I'm going to try again."

Phoenix remained gazing over the water, so Ash took that as permission and dove in.

"I care about you Phoenix. More than I think you know. And I think you care about me too." Ash knew she was fishing for a reaction, but she didn't know how else to draw Phoenix out of her shell.

"Of course I do," Phoenix interjected sourly. Not the most romantic declaration but Ash would take it.

"Good. For the past two months I've heard you casually put yourself down. And today, when I realized what you put yourself through just to avoid disappointing me, it clicked. The two behaviors have the same root. And whatever caused it, that connection equates to how little you value yourself."

Phoenix deflated and Ash's heart broke for her.

"I wanted you to see yourself how I see you, but I handled it all wrong. I'm sorry for that."

After several long moments Phoenix said quietly, "you only see a small part of me."

"I see more than you realize. That's why I was so frustrated tonight. After you shut down your solution was alcohol, and not just a single drink. I'm not a prude but something changed. You weren't yourself."

Phoenix turned, her eyes flashing. "See, that's the thing. That's often exactly who I am. You just don't realize because you've only seen carefree Phoenix."

"Do you normally respond to stress with alcohol?" Ash asked cautiously, trying to keep the judgment out of her voice.

"No, I prefer sex to alcohol if you really want to know," Phoenix replied bitterly. "But given the situation I decided alcohol was the better solution."

Ash recoiled. What could she do with that information? Sierra flashed in her mind. If she hadn't followed Phoenix into the bar, what would have happened? *Don't go down that path, Ash. You know it won't help.*

Unspoken thoughts filled the air between them. The wind and gentle waves offering solace as each struggled with their emotions.

After several minutes, Ash spoke. "We're really two different people, aren't we?"

"Too different?" Phoenix asked genuinely.

"God, I hope not."

"Yeah," Phoenix replied softly.

Silence fell again, the tension as fragile as an ice shelf strained almost to the point of cracking.

"Phoenix, I stepped on a land mine and I still don't know what it was and that's a problem. Can you help me out here? Give me something to work with?"

Phoenix's eyes flicked down, her only acknowledgment until she spoke.

"I haven't been a kid for a damn long time. I'm not talking about my teen years either. I grew up way too young. But you know what never failed to set me off? That one day a year my mom or dad would decide to be a parent and treat me like a child. Like they forgot for a moment I hadn't been taking care of myself or them all that time. They had no clue. They were just playing the role of parent for a minute until getting drunk again."

Phoenix picked up a black pebble, turned it in her fingers, and threw it into the water.

"At risk of saying something completely wrong, don't you worry about using alcohol to cope?"

"I know my limits Ash," Phoenix replied tiredly. "I may not make the choices you would necessarily make for yourself but that doesn't make me a child."

"You're right, I'm sorry. I'm trying to understand but there is so much I don't know about you. I want to know all of you though," Ash added hopefully.

Phoenix gave Ash a tentative look. "It isn't all sunshine and rainbows. There's also an awful lot of thunderstorms and tornadoes in my life, and not just in my past."

"We can't control the weather, but maybe we can move someplace less storm prone?"

Something shifted in Phoenix's eyes. "That's why I'm here, in Antarctica I mean. I just hadn't put it in those terms."

Ash reached for Phoenix's hand, palm up, offering but not forcing the touch. Phoenix took it, intertwining their fingers and wrapping her other hand around their clasped hands. Relief flooded through Ash. The ice between them was finally melting.

"Do you trust me?" Phoenix asked evenly, pulling Ash from her moment with a kick to her gut.

"What? Why do you ask?"

"Because you make it sound like I'm not capable of making my own choices about what I do or how I cope with life. But I know what I'm doing... mostly. And if I agree to go down a scary death trap of a pipe, it's because I weighed my options and decided it was worth it. Can you trust I put thought into a decision?"

"That's fair. But what convinced you to overcome your fear of the pipe?"

Phoenix gave her a look that said her question was ridiculous. "You did. Admittedly I might have done it for any pretty girl, but I actually trust you and could set aside the worst of my anxiety because I knew you were there waiting for me."

Ash's heart melted into a puddle in her chest. She scooted over, closing the distance between them and kissed Phoenix on the cheek. "Would you be willing to tell me when a situation makes you uncomfortable? There might be a solution that we hadn't thought of that makes it better for both of us."

Phoenix furrowed her brow and then replied sheepishly. "I don't want you to think I'm a wuss."

"It takes courage to advocate for your own needs. Far more than pretending something doesn't bother you. I will never think you're a wuss." Ash smirked up at her. "Unless you're afraid of spiders. Do you scream like a baby when you find a spider, Phoenix?"

Phoenix recoiled in mock horror. "Now you know my deepest, darkest secret. How could you ever be with me?"

Ash laughed against Phoenix's side. "Don't worry, I'll protect you and relocate all non-poisonous spiders outside for you."

Phoenix wrapped an arm tight around Ash's shoulders, warming her all the way through.

CHAPTER TWENTY

PHOENIX

One-night stands might be easier in theory, but looking down at Ash wrapped in her arms, Phoenix wouldn't trade her for a thousand women. She'd have to keep working on this talking through issues thing.

After yesterday's derailment, they spent the rest of the day enjoying each other's company and doing absolutely nothing adventurous. Today would be their last day in McMurdo and Phoenix was determined to spend as much of it in the open air as possible. No more confined spaces, indoors or out.

Phoenix turned the TV on to check the weather. The forecast looked promising, sunny with a high of 30 degrees Fahrenheit. A perfect day for a hike.

Ash nuzzled into Phoenix, though she wasn't sure they could be any closer. Maybe she read too much into the movement, but it felt good to be wanted. Phoenix was used to women desiring her. But they didn't value her for anything but her skills in the bedroom, or wherever they happened to be.

But Ash? She valued everything about Phoenix. In many cases Phoenix would argue Ash overvalued her, but she was trying to silence those thoughts. There was no need to revisit yesterday's argument. No one besides her grandma and Aunt Diane had ever made Phoenix feel like she mattered for anything beyond what she did for them. Did Ash know how much that meant to her? *How could she, you haven't told her, dumbass.* Phoenix scowled at herself. The voice in her head was right but she didn't need to be a dick about it.

Looking at Ash again, Phoenix wished she could just tell her everything already, her past, her fears, her hopes, her feelings. But then, what would happen if things went wrong? Last night was hard enough, she wasn't sure she could survive her heart breaking so thoroughly from the inside out. Most days her heart felt like it was hanging together by a thread. Most days before Ash that was. Now... she was afraid to look and risk everything unraveling.

Phoenix kissed the top of Ash's head, looking for an escape from her thoughts. She lightly ran her fingers along Ash's back until she stirred.

"If you keep doing that we'll never get out of bed," Ash said sleepily.

"Would that be so bad?"

"If this wasn't our last day of civilization, I'd be all for it."

"You and your sound logic," Phoenix said, punctuating her point with a quick forehead kiss. "How does some hiking sound? Maybe we will find some penguins."

"Sounds perfect."

After showers, because seriously, why wouldn't they take as many showers as possible while they could, they walked hand in hand to the galley. Phoenix slowed as she recognized Sierra heading their way. Ash paused, but then walked straight for her, surprising Sierra and Phoenix alike.

"Hey Sierra, I want to apologize for last night. I was rude and hope I didn't ruin your night."

Stunned, Sierra took a while before replying. "Thanks. I probably owe you an apology as well. I shouldn't throw terms like ice wife around. It doesn't look like I did too much damage though." Sierra glanced at their joined hands.

Phoenix smiled at Ash, adding, "We worked it out."

"I bet you did. Sorry I missed it," Sierra said before catching herself. "Anyway, I need to get to work. Have fun."

Phoenix gave her a small wave before turning and staring at Ash in awe.

Ash tilted her head and asked, "Why are you looking at me like that?"

"Why did you apologize to Sierra?"

"Because it was the right thing to do. It was unfair to treat her poorly when I was struggling with things that had nothing to do with her. Clearing the air was the right thing to do."

Her answer did nothing to clear up Phoenix's confusion. "But people treat other people unfairly every day and never apologize for it."

"Exactly. Wouldn't it be a nicer world if people apologized for their poor behavior?"

"Well, yes, but..."

"I realized a few years ago that there was little I could do to make the world kinder, not on a large scale. But this was one thing I could do. I could apologize when I did wrong, even if it didn't seem like a big deal to anyone else. And maybe that would inspire others to do the same. And bit by bit the world would be a nicer place." Ash gave a small shrug and Phoenix shook her head.

"Do you have any idea how amazing you are?" Phoenix asked sincerely.

"Isn't it sad that something as simple as apologizing makes someone stand out?"

Phoenix pulled her in for a hug. "Yes, it is, but you're still amazing to me."

ASH

The walk to Hut Point was fairly flat and about a quarter of a mile away. Hut Point was a historic site hosting the Discovery Hut from Robert Scott's expedition in 1902 and a common destination for visitors.

The square wooden building was undergoing preservation after over 100 years of harsh Antarctic weather, but it was still a unique site. Inside, everything was weathered, from the wood which was almost black, to the metal provision cans slowly rusting. Phoenix did some quick sketches, but nothing in detail because the small windows didn't allow much light in.

They regrouped outside, walking to where the ground sloped steeply to the ice below. It was so starkly beautiful, the white ice and the black volcanic rock, with the only natural color coming from the blue sky above. Phoenix nudged her arm and pointed below them.

"Penguins! How cool is that?" Ash asked, beaming. And then she laughed. "I just realized that everything here is some variation on black or white. Even the penguins!"

"It is, isn't it? Do you mind if I sit and sketch for a while?"

"Of course not. That's why we brought our notebooks."

ASH

The rocks weren't the most comfortable, but their snow pants provided some padding. Ash pulled out her notebook and started going over the events of the trip, not only for her documentation, but to try to find the core of a storyline for their comic.

Looking at everything that'd happened so far, though, she wondered if anyone would even believe them. It sounded too good to be true. In so many ways, Phoenix was a unicorn, this mythical creature that took Ash's asexuality in stride. But if they presented Al as a unicorn in the comic, would readers discount the possibility for their happy ending?

That seemed like a good place to start. Phoenix was happily sketching penguins so Ash dove into her idea.

Paige: Al is like a unicorn. She's got red hair and a horn. Wait, that's not right. She does have some pretty awesome red hair, but it's short. And she doesn't have a horn.

Al: Well...

Paige: No smartass comments when I'm complimenting you! What she does have is a true acceptance of my asexuality. For a lot of aces, acceptance is so rare it might as well be mythical, like a unicorn. But, what if people like Al are less unicorns and more like albino horses. Rare, but very much real.

Al: Oh! I see where you are going. Why search for a unicorn when they don't exist?

Paige: Exactly. And if there's one thing I want my fellow aces to get from our story, it's that there are more people who are willing to understand us than we think. They may be rare, but if we don't recognize the possibility of a romantic relationship filled with love and happiness, it becomes more difficult to find.

Al: Wait, I didn't think that kind of relationship was realistically possible until I met you, and I'm not ace.

Paige: The second thing I want to share is that I constantly make assumptions about Al and her allosexuality that get me into trouble. That's why this comic isn't an Asexuality 101 comic. It's the two of us, sharing our story, which includes learning about each other's lives. And maybe we'll help a few people along the way.

Ash looked up and caught Phoenix smiling at her.

"You look pleased with yourself. What did you write?"

Ash handed over the notebook. "Maybe an opening for the comic, after character introductions. Let me know what you think."

Phoenix began reading it but met Ash's gaze within seconds. "Do you know how badly I want to make a horny joke right now?"

Ash laughed. "Yes, I do. But if I write that in, we'll inadvertently turn people off."

"You have a point," Phoenix said before returning to her reading. "This is an interesting approach. I'll have to play with it a bit to break the dialogue into panels, but I'm sure I can work it out."

"I forgot about that. It's going to take some adjustment to be less wordy."

"We have all winter."

Ash scooted closer to Phoenix, leaning into her as she took in the scene before them. "I'm really glad we got to do this trip together. Thanks for inviting me."

"This trip was infinitely better because you were with me. But, can we make a deal? No more surprise trips to the cockpit. I think I've had enough life endangering excitement this week."

"Absolutely," Ash replied, pleased that Phoenix was expressing her needs. Their fight may have sucked, but it was already proving beneficial.

CHAPTER TWENTY-ONE

PHOENIX

*B*ack at the Pole, they slipped into their normal routine easily, but with some subtle differences. They spent more time outside, going for walks or using the climbing wall. And they gave up completely on having two rooms.

Phoenix felt more comfortable in Ash's room, perhaps because she decorated her space to feel more lived in. Or maybe it was a leftover of her old life where she didn't bring anyone home if she could avoid it. Either way, Ash's room was now solidly their room. Phoenix tucked her toiletries and some clothes in a drawer which she refreshed every couple of days. It was cozy and more domestic than she'd ever experienced.

They'd been back about a week when Phoenix was interrupted at the end of her workday by Jimmy.

"Hey Phoenix, you've got a phone call in Comms."

Confused, Phoenix asked who it was as she washed her hands. When Jimmy couldn't answer, her mind began to race through options. Diane said she'd be the only one to call, and she'd only call if it was an emergency. What could have happened now, when she was finally happy? Her heart pounded as she rushed down the hall, praying it was a misunderstanding.

She slowed at the door to Comms. "Umm, Jimmy said I have a phone call."

Shawn waved her over to a chair next to the phone. "He said it was an emergency but try to keep it short."

He? Was Diane ok? She tried to keep her voice even as she answered the phone. "This is Phoenix."

There was a slight delay from the satellite, and the audio wasn't the best quality, but she knew the voice immediately.

"Hi kiddo."

Phoenix clenched her jaw, caught so off guard she couldn't respond.

"Are you there?"

"What's wrong, Dad. Is something wrong with Diane?"

"Not that I know of. Why?"

Phoenix closed her eyes and fought back the anger rising in her gut. She didn't want to lose it in front of Shawn. She seethed as she spoke.

"Because you called me on a very expensive satellite phone from across the world claiming an emergency. You sound fine, so what's the emergency."

"Oh, well, I wasn't feeling so good and Brenda made me go to the hospital and they said my sugar was through the roof. They did a bunch of tests and said I have the diabetes. Warned me to take my insulin and pills because if I don't I could end up in a coma. Or lose a limb."

Phoenix closed her eyes again, wondering just what she could do. This was information that Diane could have told her in an email or chat, and he had to know that. There's no way Diane would have given him the number to call, and he didn't have a computer or enough Google knowledge to find the number himself.

"How did you get this number? If you'd asked Diane she

wouldn't have told you, because this isn't a phone call even close to being an emergency." Phoenix's voice was as cold as the ice she saw through the window and she didn't care.

"I had your cousin Junior look it up for me. I thought you'd want to know. I could die from this."

"Only if you don't listen to the doctors. Which is why you seriously crossed a line calling here. Diane would have told me everything I needed to know. Why are you really calling?"

"I wanted you to know, just in case."

The line went silent and Phoenix refused to speak. She could wait him out.

"And you know, they've put me on a lot of medication. That's not cheap. Maybe you could loan me a little money?"

Rage roiled in Phoenix's gut as his words sunk in. This far away and he still found a way to reach her, lie to her, and use her. No more.

"You're on Medicaid, Dad. They pay for your meds. I can't believe you called here asking for money. I'm done. Don't call me again. Not here, not when I'm back home. Never. Period. I'll reach out to you if I ever want to. Until then, this is over. Goodbye."

Phoenix used her last ounces of self-control to set the phone down gently on the cradle, apologize to Shawn, and walk back to the galley to finish her cleanup, unwilling to leave it messy for the breakfast shift.

For the first time since she'd arrived on station, Phoenix did the bare minimum to finish and ran off to her room. She discarded her uniform in the corner and threw on a pair of basketball shorts and a t-shirt. Then she retrieved her phone and the new bottle of vodka in her closet, her mind focused on how she would work off some of her repressed anger.

Phoenix opened the bottle and took a large drink. Before setting it down she glared at the vodka in her hand. *How can you be a problem and a solution at the same time?*

Rage churned in her gut and she needed to let it out before she hit something that would get her in trouble. Like a wall. Phoenix grabbed her things, leaving the vodka behind, and rushed off to the fitness center. Thankfully the room was empty when she arrived, so she opened her music app to the playlist she didn't think she'd need anymore, the aptly titled Pissed at Dad.

ASH

Ash checked her watch again. Phoenix was late, and that never happened. Especially not for writing sessions which they were making a lot of progress with. What could possibly have kept her away? Ash slid on her shoes to find her, attempting to silence her worry with action.

Phoenix wasn't in her room, or the kitchen, but she found Jimmy who explained what he knew. Given the rarity of phone calls, usually restricted for emergency use or special occasions, Ash picked up speed toward Comms. She slowed as she neared the room but didn't hear anyone talking.

"Hey Shawn, was Phoenix in here?"

"Yeah, she had a phone call a bit ago from her dad. I try not to eavesdrop, but she seemed angry when she left."

Ash's heart sank. Phoenix shared enough about her parents' behavior to know this couldn't be good. Where could she go when limited to the station?

Ash checked the communal areas on the first floor and headed upstairs. She froze at the sight of Phoenix framed by the round window in the fitness center door, pummeling the heavy bag.

ASH

Ash eased the door open, the sound of heavy metal music spilling into the hall. Phoenix hadn't noticed her, so Ash took a moment to figure out what she was walking into. Phoenix had removed her t-shirt, leaving a sports bra to cover her upper body. Her skin glistened with sweat as she struck the bag with power, but her fatigue was obvious.

Ash walked into Phoenix's field of vision but didn't touch her, stopped by the anguish dominating her expression. What could have happened?

"Phoenix?"

"Go away Ash," Phoenix said, her voice even but cold as she struck the bag again.

Ash flinched but didn't move. She wouldn't let Phoenix move backward in their relationship.

"I'm not going to leave when there is clearly something wrong."

"You don't need to know."

Ash scowled and stepped closer, barely controlling her anger.

"Hey!" Ash said forcefully. Phoenix stopped punching the bag, finally, and faced her. "Don't shut down on me again. I won't treat you like a child but please talk to me."

Phoenix looked at the floor and shifted her weight from side to side. Finally, she answered in a defeated voice, "My life is so fucked up, I don't want you to know how bad it's been. Or still is."

Ash lifted Phoenix's chin to meet her eyes. "Phoenix, you are one of the kindest, most considerate people I've ever met. That's not something you just decide to be one day, it's who you are in here." Ash pressed her palm to Phoenix's heart. "Let me in, please."

Ash took Phoenix's hands, causing her to wince. The knuckles were red and swollen. "Phoenix! Doesn't this hurt?"

Phoenix shrugged. "Couldn't feel it until now."

Ash blinked. *How was that possible?*

"You need ice and maybe the doctor. Then we can go back to our room and you can tell me what happened, at least what happened today."

"Ash..."

"Nope, no arguing. Let me take care of you." Ash picked up Phoenix's shirt and pulled it over her head, carefully dressing her.

"When did you get so bossy?" Phoenix said, resignation in her voice.

"Today. Now come on. We should get those hands X-rayed."

"No, I'm fine. This is normal swelling that will come down with ice. Besides, if the doc thinks I can't handle the upcoming winter they could send me home."

Ash eyed her skeptically.

"Trust me Ash, I know what a broken bone feels like. I will be fine."

Ash gave in, realizing Phoenix was right about one thing at least. If the doctor or program director thought she couldn't mentally handle the upcoming season they'd replace her. The thought made her blood run cold. She couldn't go all winter without Phoenix when they were just getting started.

Ash handed Phoenix her phone before asking, "Phoenix, where is your water bottle?"

Ash winced, realizing she sounded like a scolding mother. Phoenix didn't react beyond a shrug of her shoulders. Her lack of reaction was worse than their argument in McMurdo. Right now, Phoenix appeared deflated and Ash could only hope to put a spark back in her eyes.

Ash grabbed Phoenix by the front of her shirt, not wanting to put pressure on her hands in case she'd injured herself, and pulled her out the door. They stopped for ice and water in the kitchen before retiring to their room. Ash nudged a begrudging Phoenix onto the bed, a bag of ice on each hand.

"Will you tell me what happened today? What made you so angry?" Ash asked gently.

Phoenix clenched her jaw as she took a tense breath, her gaze landing on the wall across from them

"My dad called me today. He conned the right people to get the number for here, claiming an emergency. But there wasn't an emergency, he just wanted money."

That didn't seem bad enough to explain Phoenix's reaction. There had to be more to the story.

"Does he do that a lot? Ask for money?"

Phoenix laughed bitterly. "Since before I was old enough to work legally. The man is an irresponsible, selfish addict who uses everyone around him. He's the biggest reason I left home because at least he couldn't just show up at my door. Except he has a phone and calls when he needs money. Then I went to the literal bottom of the fucking planet, where my aunt could run interference, and I thought, finally I would be free for a year."

Phoenix shook her head and sneered. "Of course, I should have known he'd find a way. It's easier to use me than to support himself."

"So he can't work?"

"Or won't. When he has a job he's always complaining about his incompetent supervisors and either ends up getting fired or quits. Of course, it's never his fault. Always someone else's." Phoenix sighed. "Physically he can still work, but not mentally."

Phoenix finally turned to face Ash, only briefly meeting her eyes. "My dad's bipolar. I get that mental illness is challenging, but I don't think he's even trying. He doesn't take his medication. Doesn't go to his appointments most of the time. After half a lifetime supporting him financially, my patience is down to zero."

Ash didn't know what to say so she remained quiet, hoping Phoenix would fill in the gaps.

"It's not even about the money. If it were a legitimate emergency, I'd help. But we had a system worked out. Diane would call in an emergency, no one else. My dad thinks boundaries don't apply to him, nor does he care how much damage he causes when he ignores them, or what it costs to help him. He didn't care when I was working two jobs to cover his bills and mine. He didn't care when I was 14 and fighting for money. He didn't say thank you, didn't ask where a bruise came from, or a black eye, he just asked for more.

"And I gave it to him, because he always had an excuse and if he didn't have electricity, I didn't have electricity. If he didn't have food, I didn't have food. And I was raised by my grandmother to stand by family. I never questioned how far that rule went."

Ash couldn't imagine what that did to a kid, to feel responsible for their parents, working at an age when they should be hanging out with friends and focusing on schoolwork.

"Phoenix—"

"No. No pity." Phoenix's voice was hard again.

"Ok, no pity." Ash wanted to comfort Phoenix but she didn't know how. If she kept Phoenix talking maybe Ash could discover what Phoenix needed. "What did you mean by fighting for money?"

"I needed an outlet for my anger towards my parents. I found a boxing gym that let me trade work for gym time. I took to the training immediately and it got me in the best shape of my life. Then I heard about these underground fights, how they paid out the same day, win or lose. No one asked questions and it was better money than I could make working anywhere else at 14."

"Didn't it hurt?"

"Going to bed hungry hurts too. At least this pain had a purpose in the end."

Emotion warred in Ash's body until she was fighting tears. Shock, sadness, anger, a desire to make it all better somehow.

She wasn't sure any of those emotions would help the situation, which frustrated her, but she couldn't change Phoenix's past.

"Where was your mom during all this?"

"Drunk. At least she worked and had the decency to say thank you when I gave her money, but then she would spend it on more booze. I started paying the utilities directly when I could. And buying food that I knew she would have to cook rather than giving it all to her in cash."

"And your grandma and aunt?"

"Didn't tell them how bad it was."

"Why?" Ash asked, incredulous.

"They already helped a lot. And I thought I was doing what I was supposed to. I was taking care of my family."

"But you were a kid. You shouldn't have had to do anything. They were supposed to take care of you!" Ash felt her righteous anger take hold as her voice grew more intense.

Unexpectedly, Phoenix grew quieter.

"That would require caring about anyone besides themselves. At least when I gave them money, I existed for all of a minute. I could trick myself into thinking they loved me." The defeat in Phoenix's tone was worse than the anger and Ash's heart broke for her again. So many things made sense now.

Ash sat up on her knees, directly in front of Phoenix. "They suck and don't deserve you," Ash said, more intensely than she intended. She softened her tone. "I'm sorry your parents can't see what an amazing person you are."

"What if I'm not? Maybe I've fooled you and one day you'll realize I'm not worth your time either."

"What? Is that what you think? Nothing you've said changes how I feel about you." Ash's heart ached for Phoenix, for the pain she must have carried around her whole life. How could any parent make their child feel this way? Why would they?

Shaking her head, Phoenix slumped her shoulders. "Parents

are supposed to love their kids. There must be something wrong with me if they don't."

Ash sucked in a breath, understanding every moment of self-deprecation in a new way. Her chest filled with love and affection for Phoenix who'd managed to become a caring person in spite of parents who seemed not to care for her.

How could she get through to Phoenix if words weren't enough? Ash's gaze fell to Phoenix's hands, the swelling now coming down under ice. She gently removed the ice bags, dropping them to the floor. The skin was red and cold under Ash's thumb and she wanted more than anything to remove the pain from Phoenix's body and heart.

"Phoenix, you haven't done anything wrong. Their actions have nothing to do with who you are. Their issues are their own. I won't pretend to understand them, but I feel like I've gotten to know you pretty well these past three months. And I sure as hell think you're worth knowing and loving."

Phoenix's eyes glistened as she looked away.

"I didn't understand why you couldn't see how great you were, until now. I know you won't believe me yet, but you're worth it Phoenix. Anyone that can't see that doesn't deserve you."

Ash rose up on her knees, continuing, "I don't expect my words to undo everything they've done." Phoenix's head shot up when Ash threw a leg over to straddle her. Ash ran her fingers through Phoenix's hair, letting them come to rest behind her neck and leaned in to kiss her, pouring all her love into the gentle caress of her lips.

Phoenix wrapped her arms around Ash's waist, drawing her tighter as they kissed, her hands rubbing Ash's back.

And to her own surprise, Ash felt her body respond with a level of desire she hadn't ever felt for another person. Ash broke the kiss and pulled off her t-shirt, knowing exactly how to make Phoenix believe her.

CHAPTER TWENTY-TWO

PHOENIX

"Ash, what are you doing?"

"Making you feel better. You need to see how much I care for you." Ash closed her eyes briefly before meeting Phoenix's. "No, I need you to know how much I love you."

"Love?" Phoenix's stomach flip-flopped at the word. Those were powerful words, often misused and abused. Could she trust Ash when she said them, especially after such an emotional night? Did Ash expect her to say it back?

"Yes Phoenix, love. I suspect this isn't easy to believe or respond to. But you need to understand just how deep my feelings are for you. You are absolutely loveable." Ash reached behind to unclasp her bra, but Phoenix grabbed her arms, shocking herself.

"I can't believe I'm saying this, but you don't have to."

Ash gave her an understanding look and spoke softly. "I know. Your consideration for me is one of the reasons I love you. You allowed me to find my comfort level every time we've been physically intimate. Right now, I know what I want. Nothing feels more natural than for you to make love to me."

With Ash this close Phoenix couldn't think. She closed her

eyes, overwhelmed by the emotions those words stirred within her. Her heart raced and a part of her wanted to run from everyone. From her dad because he made her feel so awful. From Ash because she made her feel too good.

Instead she opened her eyes to meet Ash's teal eyes, filled with kindness and love. Phoenix looked closer but couldn't see anything else, like pity. That was good, Phoenix couldn't handle pity. She wasn't completely sure she could handle love either, but she would try.

"Is this one of those times when I should just believe you?"

Ash grinned and kissed Phoenix sweetly, melting her defenses. Her normal alarm bells were silent as her body quickly responded even as her brain struggled to catch up. Ash loved her. Loved. Her. How?

Ash tugged at Phoenix's t-shirt, bringing her back to the moment and what they were about to do. It didn't matter if Ash woke up tomorrow and changed her mind. For tonight she was loved. Phoenix lifted her arms, letting Ash pull her shirt off, and used the break to check in.

"Anything off the table I should know about?"

Ash tossed the shirt to the floor before replying.

"I know what's usually off the table, but nothing is the same with you. I don't want to assume anything."

"Why don't you tell me what normally doesn't work?" Phoenix asked carefully, gently rubbing her thumbs over Ash's ribs.

Ash averted her gaze before answering. "There are probably a million lesbians that would take away my gay card for this, but I'm not comfortable giving oral. I enjoy the sensations of receiving, but there's the expectation of an orgasm, and if that doesn't happen things get awkward."

Admittedly Phoenix didn't understand, but she didn't need to. "What if we approach tonight like a massage. No orgasm expectations and your gay card will never be in jeopardy."

Ash met her eyes and nodded. Phoenix reached around for Ash's bra strap but winced when her swollen knuckles complained. Of all the days for Ash to offer herself, it would be after overdoing it on the bag. *Way to go Phoenix.*

"Should we wait?" Ash asked.

"No! Now that you're ready I may not survive an additional wait. Maybe you can help?" Phoenix asked hopefully.

Ash smiled, making quick work of it, adding her bra to the discarded clothes on the floor. Then she pushed Phoenix's up and over her head, leaving them topless, with Ash still straddling her lap. Phoenix ran her hands over Ash's hips, finding herself uncharacteristically unsure of how to proceed. Phoenix wanted her more than anyone in quite some time, but she didn't want to cross a line.

Ash eyed her inquiringly. "Are you sure we shouldn't wait? What's going on?"

Phoenix's cheeks flushed with heat. Was she actually blushing over sex? What had Ash done to her? "I'm sure, just worried I'll lose control and screw this up."

Ash chuckled and cupped her cheeks. "Are you seriously turning my green light into a yellow? Let me make this clear. I'll tell you if something isn't working, but I want you Phoenix. I want you all over me, and inside me, and I want to make you feel so good you forget everything that came before this moment, ok?"

Phoenix's mouth went dry as every fluid seemed to rush between her legs. "That's a damn good start."

"Well, I am a bit of a writer and you inspire me." Ash kissed her deeply and Phoenix let go, her arousal skyrocketing as she set aside her concern. She ignored the pain in her hands as she fought with Ash's pants, until she noticed Ash's hands covering hers.

"Let me help you before you hurt yourself some more."

Phoenix sighed in frustration. "I can't believe I've waited all this time and I can't undress you properly."

Ash sat back with a glint in her eye. "I'm sure we can find a solution to this problem." Ash slid off Phoenix's legs and the bed before shooting Phoenix a mischievous grin. "Come here."

Phoenix practically leapt off the bed but was met with a hand on her chest and a cocked eyebrow from Ash. "You said properly, did you not?" Ash slid her hand down, between Phoenix's breasts and lower, until reaching her shorts. Phoenix trembled and prayed she had the self-control to follow Ash's pace as she slipped her fingers inside the waistband, sending shockwaves of anticipation through her.

Barely breathing, Phoenix managed a yes in reply, absolutely loving Ash's willingness to keep her in check. Ash's eyes gleamed, a vivid teal Phoenix knew she'd never forget.

Ash slid Phoenix's shorts and boxer briefs down in one motion with no hesitation or teasing. Phoenix met her with a hungry kiss before reaching for Ash's waistband again. She was stopped by Ash's hands over hers, brushing them away to undo the button and zipper herself. But then she lifted her hands, filling Phoenix with affection in response to the love in that simple act.

Phoenix knelt, pulling Ash's jeans down, letting her kick them off to reveal simple cotton briefs. This close Phoenix took in her unique scent, placing a kiss on the newly exposed skin, then lower through the underwear. Peeking, Phoenix saw Ash's eyes close, the smallest smile on her face. Her expression didn't change when Phoenix hooked a finger into her waistband. Ash's emotional light was still solidly green as she removed the final barrier between them.

"You smell amazing," Phoenix said reverently. Ash tensed. "What's wrong?" Phoenix asked, gazing up at her.

"I just realized it's been a couple days since my last shower..."

Phoenix stood and took Ash into her arms. "That means you will taste more like you which is a very good thing." Phoenix didn't hold back her desire as she kissed Ash, hoping to wipe away any concerns. Hands around Ash's waist, Phoenix pulled her close and for the first time there was nothing between them. No clothes. No walls. The newness of it all made Phoenix's head spin.

Desire surged through her, minimizing the pain in her hands as Phoenix lifted Ash onto the bed. Ash laughed but quickly added, "Lizard brain."

The words took an extra second to filter through the fog of arousal before Ash's words made sense and Phoenix laughed along with her. "Oh, you like that?" Phoenix pulled Ash firmly against her, feeling Ash's wetness against her thigh. Ash's expression immediately changed from playful to wanting. Seeing that look on her girlfriend's face was perfection.

Their eyes met. Phoenix fought the urge to shut down, to protect herself from the intimacy. Ash was completely open to her and seemed to sense Phoenix's struggle.

"It's ok," she whispered. "I love you. I won't hurt you."

Phoenix's gaze dropped, but she returned to Ash's eyes and gave the slightest of nods before letting her eyes close. Ash's kiss was gentle and heartfelt and Phoenix returned it in kind, letting her body say what her words couldn't.

Phoenix kissed her way down Ash's neck until her pulse quickened and small sounds of pleasure vibrated in her throat. Phoenix released her hips and encouraged Ash to lay back on the bed, positioning herself between Ash's thighs in anticipation.

Ash bit her lip, taking in a lungful of air as Phoenix pressed her hips against Ash's center, enjoying the sensations of just being together. As much as she wanted to taste all of Ash, Phoenix wanted to maximize her pleasure by taking it slow.

Phoenix peppered kisses along Ash's collarbone, licking the dip in her neck while slowly moving her hand to Ash's soft breast. The nipple hardened under her palm as Phoenix kissed her way down Ash's chest until reaching her other nipple with her tongue. Her teasing had Ash moaning, her hand gripping the back of Phoenix's head to keep her there. Phoenix lavished her breast until Ash relaxed her grip and Phoenix turned her attention to the other. Again, Ash told her just what she wanted through subtle pressure and sounds of pleasure. Phoenix didn't know how much more turned on she could get.

Looking up, Phoenix studied Ash's reaction when she asked, "Can I taste you?"

The corner of Ash's lip twitched. "That light is still solidly green." Phoenix didn't hide her joy.

"I'm going to need a pillow," Phoenix said, reaching for hers next to Ash's head.

"Why?"

"You'll see."

Phoenix tucked the pillow beside her, still planning to take her time building Ash's arousal. She shifted back on her legs, her hands caressing Ash's hips and thighs while placing featherlight kisses over her belly. Flicking her tongue in Ash's belly button earned Phoenix a playful slap as Ash giggled.

"I take that as a no?" Phoenix asked with a chuckle.

"Definitely a red light."

Phoenix loved Ash's playfulness, keeping their moment from becoming too heavy and serious. "That's fine, I have much more enticing places to explore."

"Yes, you do."

Phoenix flashed her a grin and slid lower, reaching for the pillow. "Lift your hips." Ash raised a skeptical eyebrow but happily complied. Phoenix slipped the pillow underneath, revealing Ash's swollen wetness. So beautiful.

Phoenix smoothed her hands over Ash's calves, gently positioning her legs. She kissed the inside of each knee, delighted to hear suppressed giggles.

Moving ever closer, Ash's hips rocked slowly, encouragingly. She brushed a finger over Ash's sex causing her to suck in a breath. The anticipation was palpable as Phoenix's heart thumped in her chest. Phoenix finally closed the distance, breathing Ash's scent in again before taking her first taste. Phoenix moaned, taking a moment to compose herself.

Slowly Phoenix discovered where and how Ash wanted to be touched. She found a rhythm with her tongue before reaching up to find a breast, gently squeezing the nipple with her fingers. Ash bucked her hips and Phoenix repeated the action, bringing Ash closer and closer to climax.

Remembering Ash's words from before, Phoenix circled her entrance with a finger, teasing and covering it with Ash's wetness. Her thumb took over circling Ash's clit before she asked, "What do you want, Ash? Do you want me inside you?"

"Yes... please."

Phoenix entered her slowly and easily, savoring the moment as Ash's inner muscles adjusted to her presence. With an erotic sound of pleasure, Ash's hips slowly moved against Phoenix's hand. After resuming her exploration of Ash's folds, Ash clasped Phoenix's free hand, threading their fingers, a connection unexpectedly as intimate as being inside her.

Phoenix's own arousal rose with Ash's, her breathing growing just as ragged. She wanted to be touched but her position made it impossible. Phoenix did the next best thing, imagining Ash stroking her, bringing her closer to orgasm with Ash.

When Ash's body spasmed, Phoenix felt it everywhere. From her hand, almost crushed by Ash's, to her fingers held in place by Ash's inner muscles, daydreaming of this moment couldn't touch the reality. Feeling Ash's body tense, Phoenix held nothing back, coming along with her. The shock and pleasure on Ash's face was worth the pain returning to her hand as the adrenaline eased. Every bit of pain was worth it.

Phoenix kissed Ash just below her belly button which made her jump and giggle, placing a hand on Phoenix's forehead.

"Too much?"

"Seriously? My nerves are on fire. It's like a fireworks display down there. What did you do?"

A surge of cockiness threatened but Phoenix controlled it, not knowing how Ash would respond. Phoenix opted for safe and charming.

"All I did was listen to your body and follow its directions."

"Sure, that's all," Ash replied sarcastically. "This may be normal for you, but definitely not for me. You went way beyond my expectations."

Phoenix wisely swallowed her sarcastic retort, moving alongside her while being careful to avoid sensitive areas. "Why would I give you anything less than my best?"

"Just another reason why I love you."

How quick those words grew on her, lighting Phoenix up with joy. Phoenix stroked Ash's cheek and leaned in. "Is it ok if I kiss you, or should I drink some water first?"

Ash's eyes opened wide and then softened as she reached her arms behind Phoenix's neck and pulled her in for a slow, deep kiss. It was a perfect moment and Phoenix thought her heart might burst from joy.

"Thank you," Ash whispered against Phoenix's neck as Ash held her tight. "Tonight was... unexpectedly wonderful."

Phoenix nestled closer, hiding the grin she couldn't contain. "No need to thank me. I enjoyed it as much as you did. Possibly more."

Phoenix felt Ash's smile against her skin before Ash leaned back.

"Are you really that unaware of how sweet you are, or are you messing with me?"

Phoenix answered earnestly, "I'm not messing with you."

Ash shook her head, smiling. "Then I'll elaborate. Thank you for asking before you kissed me. No one has ever done that."

"It was the right thing to do. Not a big deal."

Ash shook her head. "Yes, it is a big deal, because you aren't assuming anything. You're amazing."

"Yeah, this is going to take some getting used to," Phoenix admitted.

"Well, you'd better get used to it because I plan on frequently telling you just how amazing you are, and how much I love you."

Phoenix scrunched her face, acting annoyed, but she quickly broke into a grin, sensing the futility in fighting Ash. "Deal."

A part of Phoenix knew she was just as in love with Ash, but the scared part of her snuck back to the front, holding a giant stop sign. As they lay together, Phoenix wanted to say something, even if she couldn't admit her feelings yet.

"Ash? I... wish I could say everything I feel for you. But, it's hard. Not because of you—"

"Shush. Phoenix, I know what you feel. Maybe not in words, but in your actions every day and the way you just touched me. I can relax with you and actually have an orgasm because you reveal your feelings for me in your eyes."

Phoenix averted her gaze but Ash reached for Phoenix's chin, turning her to meet her gaze.

"Oh no, no hiding now. I need you to stay here with me. I'm not going to claim to understand what you've gone through in your life, or what you've had to hide, but you're safe with me."

If only it were as easy as saying the words. But Phoenix knew Ash believed what she was saying, so silenced her doubts.

"I've never been safe anywhere, except at my aunt's or grandma's. And besides them, I've never had someone love me before, not even my own parents. Hearing you say these things, knowing you actually mean them... it's more than I know how to deal with."

"Take your time, I'm not going anywhere."

ASH

Ash's eyes met Phoenix's the moment she awoke and she smiled sleepily. Phoenix was still here, she was awake, and Ash was pretty sure she wasn't going to freak out, but she'd proceed cautiously just in case.

"Mornin' beautiful," Phoenix whispered calmly, easing Ash's concern.

Ash hummed, "Good morning to you too. How are you feeling?"

"Like the luckiest woman on the planet thanks to you."

"And your hands?"

Phoenix shrugged. "Nothing some anti-inflammatories won't fix. That's the benefit of good technique. I'm just bruised, not broken." Wasn't that the story of her life? Often bruised, but never broken. At least Ash hoped that was the case.

Ash cradled Phoenix's free hand gently in hers, not sure what to think about the bruises, but she had to trust Phoenix. It was her body and she was the expert. She kissed each knuckle lightly before setting it on Phoenix's bare belly.

"What do you want to do today?" Ash asked. "It's Sunday,

right? My phone is in my pants, somewhere in the pile, and without it I completely lose track."

Phoenix blindly reached for the alarm clock on the shelf above her head and pulled it far enough in front of her face to verify the day. "Yes, a day off!" She set the clock back on the shelf and rolled onto her side facing Ash.

"I can think of a few ways to spend the day," Phoenix said seductively, running a finger from between Ash's breasts down to her belly button. Ash shivered, arousal building in her center, but not enough to take Phoenix up on her offer yet. Was there a way to tell her without it sounding like she just wasn't interested in Phoenix herself?

Phoenix tilted her chin up to face her. "Hey, we don't have to. I just want to spend the day with you."

"It's not that I don't want to, well... ugh." Ash took a deep breath and tried again. "I kind of want to? I mean, my body is responding to your touch but just not enough to put my brain into sex mode. Does that make any sense?"

"I think so. Does that mean you don't want me to touch you right now?"

Ash interlaced her fingers with Phoenix's. "I'm good with touch, but that touch isn't going to lead to more anytime soon. Maybe after a shower, and some food, but I can't predict it."

Phoenix rubbed the back of Ash's hand with her thumb, the simple gesture seeming to say so much more than Ash could describe.

"Ok," Phoenix said. "I think after last night we've earned a shower and a lazy Sunday."

"Maybe a semi-lazy Sunday. We're supposed to work on the next comic, remember? We need to have a few ready to go before we start posting."

"Fine," Phoenix said with exaggerated drama, "a lazy Sunday *morning*. We can work on the comic later."

"Deal." Ash gave her a quick kiss before rolling off the bed, in desperate need of water and then the bathroom. She downed a good amount of water before reaching for her pants.

"Hey, where are you going?"

"Bathroom. And while people tend to be pretty chill, I'm sure I should wear clothes while walking down the hall."

"But I envisioned a *naked* lazy Sunday morning," Phoenix complained.

"Then you'll have to undress me when I get back, won't you." Ash surprised herself with her reply. She threw Phoenix's shirt at her. "You might as well come with me. We can grab some snacks and spend the next few hours doing almost anything you want," Ash said, careful not to send Phoenix mixed signals or tease her too much.

Phoenix sat up and pulled her shirt over her adorably mussed hair. With their wrinkled clothes and bedhead, Ash was sure people would guess what they'd been up to last night. Then again, everyone likely assumed they'd been having sex for weeks now.

While she wasn't ashamed of anything she'd done, there was a part of her that felt like a fraud, not asexual enough because she'd fallen in love and enjoyed sex with Phoenix. She didn't understand what it was about love that allowed her brain and body to experience sexual attraction. It wasn't like her brain now went from not thinking about sex to constantly desiring it and initiating it either. Phoenix needed to know that. Perhaps this would be the perfect topic for their comic this afternoon.

Back in the room with bodies refueled and an attempt to tame their wild hair, Phoenix surprised Ash by dismissing her stripping suggestion.

"I honestly don't think I can do it without torturing myself. Maybe after we've showered?"

"A shower sounds so good, but I'd rather not wait in that line right now. So, what's on your lazy Sunday agenda?"

"Music." Phoenix woke up her tablet and scrolled through

her music until the timeless sounds of Carole King filled the room.

Ash cocked her head. "Really?"

"Don't tell me you dislike Carole King, because that's a major deal breaker," Phoenix was clearly teasing, but there was defensiveness in her voice.

"I'm just surprised. I'm not sure I've ever listened to any of her albums, but this is nice."

Phoenix's eyes widened. "Come, sit. Tapestry is one of the greatest albums of all time. She portrayed all the emotion of her divorce and new life in these songs, without being depressing."

Ash smiled and sat next to her on the bed, enjoying Phoenix's enthusiasm. "Tell me more."

"Just listen," Phoenix said with a wink.

Ash rested her head on Phoenix's shoulder and listened to Carole's uniquely beautiful voice. When was the last time she'd listened to music like this, without anything else to distract her? Well, to be fair, Phoenix was a little distracting. She looked so content that Ash was ready to declare every Sunday a music morning.

They'd known each other for three months now and it felt like Ash was finally seeing the real Phoenix behind her mask. Sensitive, romantic, hurt but still so caring. A surge of love caught Ash off guard and suddenly Phoenix was too far away, Ash's heart feeling physically pulled to Phoenix's. Ash wrapped her arms around Phoenix's neck and kissed her intensely, pressing her body firmly against Phoenix until she felt the need ease.

"What was that for?" Phoenix asked breathlessly.

Feeling a little embarrassed at her intense reaction, Ash hesitated, but then realized how ridiculous her response was after everything they'd been through. She shook off the embarrassment and spoke truthfully.

"I was just thinking how lucky I am to have found you. I

don't even care how improbable it was. My entire career is built on improbabilities, why wouldn't my love life be just as unpredictable too?"

"The way I see it, any good relationship is improbable. Before you, I didn't think it was worth looking for, but with you it's finally worth the risk to try. I don't know what I would have done last night if I'd been left to my own devices. Back home I would have ended up incredibly drunk at a strip club. Or a bar, hoping for a simple hookup. And then I would have woken up just as angry as before."

"And now?"

"Now I'm as much sad as angry that this whole situation with Dad had to end like this. But even more, I'm ecstatic to be lying here with you, and would be even without last night. That's an improvement I think, and that's because of you. Thank you."

Phoenix may not be able to say she loved Ash, but her admission said so much more. Ash's heart swelled with love and hope that they'd finally crossed the threshold into the intimacy she'd only dreamed of.

After lunch they sat on the bed, Phoenix with her sketch pad and Ash with her lined notebook, ready to work. Ash took the opportunity to voice her early morning thoughts.

"There's something I need to talk to you about, and since it falls under the ace education umbrella, I thought it would be good to use for the comic too."

Phoenix folded her hands in her lap and gave Ash her full attention. "Ok, go for it."

"There's a lot of debate— No, disagreement, in the asexuality community that if a person ever feels sexual attraction then they aren't asexual. It doesn't matter if 99% of their life is spent without attraction, those gatekeepers still think it negates their asexuality. Thankfully, the general consensus is that asexuality is on a spectrum.

"I didn't know if I was going to be sexually attracted to you when I realized I was interested in you as more than a friend. I've been romantically attracted to people before, just to have it disappear or return to friendship once we started dating. Attraction is so complicated.

"With you, not only was the romantic attraction there, it grew stronger every day. You're kinda awesome, you know?"

Phoenix gave her a cocky smile that she felt deep inside. The confidence that originally turned her off a few months back now sent heat to her belly. Ash chuckled.

"Case in point. A few weeks ago, that smile wouldn't have affected me like it does now. Something changed once you let me in. But here's the thing I need you to know."

Ash paused, searching for the right words. "Sex is still not my priority. When I'm away from you, it's highly unlikely that I'll be thinking about sex. I'm not going to seek you out for a quickie because sex just doesn't take up that much space in my brain."

"But you initiated it last night," Phoenix said as she cocked her head.

"That's where it gets confusing for me too. Sometimes being near you arouses me, but I don't want to have sex. There's a disconnect. Last night was different. You needed the physical connection, and I wanted to give it to you. Thankfully, my body was ready as well so I could give you what you've been wanting."

"And if you hadn't been turned on, then what?"

"I would have found another way to make you feel better, like any other time. But honestly, just being near you makes me feel at least a little aroused. It's distracting."

"Now you know how I feel sitting on this bed with you. I've had blue ovaries since you kissed me."

Ash flinched. "I know you don't mean that as a criticism, but other people have. It brings up some painful memories."

"Sorry," Phoenix replied genuinely. "Consider it banned from my vocabulary."

Ash nodded and tried to regain her train of thought. "How often do you think about sex during the day?"

"I've never really thought about it, but quite a few times. I'll see an attractive woman and wonder what she's like in bed. Not that I'd act on it anymore," Phoenix added quickly. "But it's how my brain works."

"You don't have to defend how you're wired. But I want you to understand that where you might have thought about having sex all day, I probably won't until we're in bed. If you're really wanting it, you need to broach the subject."

A pensive expression filled Phoenix's face. "I'm completely capable of having sex every day, so if I ask every time the urge strikes, wouldn't that make you feel pressured?"

Nervous butterflies filled Ash's gut, worry over their long term prospects, but she knew the best way for this to work was to be honest and look for a compromise. Assuming the worst wouldn't help.

"You're probably right to worry. Daily would feel like pressure. What if I do my best to initiate when I'm feeling like sex, and you tell me when you're more aroused than usual. Does that sound fair?"

"As long as you don't make yourself uncomfortable just to satisfy me. I don't want that for you."

"Neither do I." Ash had tried just that for her prior girlfriend and it hadn't turned out well. Her ex had been happy enough but Ash felt wrong, almost dirty afterwards and it quickly soured the relationship. It took years to understand her sexuality and, now that she did, Ash was determined to value her needs just as much as Phoenix's.

Phoenix kissed her. "To seal the deal. And because I suspect that wasn't easy for you. We're being, like, real adults or something."

Ash laughed, and while she knew it wouldn't always be easy, she was truly excited about the possibilities of her and Phoenix as a couple.

CHAPTER TWENTY-THREE

PHOENIX

Sunday night, Ash fell asleep easily but Phoenix couldn't wind down. After such an emotional weekend her mind raced, but not in an orderly fashion like the Indy 500. Instead, Phoenix felt like she'd been covered in catnip and dropped into a box of kittens who hadn't learned to retract their claws yet – with a dozen laser pointers controlled by overexcited toddlers. While there were soft, warm fluffy thoughts of Ash, there were also countless painful thoughts of her father. And as anyone who'd attempted to herd cats knew, the chaos was impressive.

She needed to talk to Diane, but it was still early on Sunday morning. It wouldn't hurt to try to reach her, and even an email would help. After waiting an extra few minutes to ensure Ash's breathing remained deep, Phoenix slipped from her embrace regretfully. At least she wasn't trapped against the wall. Ash briefly stirred but remained asleep.

Phoenix grabbed her tablet and sat at the desk, keeping the light as low as possible. Diane agreed to keep her messaging app open so Phoenix sent a quick greeting and waited, opening her sketchbook to pass the time. She found herself sketching a kitten, a soft ball of fluff curled up next to Phoenix's heart – an anatomical heart, not the cartoon kind. She added markings around its eyes, like the glasses Ash occasionally wore. Did Ash like cats? It was another thing to learn about her.

Without thinking, Phoenix was drawing a big old tom cat, weathered and worn, with a torn ear and patches of fur missing. His claws were extended menacingly, about to swipe at the heart from the other side. How much damage could he do in a single swipe? Thinking of her dad now, the answer was 'quite a lot'.

Phoenix checked her screen, and seeing no reply began drafting an email to her aunt, but where should she begin? She didn't know what Diane knew and doubted her dad would tell her how bad he fucked up. That was as good a place to start as any.

> Hi Diane,
>
> I know you did your best, but Dad found a way to reach me and called Saturday. He claimed a medical emergency but ultimately wanted money. I'm officially done. I told him not to contact me ever again. I doubt he'll listen, but I'm sticking to it. He's out of my life until I decide I want him there again.
>
> He made me so angry! You'll be happy to know I didn't punch anything except the heavy bag, and I didn't even break anything. But that might be because Ash found me and made me stop, iced my hands and then asked me what was going on. So I told her. I actually told her about my childhood and she didn't freak out. In fact, she told me she loved me and then things happened that you don't want to know about. Needless to say, it was a good night.
>
> But now I'm so confused. I think I love her, but I don't trust myself to know what that even means. She's the most amazing woman I've ever known, and I want to do right by her, but...

I've never been so happy and scared in my life and I don't know what to do.

Phoenix glanced at her sketch and took a picture, attaching it to the email.

I drew this tonight while waiting for your reply on messenger. It might make more sense than words.

"Phoenix?" Ash asked sleepily. "Is everything ok?"

Phoenix didn't turn, wanting to send the email before Ash could read it. "Yeah, just needed to send my aunt a message. I'll come back to bed in a minute."

Ash just woke up, so I'm going to send this and hope for a reply when I wake up in the morning. I love you.

With the email sent, Phoenix crawled into bed and wrapped her arms around Ash, allowing her girlfriend's contented hum to act as a balm for her confused heart.

Phoenix didn't read Diane's response until Ash was in the bathroom the next morning.

Oh, that father of yours is lucky he is too far away to knock some sense into. I have a damn sturdy cast iron skillet, but your grandmother discovered how ineffective that was due to his thick head. Maybe cutting him out of your life is the only solution left. I'm so sorry I couldn't protect you better baby girl.

Seems to me that everything is working out for the best. You met someone that has you asking the right questions. Give yourself the time to discover the answers. You have months.

Just tell her what is going on and I'm certain she'll wait for you to figure it out.

Focus on Ash and who you are with her. Build your future. Your past isn't going anywhere anytime soon. But your future could if you aren't willing to be vulnerable. Be strong Fee. It sounds like she's worth it.

Phoenix drew in a shuddering breath, feeling the truth of every word. Ash was more than worth it, but that didn't make Phoenix any less afraid. It was time to man up. Woman up? Whatever, she needed to find a way to talk to Ash, but not today.

Phoenix did an admirable job finding plenty of excuses to avoid talking about her feelings. Monday, Wednesday and Friday mornings were spent in the fitness center, which wasn't conducive to emotional discussions. Monday night the weather shifted, further reducing the available oxygen resulting in piss poor sleep. The whole station seemed to be on edge.

Luckily Ash was patient and didn't push Phoenix at all, so she didn't even need an excuse on Thursday. Except Phoenix knew she was avoiding the issue, and that nagged at her. She felt even worse when Saturday dawned with a short email from Diane.

> I am starting my weekend alone because I never let myself be vulnerable enough to make a relationship work. Learn from my mistakes Fee.

Damn, Phoenix felt that in her gut. Diane wasn't pulling

punches anymore. She didn't want to see how tough Diane's love could get. Maybe she could talk to Ash after work.

But before Phoenix could ask to talk, Ash mentioned going to the movie playing in the gym. So Sunday became the day.

"Are you up for some gaming today?" Ash asked as they lounged in bed. "It's probably our last chance before the rest of the summer crew leaves."

"Yeah, that sounds fun," Phoenix replied distractedly, Diane's words echoing in her mind. "But first, we need to talk." She winced at the same time as Ash, realizing how that sounded. "Not about anything bad. Just... you asked me to let you in, right? I'm trying to figure out how to do that."

"Oh!" Ash rose up on her elbow, facing Phoenix. "Sure, we can talk about anything you want."

Ash's expectant look was all Phoenix needed to freeze up, her mind blank. There was too much to say and nowhere to start. Maybe that was the solution.

"I don't exactly know where to start. Last week I emailed Diane because my head was too full to think clearly. She knows me better than anyone, so when she gave me advice, I knew she was right. I just don't know how to follow her advice."

"What did she recommend?"

Phoenix played with a loose string on Ash's blanket, not meeting her eyes. "To open up to you about what I'm dealing with."

"I'd really like that. But I don't want you to feel pressured." Ash placed a hand on Phoenix's forearm reassuringly.

Phoenix took Ash's hand, interlacing their fingers. It was so easy, so natural, how could she not do everything to keep moving forward?

"Sometimes a little pressure is a good thing. It pushes you to do things that you wouldn't otherwise. I've spent too many years hiding because the people closest to me didn't take care of me."

Phoenix traced circles on the back of Ash's hand, then met her soft gaze. "You told me you loved me, and I couldn't say it back. Not because I don't love you, because I probably do, but I don't trust myself to know. My heart has been broken so many times that I couldn't tell you what love should feel like."

Phoenix rolled away to reach her sketch pad, flipping through the pages to find the sketch she sent Diane. "I drew this last week. You're this adorable kitten that makes me feel so happy. But always lurking is this nasty cat here, taking swipes at my heart every chance he gets. For now he's out of my life, but it's never that easy. My wounds need to heal. And he isn't the only problem, just the most pressing. Somewhere, hiding, is my mom. And every so often, a random family member who can't see that I'm not my parents."

Phoenix exhaled at the realization of how many people seemed to enjoy fucking with her head and heart. "I need some time to figure this out. While I do, please believe me when I say you're the best thing that's ever happened to me."

"Take all the time you need. I'm not going anywhere," Ash said before placing a chaste kiss on Phoenix's lips. "Was that all?"

Phoenix could almost feel Diane slap the back of her head. She rubbed it reflexively and smiled sheepishly. "You let me off the hook way too easily, you know that?"

Ash furrowed her brow. "I love you and don't want to see you hurt, but that doesn't mean I'm being too easy on you. Don't worry, I will call you on bullshit when I see it, hopefully more effectively than in McMurdo."

Phoenix fixed her eyes on Ash's. "I hope you mean it, because I am capable of a lot of bullshit."

"And I've built up my shoveling muscles while here, so shit away. I can handle it."

"Now that's a visual for later," Phoenix said with a chuckle. She took a deep breath and let her words spill out. "Diane said

RISING FROM ASH

it's ok that I cut my dad out of my life, but I can't stop hearing my grandmother's voice saying we take care of family and the guilt is eating me up inside."

"Do you really think she meant to let him hurt you repeatedly?" Ash asked carefully.

"Probably not, but I don't know. It's not like she didn't enable him when she was alive."

"That may be true, but how did she react to his treatment of you, when she knew?"

Phoenix thought back through her memories, trying to separate just those involving his screw ups around her. Missed appointments, missed basketball games, showing up to visits drunk. Phoenix chuckled at one story in particular that Diane reminded her of. "Diane told me this story many times over the years. When I was still a baby, he showed up to my grandma's place drunk and planning to leave with me, while still drunk. Grandma actually hit him with a cast iron skillet, just like in the cartoons."

"Wow, I didn't know people actually did that!"

"Beware the tiny, old southern woman," Phoenix said with a grin. "They couldn't save me from my life, but they did their best to minimize the damage. I always had a safe place to go and a hot meal if I needed it. There were times when I was there every night after school so I knew I could guarantee getting a hot meal. She didn't make me feel bad about it either, just asked what I wanted to eat."

"I'm glad. So why would she want you to keep putting up with your dad's crap?"

"She wouldn't, but when you hear things like 'family sticks together' often enough, it's hard to let it go."

Ash took a moment to respond. "You've heard the dangers of rescuing a drowning person, right? That sometimes the person is so frantic they end up killing their rescuer in the process? It sounds like your dad is drowning, and you've tried to rescue him all your life. But now it's time to save yourself and let him learn to swim on his own."

"He knows how to swim. He chooses not to."

"Even more reason to let him go, don't you think?"

Something shifted inside, the heaviness at talking about her dad releasing. Perhaps that old tom cat was going for a walk and leaving her in peace for once. But looking at Ash she could see that little kitten go all feral on that tom cat and scare it away. Emotion swelled in her chest. Phoenix covered the distance between them quickly, kissing Ash hard.

"Thank you." Phoenix said sincerely. Those last three little words were so close to her lips, but she needed to be sure. When she said them to Ash, she needed to know that there was no doubt remaining.

"Thank you for trusting me."

Phoenix nodded. "So, gaming today? I look forward to watching you beat me because I will probably give you anything you ask for at this point."

"That's strangely romantic. Maybe I'll go easy on you."

"Or maybe we should partner up and destroy everyone else," Phoenix suggested.

"Now you're talking."

ASH

Ash glanced at the monitor on her way into the galley, taking in the daily news: today's menus, temperatures, weather forecasts, and a list of the week's birthdays where she found Phoenix's name. February 7, only three days away. Did they seriously forget to ask for each other's birthdays? There should be a checklist for dating so they wouldn't forget all the little details like birthdays, favorite color, favorite dessert, whatever you were supposed to know about a person by the time you'd fallen in love with them.

To be fair, they'd only been dating a month if she counted from New Year's. Maybe there was something to those cheesy pickup lines. If you know someone's astrological sign at least you could narrow their birthday down, and even ask without it being creepy. In any case, she knew now, and she needed a plan. Would Phoenix like a party? What else could she do that they hadn't already done?

Perhaps Jimmy could help. Phoenix was probably closer to him than anyone else besides her. She resolved to find him after dinner and devise a plan to give Phoenix the best birthday she could. For now, she'd test the waters with Phoenix.

"Hey babe, how's work going today?" Phoenix asked when she saw Ash approach the serving line. Ash still wasn't used to this particular term of endearment and she tried not to show how gooey it made her feel.

"Same as usual. Nothing exciting, which made the news monitor even more interesting today."

Phoenix cocked an eyebrow in response.

"It turns out it's someone's birthday this week. Someone I happen to know intimately," Ash said pointedly.

Phoenix had the decency to look a little abashed. "Can we talk about this later? It's... private."

Ash softened her tone, not wanting Phoenix to think she was genuinely upset. "Of course. And maybe I'll even remember to tell you mine so you're prepared," Ash added with a playful smile.

"And ruin the surprise? That will give me too much time to think."

"Maybe I'll give you a fake date then, just to keep you on your toes."

Phoenix laughed and waved her hand in dismissal. "Go eat and let me work. You're distracting."

Ash smiled mischievously. "Mission accomplished."

Ash decided to wait for Phoenix in the galley, having bailed on work earlier than usual. Her data analysis program would run for a few more hours so there was no reason for her to hang around. Instead she worked on her latest fanfic idea.

For the first time she seriously considered what it would be like for Faith and Willow to end up together. They were the least likely pair in Ash's opinion, ignoring creepy and illegal combinations, but her experience with Phoenix inspired her to give it a try.

The pairing was so unlikely she couldn't come up with a story yet, not without re-imagining the characters first. It was proving to be a fun exercise.

"This is a surprise. What are you working on?" Phoenix asked, sitting down next to Ash. She quickly closed the notebook, not comfortable sharing the earliest parts of her process, even with Phoenix.

"A new story, if I can find a plot, that is. Right now it's just an idea."

"What's the idea?"

"What would happen if Willow and Faith got together?"

"Oooh, I'd read that. Wait, when Faith goes dark, does Willow go dark? Or vice versa?"

"That's a really good question." Ash opened her notebook and wrote the questions down. Those questions might be enough to create a series of stories. She closed her notebook again.

"Are you done? I thought I'd walk you home for a change," Ash asked lightheartedly.

"Yep. But I'm feeling antsy and really don't want to go back to the room yet. Up for a walk?"

"Sure. Would you like a tour of the IceCube site? It's not very exciting, but it's a new destination and soon it will be too cold to be an enjoyable walk. As an added bonus I can claim I was working late."

"Considering our options, new is all I need, but I'd love to see your world."

"Well... the wires are impressively organized."

Ash chuckled at Phoenix's attempt to find something redeeming about the elevated blue building. It was basically a giant insulated box to house the electrical hardware for the system frozen far below them. Just racks of equipment, an impressive amount of wire, and blinking LED lights.

"I told you, not very exciting, but really important to keep everything working properly. Clean, organized wiring is a part of that."

Ash pointed out what each piece of equipment did, tracing the path up from the ice, into the building, to the various racks, and then out the other end of the building to the station where the science lab was located. "And that's about it. Everything I work with is digital and doesn't make much sense until we can display it in 3D."

"Huh, it doesn't look very sciency."

"It's funny. In high school and entry level college classes we do physics experiments with tangible objects. Then we go to grad school and so much of what we do is computer based that it feels more like programming than actual physics because we need that level of precision and computing power. But I don't mind. We're doing basic science that can revolutionize our entire understanding of matter. I wouldn't give that up."

Phoenix leaned casually against a desk. "So, what happens when you finish your PhD?"

"Ideally I find a position with a university that is still affiliated with this project. There are currently fifty different universities around the world. I'm not picky where I end up. It might be nice to stay in Madison for a post-doc position so I can get my feet under me before going somewhere else."

Silence fell, Ash realizing all the plans she'd made were before meeting Phoenix, and from the look on Phoenix's face, she'd realized that as well.

"Did you have specific plans for your time off the ice?" Ash asked cautiously. She purposely didn't ask what Phoenix's plans were now, that was too risky when Phoenix was still working through her emotional baggage.

"I didn't even plan to come here, I sure as hell didn't have a plan for after. My stuff is at my aunt's and in storage, so I need to go back to Colorado. I quit my job before I left, so I guess I'd look for a new job and go back to working hard and avoiding my parents." Phoenix frowned.

Ash wanted to tell Phoenix to come with her, but it was too soon. What if Phoenix freaked out and closed down again? They had plenty of time to discuss the future.

"Well, you'll have this on your resume and that should make finding a good job easier. Or you can get a food truck and be your own boss." *With a business you can drive anywhere*, Ash added to herself.

"Keep dreaming, no one is going to give me a loan and I don't have the money, not even saving all my earnings this year."

Ash dismissed her argument, certain there had to be a solution. "I'll keep dreaming for both of us then."

Phoenix pushed off the desk and took a step toward Ash, her eyes showing exactly what was on her mind. "You do that. I, for one, have a different dream. One that's far more attainable." Phoenix looked around the room purposefully. "The building looks pretty private to me," Phoenix said suggestively.

Ash took a step toward Phoenix, within reach now. "Yes, very private, which means you can tell me why you don't like birthdays."

Phoenix closed the distance and took Ash in her arms. "That's not what I was thinking at all."

"I don't doubt it. But we need to talk so I don't trigger a birthday land mine." Ash pulled Phoenix over to a small couch in the corner of the room. Phoenix plopped down begrudgingly while Ash sat at the other end facing Phoenix. She waited, offering Phoenix the space she needed to open up.

"The short answer is that birthdays always sucked. If my parents didn't end up in a drunken argument it was a miracle. I stopped having family birthdays by the time I was ten just to avoid having them in the same room together. Not that they cared. Without being told by my grandma to be at her apartment for my birthday they tended to forget."

"That's awful!"

"That's why I don't like birthdays. I don't like the memories, except with Grandma. She made the best coconut cake," Phoenix said wistfully, her eyes unfocusing. "It took three days to make, which she reminded you of if you dared complain about anything." Phoenix's lips curled up into a sweet smile before turning conspiratorially to Ash. "She didn't make that cake for my dad. He got a basic yellow cake. One year I asked about it and she said, *baby, I gave that boy enough of my time. He doesn't deserve my coconut cake.*" Phoenix chuckled and Ash joined her.

"I'm betting she made you that cake every year."

"Damn right," Phoenix said, but then her whole demeanor shifted. "I wish she was here to make my cake now."

Ash took Phoenix's hand and kissed it. "I wish she was too."

"She'd like you," Phoenix said thoughtfully. "She'd like that you're smart, considerate, and adventurous. Did I tell you about the year she went to Alaska?"

Ash felt the smile forming as the excitement returned to Phoenix's voice.

"Ok, you know how I told you that Grandma hosted Thanksgiving, and how I'd always help? Well, that was a lot of work, even when I did a lot of it. Even worse was the drama from supposed adults. When I was 15 she said to hell with it and booked herself a trip to Alaska, at 70 years old! Even better, she didn't tell anyone. I showed up to an empty apartment. Of course, I called Diane and she was just as confused. As we stood around making jokes about the reckoning, alien kidnappings, and other unlikely scenarios the phone rang and it was her calling from Anchorage. It was epic."

"Wow, what did you do?"

"Cooked dinner. There were a few dishes we didn't make

because Grandma was often the only one eating them, like oyster dressing. All in all, the food turned out reasonably well but it kicked my ass. I understood why Grandma didn't want to do it anymore."

"She sounds like quite the woman. Did she take a trip every year?"

"No, but I handled almost everything from then on. She taught me every little detail in the subsequent years."

"Well, my stomach is grateful that she did," Ash replied, patting her belly. "She taught you well."

"Yeah, she was pretty amazing." Phoenix's wistful smile made Ash wish she could drop her questions, but she was still at a loss regarding her girlfriend's birthday.

"So, most of your family sucks," Ash said, returning to the subject at hand. "What about birthdays with friends?"

"If I had friends around that knew it was my birthday, then we likely went to the bar or strip club, whatever sounded fun that day. They'd buy me a drink, or a dance, and that was that."

"No parties then?"

"No. I'd rather not make my birthday a big deal."

Ash added that information to her mental notes as some options floated forward in her mind.

"So, almost-doctor Ashley Bennett, have you ever fooled around at work?" Phoenix asked playfully, putting an end to discussion of her birthday.

"Never even considered it," Ash answered honestly.

Phoenix brushed a finger up Ash's arm, across her collar bone, down her chest and circled her nipple, her skin burning under Phoenix's touch. She was certain anyone looking through infrared goggles would see Phoenix's path glow with heat.

"What about now?" Phoenix asked suggestively.

"Well, you are objectively more tempting than any of my colleagues," Ash said coyly.

"It would be another experience to add to your list of South Pole adventures."

"Well, I do like lists..."

Phoenix's grin was almost wicked as she met Ash's mouth for a kiss. As she laid back on the couch, Ash realized just how long her adventure list was becoming, and it was still only February.

Given Phoenix's dislike of birthdays, and their lack of options, Ash had to be more creative than ever. Maria, the station baker, agreed to make a coconut cake when Ash explained the situation. It wouldn't be the same as Phoenix's grandmother's, but perhaps it would make the day a little special.

With the first part of her plan in place, Ash brainstormed ways to make Phoenix feel loved and appreciated. The absence of love seemed to be the root of every hurt in Phoenix's heart. Breaking her own rule, Ash emailed Cole at work for help and they suggested writing down all the reasons Ash loved Phoenix, so whenever Phoenix was feeling down she could read them. That sounded perfect, so once Ash hit run on her program she snuck off to the salvage and recycling area outside which housed all manner of discarded materials that had potential for reuse. After a bit of searching she found a small container with a lid that snapped shut and headed back to the station.

Her next stop was the arts and crafts room. She didn't consider herself artsy, but she wasn't planning anything fancy. Just some colorful paper, of which there was plenty. As she cut out paper hearts, she tried to remember the last time she'd done anything similar. Middle school? Seemed appropriate, given how often she felt like a kid with Phoenix. And that gave her another idea to add to the container.

She was running out of time so focused on adding the decoration. She wrote, *reasons why Phoenix is my favorite person on the planet*, on one square of bright pink paper. On another, which she placed underneath, she wrote, *or why I love her*. Then she added the red hearts she'd cut out to decorate the rest of the container. After ensuring it was well protected, covered in clear tape, she returned to her lab to work on the next part of her plan, writing all of the reasons onto scraps of colored paper.

CHAPTER TWENTY-FOUR

PHOENIX

*P*hoenix knew she was dreaming because as real as it felt to be lying between Ash's legs, the bed was too large and the sun shone through the windows which were open, allowing in a warm breeze. But she could feel everything as if it was happening. Ash called her name, increasingly excited as she came closer to climax. But before she did Phoenix awoke in their dark room to a confusing mix of sensations. Her mind quickly adjusted from the dream to reality, from Ash enthusiastically calling her name to Ash whispering in her ear from behind, the gentlest fingers stroking low on Phoenix's belly. Phoenix's hips were already moving, her center pulsing and on fire.

"Ash?"

Ash kissed the back of her neck, her ear, before whispering, "Happy birthday, Phoenix."

The act sent shivers over her body, already so turned on from the dream she couldn't think straight and she soon gave up trying. Phoenix turned in Ash's arms, capturing her mouth in a deep kiss. Ash's hand dipped into Phoenix's shorts, finding her wetness. Phoenix moaned, already so close to climax. Ash seemed to sense this because she didn't tease, stroking her while finding a nipple with her mouth, moving with Phoenix's body, matching her pace.

"I want you inside of me," Phoenix said through gasps. Phoenix opened her legs wider, rising to meet Ash's hand as she slipped two fingers inside. Her thrusts hit just the right spot for Phoenix to crash over the edge in seconds, sending spasms through her core.

The room was still dark as her body slackened and she used the last of her strength to curl around Ash. "As birthdays go, this one isn't bad."

"Isn't bad?" Ash challenged, brushing her fingers over Phoenix's sensitive center.

Phoenix sucked in a breath but laughed. "It's fucking fantastic."

"Better. You didn't ask, but I had a feeling this would be your favorite way to start the day."

Phoenix kissed her, her brain working well enough now to realize how much of a gift that orgasm was, coming from Ash. "Thank you feels so inadequate, but it's the best I've got."

"It's ok, I'm learning to speak Phoenix. I felt your gratitude all over my hand, on my lips..."

Phoenix kissed her again, truly in awe of the woman lying in bed with her. When she broke the kiss, she could just make out Ash's cocky smile in the dark. It sent another surge of arousal through her and she wanted Ash below her, feeling the pleasure she'd just experienced. Phoenix tugged at the waistband of Ash's panties.

"Can I?"

"Yes," Ash whispered while covering Phoenix's hand with hers and guiding it down. Never had a simple act felt so erotic. This was going to be a good birthday.

The alarm went off as they recovered and Phoenix turned on

a small light. "For the first time in my life, I wish I had the day off for my birthday. I don't want to move."

"Glad to hear you've achieved goo status."

"Incredibly gooey, thanks to you. But if you keep looking at me with that confident smirk on your face I might just hit a third wind."

Ash pulled her face into a frown and spoke in a low, gruff voice, "Does this help?"

Phoenix pulled her close as she laughed. "Now you're just adorkable, and that apparently does it for me too. It's probably a good thing I need to work or I wouldn't leave this bed today."

"Sounds like a plan for next year." From the look on Ash's face, she didn't mean to say it, but Phoenix didn't feel an ounce of panic.

"I fully support that plan."

The room fell silent until Ash's stomach grumbled. Phoenix checked the clock again and realized it wasn't set for their normal morning of 9 am, but 11. Ash had clearly planned ahead. What else had she done?

"It's late and we need food. We must have burned a thousand calories this morning."

Ash gave her a quick kiss. "Time to get dressed, birthday girl."

Ash practically pushed Phoenix to the dessert table at lunch, but she soon saw why. "Is this coconut cake your doing?"

"I may have mentioned it to Maria. It's not the same, but I was hoping the flavor would be close enough. Happy birthday my love."

The warmth in Phoenix's chest might just make her explode at this rate. "I don't care what it tastes like. You made the effort to get Maria to make it." Phoenix took a piece, as did Ash, and they found a spot to eat with enough space to provide some privacy.

Phoenix immediately dove into the cake and tears welled in her eyes. It wasn't the same, but it was close enough to remind her of her grandmother. She closed her eyes and willed away the tears, wishing her grandma was here now. To see her adventures, to meet Ash, to see just how much Phoenix had already grown during their short time together.

She felt Ash's hand on hers and she brushed away the moisture before facing her. But there were no words for how she felt. This was why she drew. She didn't need to find words, just keep moving her hand until the picture represented what she wanted to express.

"You're welcome," Ash said quietly before taking a bite of cake and smiling. "And I owe Maria big time for this."

"I'll find out what her favorite food is and make sure to work it into the meal plan next week."

Ash was waiting outside the galley when Phoenix finished work.

"Are you ready for your present?" Ash asked in greeting.

"Wasn't this morning my present?"

"Yes, smartass. Are you ready for your other present?"

"I think so?" Phoenix replied nervously, but let Ash lead the way back to their room. Once inside, she made Phoenix close her eyes and hold out her hands. She felt the weight of something cool being placed in her palms. When Ash gave the all clear, Phoenix opened her eyes and studied the object she held, reading the labels, her heart skipping as she read, *reasons I love her.* Phoenix raised an eyebrow at Ash who shifted her feet nervously.

"Go ahead, open it."

Phoenix carefully lifted the top off to find small strips of paper. She pulled the first one out and read it to herself. *Scal-*

loped corn. Phoenix chuckled and pulled out another strip. *Patient.* Well that was arguable, but Phoenix was curious now and kept pulling more strips out. *Cute drawings. Good listener. Supports my dreams. Kind. Accepting. Strong. Kickass hair.* That one made her laugh out loud. *Muscles. Playful. Flexible.* Phoenix set down the container and gazed at Ash, fighting the urge to sob. If this wasn't love, she didn't know what more it required. To be so seen, appreciated, and loved, how could she not love this woman?

"This is the best gift anyone has ever given me, Ash." Phoenix pulled her into an embrace, kissing the top of her head. "Though I don't know how I'm the patient one. Maybe stubborn is more like it. But you've waited for me to catch up to you, more understanding than I knew a person could ever be."

Phoenix squeezed her tighter, feeling foolish for questioning her feelings for so long.

"I had reasons for being cautious, but they sound ridiculous in the face of all you've done for me." Phoenix paused, gathering her courage. She loosened her embrace and met Ash's eyes. "I love you, Ash."

Ash's eyes glistened with emotion. Her smile slowly filled her face as she replied, "I love you too, Phoenix. But I already knew, that's why I could wait for you to slay your demons. I knew you would eventually."

Something about that idea, that Ash knew, gave Phoenix mixed feelings. It was such a big moment for Phoenix, was it not for Ash? She must have let her disappointment show for Ash to catch it.

"Did I say something wrong?" Ash asked, studying her face.

Phoenix shook her head, at her own reaction rather than Ash's question. "Just wondering if I made this a bigger deal than it should have been, if you already knew."

Ash lifted her eyebrows and answered intensely. "No, this is a damn big deal. I'm so proud of you for working through everything. I'm not dismissing your feelings. My intention was to explain that I have felt loved by you for much longer than just today. Words aren't necessary, but I can't describe what it feels like to hear them.

"I've written them countless times between characters. I've imagined what it would feel like to hear them from someone I loved just as much in return. But nothing compares to hearing you say those words for the first time. Nothing. If I write an autobiography, this moment will be marked as one of the greatest of my life. Is that clear enough for you?"

Ash's sincerity blew Phoenix away. She was genuinely beginning to question if a person could die from too much love. Phoenix released Ash and flopped on the bed. Ash eyed her curiously. Phoenix answered her with a question.

"You know the phrase, bowl me over with a feather? Well you just about knocked me out."

"Words may not be necessary, but they are powerful. Scoot over."

Phoenix moved against the wall and opened her arms for Ash, enveloping her with her body. In that moment Phoenix understood why people searched for 'the one'. She hadn't dared dream there was a person for her, and now she didn't have to, because she was lying in her arms.

"So when is your birthday? You've set the bar so high I'm going to need every minute to prepare."

"It's June 26th, but you don't need to do anything special. Just make me some more chicken nuggets and I'll be happy."

"Chicken nuggets, that's all? Can I draw you something at least?"

"Always."

Phoenix knew she'd do way more than that, but she had months to work out the details. For now, she was content to bury her face in Ash's freshly shampooed hair, the scent relaxing her as she let her heart be healed by Ash.

ASH

You were right.

It was amazing what impact three little words could hold. Like *I love you,* they said so much. And even if Cole gloated, Ash couldn't be mad. She had Phoenix because of Cole's wise encouragement.

Cole's initial response was to send a picture filled with hearts back. Yeah, that about summed it up.

I need to fill you in on everything but I figured you'd want to know the end first. You were right and I couldn't be happier.

Ash proceeded to recap the days, starting with the punching bag incident. She kept the details vague, protecting Phoenix's story since it wasn't hers to tell, but poured out her own heart.

How does this even happen? I'm beyond grateful, and amazed, but it's all so improbable. I wish I knew how it all worked. How people find just the right person for them, in spite of their foibles and the things they think make them unlovable.

Cole pulled out some of their timeless wisdom in response. *That's one of those impossible questions, isn't it? Philosophers spend lifetimes pondering that very question. Even if it was possible to know how love worked, what would it change? Would you love Phoenix any more than you already do? What if it's the mystery that enhances the experience?*

Ash smiled to herself. *You're right, again. And because you are right, I believe I owe you a story. It's going to take a little while, and I'd like to do it as a graphic novel with Phoenix, but I think the world could benefit from your wisdom creating our story.*

The string of excited GIFs Cole sent left Ash rolling with laughter. She didn't have a chance to respond before they typed a reply.

I'm glad I was able to be your catalyst, but you did the work. I look forward to meeting Phoenix at C2E2 next year.

That would be great! I don't know if she's been to a comic convention before. I'll add it to the list of things to discuss this winter. It's a long list.

I envy you Ash. You have so much time to get to know each other without the stress of civilization. That's going to build a rock-solid foundation for you two.

Civilization. They hadn't discussed what life would be like once they left now that they were a couple, but Ash didn't think it would be smooth sailing. Cole was right. They were in a relatively stress-free situation now. Sure, work could be difficult, but they didn't have to worry about money, or food, or even mundane things like traffic. What would happen once they left the ice?

I hope you're right. I fully intend to take advantage of the remaining eight months here. We'll figure out the rest as it comes. For now, I want to enjoy being happy and in love for myself instead of living through the characters I'm writing.

That sounds brilliant, my friend.

AFTERWORD

This book began simply as a desire to set a story at the South Pole, a place I had the pleasure of visiting in December of 2002 and January 2003, before the new station was completed. As I brainstormed the idea with friends, key aspects of this story kept falling into place. Their names are an example of the synchronicity that reminds me why writing is so addicting. In fact, it took a whole minute to put together Phoenix and Ashley and get to the title of the book.

Once I had the character names I spent a lot of time considering the types of people who go to the Pole, and who would be the most challenging to each other. Before long the story became a way to share the best qualities of my wife through the story of Phoenix. At the same time I wanted to explore my understanding of asexuality and Ash was born. Through the researching and writing of this book, I've become a lot more understanding of my own sexuality. More than anything, I want readers, asexual or allosexual, to gain an awareness of the many ways relationships can work.

Phoenix and Ash's story doesn't end here. Their return to

AFTERWORD

the real world means new problems, but as always, I promise a happy ending for them both.

Thank you for reading!

ACKNOWLEDGMENTS

I'm blessed to have a group of people who actively support me as I write. Between the Lesfic Love Slack group, Twitter, and Facebook groups, this book would have taken significantly more time to complete. A few people, in particular, stand out.

To Rae, I can't believe we've only known each other a few months, but you might know me better than 95% of my friends. Your willingness to share your experiences with me has been crucial to writing Ash authentically. Thank you for providing their ship name and a few other Easter eggs. I look forward to many years of friendship and collaboration.

To my friend who refuses to be acknowledged, you know who you are, and you know what you did. I'm grateful for all your very gay contributions.

To Jeffrey and Kathrin who answered my questions about life at the South Pole you gave me the little details that brought the setting to life. Jeffrey has a great blog that I referenced frequently. http://www.jeffreydonenfeld.com/

To my beta readers, now reaching a number too large to list, thank you. Your feedback and support is invaluable. A few have been extra involved and deserve extra acknowledgment: Rae,

JD, Kim, Gwen T., and Mildred, I hope you enjoy the finished story!

To Em, who helped me brainstorm and dig myself out of a hole twice, your perspective was incredibly beneficial. I look forward to future brainstorming.

To Claire, my editor, you challenge me to view my story with fresh eyes, making it even better. Thank you for your patience.

To Gwen K., who patiently made adjustments to the cover art until it was just right, I love it. Seeing Phoenix and Ash brought to life makes me smile every time. I can't wait to see what you do for the next book.

To Amanda, who put words to Gwen's art and made another beautiful cover, thank you! I couldn't do what you do.

To my wife, who didn't veto this story idea even as I borrowed stories from her life. It means the world to me. I hope you like the result.

To my daughter, thanks for bringing me joy and being old enough to understand that mama is working. I promise it's worth it.

ABOUT THE AUTHOR

Jax grew up in rural Wisconsin with a love of nature, sports, and music. Her first book, Dal Segno, was published in 2018. A list of her books can be found through http://author.to/JaxMeyer. Writing has become more than a hobby and is now the highlight of her workday.

She spent one year, ten months and ten days in the United States Marine Corps before being honorably discharged under the Don't Ask, Don't Tell policy, during which time she reconnected with her first girlfriend. They have been together since 1999 and had a daughter in 2015. Jax and her family call the Denver metro area of Colorado home.

For more information than you may want to know, you can find Jax frequently on Twitter – http://twitter.com/butchjax, on Facebook – http://fb.me/jaxmeyerauthor and on Instagram - http://www.instagram.com/jax.meyer.author/. You can also email jax.meyer.author@gmail.com or visit her website to subscribe to her newsletter. https://jaxmeyerauthor.wixsite.com/website.

Printed in Great Britain
by Amazon